★★★
BLACKTHORN
DYNASTY OF MARS

The BLACKTHORN Saga
from White Rocket Books

Blackthorn: Thunder on Mars
(anthology; edited by Van Allen Plexico)

Blackthorn: Dynasty of Mars
(novel by I. A. Watson)

Blackthorn: Spires of Mars
(novel by I. A. Watson)

Blackthorn: Sorcerers of Mars
(anthology; forthcoming)

BLACKTHORN
DYNASTY OF MARS

I. A. WATSON

Blackthorn Created by
Van Allen Plexico

WHITE ROCKET BOOKS

This one goes out to the old-time comics guys who taught us about power and responsibility, about criminals being cowardly and superstitious, and about coming together to fight the villains no single hero could withstand. Blackthorn's Mars in my head is variously pencilled by Kirby, Ditko, Wood, Ploog, Eisner and Starlin. Blackthorn's stories owe as big a debt to Lee, Thomas, Fox and co. as they do to Burroughs, Verne, Wells, Howard and Lovecraft.

And perhaps this one should also be dedicated to Princess Aria's greatest advocate and most vocal defender, my daughter Rhiannon, who has strong and loud views on the mythological, cultural, narrative, and practical aspects of being the Lady of the Land and is in danger of becoming one.

Special thanks to Van for inviting me to play on his planet, and Adam for so brilliantly illustrating its most spectacular view on our front cover.

--IW

BLACKTHORN: DYNASTY OF MARS

Copyright © 2012 by I. A. Watson

Cover art by Adam Diller

Original Blackthorn Logo by James Burns

A White Rocket Book
www.whiterocketbooks.com

ISBN-13: 978-0-615-67654-8
ISBN-10: 0-615-67654-5

First printing: August 2012

0 9 8 7 6 5 4 3 2 1

Introduction

I'll keep this brief, because you've got a heck of a novel ahead of you to read here, and you shouldn't waste any more time than necessary in getting to it.

The tale of how the Blackthorn Saga came to exist as a literary phenomenon has been told elsewhere (the Introduction to the *Thunder on Mars* anthology, to be precise), but here are the basics: In 2011, I hit upon the idea of doing stories set in a universe where far-future Mars has been terraformed, has achieved the pinnacle of high-tech civilization—and has then collapsed into barbarism. Four powerful but evil beings arose who were able to harness the remaining scraps of advanced technology and use it to make themselves effectively the Sorcerers of Mars—the First Men, in Blackthorn parlance.

The average folk of Mars suffered under their oppression for generations, until the coming of one man—a man from Earth, in the now-distant past—who dared to challenge them, and who sought to unite the downtrodden masses against their tyranny. His name was General John Blackthorn. And one of his first recruits, as seen in *Thunder on Mars*, was the Princess Aria.

But questions lingered. Who, exactly, was the Princess? What was her connection to the First Men? Why did she decide to join up with this "barbarian" from old Earth? What, exactly, was she a "princess" *of?* What was her story, anyway?

To tackle those vital questions, I turned to the one guy I knew could handle them with ease—and give us a rip-roaring adventure story in the process: I. A. Watson.

Man, was I ever right.

So—here we are, with *Blackthorn: Dynasty of Mars*. The answers you seek are here, plus a whole lot more, in a novel that covers a vast epoch of time and incorporates everything you've come to love about the Blackthorn Saga.

Now: Enough! Get to reading. You can thank me—and the good Mr. Watson—later.

--Van Allen Plexico
Somewhere in Southern Illinois
July 2012

"The first men to be created and formed were called the Sorcerer of Fatal Laughter, the Sorcerer of Night, Unkempt, and the Black Sorcerer...They were endowed with intelligence, they succeeded in knowing all there was in the world. When they looked, instantly they saw all that is around them, and they contemplated in turn the arc of the heaven and the round face of the earth... [Then the Creator said]: "They know all...what shall we do with them now? Let their sight reach only to that which is near; let them see only a little face of the earth! ... Are they not by nature simple creatures of our own making? Must they also be gods?"
                    --From The Popol Vuh of the Quiche Maya

"Any sufficiently advanced technology is indistinguishable from magic."
                    --Arthur C. Clarke

Prologue:
New Leaf

The fighting had reached the landing below the library now. Adept Anselm found it hard to ignore the death-squeals of the shadowmen.

He forced himself to concentrate on the task in hand. He carried his armful of scrolls into the reading carrel where Father De'bias was studying. The old man accepted the documents with muttered thanks and added them to the high pile of papers already cluttering his writing desk.

"Perhaps we should do something else?" Adept Anselm ventured. "Move to somewhere less... disturbing?"

Father De'bias made a notation in the margin of the book he was studying. "Anselm of Corozin, isn't it?" he checked. "You wrote your dissertation on the final stanzas of the holy book?"

"Er, yes." The young adept was surprised that the ancient scholar should know of his work.

"Diligent effort, Anselm."

"Thank you, Father. There appears to be swordplay outside the scriptorium..."

"Quite wrong, of course."

"What? You mean – my thesis?" Anselm couldn't believe that the old man was choosing now for literary criticism.

A small explosion shook the Ghost Tower. Dust fell from some of the high shelves.

"Don't be ashamed, Anselm. You did well with the materials available to you. You didn't have access to the great repositories of the Hall of Tatters or the lost works of the Isidic Bards. You extrapolated your conclusions quite logically from your sources."

"Father, someone or something is invading. It's cutting its way through the shadowmen. The guard-banshee has been overcome."

Father De'bias shifted his candle to light another obscure manuscript. This parchment showed four objects linked by scrolling lines. A circle that might have been the world encompassed a cup, a stave, a stone, and a sword. The old scholar made another notation.

"The Ghost Tower is one of the best defended places in Elysium," Anselm pointed out. "The Sorcerer of Night himself appoints the library guardians. Anything that can break through the greater wights and cursemorts in the lower halls…"

The sonorous toll of the alarum bell echoed from the belfry above.

Anselm jumped. "The signal! Father, we have to leave! And we have to take what documents we can to safety. The Ghost Tower is compromised. It is to be destroyed!"

Father De'bias sighed. "Your error, if you don't mind me saying, Adept Anselm, was in assuming that the holy book was complete. All of your assertions about the various sources of those tangled final passages assumed that they were indeed the final passages."

"You believe some of the *Ojer Tzij*[1] has been lost?" Despite his concern about imminent death the young researcher found himself drawn to defend his conclusions. "No credible evidence of additional Ancient text has ever been found."

"I agree."

"Then how could you say…?"

Another blast rattled the chamber. The candles guttered. A flash from the hall lit the gap under the library door.

Anselm winced. "If that is one of Lord Ruin's suicide squads breaking in they will have no mercy for scholars. They'll burn this collection and us with it - if we are fortunate. If it is the Lord of Fatal Laughter who invades then our deaths will be long and creative. We have to escape!"

Father De'bias drew another parchment before him. The yellowed paper was a diagram of some kind of cauldron, a large basin of water

---

[1] Mayan for "Ancient Word"; used here to refer to the Martian book recounting the Ancients' prophecies.

attached to chemical and electrical engines that were shown in cross section with accompanying descriptions. Old Daedalian script identified the device as the Pool of Rainbow Waters, technology of the Ancients acquired by the Black Sorcerer of the West.

Anselm blushed; the image also depicted a rather realistic black-haired beauty rising naked from the bath.

"Princess Aria rose from the crystal pool, nude and perfect," Father De'bias said. It sounded like a quote but the Adept couldn't place it.

Something heavy hit the library door. There was a screech. Black blood trickled under the barred portal.

"We have to go!" Anselm said. He cast around, selecting the rarest volumes he could see. "Help me carry these, Father! We can activate the shadow door and carry at least some of the books to safety."

"The bell will peal six hundred and sixty-six times," De'bias reminded the young scribe. "It takes that long to raise the daemons of entropy. At one toll every three seconds we have over half an hour to evacuate. Pass me the Tyrhennian Codex, would you? The pre-Numian edition with the obscene engravings."

The Adept reached the heavy brass-bound volume by habit. He'd fetched books for scholars here in the Ghost Tower for nearly five years.

Then he rushed to the black altar in the center of the tower. He dipped his fingers into the little pot of blood standing ready and touched his hands to the jeweled skull atop the ebony stand. "Invoke, in the name of the Lord of Night!" he commanded. Nothing happened. "Hello? Invoke!"

"The shadow door is jammed, Adept," the old scholar warned. "Its magics have been cracked and scrambled."

"It's not opening!" Anselm cried. "What am I doing wrong?"

Father De'bias sighed. "Apart from working for the Sorcerer of Night, you mean?" He tapped the thick wyvern-skin copy of the *Ojer Tzij* in the pile on his desk. "I do not assert that there are other Ancient sources that complete the holy text. I just think that the rest of the story is yet to be written."

Anselm looked at the old man in disbelief. He wasn't sure what shook him most, the invasion of the Ghost Tower, the blocking of the emergency shadow door, or the white-bearded scholar's suggestion that Mars' sacred text might need a few more chapters adding.

Father De'bias smiled cheerfully at him. "Oh come on, Anselm. You have a good mind. Use it. Don't you think we need to hear rather more about the Harmony Spires and the Four Hallows? About the Sleeping Army of the Last Man? About the Princess of Mars?"

"Maybe. Not when monsters are breaking down our door!"

"When monsters are coming for us is exactly when we need the Hallows and the Princess," chuckled the old scholar.

Adept Anselm seized up an inspection lens and peered closely at the rune-engraved skull on the shadow altar. "I'm not yet ordained in the necromancies of the Tower, but I'm sure something's been done to this spell. It's like the shadow door has already been triggered... but in reverse. Or something. Anyway, it's useless!"

"You regret not joining the unliving ranks of the senior librarians here, then?" Father De'bias enquired.

Anselm shuddered. "Hardly. I mean, I know it's a great honor and everything, but... dying and coming back – or part of me coming back – gives me the screaming heebie-jeebies! But there's no advancement, no access to the forbidden books, without joining the ranks of the seniors."

Even as he spoke, the youngster realized that Father De'bias didn't have the corpse-pallor and stiff movements of a revenant; yet he had access to everything. A dozen of the proscribed texts were piled on his desk even now.

A foul stench billowed through the cracked door to the landing. Energy weapons discharged. There was an inhuman multi-voiced shriek.

"That was the terror-seeming! They're right outside!" The stricken young scholar piled the books up behind him and seized a quill-sharpening knife to stand guard over them. "We have to protect the books. This knowledge is priceless."

The sounds of conflict in the hallway ended. The tolling bell continued its countdown.

Father De'bias put down his pen. "Anselm, are you happy here in Lord Night's Ghost Tower, poring over dusty manuscripts written in extinct tongues? Spending your days hoarding knowledge and preserving texts that most people have never heard of? Copying crumbling documents that no one has read for half a millennium?"

"Yes," admitted the young scholar.

"But you're not as keen on joining the senior librarians in their unliving servitude of ages?"

"Who wants to die? But I knew when I was recruited, when I was taken from my home to be specially taught for this post, what my eventual destiny would be. I... I don't know what else of me will survive the dark awakening but I'm certain the part that loves books will endure."

"So you are a loyal supporter of the Sorcerer of Night. And of all he does."

Adept Anselm hesitated. "I..." He glanced towards the battered door. "Not *all*. I mean, everyone knows that... well, not everything is right. The culls and the tithes. The blood-thirsters and the nightmare-crawlers. The growing shadow. Even in the Ghost Tower we hear whispers of terrible atrocities. But what can be done? The Lord of Night has ruled this land since the First Men came to power so long ago. What is the alternative?"

"I was about to ask you, Adept."

The scribe's hands strayed to the geography texts. "The Lord of Night's dark cloak protects us from worse. The cold regimentation of the Black Sorcerer, the endless war-lust of Lord Ruin, the cruel madness of the Lord of Fatal Laughter? How are those things better?" Anselm's gaze strayed back to the battered door to the tower landing. One by one the lintel wards were turning black and crumbling to ash.

"Are those the only alternatives, then?" Father De'bias asked.

"What else could there be?"

The old scholar tapped the holy book. "A different ending. A proper one that ties up the plots and themes and makes sense of all the jumble."

Anselm couldn't cope with blasphemy while raiders were breaching the library. "What happens all across Mars is terrible. But someone has to look after the books."

"Why?"

The young scribe blinked, surprised he should be asked such a self-evident question. "Books preserve the past, record ideas, tell stories. They teach and inspire. They lift us up – and we so need lifting! They..."

De'bias raised his hand for silence. "Enough. Good answer, young Adept. You can come and stand over here by me."

Anselm wasn't sure why he scooped up his treasure horde of tomes and hurried over to join the old scholar. Now he came to think about it he wasn't even sure what Father De'bias' status was in the Ghost Tower. The old man just wandered the library as if he owned it. Even Wight-Lord Ash-na-Dhrak hadn't questioned it.

Father De'bias examined a woodcut of a fierce warrior with a blazing sword, flanked by a sorceress and a hairy beast-man. He carefully slid it under his other papers.

The library door burst open. Anselm yelped.

A fierce warrior with a blazing sword strode in, ready for combat. He was flanked by a raven-haired sorceress and huge hairy beast-man.

"General Blackthorn," Father De'bias called out to the swordsman. "Princess Aria. Oglok. Hello."

A stray rend-shadow lunged from the landing, its terrible claws extended ready to kill. The Mock-Man Oglok sliced it in two with a vibra-axe.

"Hello, Father De'bias," Blackthorn called back to the old scholar. "You're not an easy man to find."

"People don't value what comes easy, General. Besides, this Lord Ash-na-Dhrak needed to fall. I trust you've given him a suitable push."

The Mock-Man growled something in his guttural, glottal tongue. It sounded fierce and urgent.

"How can you smell wight dust on your fur over all the other stenches?" Princess Aria objected.

Father De'bias gestured to the trembling Adept beside him. "This is Anselm. He works here. But he doesn't like the Sorcerer of Night and when the tower was attacked his first instinct was to save the books, so please don't kill him. I'm going to get him a better job."

"Father, we've come a long way - with a whole bunch of things trying to kill us - to ask you some more questions," Blackthorn declared. "Is there any chance at all we'll get any straight answers this time?"

"No," replied De'bias, giving him a straight answer. "Not here anyway. The Sorcerer of Night has worked out that you're plundering his personal library. That annoying bell is a countdown to self-destruct. The Lord of Night would rather have his library destroyed than let it be captured – which tells you what kind of scholar *he* is!"

"We have to save the books!" declared Aria.

De'bias indicated the precarious stacks on his desk. "I've already identified the unique ones." He gestured to the worried scribe clutching an armful of tomes. "Adept Anselm has picked some more. I wish we could evacuate everything, but then again I didn't trigger the entropy daemons in a fit of pique."

"W-who are you people?" Anselm ventured. "How dare you disturb the library of the Ghost Tower?"

"We're the people who don't like what the Lord of Night does to his subjects, or the use the arcane knowledge in this tower gets put to," Blackthorn answered. "We're the people who intend to see an end to him and the other First Men and make Mars free."

"We're also the people who disapprove of Lord Ash-na-Dhrak," Princess Aria added. "Well, we did. Now he's just another stench on our resident Mock-Man."

The alarum toll reached its mid-way point. De'bias was counting.

"That's your wake-up call," he told the intruders. "Time to go. You don't want to be here when the daemons arrive. I certainly intend to be absent. Let's set up an appointment during office hours somewhere else, shall we?"

"Hold on!" Blackthorn objected. "We came all this way to…"

"I'm sure you've done very well, General. Call that meeting you've been planning. Call Nanzak and Reith and Sihla and the rest. I'll see you there."

"How? You're like a ghost. You might be a ghost. Last time we talked you just vanished like…"

Father De'bias snuffed out the candle on his desk. Darkness crowded round the old scholar and Adept Anselm.

When De'bias struck a match and re-lit his sconce they were somewhere else. Blackthorn and his companions were not with them.

"What?" gasped Anselm. "That was… we traversed a shadow door. Like the one in the Ghost Tower!"

The old scholar shrugged. "I rather cannibalized that spell a while back to project myself *into* Lord Erebus's library, I'm afraid. Why do you think the emergency escape wouldn't work? I'd already borrowed it. And here we are – gone."

Anselm looked around his new surroundings for the first time. He was in a frozen cave; a cave filled with more bookshelves than he'd ever seen. Ancient ragged banners hung solemnly over hundred of thousands of tomes.

Father De'bias rose from his seat. "You know where you are?"

"The… the Hall of Tatters doesn't exist!"

"Really? Are you sure?"

Adept Anselm stared around him. "Who are you? Who were those three people that dared invade the Ghost Tower? What is really going on?"

The whole table and all the rare volumes piled on it had traveled with Father De'bias. He tapped the thick sheaf of notes laying on his desk. "I think you have some reading to catch up on," he suggested.

"What is it?"

"Just some scribblings. Maybe the next few chapters of the *Ojer Tzij*?" The old scholar patted the young scribe on the shoulder. "You enjoy yourself. I'm off to warn the Mapkeeper that he's got a new staffer."

Anselm sat down heavily.

Father De'bias turned back to add, "Don't worry, Adept. This place is the home of all dutiful academics. Here you don't die until *after* a long and fruitful life working on the lost knowledge of the Ancients. You will be happy here."

The old man wandered off between the stacks. Anselm rubbed his temples and wondered what had just happened to his life.

The manuscript called to him.

It was heresy, of course, but...

The first line can't hurt.

Adept Anselm lifted the top leaf and began to read.

One:
Memory

Princess Aria rose from the crystal pool, nude and perfect. She shook the water from her coiling black hair, spraying rainbow droplets back into the glowing basin.

She stared around her at the blue-lit cavern and its ancient machinery. Apart from the pool's underlighting the main illumination came from the glowing glass columns of nano-nutrients lining the walls.

"Where am I?" she asked. After a moment's pause she added, "Who am I?"

Nan Vidi moved forward into her field of view. The old nurse was a pre-human hybrid. Her Neanderthal features were framed with graying red hair that was mostly covered by her wimple and robe. Her smile was loving and reassuring. "You know where you are, lovie," she answered the princess. "You know *who* you are."

Memories began to register in Aria's waking mind. "This... is the Chamber of Rainbow Waters," she remembered.

"Very good," Nan encouraged. "And you?"

"I am Aria, Princess of Mars."

Nan nodded as if her ward had passed an important test. She made a note on the data module she clutched like a clipboard. "There's always a period of disorientation after time in the reconstruction pool, lovie. Your memories will return soon enough. Don't force them, but when they cascade back don't fight them either. It's all a natural part of waking up again. You know that."

Aria vaguely recalled that same nun-like woman saying those same things to her before. More than once?

Nan gestured to the women flanking her. As the princess stepped from the pool they both came forward to meet Aria. The younger of the two was surely no more than nine Martian cycles - eighteen in old Earth terms[2]. She had braided flaxen hair and wide blue eyes. Her twisting bronze adornments and translucent gauze strips proclaimed her a senior house slave. It was she who wrapped a linen towel around her mistress to dry her off.

The other retainer had ebony flesh, milky-reflective eyes, and the cranial jack implants of a Sensorine, a walking data-store and diagnostic device. The Sensorine spread graceful fingers and almost brushed the princess' flesh as she conducted her examination.

Recognition of a Sensorine reminded Aria of her father's usual diagnostician. "What happened to Elicogna?" she asked.

"Elicogna was captured by the Lord of Fatal Laughter, highness," this Sensorine replied. "It is reported that she still screams on his pain wracks after all this time. She was replaced by Nerisantha, who was torn apart by Lord Ruin's War Dogs - although she was able to transmit her final perceptions out in a data surge before she perished. Then came Amanura, who was lost in conflict with Brides of the Lord of Night. I am Malathea."

"I can see there have been some changes while I was gone," Aria recognized. She tried to remember exactly what had happened just before her last extended sleep in the Chamber of Rainbow Waters, but those facts were still denied her. "How long was I submersed this time?"

"About eighty cycles, lovie," Nan answered before the more literal Sensorine began a precise chronological report. "Of course, biologically it was no more than six or seven weeks for you, but I've been transplanted into two new bodies since we last talked."

---

[2] A Martian year, one rotation of the sun, takes 687 Martian days, each of 24 hours and 37 minutes in Earth time. Humans on Mars mostly divide Martian days into twenty-four slightly longer hours. They generally use the term 'year' to refer to old Earth-length periods of 365 days and 'cycle' to indicate one complete Martian solar rotation with its progression of seasons. Martian calendars consist of twelve 57-day months and a three-day "Fool's Holiday".

Aria remembered that her father had the technology to transfer his favored servants minds into fresh cloned bodies so that they could continue their service for many generations.

And thought of her father triggered the next association: "I am the daughter of the Black Sorcerer, who is lord of Western Mars from the Amazonis Sea to Far Tempe and the Valles Marineris. He is one of the First Men, the four who mastered the technology of the Ancients and became all-conquering mages."

"That is correct," confirmed Malathea. "Although at the moment the Black Sorcerer's lizard men have pushed back the Lord of Fatal Laughter's mecha-clowns as far as the Foundries of Cryce, whilst one of Lord Ruin's Chain Cities has penetrated as far north as Solis to devastate the hinterlands."

The servant girl folded away the towel-sheet and fastened an ornate silver-linked belt around Aria's hips. The garment's programming activated as soon as the clasp closed. The pliable matter shifted and twisted, spawned fabric and metal, snaked out silver threads to form calf-high sandals and matching bracelets and armlets, unfolded long translucent panels of cloth into elegant silken skirts then stitched them with delicate silver chains. Wires twisted upwards to create an elaborate bustier, then more fabric formed to offer it decency. Within seconds the princess was clothed in the noble raiment of the royalty of Daedalia.

"Daedalia is long dead," Aria whispered as a full-blown memory surge overwhelmed her.

Aria was small, barely six in Earth years – and how curious that after so many centuries on the red planet people still tended to count time in the annual cycles of their lost home – when her mother first showed her the capitol of Mars. It stood high and gleaming over a blue lake basin, surrounded by fertile fields and broad canals and great stands of spiney apples as far as the eye could see. Its isolation in a vast prehistoric crater had spared it much of the Great Burn's devastation. Even in its declining days they called it the City of Joy.

Aria saw tall glass towers and fluted bridges over the sparkling waters of the crater lake. The whole of Daedal stood on graceful pedestals over that azure water.

"This was once the greatest city on Mars," Queen Rhapsody told her daughter. "Centuries ago, before the First Men of the *Popol Vuh*[3] and the Great Burn, before the Long Decline, even before the chaos times, right back to the days of the Ancients, our city was the capitol of Mars. Every nation came here and paid tribute to us." She stroked Aria's cheek. "It is your heritage. These are your people."

Aria had spent her first years in the quiet sanctuary of domed Crystalia, where the graceful cathedrals were translucent and pale. The glass pleasure-steeples of Daedal were stained with rich bright colors, each hue complimenting the others, plaited together in fabulous variations. Even those towers that were now shattered seemed elegant in their ruin.

"Why did you never bring me home before this?" Aria asked her mother. "You are Queen, Queen of Mars."

As always, Rhapsody was beautiful but sad. "Queen of Mars in name only, now. It is many generations since we could claim any power, though our royal line is Ancient, back to the legendary times of old Earth. The City of Joy is a wonder but no longer powerful. It is protected, but only by the whim of a Sorcerer. I did not bring you here before because it was not safe."

"Is it safe now, mother?"

Rhapsody shook her head. "It is never safe to be a Princess of Mars, little one. Never safe to be a Queen. I only brought you here now because you have to be here, see this, before it is too late."

Aria didn't like the distress in her mother's voice. "What do you mean?"

Rhapsody stroked the child's hair. "The Black Sorcerer is cunning and not easy to fool. He believes you dead but that deception will not last forever. One day he will come for you and I will not be able to stop him."

Aria shuddered. "Why would a First Man come to get me?" she asked, trying not to let her voice tremble.

"Because he is your father," Queen Rhapsody replied.

---

[3] The Mayan "Book of the People" is a collection of myths and histories of the K'iche kingdom of Guatemala. Lines 4940 ff. include mention of four "First Men" whose titles have been taken by the four sorcerers ruling Mars. Somehow the Mayan myths have become mingled with Martian legend.

"Highness?"

Aria blinked and returned to her present surroundings. The blonde attendant was looking at her in alarm. It was she that had called out.

"Leave her be, Nepenthe," Nan scolded. "I said she'd have memory dumps, didn't I?" She turned to Aria. "What came back to you, lovie?"

"My mother," the princess replied. "I was so young. She showed me the City of Joy."

"That was a long time ago, then," Malathea commented. "Daedal was destroyed almost a thousand years ago."

Nepenthe's eyes grew even wider. "A thousand years?" She eyed Aria with surprise. The question that she dared not ask was written plainly on her face.

The princess remembered that answer now. "I'm not very much older than you are, Nepenthe. I've spent almost all the intervening time suspended in the Rainbow Waters."

The blonde attendant glanced at the marvelous pool.

Aria explained better. "My father wished me to be a sorceress. You know that sorcerers channel the arcane telluric energies of Mars, yes? Some use ancient artifacts or indwelling parasites, but a few – and the best – have bioware implants, mesh that weaves along their central nervous system and becomes a part of them. Many go mad or simply die. The Black Sorcerer made sure I had the finest possible implants and took centuries growing them in me as I slumbered in this Chamber."

Aria raised her hand and concentrated. A lilac aura rippled around her fingers, crackling like lightning.

"So easy now!" she admired. "I presume I was upgraded again during my recent bath?"

"Completely, this time," Nan promised. "Your arcane nerve-web is fully grown, your wetware as tuned as it can possibly be. You are an adult now, Princess Aria, and as fine a sorceress as any on Mars."

Aria located the occult knowledge that had been downloaded into her mind while she slept. The data-lore had been significantly increased since last time she'd checked. It would take months, maybe years, to sort through everything that had been stored in her brain.

Malathea raised her pale hand again and registered what Aria was doing. "You are drawing seven thousand two hundred geothaums per second from the planet's ambient energy field," she reported. "You seem to have an internal biocapacity to store around seven terrathaums for practical application."

Nepenthe looked worried again. Aria translated for the handmaiden. "My body pulls magic from the world like a flower absorbs sunlight. When I want to use that power I radiate it out again. Like this."

The princess gestured and all the instruments on Nan's workbench spun up into the air and twisted round in a complicated spiral. Not one of them crashed into another. Then Aria laid them all back exactly where they had been before.

"Your fine control has improved too," the old nurse approved. "Not that you won't have to practice to translate all that theoretical knowledge into practical experience."

The Sensorine had recorded it all, of course. Perfect recall was an essential part of her job. "Your projection of energy over range seems to have improved approximately 17.4 percent since your last biometric survey. Of course it is not possible to determine what extreme biological conditions might do to your arcane capacities."

"You mean you can't tell what I might be able to do if I'm hurt or scared," Aria surmised. "Or really really pissed."

"Only empirical observation will allow accurate extrapolation."

Nan put her datapad block down and patted Aria on the shoulder. "Enough of this for now, sweetness. You've just woken up from a very long sleep and you need some fresh air and a change of scenery. Your chambers are just as you left them. Why not go and settle back in until your next memory cascade?"

That seemed like a good idea to Aria. "Is my father here?" she wondered.

"The Black Sorcerer is in the South with his war machines, hunting Lord Ruin's Chain City," Malathea reported. "You awoke 9.4 days before his projections."

Aria didn't know why she was relieved, but she was. There were obviously more things about her father that she had to remember.

It seemed to Aria as though she had only left her silk-draped chambers mere days before. She knew that actually it was many years, but so much of the Nix Olympus volcano bastion of the Black Sorcerer was ancient that a mere eighty years made no difference at all. The same iron-framed windows looked over the red crags to Arcadian forests and the Lycos grasslands beyond. To the west was the faintest blue ribbon of the Amazonis Sea.

Aria returned to her familiar rooms and found books beside her bed that she'd last opened before her attendant's mother was born.

"We have tried to anticipate your every need," Nepenthe promised. She still sounded terrified. A displeased princess could have her tortured or killed.

Aria winced at the fear in the girl's voice. "How long have you been in the Black Sorcerer's service?" she wondered.

"Not long," the blonde maid confessed. "I was one of the last tribute tithe from Tempe, five months ago. Nan picked me to be trained as your handmaiden because she knew you would be rising from the Rainbow Waters soon."

"And I suppose she impressed upon you that you must be absolutely perfect in every aspect of your work?"

Nepenthe made a nervous curtsey.

Aria smiled to put the girl at ease. "Nan impressed the same thing upon me. For most of my life she's been reminding me that I am the Princess of Mars and the Black Sorcerer's daughter and that as such I have many duties and responsibilities."

Nepenthe bobbed again. "I did not understand, until they told me… I mean, there are many princesses from many lands sent in tribute to the First Men. Several occupy the master's Sealed Harem even now. Everybody knows that you rank higher than all others but few know why. I had thought you just another tithe, raised by the Black Sorcerer for his purposes."

"I'm sure I have been raised for his purposes. But few outside the Bastion know I am daughter to Queen Rhapsody of Mars and less that I am the Black Sorcerer's only surviving offspring."

Nepenthe's eyes flickered. The girl was curious but cautious. "Surviving offspring?"

"Have you not wondered why none of the First Men have long dynasties by now?" the princess noted. "The same energies that gave the great Sorcerers their power seem to inhibit their ability to engender children. Even arcane science cannot overcome the problem. Those rare quickenings that do occur end in abortion or death, often for mother as well as child. Of the hundreds of heirs the Black Sorcerer has tried to sire I am the only one to live more than a few weeks."

"Why?" Nepenthe could not help but ask.

"Father speculates that my mother's bloodline made the difference," Aria remembered. All the knowledge and experience she'd had before lay dormant in her mind, merely waiting for her to find need for it. "Rhapsody Arcantrix was the last ruler of Daedal, which the *Ojer Tzij* calls the capitol of Mars. She was of an ancient lineage – probably an Ancient lineage."

The princess sounded the capitalization in her second use of 'ancient'. The Ancients were the legendary beings who had first settled Mars from old Earth-that-was. The holy book spoke of them taming the red planet, setting the magic-like technologies that altered the world's gravity and atmosphere so that men could dwell there, embedding great machines in Mars' mantle that still preserved the biosphere today. The planet had been shaped by the Ancients, molded for their use and pleasure, long before the First Men had gathered the scraps of their shattered sciences to rise to dominion over a sundered globe.

"You are the Princess of Mars," Nepenthe recited. She sounded like a little girl saying her Quiche Maya devotions. "*The* Princess. Of *Mars!*"

"Does that matter? It's a very old title."

"Everyone knows about the Princess of Mars," the handmaiden dared to venture. "Rumors, legends, old stories. Why do you think so many girls are named Aria? You say few know of you outside your father's Bastion? My lady, *everyone* knows of you! Or about you. You're nearly as famous as the Crystal Lady!"

"Maybe I am," Aria allowed. "I don't get out much. But if we're to be friends then you need to stop being frightened or awed by me." She took Nepenthe's chin and lifted the girl's head so they could look each other in the face.

"Friends?"

"Why not? If Nan chose you she must of thought we'd be suited for each other. Tell me something of yourself. You're highborn of Tempe, aren't you?"

"Yes, highness. Only the nobility of Tempe are considered for the tithing, in their eighth cycle as they approach adulthood. I am a younger daughter of the Sub-Pasha of Scamander."

Aria had barely heard of the place, another of the distant provinces of her father's empire, but she asked more, to set her new servant at ease and because she was interested in new information. "What's it like in Scamander?"

Nepenthe's face grew wistful. "Beautiful in spring and first summer when the redgrass blooms. Dramatic as the trees turn amber in autumn. Terrible during windtide[4] and winter. Our citadel has

---

[4] Like Earth, Mars' orbital inclination causes a progression of seasons. The lengthier year means that each season is longer, allowing for two or more

spectacular views over the Eridanian icefields and the Mare Cimmerium. It nestles right in the shadow of a Harmony Spire that hums with the music of the gods."

It was mention of the Harmony Spire that triggered the memory cascade that took Aria back to her childhood.

"What *is* it?" nine-year-old Aria asked her mother in wondering tones. She leaned so far over the side of the sea-skimmer that the Knights of Daedal dutied to guard her twitched in panic lest she tumble into the deep waters.

Queen Rhapsody guided her daughter's feet back onto the deck of the glass and ebony sailing ship that sped them towards the distant Harmony Spire. They were still half a day's travel from the half-mile high structure but it glimmered clear and beautiful on the horizon.

"That, and others like it, are the legacy of the Ancients to all the creatures of Mars," Rhapsody told her daughter. "Nobody now understands how they were made or how they work, not even the First Men. But everyone knows it is these towers that allow us to live on Mars."

Aria stared fascinated at the twisted crystalline needle. She thought it looked like a giant unicorn's horn made of gem and pearl. "How can it let us live?" she puzzled.

"Mars was not always the world it is now," Rhapsody lectured. "The Ancients tamed it to their will, with their powers and machines. The Harmony Spires changed our planet's gravity, created air we could breathe, made an unseen barrier to stop the sun's invisible particles from ripping our new atmosphere from us. They hold Phobos and Deimos in the skies and transmit magic into the earth."

Aria looked at the elegant column with more excitement than ever. "Can we go inside?" she wondered.

"Nobody ever has. They may even be solid," her mother replied. "Or perhaps you will be the first. Hold out your hand to the Spire, Aria."

The girl did so. She yelped a little as a faint purple glow flickered across her skin. "That tickles! What is it?"

---

harvests in a long summer but a much worse and more extended winter interval. Between autumn and winter the natural geology of Mars causes a fifth, "windy" season of powerful gales and storms.

Rhapsody held up her hand to display the same effect. "This is proof that we are of the line of the Ancients. Our lineage allows us to sense, even capture, the great energies of the field the Harmony Spires wrap about Mars. Their magic."

Aria found that if she touched her fingers together then drew them apart she could make little lilac sparks.

"Once our line could draw upon those energies to perform great deeds," the Queen revealed. "But that was before the Fall. Now only the First Men and the Crystal Lady have the technologies to harness the higher magics of the Spires."

Aria remembered the Crystal Lady from her infancy in the sanctuary of Crystalia. She still wore the Lady's parting gift, a wonderful chain that became whatever colored clothing she desired. "The Crystal Lady could show us how to do the magic," the princess suggested.

"But she will not," Rhapsody answered tersely.

Aria looked over at the stately tower that stretched to the dappled sky. The wind pushed the sea-skimmer straight towards it over the Amazonis Sea. Half a dozen giant armored waterworms paced them, undulating above and under the waves. Their bulk and strange appearance had alarmed the girl until her mother had showed her the vibration box in the ship's prow that sent out pacifying subsonics to keep the creatures content.

"How many Harmony Spires are there?" Aria wondered. "Can we visit them all?"

"Nobody knows their number, except perhaps the First Men. Dozens, certainly. But less than there once were. Every century or so another Spire turns black and falls silent. When they all die then the magic will go from Mars and all life here will perish."

"Perhaps the dead Spires can be fixed?" Aria suggested. "I'll try and mend them."

"Perhaps you will," Rhapsody said indulgently but a little sadly. "Anyway little one, by tonight we'll sail up to the base of this Harmony Spire. You can touch your hand to its smooth side and feel the pulse of all Mars run through you. I want you to feel that once, while you're still with me."

"Still with you?" Aria suddenly felt alarmed. "Mother, what do you mean?"

Two days later the courier boat caught up with them, with a hasty summons to return to the City of Joy. The Knights of Daedal changed from their ceremonial finery to steel suits ready for battle. Their beautiful antique honor blades were replaced with laser rapiers and percussion staves. The mood of the voyage changed as the skimmer hurried home.

"What is happening?" ventured Aria, worried and a little frightened by the grim demeanor of the adults around her.

"War is coming," Queen Rhapsody told Aria. "I averted it for a while, but now the doom of Daedalia is upon us."

Aria looked at the strong brave soldiers that surrounded them. "The Knights of Daedal can overcome anything," she proclaimed with confidence.

Rhapsody didn't contradict her.

"Can't they?" Aria insisted. "Mother?"

Rhapsody took her aside where they could speak privately in the lee of the main cabin. "Do you think our knights could prevail against a First Man?" she asked.

"No," the princess reluctantly admitted. "But they don't have to. We are *protected* from the other First Men by the Black Sorcerer himself!"

"And what if it is the Black Sorcerer who makes war against us?"

Aria had no good answer for that. "But why would he?" she blurted. "I thought he liked us!"

Rhapsody's smile was bitter. "He liked me well enough once, or so I told myself." She smoothed her daughter's hair, the same raven black as her own, and made her confession. "Our nation's doom was upon us when the Black Sorcerer first desired me. He had decided that my genetic heritage made me compatible with him, a suitable candidate to mother his children."

"We can make magic sparks at the Harmony Spires," Aria understood.

"Yes. So I made a black bargain with the Black Sorcerer. I became his, to have and to hold, and Daedalia was spared and had peace. Each year I visited him in his great volcano, or wherever he had chosen to base himself at that time in his endless schemes and campaigns, and I stayed with him for a time as he attempted to quicken me."

"He was trying to give you a baby," comprehended Aria. She was unclear about the mechanics but she knew about mothers and fathers, and that she had no father as other little girls did.

"In the end he gave me a baby," Rhapsody told her. "You. But I did not want the child of my flesh to grow up in the Black Sorcerer's laboratory and never see her again. So with the help of loyal friends I deceived him, who is so good at deceiving others. He thought my child had died like all his other get. I fled to the Crystal Lady to recover and smuggled you with me into her Crystal City."

"The Crystal Lady is kind," Aria remembered.

"And terrible," Rhapsody noted. "Time runs differently in her domain when her borders are closed. A stay of six short years for us was a lifetime out here. When at last I returned to my kingdom everyone I knew had passed on. But return I had to, because there were things I had to show you, things I had to teach you, before the Black Sorcerer came for you."

"But he thinks me dead!" Aria squeaked. "Doesn't he? Mother?"

Queen Rhapsody shook her head. "He knows now that you live and thrive, little one. He is coming to take you, and to punish me. The doom of Daedalia has come at last."

The glass spires of Daedal were shattered jagged stumps. The graceful bridges were all broken. Millennia of art and literature burned in their galleries. The City of Joy was fallen.

The Black Sorcerer's formidable war-machines waded across the lake waters on spider legs, spitting fire and lightning. Rusty iron robots clanked unstoppably through ranks of Knights, crushing all resistance. Fierce brutal handlers led packs of the Sorcerer's newly-bred lizard-men pets on spiked chains to unleash upon the fleeing citizens.

The Jeweled Citadel was surrounded, cut off, while the rest of the capitol was demolished.

"You must flee now, majesty," Rhapsody's Knight Commander advised her. "We may yet be able to break through the besieging ring with one last supreme effort. You can seek refuge in Solis or Syria, hide out in the Sirenum swamps…"

The Queen shook her head. "I would not bring this devastation on anyone else. Wherever I run, the Black Sorcerer will follow me."

"Then the princess," the Knight Commander offered, "We could spirit her through the Shadow Door to the Hall of Reflections, hide her until…"

"You do not understand," Rhapsody told the battered officer. She gestured to the gallery where Aria watched the City of Joy burn and wept. "I knew that this day would come from the moment I conceived her. From the moment the Black Sorcerer's Herald brought me word of his desires. There was no other honorable end."

"Majesty?" The Knight Commander was baffled. Almost all his men were slaughtered now. The rest would not last the night. The capitol of Mars was destroyed, its population eradicated. He did not understand why.

"If I had not gone to the First Man's bed he would have destroyed Daedalia and taken me anyway," the Queen explained. "If I had borne him a living child and left her to his care then I would have allowed him a dynasty that would ensure tyranny on Mars till the last Harmony Spire dims. But Mars must not always bow to tyrants, and the First Men must be destroyed."

Aria looked over at her mother, unable to take in what she was hearing then. She remembered it all later.

"My daughter, the Princess of Mars, was raised in the Crystal Dome. I have shown her the secret places of this world. She has visited the Hall of Tatters and the Harmony Spires, spoken with the Brothers of Maya, been seen by the Bards of Isidis. Everything I could teach her I have taught, including the duty of a ruler. There was one last thing she had to see to become the weapon that will one day cast the First Men down into the dust." Rhapsody gestured to shattered Daedal. "This – and what comes next."

The gates of the Citadel blew off their hinges and splintered. The Black Sorcerer had arrived.

The Knight Commander stared at his Queen and his princess, torn between the desire to protect them and the need to attend to the breach.

"Go and end your life with honor," Rhapsody granted him. "Thank you for your service. You and all your fellowship, all of the City of Joy, your sacrifice *will not* be forgotten. All of it will be remembered in my daughter's eyes. One day your valor will inspire the freedom of Mars."

The Knight Commander saluted, then raced to his death.

There were more explosions in the courtyard. Some of the tripods had managed to climb the outer walls.

"What will happen now?" Aria finally dared to ask.

Rhapsody Arcantrix embraced the child. "I will always love you," she promised her daughter. "Remember."

"I will."

The chamber doors opened. There was no massive explosion or show of power. The Black Sorcerer merely turned the handle.

He entered the room alone, mantled in a plain black robe, bearing a serpent-crested staff. His thin pale face was intent and humorless. His hood was back, revealing a shining bald pate.

The Queen turned to face him. "Noir," she said.

"Rhapsody," he replied.

Aria peered from behind her mother, scared but still curious about the terrible bogeyman that even the holy book talked about. Her father.

"So that is Aria," the Black Sorcerer noted. "Hello, my daughter."

The child managed a fumbled curtsey. She did not want the First Man to think her rude – or frightened. She still clung to her mother's skirts.

"I thought once that you loved me," Rhapsody told the Black Sorcerer.

"And you used that affection to make me a fool," the First Man replied. "That cannot be forgiven."

"So I see." Outside, Daedal burned and crumbled into the lake. "What do you intend?"

"Aria is mine. I will care for her now."

"Will you? Care for her, I mean? Noir, she's only a child, your flesh and mine. Will you truly look after her? Or do you only want a pawn, another test subject in your endless machinations?"

The Black Sorcerer looked at the girl. "I honestly do not know," he admitted. "It will be instructive to find out."

Rhapsody stiffened. "And what of me, then?" she dared to venture.

There was no affection in the Black Sorcerer's gaze. "For you," he promised, "there is only pain."

Aria never saw her mother again.

"Now, lovie, you mustn't cry," Nan Vidi chided little Aria gently. "I know I'm a funny old stick to look on, what with being one of your father's genetic experiments and the like, but I'm only a silly old woman who wants to see that you're properly looked after."

Aria blinked away her tears and looked around. "Why am I in a bath?" she wondered.

Nan Vidi chuckled and guided the little girl out of the Pool of Rainbow Waters to where house slaves could dry and dress her. "Creator love you, child, but that's no mere bath. That's a wonder of the Ancients, that is, restored for you by the Black Sorcerer himself. It's a magic well, and when you're dipped in it you sleep for a long time, then wake up changed."

Aria looked at herself. She didn't feel that changed. She didn't think she'd slept that long, and said so.

"Three hundred cycles, lovie," Nan told her. "It's been that long before your father was satisfied that the neural grafts had taken. And to be honest, before he was ready to face his daughter, I think."

"I don't know what you're saying."

"But you know about magic, don't you?" Nan encouraged the princess. "You know how sorcerers can draw upon the magic of Mars and focus it to do things?"

"Yes. Some have magic wands, or strange gems planted in their foreheads."

"Some do. But the best sorcerers – the ones who can do the most and who don't go insane when they call on their powers – they have what lets them do magic planted inside them. Little silver fibers run through their whole body like nerves and let them draw upon magic just by thinking about it."

Aria checked her fingers but she couldn't see any silver wires.

"Your father has given you a neural net," Nan supplied. "Grown it within you while you slept like a fairy tale princess. Oh, it'll take time and years to fully implement, and several more long sleeps in the Rainbow Waters, but one day you'll be the finest sorceress on Mars, second only to the First Men themselves."

Aria was fascinated by the idea, but now her memory was returning properly. "Where's my mother?"

Nan's face fell. "You slept an awful lot of years, lovie. It's hundreds of years since your mother's time." She offered no other detail than that.

Aria felt like a lump of ice had been put where her heart should be. "Daedalia burned," she recalled.

"Nobody is allowed to defy the Black Sorcerer," Nan explained. "Our first loyalty must always be to him."

"He is a monster. And I am his daughter."

The nurse had no answer to that. "He is waiting for you," she told the princess. "Come and meet your father."

Aria awoke with a gasp. It took her a moment to register that she was an adult now, a grown woman with the perspective of twenty-two Earth-years' experience – albeit ranged over near a thousand years of history. She held up her hand to see the differences from the one that child-Aria had inspected all those years before.

Nepenthe was staring at her, worried and uncertain.

"Just one of those memory catch-ups that Nan was talking about," Aria reassured the handmaiden. "Nothing to worry about."

She turned her attention to her old room. For all the great chunk of experience that had just returned to her, Aria knew there were far greater swathes of herself still to discover. She looked about her chambers for clues that might prompt her recollection.

There was a mirror, and a table covered in bottles, cosmetics and potions for her daily use. The books by her bed were an eclectic mixture from high Isidic poetry to ribald Acidanian pulp, from an academic treatise on the barter economy of wild Phoenix Landing to a manual on the repair of servo-motors. Her wardrobes were expensive and tasteful, although Aria still preferred to wear her gift from the Crystal Lady.

All in all the room gave little away about the princess, as if it were a mask rather than a portrait.

"How much did they tell you about me, Nepenthe, when they prepared you as my maid?" Aria wondered.

"Everything that I needed to know," promised the blonde girl, bobbing her knees again. "You take a grapefruit and a spiney apple at breakfast, with tinoro leaf tea sweetened with honey. You favor a temperate bath with Olympian salts. You do not care for spiders or undead. You do not like being disturbed when you are in your workshop."

"Helpful to know," Aria considered. "It's possible that for the moment you know me better than I do. What are my interests and hobbies?"

"You conduct your experiments, of course. Sometimes you even borrow the master's sanctum. You practice your sorceries. You read extensively, ride on the grasslands, hear the testimony of whatever travelers you can meet and sometimes record it."

"Who are my friends? Or who were they, before my latest long sleep?"

Nepenthe shook her head. "I cannot say, highness."

Aria sensed an evasion. "Cannot say or do not know?" she clarified.

Nepenthe paled. "I haven't been briefed," she promised.

"There must have been people I talked to, spent time with," Aria reasoned. "I remember late-night discussions – arguments – with the Black Sorcerer. And Nan, of course, and the Sensorine Elicogna, Malathea's predecessor. Who else? A confidante? A suitor?"

Many of her father's warlords and specialists courted her, of course, desperately seeking advancement but respectful of her position; but it felt as if that memory was... incomplete.

"I don't know about suitors," Nepenthe confessed.

"So you have found none for yourself, before or since you came to Nix Olympus," Aria teased.

Nepenthe blanched, and the princess realized she'd made some mistake. "Was there someone special at home you had to leave behind when you were chosen for the tribute?" she guessed.

The maid shook her head. "I was a maiden when I came here, of course. It is the law."

"But now you are... not?"

"Herald Maximal desired me. He was... insistent."

"Ah."

"That was before I was selected as your handmaiden," Nepenthe added hastily. "He committed no disrespect to you."

"I do not know this Maximal. He is new."

"You will know him," Nepenthe replied. "He is high in the master's favor. It is rumored that the Black Sorcerer may even bestow you upon him some day."

"Bestow me?" Aria snorted. "I think not." She suppressed her revulsion at the idea of being awarded like a good conduct certificate, shelving it away to be considered another time.

"If you would prefer a handmaiden who is more pure I will explain my shame to Nan Vidi and ask for a replacement," Nepenthe offered in a trembling voice.

"I don't judge my handmaidens on grounds of 'purity'," Aria insisted. "Loyalty, intelligence, diligence, good counsel, yes, but not on what man happens to have pawed at her when she didn't have any say in it. My last maid Coda, now she was the most outrageous..."

Aria halted in mid-sentence. How had she forgotten Coda, who had attended upon her before her most recent time in the Rainbow Waters? Wild, outrageous Coda, with her irreverent humor and devastating candor? Coda who had disgraced herself so enthusiastically with her secret lover and had reported on it in such confiding minute detail to her mistress?

That thought caused another memory to click. "What happened to Coda?" she asked Nepenthe suddenly. "What became of Coda of Prima Prevura?"

"Coda?" Nepenthe blinked and the fear crossed her face again. She could only repeat what she'd heard. "Coda died."

And just like that, the next memory cascade began.

Coda was a typical Prima Prevuran, tall and graceful with smooth coffee skin and elaborately-cornrowed hair. She wore the bronze and gauze house uniform of a residence-level slave like a fashion statement. She moved like a ballerina or a huntress.

"Could have been a whole lot worse," she'd said, when Aria had sent for the girl to tell Coda that she was assigned as her new attendant.

"I'm pleased you think so."

"No offence," Coda assured her new mistress. "Just that there's so many bad things can happen to a girl who wins the lottery, you know?"

Aria was vaguely aware that the peoples of Prima Prevura held an annual draw to determine which sons and daughters of their noble houses were sent in tribute to their First Men overlord. Since Prima Prevura lay in disputed territory between the Black Sorcerer and the Lord of Fatal Laughter, the city elders chose to send seven young men and seven young women to both warlords.

"You did not volunteer for this duty then?" the princess surmised.

Coda shuddered. "Who would? Everyone knows what happens to the boys and girls that the Lord of Fatal Laughter gets his oh-so-creative hands on. He has a very sick sense of humor, that one. Sometimes he even sends back what he's made of his tribute when he's finished with them. And your father, with respect highness, well…" The black girl fell silent, realizing that she'd already said too much.

"You may speak freely with me, Coda. I expect confidentiality of you, and loyalty to me above all others, so you may expect confidentiality and loyalty from me also."

"Your father is the Black Sorcerer," Coda pointed out. It almost sounded like an apology. "The women of his harem aren't always treated well. Those tribute-slaves who serve in his experiments even less so." She managed a brave smile. "So yeah, I'm happy to be on Team Aria."

"What is Prima Prevura like?" the princess wondered. "I've seen images of the snake-people of Secunda Prevura. Do you have them in your state too?"

"Not for long if we see 'em," Coda answered honestly. "The boys hunt 'em down with long javelins. Chase 'em for days through the swamps and bayous if they have to."

"The women don't hunt, then?"

"With men to send out and do the hard stuff? Why should we?" Coda grinned. "In Prima Prevura it's the women who make the decisions. The Matriarchs run the show. The menfolk get to chase through the leech-groves."

"So you have wetlands," Aria recognized. "And men."

Coda's brilliant smile widened yet more. "Oh sure. The wetlands to make sure we're bitten during the day, and the men..." She winked.

Aria blushed. Nan had programmed a theoretical understanding of the exchanges between men and women but, as the old nurse was fond of reminding her, theory could only become proven through practice. So far Aria hadn't had the opportunity.

"So you...?" Aria asked Coda in a low voice.

"Never got the chance," the maid replied. "The tributes all have to be untouched for the First Ones. We got laws and serious penalties for girls who make themselves ineligible for the lottery. That's not to say I haven't had a few hot moments with a few hot boys, y'know, but nothing could ever come of it till I'd passed my lottery year." She gestured around her. "And we know how that turned out!"

Aria realized that she and Coda must both be exactly the same age. "Well, my last handmaiden caught the eye of one of father's top Robot-Callers and got permission to wed him," the princess revealed. "So maybe after a few years you'll be able to find true love as well?"

"True love?" Coda snorted. "Girl, it's not true love I want, it's ---"

Aria blushed again as the Prima Prevuran revealed exactly what she wanted from a man.

"Perhaps we should just stick with your regular domestic duties for now then," the princess suggested prudently.

"You wanna see something *hot*?" Coda asked Aria one afternoon.

It was the dog-days of the late Martian summer, when the air was thick and still and the skies were purple-blue. Phobos hung high in the sky like a half-closed red eye. Aria was bored and restless so she was ready for an adventure.

"What is it?" she asked Coda as she jumped from her bed. She mentally configured the gossamer strips of her gown into something more substantial and seemly for public wear, staining them green and gold to match the season.

"The handsomest guy I've seen since Prima Prevura," Coda told her. "C'mon. You can use your magic to over-ride the ventilation ducts, right?"

Aria followed after her impetuous maid, out of the residential floor and down the Iron Stairwell past the bionics labs and robotech bays to the Intelligence level. There she flared her arcane bioenergies to fool a maintenance hatch locking system so that Coda could prize the rusty grill open.

"It's filthy in there!" Aria objected as the maid crawled into the shaft.

"Does that dress of yours ever get dirty?" Coda challenged.

Actually, the princess' favorite garment could be stained and damaged but it cleaned and repaired itself. Aria was intrigued enough by her handmaiden's enthusiasm to overcome her distaste of the dusty duct and follow after.

"Could you please tell me *why* we're disturbing every crawler in the palace?" the princess demanded.

"We need to get to the Holding Quarters," Coda explained. "Should be left here, I guess."

The handmaiden crawled over to a mesh that looked down into the gunmetal-walled interrogation block. Aria squeezed in beside her.

"Look there," Coda whispered, pointing down at the lizard-men who'd just entered the guard room.

The reptilian servants of the Black Sorcerer had a new prisoner. He was tall and muscular, brown-skinned like Coda, and he struggled with his captors until one of them dropped him to his knees with a pain wand.

"Mm-mm," approved Coda, not of the captive's treatment but of the way sweat glistened on his heaving chest. "I know you don't have much experience to call on, highness, but that there is a fine, fine man!"

"He's quite handsome," Aria agreed. She felt she had to say something.

"He is the kind of boy I would like to have met if I hadn't done been picked in the lottery," Coda confessed. "Now how we gonna rescue him?"

"Rescue him?" Aria frowned. "He's in father's Holding Quarters, surrounded by General Hasst-Gak's lizard-men. How can we rescue him?"

"Look at those pectorals, girl," Coda responded. "How can we not?"

Aria's mind turned naturally to strategies and plans. It wasn't enough to get the handsome man out of the interrogation suite. He had to be got away from Nix Olympus, to where he could flee to freedom. And it had to be done without leaving a trace of the princess' interference.

"Easy," she said to herself as much as to Coda. "Back up the shaft, please. We need to navigate these ducts to a security terminal."

Coda shuffled in reverse until she reached the T-junction, then let Aria take the lead as the duct crossed over the Iron Staircase and passed into the Data Reservoir.

Once inside the great chamber where the Black Sorcerer's ancient thinking machines wheezed and clattered in constant calculation, Aria charmed another security door and gained access to the programming deck. Her hands flared turquoise for a moment as she used her magic to bypass the lockouts on the interface terminal.

"What you got in mind, princess?" Coda asked, intrigued.

"Well, if we're to rescue your handsome paragon we need to send a few messages," Aria explained. Her fingers clacked over the typewriter keyboard, each stroke shifting a bar that struck a data-feed pad. "This one's to the Duty Inquisitor in the Holding Quarters instructing the new prisoner's immediate transfer to a specimen cage in Bio-Lab Three. And this one's an order to secure a package from Bio-Lab Three in an hour's time and transport it to the shores of the Xanthe Sea and set the contents loose in the wild. Your hero should be able to find his way home from there, don't you think?"

"Just like that?" Coda asked, impressed. "You can do it that easy?"

"Oh, the hard part is this," the princess admitted. She pressed her hands against the cracked old monitor screen and used her power on the vast sluggish data systems to which it connected. "I've got to erase all trace of those orders and delete all record of the prisoner from the system." Information flooded through her mind. "His name is Dane, by the way."

"Dane." Coda tasted the name and found she liked it. "Okay."

Aria's probing coursed Dane's whole capture file through her mind for a moment before she deleted it from the system. "Oh!" she gasped.

"You alright, princess?" Coda asked as Aria turned pale.

"I think so. But we might have made a mistake, Coda. A bad one."

"What kind of mistake?"

"That Dane," answered Aria. "He's one of the rebels. He's a major enemy of the Black Sorcerer!"

Bio-Lab Three was shut down at the moment. Its huge Van de Graaf globes and computer-controlled surgical arms were powered-off and silent. Tesla coils and protomatter pumps were covered in cobwebs.

Dane was secured as ordered in one of the black iron cages suspended around the dissection slab. When he heard someone coming he shifted round, setting his box swinging.

Aria paused as she approached the captive rebel. She hadn't expected that they'd confiscate his clothing.

Coda on the other hand seemed quite encouraged. "Hey, brother!" she greeted the prisoner. "This looks like it's your lucky day."

It took a moment for Dane to realize that the young women were not part of the ordeal he expected to face. "Who are you?" he asked in wonder as Aria sealed the Bio-Lab for privacy. "Why are you here?"

"I'm Coda, that's Aria," the princess' handmaid revealed. "This is a rescue."

"This *may* be a rescue," Aria qualified. She shifted closer to the metal cage where the naked man hung – but not too close. "I have a few questions."

Dane snorted. "So that's it! This is some kind of trick to get me to talk, to pry information out of me by some stinking ruse! I guess next you're gonna offer me your bodies if I tell you what you want to know."

"We most certainly are *not!*" snapped the princess, over Coda's mumbled consideration of the proposition. "Nor is this a ruse. We have risked considerable censure in making these arrangements to speak with you. However, before I allow the other part of our plan to release you to proceed there are certain assurances I need to have."

Dane frowned, torn between hope and suspicion. "What do you want, lady?"

"Your file said you were a rebel," Aria began. "Rebelling against what?"

"Against what?" the black man echoed. "Where you been living, lady? Against the First Men, that's what – and who. Not everybody's so cowed and terrified that they'll just roll over and be slaves to the Sorcerers. There's some folks will die free rather then live as slaves."

"Like you?" Coda asked, admiringly.

"Hell yeah! Like me and plenty of others. The Black Sorcerer and the rest, they have the magics, they have the weapons, but they don't have our souls."

"The Sorcerer of Night might," Aria added warningly.

"They don't own us, only imprison us. Magic can be got. Weapons can be got. The First Men can be taken down."

"It's been tried before, many times," Aria retorted. "Right back to the Resistance of Daedalia. Nobody has ever succeeded."

"Don't mean nobody ever will," Dane spat. "But that's all you get from me. No dates, no times, no people. I'll die before telling you or anyone zip 'bout the Runners."

"Don't be a damfool!" Coda scorned. "Dane, there's folks here who could have you singing like a bird on their torture racks. There's beings could just scoop the knowledge clean out of your mind, leaving you empty as an old jam-pot. They could put visions in your head make you think you're talking with your oldest best friends and make you jabber everything you know. This is the Black Sorcerer's lair, Runner, and there's 'bout a million ways he could make you talk. So you're damned lucky me and Aria decided to look out for you and send you home."

"How can you do that?" Dane demanded.

"I planted some orders," Aria explained. "In a few minutes the lizard-men will come and transport you to the sea-shore and set you loose. Their commander will probably assume we've implanted you with a tracker or some time-delayed virus and sent you back to destroy your comrades. But before I allow you to go I have to understand why I should."

"Why? 'Cause the First Men have to be put down is why!" the rebel insisted.

"Be specific," Aria told him. "Explain to me why you believe Mars would be a better place without the First Men controlling it."

Dane realized that the girl was serious. "Alright then. How 'bout this? The *Popol Vuh*, the holy book of the Maya, it says the First Men were the first formed and they ruled because they gained knowledge of all the world. But even the book admits that there was already a world before them. There was a Creator and there were people that lived without four tyrants lording it over them. So we know men can live free."

"It's just a story," Coda suggested.

"What about the Ancient ruins all 'cross Mars, then?" Dane challenged. "The First Men didn't make those cities. Destroyed them, maybe, but not built them. What about the Ancients' technologies that the Sorcerers are always digging up to use in their endless wars with each other? Why should a whole world get wrecked and ruined just so four massive egos can use it as the playing board for their brutal war-games?"

"You're arguing that there was a time before the First Men," Aria summarized. "So what if there was? The Sorcerers rule now and their grip is nigh absolute. How can futile rebellion change anything?"

"How can anything change otherwise? How can the races of Mars grow back to what we once were 'fore something awful happened? How can we rebuild our cities and canals? How can we raise our families in peace? How can we even survive in the long run, while the First Men use us as disposable toys and test subjects?"

"You have a family to raise?" Coda asked, disappointed.

"Not while I'm a rebel," Dane answered with a rakish smile. "Maybe some day."

"Well damn!" answered the handmaiden.

Aria still wasn't satisfied. "You're talking about a dream of freedom, not about a practical way of achieving it. Dying for a cause is very noble, but also stupid if there's no gain."

"Well like I said, I'm not giving away anything while I'm locked in the Black Sorcerer's Bastion. Maybe you're right that he can rip whatever information he wants from me but I'm not giving it away for free. Not here."

"Then where?" asked Coda, suddenly breathless.

Dane paused a moment and looked at the young women. "You serious?" he checked. "You're both highborn, I can tell, and you're dressed like a top-notch house slave and you..." he gestured to Aria, "...maybe you're one'a the Sorcerer's harem or something. Why would you want to learn about rebellion 'gainst the First Men unless it was to sell us out?"

"I have a curious mind," answered Princess Aria.

Dane snorted again. "Alright then. I can't make no promises for the others, but here's my best offer. On the South shore of the Cimmerium Sea, right in line with Mount Draconis, there's a bay with a waterfall, and a broken statue rising out of the water. You be at that statue, just the two of you, at midnight, in three weeks when Deimos is full, and I'll answer your questions. If you dare come. But if there's even a whiff of trap about it you'll never hear from me again."

Coda's lips moved to answer but she restrained herself. The maid knew that this decision was Aria's alone.

Purple Deimos hung low in the Southern sky, its irregular shape fully lit against the backdrop of stars. Phobos had not yet risen[5], so

---

[5] Mars' two moons are tiny; Phobos at 8.9 miles across and Deimos at 3.9 miles across are dwarfed by Luna's diameter of 2,160 miles. At full moon in the present skies of Mars they appear no larger than a golf ball and a

the Mare Cimmerium was bathed in violet moonlight, each rippled wave topped with purple spume.

Aria coaxed her personal flyer low over the clifftop and dropped it down almost to water level beside the high waterfall. Coda, never the best traveler anyhow, emitted a shrill shriek at the sudden descent.

The broken statue was easy to spot. It still stood seventy feet out of the water, a robed figure carved from green stone, shattered at about knee height. It was impossible to say whether the image had been man or woman, or even human. The shallow bay washed around the crumbled base. Huge fallen fragments were now the rounded-off boulders dotting the inlet.

Aria pushed her flyer's sensors to their maximum, pressing through the all-pervading static fuzz that prevented long-distance communications and long-distance surveillance across the entire planet. She could detect no sign of life and no electronic signatures.

"So we're doing this?" Coda asked, nervously.

"I thought you wanted to meet Dane again?" the princess teased. "You certainly seemed keen enough when we discussed it."

"Sure. That was back in Arcadia. Before we ran off without telling your father or Nan Vidi where we were going." Coda shifted uncomfortably. "If you annoy the Black Sorcerer he'll probably cut your allowance. Me he'll flay."

"If you think the risk too great…" Aria began.

"No. I'll go. But before I do… girl, there's something I have to tell you."

"Is it about what else you'd like to do with Dane? Because I heard quite enough of your ideas on the flight here, and frankly I think the poor man would die of exhaustion."

Coda didn't answer Aria's smile. She stayed deadly serious. "I already know what Dane's going to say, princess," she confessed. "I know about the Runners."

---

marble respectively. Phobos whizzes around the planet every 7 hours, 40 minutes. Since it moves faster than Mars turns it rises in the west and sets four and a quarter hours later in the east. Deimos has a synchronous orbit over Mars' equator, where it appears to take around 2.7 days from rising to setting west to east. For the purposes of this novel it is assumed that the Ancients who engineered changes to Mars' gravity and atmosphere likewise altered the orbits of its moons, bringing them much closer and holding them in place with the same technologies that maintain the other physical changes. Thus Phobos and Deimos have the same orbital characteristics but appear much larger in the sky. They likewise exert gravitational and tidal forces far beyond their natural mass.

"The rebels?" Aria clarified.

"There's lot of rebels. The Nots hold out against the Lord of Fatal Laughter. The Wisengot resist in the Sorcerer of Night's Utopian Forests. The Corsairs sail free on the Amazonis Ocean. The Runners are the ones who connect the rest, link them up to exchange news and trade weapons, to share intelligence and stay ahead of the First Men's forces."

"And you know this how?"

Coda shrugged, embarrassed. "Because my brothers were Runners, Aria. Both of them. Albin was caught and eaten by the Night Sorcerer's wights. Nobody knows what became of Tobit down in the Warfields. Both of them died doing what they thought was right."

The Princess regarded the Prima Prevuran. "You've been my maid for over two years and you never mentioned this?"

"What was I supposed to say to the Black Sorcerer's daughter? 'Oh, and by the way, mistress, my family are all active rebels working to overthrow your pa and all his works?'"

"So your coming to me was not an accident."

"I swear it was. The lottery fell on me and, well, we figured that maybe I might be able to do something useful before I died. Sabotage something or spy something out, maybe? If I had to go to your father's bed or the Lord of Fatal Laughter's Delirium Dome, maybe I could even get close enough to hurt one of them? It wasn't any more planned than that. But then I came to you and you... you weren't what I expected at all!"

"What did you expect then?"

Coda spread out her hands in an I-don't-know gesture. "Something bitchier? Some overprivileged spoiled monster, cruel and thoughtless? Maybe someone just like your father. Not you. Not someone I could talk with and respect. Not... a friend."

Aria saw the tears in the handmaid's eyes. "What about Dane, then?" she asked.

"I heard 'bout him from the servants' grapevine. A rebel captured, they said, maybe even a Runner. Being brought for interrogation and execution. I saw him being dragged through the outer bailey and I thought maybe this was the moment I had to take a chance and let you see what was really going on."

"Turn me against the Black Sorcerer, you mean?"

Coda looked at the princess. "Aria, you're not just the Black Sorcerer's daughter. You're heiress of the legendary Queen Rhapsody. You're the Princess of Mars! *Our* princess." The maid faltered. "I had to take the chance that maybe, just maybe, you'd listen."

"I'm here, aren't I?" Aria demanded. She gestured to the green statue beyond the flyer's window.

"You are. But I didn't want you to go out there without knowing everything. I owe you that. Princess, I don't know what they're planning. They might tell you what's really happening – I hope they do – but they might try and hold you hostage, or torture you for information, or simply kill you. It'll be dangerous."

"A princess is always in danger," Aria remembered. "But thank you for telling me, Coda. And for being my friend."

She lowered the flyer to land on the plinth beside the statue. Then she waited.

Around midnight a light showed on the cliff above the waterfall. It flashed briefly then went dark again. Shortly after, Coda and Aria gasped when two dark shapes launched themselves off the clifftop and dived straight down into the bay below.

Dane and his companion swam with fast overarm strokes out to the plinth of the broken statue.

"Man knows how to make an entrance," Coda admitted.

Dane and his companion reached the crumbling pathway that joined the statue to the shore, and climbed up. The other Runner was stockier than Dane and had the pale white skin of a far Northerner, but he had the same rakish swashbuckling air and an easy handsome countenance.

"Halifax," he announced himself with a little bow. "Pleased to meet you, Princess Aria."

So the Runners do their research, the princess reflected. She should have realized that her own diligent preparation for this meeting would have been equaled if not exceeded by that of the rebels. They needed to stay one step ahead of the First Men if they wanted to stay alive at all.

"You invited us, we came," Aria said.

Dane unslung a waterproof satchel from his back and pulled out a rusted old proximity scanner. It looked like Lord Ruin's technology, bulky and blocky and seamed with rivets. "Nobody else around," he reported at last. "Looks like the ladies kept their side of the bargain."

"I told Corrigan that he was being paranoid," Halifax replied. "That's why it's just the two of us, ladies. No-one else was dumb enough to come."

43

"But you were," surmised the princess.

Halifax's smile was dazzling. "Dumb enough for anything," he promised.

Dane moved on to business. "You wanted some answers. Before that, we need some answers from you."

"What kind of answers?" asked Aria. She tried to keep the nervousness out of her voice. She mentally checked the precautions she'd programmed into the flyer behind them; just in case.

"For starters, do you intend to go back to the Black Sorcerer?" Halifax questioned. "And if so, why?"

Aria met his gaze. "If your reasons or methodology for rebelling seem inadequate to me then I would naturally return to my father. I can probably influence him more than anyone. Perhaps I can temper his excesses and encourage him towards a more moderate reign. If your responses are compelling then I will also return to the Black Sorcerer. Logically I can do far more inside his organization with access to information and technology than I could grubbing some peasant existence in permanent exile."

Halifax and Dane exchanged glances. "That kind of limits what we can tell you," Dane admitted, "but it makes sense the way you say it."

"Stop telling me what you can't say," commanded Aria, "and tell me what you can."

Halifax nodded. "There's been resistance to the First Men's rule for as long as there's been a rule. If the rumors are true, if you were actually around when the Black Sorcerer shattered the City of Joy, then you know that. Many generations have opposed the total domination of the Sorcerers. Some gathered in marginal lands, the Amazonis archipelagos or the Sirenum Swamps. Others hid where conspiracy could be masked in towns and villages that conceal their disaffection from their overlords."

"Plenty of rebels got caught and died too," added Coda from family experience.

"Of course. After all these generations we still haven't figured how to overcome the massive advantage of the Sorcerers' magic. Maybe that's how you can help us, princess? We don't have many mages and those we do have are pretty... strange."

"Do you actually have a plan?" Aria wondered skeptically. "Long term strategy? Goals?"

"We try to stir up the conflict between the First Men," Dane supplied. "We go after whatever technology they're trying to reclaim and grab it first. Maybe one day there'll be something powerful enough for us to have the edge. The Voice of God or one of the Hallows, something like that."

"We even sent scouts into Acheron, where the Sorcerers dump their discards," Halifax confided in a hushed whisper. "None of them returned, of course."

"Mostly we just keep the idea of rebellion alive in people's minds," Dane went on. "If we can suborn a weaponsmith of Cryse here, an Elysian necrotechnician there, we stand a chance."

"So no master plan, then," said Aria. She should have known.

"Nothing we'll tell you, princess," Halifax admitted. "Not 'til we know we can trust you."

"And how will you know that?"

"You say you're going back. So then, if you decide to aid us we'll set up lines of communication. Do you know what a dead drop is? Where you hide a message and someone picks it up later or leaves you a reply? If we need information about the Black Sorcerer then you can get it for us. If you want to know what's happening outside your mountain palace you can ask us about it."

"And when the princess sends me out to shop for her, down in the Arcadian plains villages, I could meet someone and talk," Coda offered. Her eyes were on Dane.

Aria still wasn't committed. "And if I choose not to assist you?" she challenged.

"Then you go home and never speak of this again, please," Halifax told her. "But you will help us. I know it." His eyes burned into the princess'.

"I shall consider it," Aria conceded. "Suggest a location for this dead drop of which you speak. When I have taken thought I will communicate my decision."

"You'll help us," Halifax smiled. And he kissed Princess Aria's hand.

"The Black Sorcerer is furious," Nan Vidi told Aria as the Sensorines completed their scans of the returned princess. "Half the lizard-men legions in Arcadia are out looking for you, as well as the Esper Shells and the Ticktockmen."

"It was a simple flyer malfunction," the princess lied plausibly. "The vril interface coupler fused and we had to make an emergency landing. We didn't want to identify ourselves to the locals for obvious reasons, so Coda and I hid out until I could synthesize a replacement part. And now we're here."

Nan glanced over at the Sensorine Elicogna. "She is unharmed," the white-eyed scanner confirmed. "I can find no sign of biointerference, psychic modification, implanted technology or physical intrusion."

"Physical intrusion?" Aria puzzled. "What do you mean by... oh!" She blushed as she realized the Sensorine was checking whether she'd run off to be with a lover. "I told you, Nan, it was a simple accident. I'm glad to be safely home again."

"That's what you told me, lovie," the old nurse agreed; but she had an edge to her voice.

Coda returned to her mistress, likewise scanned. "The Black Sorcerer has summoned you," she warned Aria. She said it like it was a death sentence.

Aria fastened her hip-chain and dressed herself again. "I'd better not keep him waiting then," she told Nan and the Sensorines.

Nan held her gaze. "You be careful, Aria," she advised in worried tones. "The Black Sorcerer will not countenance you having too many... malfunctions."

Aria sent Coda back to her quarters and took the Iron Staircase up towards the rotunda of the Black Sorcerer's fortress. Here, under the greened copper dome beneath the roiling Martian sky, the unquestioned Lord of the West kept his laboratory sanctum.

The great chamber looked like a cross between a junkyard and a surgery. Chains of naked bulbs lit vast piles of recovered technology. Dozens of static-filled monitors fizzed and crackled. Hundreds of oscilloscopes flickered and danced. The main work-floor was ringed with reel-to-reel tape machines, constantly whirring as they drove steam-pistoned rods that programmed the bubbling nano-liquid cylinders.

The Black Sorcerer held up his hand to warn Aria to enter no further, then jammed down a huge circuit-breaker to activate his machines.

Electrical arcs played around the main platform. For an instant the dark dome was washed with brilliant blue light. Great capacitor batteries hummed in chorus as they discharged their energies. Fizzing ball lightning shimmered away, earthing through the nearby mechanisms.

The first power-bus blew, sending crimson sparks across the lab. A second, then a third coil exploded. The lightning stream went wild, arcing some of the projector nodes to slag before flickering to nothing.

Shadow returned to the sanctum.

The Black Sorcerer peeled off his goggles and approached the pyrite platform. He lifted a silver-white cylinder into his gloved palm and made a guttural grunt. "Not even warm."

Aria decided it was safe to approach now. She crossed the metal-mesh floor between the generator arches, picking her way past the melted debris of the recent experiment.

Her father passed the cylinder to her for examination. "Do you know what it is?" he enquired.

Aria inspected the artifact. It was the length of her hand, smooth and regular, terminating at one end with a crystal disc. Five buttons along the shaft were each tinted a different color. The princess pressed one at random but nothing happened.

"Something needing new batteries, I'd say," she judged.

"Elicogna has determined that item to be of an age with the Harmony Spires," the Black Sorcerer revealed. "What do you think it might be?"

Aria had expected a scolding, or threats, maybe punishment for her recent waywardness. In her worst rehearsed cases she might be subjected to mental probes or torture. She had not expected an exam.

The princess turned her full attention to the device. It resisted her arcane senses, which made it unusual for that alone. It seemed to have an energy signature but she could not discern what. It felt... locked.

Her fingers smoothed over its seamless construction. The object was heavier than it looked, but well balanced. The lens reminded her of Crystalia and its eternal Lady. It had that same subtle luster. And it was old, so old...

The relevant scriptures from the *Ojer Tzij* dropped into Aria's mind. "You can't imagine this is one of the Four Hallows?" she said to the Black Sorcerer. "It isn't a sword, a stave, a cup, or a stone. It exhibits no active power field, mortality aura, temporal weave or matter alignment matrix."

"And yet it resists everything I use on it," the First Man noted. "It absorbs whatever energies are directed at it and simply... stores them."

Aria turned the device over in her hands. "Where did you find it?"

"Ulyxis, a long-ruined colony in the ultimate North," the Black Sorcerer replied. "Or rather, the Lord of Night's wights discovered it there. General Nash'Tak relieved them of the burden when he ambushed their survey team."

"And apart from Elicogna's assertion of its antiquity and its apparent indestructibility, what makes you think this might be one of the Ancients' great and legendary Hallows?"

The Black Sorcerer paused. "A sense," he admitted at last. "Can't you feel it?"

Aria allowed herself to examine not what her mind was reporting about the item, but what her heart was feeling. "Is it... waiting?"

The Black Sorcerer snapped his fingers. "Waiting! That's the word I was groping for. Well done, daughter." He retrieved the item and placed it on one of his cluttered shelves. "I believe that might be the Sword of Light. And if it is then we must move quickly to secure another artifact."

"How so?" Aria asked, swept along by her father's intensity. She too was lured by the idea of ancient knowledge rediscovered.

The Black Sorcerer ran his hand over one of the monitors, willing it to exhibit a screed of sensor readings from the ruins of Ulyxis. "Look at the construction data, daughter. I had the Loremaster check to see if we'd ever come across comparable buildings elsewhere. And we have."

Aria traced the research trail. "Seven centuries ago our scouts reported Ancient ruins near the Cerberus Canal in the shadow of Mount Charon. The place had the same construction style and materials as the Ulyxis colony. You suspect that if one Hallow was lost or hidden at Ulyxis, then this other complex at..." (she checked the reference) "Stygis, might contain another."

"I do," agreed the Black Sorcerer.

"The only problem is that Stygis is on contested lands between the domains of Fatal Laughter and the Sorcerer of Night," Aria pointed out. "An expedition there would not pass easily nor escape unscathed."

"If I made this connection then my adversaries can," the Black Sorcerer warned. "Night at least has exactly the same data I have, and he is not a fool." He turned aside to examine the damage his recent investigation had done to his equipment. "It will take me some time to prepare an adequate expedition, Aria, but when I am ready I shall go to Stygis and take what I desire. *You* shall accompany me."

Aria's heart lurched. "Me?"

"You are ready. Your recent exploit convinces me of that."

"My exploit?"

The Black Sorcerer turned away and said no more.

The warriors clashed on the combat field, striving for perfection in the art of killing. The best of the Black Sorcerer's fighters were mere blurs of blade and fist, dancing around each other in a lethal whirl.

Aria and Coda sometimes watched the soldiers, gossiping and giggling as their favorites rose and fell. Today Aria found no pleasure in watching sweating fighters try to harm each other.

She rose. "Come with me," she told her maid. "Nan, you need not trouble yourself. I only want a walk."

The old nurse settled back into her seat and resumed her enjoyment of the training show. If she glanced warily after her young charge she did so covertly.

"Where are we going?" Coda asked when she and Aria were out of earshot.

"I've been thinking about our recent encounter," the princess said.

"With *Halifax?*" Coda teased.

The back of Aria's hand prickled where he'd kissed it. "With the Runners," she whispered urgently. "I don't know whether to believe them or not. I know father can by a tyrant sometimes, but he does protect the West from the other First Men. He's better than the obvious alternatives."

"The devil you know," Coda quoted the *Ojer Tzij*.

"Yes. It's all very well for the rebels to talk of overthrowing the First Men, but what next? Free cakes for everyone and peace and joy thereafter? Who rules in the Sorcerers' stead? Who controls the technology they once possessed? Who will prevent civil war and chaos? How will mankind come together to revive the dying Harmony Spires?"

"I don't know," Coda shrugged. "You?"

Aria was mildly horrified to realize that she was considering it. "Before I commit myself to doing something which may bring the social fabric of Mars crashing down I must be certain what we have can't be fixed. Hence our expedition."

"Expedition to where?"

"Back to the Holding Quarters," the princess declared.

Coda wrinkled her nose. "The ducts again? *Your* dress might clean itself but…"

"No ducts. Not this time. I am the Black Sorcerer's daughter, the Princess of Mars. This time I shall undertake a full and formal inspection, as is my right."

"A right you've never before asserted, girl."

"There has to be a first time."

Coda smirked. "You thinking 'bout Halifax again."

"You are obsessed with men!" Aria complained.

"And you are obsessed with… whatever the heck it is you're doing right now. Interfering. Trying to fix things. Princessing."

Aria didn't argue. She strode up to the main entrance to the Holding Quarters and spoke to the guards as they snapped to attention. "Fetch me your duty commander. I wish to take a tour."

Princesses do not vomit, Aria insisted to herself. *Princesses do not weep.*

She clenched her fists until her nails drew blood from her palms and followed the Chief Inquisitor on his round.

Aria had known, in theory, that many captives were brought to the Black Sorcerer. Slaves sent as tribute from subordinate kingdoms staffed the palace. The army was filled with conscripts who preferred servitude to immediate death.

She had known, if never really considered, that her father held prisoners for interrogation and used some of his subjects for his experiments.

She had never visited the Inquisition Bays before, nor witnessed what went on in the Red Surgeries. She had never seen a man's chest opened up like a cage, his life-force pinned in his body so he could not die no matter the pain. She had never seen one of the shambling peaceful Mock-Men shaved and impaled on a hundred pain-needles, each one testing the limits of the huge creature's endurance. She had not been shown the dark pit where the mindless victims of the brainworms crawled in idiot cannibalism.

Somewhere far away the Chief Inquisitor was delivering his lecture, oblivious to the horror all around him. "…strip away the part of the brain that filters out pain reflexes so that every nerve ending in the body becomes a screaming throbbing torment. It is a proven technique for interrogation and a simple short-cut for higher-end psychological programming…"

Coda followed close behind Aria, her mouth clamped shut so she wouldn't scream. Aria dared not look at her.

This is my father's empire too, the princess thought. *While he pioneers the restoration of the Ancients' lore, men bleed and die down here for opposing him. As his armies hold back the mad robots of the Lord of Fatal Laughter and the ghost galleys of Lord Erebus his inquisitors are peeling away the skins of Mock-Men to see what will happen. I thought his eccentricities could be tolerated for the sake of the order he brings, but I was wrong. I did not know. I did not want to know.*

She remembered her mother then, and Queen Rhapsody's prediction. Aria was the weapon she had aimed at the First Men. Nearly a thousand years ago the last Queen of Mars had foreseen the day when Aria would understand.

"Of course," the Inquisitor continued, "once the plague-moulds have begun to manifest sentience they can devise their own programs of agony on their hosts, which allows for..."

"That will be all!" the princess snapped, and turned away hurriedly. "Come Coda!"

The usually-confident handmaiden was a trembling wreck by the time they had retreated to the Iron Staircase. "They... It... There was..."

"Yes," said Aria, blinking back tears. "Now we know. We need to use that dead-drop."

And there Aria's vivid flashback ended, leaving her shaken by what she remembered seeing, puzzled at what might have happened next.

The princess sat down heavily on her bed. "So what became of Coda? Did she live to a ripe old age? Did she marry? Was she happy?"

"I cannot say, highness - I do not know." Nepenthe was distraught to be failing her new mistress so soon. "I could try and find out."

"Ask Nan. She'll remember." *I might well recall something myself soon*, Aria worried. She didn't like the gaps that last sequence of visions had left in her mind.

And Halifax? What had become of that young man and his handsome partner? With a sick sinking feeling, Aria realized that she had probably outlived everyone she'd ever met outside the Black Sorcerer's inner circle.

Aria spent some time refamiliarizing herself with her apartments. When she'd checked her household accounts, made sure the standing orders for her daily comforts were still in place, and set the Loremaster to preparing a summary of the major events that she'd missed in the last eighty cycles, the princess moved her investigations on to the rest of the palace.

It felt strange to be exploring a place she must know intimately. Nepenthe was fairly new and had kept to her room as much as possible, so the grim grand Bastion of the Black Sorcerer was fresh to both of them.

The central space was named after the huge winding steps that twisted round it. From the Iron Staircase all the different laboratories and function rooms radiated away, some into high terraced suites with spectacular views from the solar system's highest mountain, others into the security and privacy of the strong Martian bedrock.

Aria and Nepenthe found the kitchens by smell. The princess used her privileged rank to commandeer strawberry tarts for them as they passed through. The serfs were all new but the cuisine remained good.

From there the rooms were bakeries and alehouses, pantries, sculleries, butteries, butcheries, laundries, sewing rooms, and all the minor industries required to maintain a military fortress of almost ten thousand people. Nepenthe was less interested in the behind-the-scenes domestic workings of the Bastion than the upper chambers, so the ladies moved on.

The next tiers afforded more entertainment. These levels included the barracks, human and lizard-man, with their attached practice grounds and training rings, the Holding Suite and Interrogation Pits (Aria avoided them), the machine shops where the Black Sorcerer's ticktockmen maintained the baffling array of different robot servitors, the first of the tripod bays, and for some reason known to no-one, a tiny well-tended mushroom house in one corner of a parade hall.

Higher yet were staterooms and guest halls. The Black Sorcerer sent forth his Heralds to maintain his lands for him, but when he desired he would summon entire courts to attend him. Here was the required accommodation. Packed in behind the elegant marble facades of the noble's suites were cramped servant and slave quarters.

Above that, and reflecting the Black Sorcerer's priorities, were the laboratories and workshops. The main floors were stuffed with men and robots laboring at the processes their master had assigned them. A mezzanine level housed more approved scientists and technicians working on special projects or original research. A higher gantry still linked the Black Sorcerer's most favored laboratories and libraries.

Near the top of the fortress were the Black Sorcerer's chambers, the Sealed Harem and Aria's suite, almost directly below the brass and iron dome that covered the First Man's personal sanctum.

On that penultimate tier Aria and Nepenthe found a cluttered museum piled high with trophies and curiosities from all over Mars. A broken Martian orrery leaned next to a stuffed moth-eaten Mock-Man. A waterworm jawbone longer that Aria's torso lay beneath a pile of brightly colored headdresses. Nepenthe admired a silvery-sheened substance like fish-skin until Aria revealed that it was cut from the flesh of a mermaid of the distant east.

"If there was ever an order to this my father gave up on it long ago," Aria admitted. "Everything's just jumbled together and covered in dust. Look, those are corrosive clown masks that the Lord of Fatal Laughter glues to the faces of his enemies. And there, below them, a petrified *shamir* from Lord Ruin's biolabs. It can disintegrate everything except silicone. That bloody bridal dress there belonged to one of the Sorcerer of Night's wives, I think."

Nepenthe looked at a stack of flags and battle-standards leaned in a corner. "So many kingdoms pay tribute to the master," she observed. "Look, there's the red tree of Tempe. And on the floor there the checkered helix of Scamander, my home. My former home."

"I think this rug must be warhound," Aria suggested. "And that's a Tyrrhenian honor sword."

The disarray of so much history upset Nepenthe's sense of propriety. "This should be tidied up," she insisted. "If the master is unwilling to trust the domestics to do it then we could take it bit by bit and do it..." Her expression faltered as her confidence failed. "If, if you would want it, highness," the handmaiden concluded.

"It might make an interesting project some rainy afternoon, yes," Aria encouraged the blonde girl. "Good thinking, Nepenthe."

It was close to the evening meal when one of the stewards found Aria and Nepenthe examining the inner workings of a mechanical battle turtle. "My apologies for interrupting, highness, but the master has returned. He commands your attendance in his rotunda sanctum."

A strange shudder ran through Aria, but she couldn't recall why. Was it the vivid memory of the things she'd seen with Coda in the Black Sorcerer's interrogation suites - or was there something else?

"I'd better go and see what he wants, then," the princess replied, keeping her voice light and nonchalant. "Wait for me back in my quarters, please, Nepenthe. If I don't make it down for dinner have the kitchen send up a cold tray for later."

Aria was proud of the casual way she made it sound as if a summons to her father was nothing to be afraid of; but no-one, even his own flesh and blood, went to see the Black Sorcerer without some trepidation.

Aria recognized the worn stairs from her memory cascade as she mounted them into the echoing dusty dome. All of the fortress had a somewhat neglected air. Even the spacious, well-furnished guest rooms had threadbare carpets and old flaking wallpaper.

Her father's sanctum was like all the rest but magnified. No chamber was more impressive and no space was so cluttered with rusting junk and detritus. A rare treasure might be piled next to a worthless machine that would never work again, and both of them be buried under a pile of forgotten blueprints that the Black Sorcerer had not worked on for two hundred years.

The First Man was in the central operating area. Indeed, he had filled that space with three bubbling incubation cylinders each large enough to contain a grown man. At the moment they seemed to contain only a fluorescent green liquid that bubbled as the First Man channeled voltage through it.

Aria was reluctant to interrupt when her father seemed so preoccupied connecting a series of nanogel think-tanks to some ancient monitor screen, but she had been sent for. "Hello father," she bade the Black Sorcerer. "How did discouraging Lord Ruin's adventures go?"

"He'll need a new chain city now," the Black Sorcerer gloated. "The bigger they are, the harder they fall." His pleased face soured as he remembered the cost. "General Ataxaus was a fool! He allowed Ruin's Bloodmaster Bale to pass through all our defenses and cause substantial damage. The Third and Ninth Lizard-Men Foot and the Sixth Heavy Robot were utterly destroyed, the Second Tripod Column decimated."

Those were serious casualties, though not disastrous. "Good commanders seem hard to come by," Aria admitted. "Didn't you have Ataxaus' predecessor executed for incompetence?"

"Just like Ataxaus. I need a new supreme commander of my armies. Again." He gestured to the equipment half-dissected on his workbenches. "I cannot afford constant distractions from my researches to go and correct the errors of my generals."

He turned back to assembling whatever he was attaching to the crackling monitor screen. The green-grey uplighting made his gaunt face look as sinister as his discipline policy.

"The steward said you wanted me," the princess prompted.

"Ah yes. Welcome back, daughter. Have your full memories returned yet?"

"No. A couple of cascades but some recent detail eludes me."

The Black Sorcerer patted the device he was wiring in to the dusty monitor board. "Do you remember this?" he wondered.

Aria shook her head. "It seems familiar, but... no, I'm not getting anything."

The First Man's thin hands smoothed antique silicone circuits into place. "It has taken me decades to reconstruct this just as it was when I found it."

"And when was that?" Aria asked.

"You'll doubtless remember soon," the Black Sorcerer promised her. "Where it came from doesn't matter," the Black Sorcerer told her. "The key is what it *will* do."

"And what's that?" Aria instinctively reached out with her arcane senses to inspect the apparatus then took an involuntary step back. "Chronal particles? That thing is charged with time energy!"

The Black Sorcerer nodded eagerly. "That was my conclusion too. It had an eighty percent charge, according to Malathea's best readings, when I first attached it. My initial experiments have run it down to forty-five. I need to get the thing working fully before the last of the irreplaceable particles are dissipated."

"What does it do, then?" Aria wondered.

The Black Sorcerer looked pleased that his daughter had asked. His earlier pique evaporated as he demonstrated his latest obsession. "I have only the first part of this apparatus working at the lowest functions. But look!"

He shifted the control keys on the command interface. The jars of nanofluid bubbled as they performed trillions of calculations a second to control the chronal particles. Lights dimmed across the laboratory and flickered throughout the fortress at the energy toll.

The cracked ancient screen fuzzed then focused, showing a black and white image of some men riding atop an armored vehicle.

"A distance viewer?" Aria puzzled. "I thought the static from the Harmony Spires prevented any kind of long-range signal broadcast or sensory scanning everywhere on Mars."

The First Man poked a thin finger toward the screen. "But that is not Mars. Look to the sky, daughter."

The image was cleaner now. It showed a long ribbon causeway and a line of unfamiliar battle vehicles driving along it. The road was straighter and smoother than anything Aria had ever seen. Dotted white lines were painted along its center. And low over the horizon...

"The sun is so big!" Aria exclaimed. "Twice its proper size!" Then, in a flash, she knew what she was looking at. "That's old Earth-that-was! Is this some kind of playback device containing data from legendary times?"

"Better than that," the Black Sorcerer crowed. "This is a window, a time window, showing us events that happened millennia past. A time window and more than that!"

Aria noticed that auxiliary screens were scrolling endless biometric data on some living specimen.

"Yes," the Black Sorcerer hissed. "You see it now? This time window focuses not on places or dates but on people. It has locked onto a sentient lifesign and now records that person's movements and condition in real time. With a little tuning I can jump forward or backward in the subject's lifeline, from birth to death."

"That is a remarkable discovery, father," Aria admitted.

"So far I have been able to refine the search enough to concentrate on military operatives, so as to observe their doctrines and strategies."

"You want to learn the war-secrets of the Ancients' Ancients."

"I want more than that," the First Man announced. "If I can only bring this machine to full functionality while it retains some power I could actually transfer sentience through it at the subject's point of death and rehouse it here in new flesh. I could recruit my next supreme commander from the war specialists of legend."

Aria glanced at the gestation vats bubbling behind the array. Half a dozen fetuses were already started there.

"You clone your key staff new bodies when their old ones wear out. It's not much harder to design new flesh for someone whose mind you transfer through history."

"Exactly. I could have Napoleon or Alexander, Grant or Caesar leading my troops. Their old memories would not transfer well, but their skills and experience could be permanently imprinted. With proper obedience conditioning I would have a General that no minion of my adversaries could ever match!"

Aria began to be excited by the possibilities. "Who will you select, if you have the choice?" She thought of all the mythological characters she'd been taught about. "Patten? Sun Tzu? King Arthur? Robert E. Lee?"

"It's not quite that simple," the Black Sorcerer regretted. "The device seems limited to certain times and locations. Each major time reset burns significant irreplaceable tachyon stores. So I must harvest all my barbarian test subjects from a roughly similar time and place from the list of observation points I have been able to fix."

Aria watched the armored column pass along the road in fascinated wonder. "You're probably wise to limit yourself to people who understand mechanized warfare," she admitted. "Hannibal might be an excellent soldier but there's no way to know how he'd perform against Lord Ruin's War Wheels or Fatal Laughter's Joker Deathsquads."

"So I decided, daughter. That is why I have been examining the career of *this* man, and of his staff. He was an excellent warrior who literally wrote the book on much of his kingdom's military doctrine. He served in a variety of conflicts in different theatres of war. He was loyal yet intelligent, disciplined yet flexible. I am seriously evaluating him for eventual transfer."

Aria watched as her father refocused the viewer on the middle of the convoy to show her the man traveling in the staff car.

"He's old," the princess noted.

"That is easily corrected. What do you think otherwise?"

Aria skimmed the datafile on the man's record. "It seems he might do, if he survives the transfer and stays sane."

"He is definitely a candidate," declared the Black Sorcerer. "I may yet have a use for him. The whole of Mars may change because of General John Blackthorn."

Nepenthe hurried to meet the princess when Aria returned to her quarters. The girl had been standing ready, even though it was three hours past midnight. "I saved you a platter," she told her mistress. "The kitchen did exactly what I told them to!"

She sounded surprised. Aria thought that her new handmaiden had not yet understood where being the princess' primary attendant placed her in the hierarchy here. Herald Maximal would not compel her attentions again.

"Set cheese and fruit on a salver," Aria commanded. "I'll eat while I bathe." She held up her hands to show the oil and grease that covered them. "I've been restoring Ancient technologies with the Black Sorcerer. It was dirty work."

Nepenthe scurried to comply. She set the iron tub filling and hurried to light candles and find unguents for her mistress' ablutions.

"The apparatus that father had salvaged seemed strangely familiar," Aria mentioned as she brushed out her hair and slipped from her gown. "Maybe when I have my next memory cascade I'll know where I've seen it before. It was nagging me all the time we were working."

"It must be very strange, going to sleep in the Rainbow Waters then awakening so many years later," Nepenthe ventured.

Aria felt a twinge as she was reminded of Coda. There was a strange ache when she remembered the rebel Halifax too. "What happened to my former maid?" she checked with Nepenthe. "Did you ask Nan?"

"Nan Vidi said it would come back to you and best not to force it," the blonde girl reported.

Aria gestured. Clips flew across the room to her hand so she could tie back her tresses. "I saw something remarkable this evening, Nepenthe. I watched a man who existed in times we hold as legendary. A man who was born and fought and died before any foot had ever trodden Mars."

"I don't understand, highness."

"Let's just say that the Black Sorcerer has some pretty potent magics. One of them let me glimpse a lost world and a forgotten hero."

Why did she almost choke when she said the word 'hero'?

"Was he slaying dragons to save a beautiful princess?" Nepenthe asked. So Aria's new maid was a romantic.

"He fought a tyrant and stood against fanatics that would have destroyed his land. Does that count?"

Nepenthe didn't seem sure. "There should have been a princess."

"Oh, princesses have always been overrated," Aria smiled.

Nepenthe didn't agree. "All the master's greatest lords want to wed you, highness. The Generals of the Staff, the Senior Technocrats, the Heralds, the Regent Princes, they vie for your hand. Maximal said..." She bit off her sentence.

"*What* did Maximal say?" Aria demanded. "Go on."

"Herald Maximal told me that the Black Sorcerer will bestow you soon, to someone who pleases him best, or to secure some major alliance. He said that it would most likely be him, to Maximal, because the master had promised it for his successful service, and that through you he would rise higher than any. Then he said... that I should turn over and stop sniveling."

"I don't believe I will be wedding the Herald Maximal," Aria promised.

Nepenthe swallowed hard. "There is another rumor... They said in the servant's wing that if you have to marry the Sorcerer of Night then I'd have to die with you, to serve you in undeath as I served you in life!"

"You needn't fear. Father wouldn't join me with any of his rivals. Not unless it gave him tremendous advantage, anyway." Aria found herself growing uncomfortable with the conversation. "Is my bath ready?"

"I just need to add these scented oils, highness. Which of these fragrances pleases you most?"

She held out the unstoppered bottles for the princess to sniff.

And those scents pushed Aria into her final memory cascade...

Coda barely returned before curfew, bearing a basket of oils and perfumes she'd acquired at Tantalus Crossroads. She unpacked her acquisitions and displayed them to Aria and Nan. "There was a gypsy selling viridian spice from Argyre so I bought a jar," she reported, "and a shabby old hillwoman who had fenrir root."

Nan inspected the twisted vegetable with reluctant approval. "Fenrir root is a useful psychotropic when properly distilled," the old nurse admitted.

"I also bought a couple of bolts of Solisian cloth," the handmaiden reported. "Aria, if you don't want it for a dress there's probably enough for new drapes. Or if you like it we can analyze its genetic code and fabricate more easily enough."

Nan rose stiffly, her broad Neanderthal shape hunched with age. Her current body was winding down. "I'll leave you girls to your gossip," she decided. "Mind you're ready for the master's formal dinner with the Southlands emissaries tonight, though." She staggered out, taking the fenrir root with her.

Aria chattered on about the pattern of the fabric until she was sure they weren't being overhead then switched mid-sentence to ask, "How did it go?"

Coda winked. "I met with Dane." Then she bit her top lip.

"You met with Dane and told him about the Black Sorcerer's expedition plans to Stygis?" Aria clarified. "Or wasn't that all you talked about?"

"That was all we *talked* about," answered Coda very precisely, but her expression gave her away.

"You *didn't!*" gasped Aria, shocked and suddenly curious at the same time. "Coda, tell me you didn't misbehave with that Runner rebel!"

"I didn't mean to," the handmaid apologized. "It just… happened. Maybe it was the tension of the moment, all clandestine meeting about life-and-death stuff?"

"Or maybe you're just a huge natural slut?" Aria suggested.

Coda shrugged to admit the possibility. "You should come next time and meet Halifax," she offered slyly.

"When I said we should help out the Runners that is *not* exactly what I had in mind," the princess pointed out. "I'm disgusted with you, Coda. Give me all the details."

"Of the information the Runners want us to try an' get to them 'bout this possible Hallows site?"

"That too. After." Aria huddled down with her friend. "Seriously, Coda, *tell me everything.*"

Aria ignored the pain in her fingertips, the spasm spreading up her arm that threatened to flare through her whole body. She gritted her teeth, bent her will, and continued to project her magics into the control system on the Black Sorcerer's data platform.

This was much harder than anything she'd attempted before. She wasn't fooling a simple lock mechanism or fabricating lizard-men command messages now. She was wrestling with the Black Sorcerer's own system, sealed by his magic and backed by his power.

Aria knew she had no chance of forcing the wardings. Even if she had the strength to overcome something set by a First Man – and she certainly didn't – then it would be obvious that the system had been breached. The only way she could get in was by convincing the interface screen that she was her father. At least they shared some DNA.

The pain intensified but the princess refused to give in. Her head started to swim. Spots appeared before her eyes but she persisted. Then as she approached her arcane limits the system suddenly yielded and granted her access.

She leaned on the system desk and caught her breath. "Take your time, Aria," she advised herself out loud. "Father is far away, dealing with undead marauders on the Amazonis Ocean. You have all the time you need."

Her voice echoed round the vast copper dome. She thought she sounded guilty.

She fingered through the many layers of classification of the millions of files on the Black Sorcerer's system. Most documents were now available to her. A few were additionally warded so well that she didn't even attempt to examine them. She extracted all the data she could find on Stygis and Ulyxis and on the Four Hallows and imprinted it on a data coin. She added in some random summaries of troop dispositions and patrol movements as a bonus.

She should have finished there, but some other files caught her attention. There was a folder titled *Aria*.

The princess flicked down into it to see what the Black Sorceress knew about her and to discover what he had planned.

Her mouth fell open. The first file contained images, hundreds of them, thousands, and they were all of her. With them were copies of her academic works, teenage poetry she had written, scans of childish handmade paintings using poster colors with cereal glued on for texture.

It was almost like the scrapbook a proud father might keep on his child.

Aria blinked back a tear and searched deeper. She found detailed biometric scans prepared by the Sensorines, annotated by Nan, that outlined each of the arcane net upgrades she had undergone. The nano-waters had also eliminated all kinds of potential diseases, given her perfect teeth, and corrected vision problems she would have developed in later life. Nan had written long, detailed accounts of every process, that showed just how much care and attention the Neanderthal nurse had lavished on the princess over so many years.

Perhaps I've misjudged them, Aria thought. *My father has done terrible things, I must not forget the Inquisitor's cells, but maybe the Black Sorcerer could change?*

A sub-folder contained the specifications for Aria's next and final Rainbow Waters upgrade. That one would complete the adult version of her arcane wetware. The finished capacity would be quite impressive. 3D projections of what Aria would look like at twenty-five caught her eye. At first she thought she was seeing images of her mother.

There were other packages to be installed during her final sleep. Much of Aria's education had been planted into her mind by the nano-waters, to be woken by the Loremaster's judicious reminders then made practical through application and experience. Aria browsed down the instruction modules that awaited her in her last time in the Chamber.

The agenda was heavy on history and politics this time, she noted. Was her father grooming her to assume authority? She'd have liked a module on war strategy and tactics but there wasn't anything worthwhile available to add to the list. She raised an eyebrow as she spotted a datafile on carnal techniques awaiting her. *Did* her father have some alliance wedding plans for her that he had not yet confided?

She didn't recognize the coding of the very last module at all, and it bore numbers instead of a title. She focused down and inspected the contents of her last instruction block.

It was an obedience program.

Aria felt a leaden weight drop in her stomach. The coding was the same as that in the obedience discs her father often installed into his principal Warlords and Heralds, except that hers was a generation more advanced, requiring no additional physical component. It would remain dormant in her mind until the Black Sorcerer chose to trigger it, but then she would treat his commands as absolute law.

Worse, that command could be transferred over to someone else: a husband.

Links in that folder took her to her medical profile. There, in Nan's careful clinical analysis, was the assessment that with the right genetic partners Aria would be able to breed viable magic-wielding offspring.

The Black Sorcerer could achieve what none of his rivals had managed. He could found a dynasty. All it would cost was Aria's free will.

The princess swallowed hard. She found herself shaking. "How could he?" she demanded in a trembling voice. "How *could* he?" She realized that Nan Vidi too was complicit in this planned breeding programme. She recalled what Nan had once told her: *Our first loyalty must always be to him.*

"Not mine," Aria argued with the memory. "My first loyalty is to my people, the peoples of Mars!"

She jammed her hands down on the control interface and hammered her will into the obedience code. At her command it reshaped itself to harmless, useless gibberish. If they plugged *that* into her head it would do nothing. Better, it would *appear* that the programming was dormant as expected until the Black Sorcerer tried to trigger it.

She left the carnal techniques package in there though, and tried not to think of Halifax.

Aria was shocked by what she'd found, but she was well trained. She closed every file she'd opened, erasing with meticulous care all traces of her intrusion. She painstakingly re-established all the interlocks she'd bypassed, though the effort left her pale and weak.

She tucked the data coin into her bodice and slipped away to her chambers.

Only then did she weep.

Nan hadn't seen the point of traveling halfway over the grasslands of Lycos just to see a mummer's show. "Send for them to be brought to the Bastion for a command performance," she'd advised the princess.

Aria had argued that that would be missing the real flavor of the show. "It's *got* to be delivered in a rural setting in front of a genuine country audience, Nan. If we drag those poor frightened players here we'll miss out the whole context and get a miserable performance."

"We'll take some guards with us to quietly secure the perimeter," Coda promised. "Besides, if Aria can't protect herself at a little rural festival what hope will she have on the master's upcoming mission?"

Hence one of the Black Sorcerer's landwalkers had trodden its multi-legged path through the broad grasslands to Iris Market so that the Princess of Mars could go incognito to a mummer's festival. Thereafter it had been simple for Aria to shift her clothing to resemble that of the local peasant women and vanish into the thronging crowd.

It took Coda a little longer to slip away, but at last the two women met in the cellar beneath the tavern, where their contacts awaited them.

"Dane!" Coda yelped as she saw the handsome black man. She bounced over to him and jumped into his arms, wrapping her legs around his pelvis as she kissed him.

Halifax grinned and held out his arms half-mockingly in case the princess felt the need to do likewise with him.

Aria returned the smile but declined the athletics.

"I have the data," she told the Runners, "but you don't have much time. The Black Sorcerer plans his expedition within the week."

"You heard the princess," Coda told Dane. "Not much time. Take me behind those barrels now!"

Aria knew that Coda and Dane had met three times before and that on each occasion there had been 'misbehaving'. She wasn't sure she could approve of her handmaid dragging a man into a cellar alcove while she was chatting by the stairs in the same room.

Halifax caught her hand. "Let 'em have their moment," he pleaded. "Dane doesn't talk or think about anything but her. He's no use to the Runners unless he's had his dose of Coda." His face sobered. "Besides, any of us might be dead this time next week."

Aria knew that the Black Sorcerer's expedition would take them into dangerous territory even before they ventured into whatever remained of underground Stygis. She hadn't realized until then that the Runners intended to go there too.

"What did you expect?" Halifax challenged her. "You know we need some edge against the First Men. What better than the Spear of Death, the Stone of Transmutation, or the Chalice of Time? Those are prizes worth risking everything for."

"Is that what Corrigan thinks, or you?" Aria wondered, referring to the elusive leader of the Runners movement.

"Both of us." Halifax moved in closer. "Great prizes require great risks."

Aria couldn't back away without tripping on the stairs. Coda's giggling echoed from the barrel stacks.

"Are you going to try and steal away my father's great treasure from under his nose?" the princess asked. Her heart was thumping.

"If I can, I will," Halifax assured her. He slid his hands round Aria's waist. His fingers were rough and masculine on her uncovered flesh.

Aria thought of the instruction data awaiting her next Chamber immersion. Then she remembered Nan's mantra that only practice made it real. "The... the Sword of Light, if that's what it really was, didn't work any more," the princess stammered.

Halifax slid one palm up her smooth spine to cup the back of her head. "Just having a Hallow would be a symbol. A sign that the First Men don't have all the power. It could be a rallying banner. Don't underestimate the power of symbols, Princess of Mars."

"I don't," Aria whispered, just before he kissed her.

It was nothing like she'd dreamed but she found she liked it. When she came up for air she wondered why she felt so dizzy. "I've never kissed a man before," she admitted. "I've never trusted one."

"Aria," Halifax told her, "*every* beautiful princess should have a hero to quest for her. Someone who'll do the impossible to win her."

"And that's you, is it?" Aria asked. In the alcove Coda's giggles had become gasps. "I'm not Coda," the princess said.

"You are Aria, and no-one else," Halifax assured her. Then he kissed her again.

I'm already learning from experience, the princess thought as she automatically tilted her head a little to avoid nose collision.

It would have been easy to melt then, to allow Halifax's experienced hands to continue their exploration, to let him complete her education without need for implanted data. Some primal part of Aria urged her surrender. But there was a colder, steelier part of the Princess of Mars, and that was the Aria that pushed Halifax away and said "Enough."

"Aria..." Halifax coaxed, approaching her again.

The princess held up her two index fingers, tips towards him, to indicate he should stop now. Flickers of azure energy sparked around them to illustrate her point.

"I do want a hero," Aria admitted. "I need someone to save my world for me, to free my people. I need one man, just one, who I can trust with everything. Entrust not just with me, but with all I must do, the things I have to accomplish. Impossible things."

Halifax made a short bow. "At your service, princess. I'm your man." He waggled his eyebrows. "Or I could be, if you'd let me."

"Then go to Styxis," Aria instructed him, "and we shall see."

The Black Wizard raised his serpent-headed stave and loosed an eldrich bolt at Princess Aria. The bubbling black energies made an unpleasant sizzling noise as they seared through the air. They smelled of sour lightning.

Aria raised an arcane shield but gave it an axial twist that span the spell aside without bearing its full force. The midnight magics slammed into the metal mesh of the practice ring and fizzed out their fury on the protective bars.

"Good," approved the Black Wizard. He loosed another blast. It separated in mid-flight into twin assaults that spun in corkscrew fashion to confuse his target.

Aria crooked her fingers and sliced a violet energy pulse to skewer both bolts, slamming them together to their mutual annihilation. She was pleased with the move but had no time to congratulate herself as her father launched another fizzing ball that split into no less than four missiles.

Aria was forced to craft a whole-body shield. She braced herself but she was still tumbled from her feet as the magic bolts slammed home. The cost of sustaining her protection was huge, sapping most of her body's arcane reserves.

She'd known that would happen though, and prepared her final gambit. She took the offensive even as she fell, peeling off a shimmering star of arcane force and searing it towards the Black

Sorcerer. She quietly followed it up, a mere inch behind, with a second such attack. She hoped that the first might dazzle her father's shields leaving him wide open to the second packet.

The Black Sorcerer was wily, though. He didn't use a conventional shield, which he might easily have formed. Instead he twisted the head of his combat stave and caused a localized dimension disruption. The straight-flying arcane bolts skewed round 180 degrees and flew right back at Aria.

Her own trick caught her out. Her weakened shields flared and absorbed the first blast but folded utterly when her second shot hit them. The seething energies slammed into her kneeling body and hurled her backwards into the practice cube's absorption mesh.

"Ouch," she said as she lay twitching.

The Black Sorcerer loomed over her. "I am not displeased," he told his daughter. "You battle with wit and strategy, utilizing your limited arcane strength with proper imagination. Against any other foe you would have probably prevailed." He reached down his hand to help the princess regain her feet.

Aria's frame ached from the conflict but she forced herself off the floor. "I'll improve," she vowed.

"We shall practice each day from now on," the Black Sorcerer announced. He gestured for Elicogna to open the magic-catching combat cage and led his daughter out of it. "Come," he commanded.

Elicogna shot the princess a look that could just have been a response to diagnostics of Aria's vital signs but might have been sympathy from any normal woman. Aria padded after the Black Sorcerer out onto the hurricane deck of his Black Airship.

The First Man clutched the guard rail and looked from the vast dirigible down over the wide Martian landscape below. They had left behind the flat red-grass Lycos plains and the mountainous lands of Cryse. The airship's armaments had defied the anti-aerial defenses of the Forgemasters, and the Black Sorcerer had passed on without taking reprisal. The orange craggy ridges that now passed below were desolate and uninhabited, little changed from the time before man had ever tamed Mars.

"This is a world of secrets," the Black Sorcerer told Aria at last. His hawklike face stared far across the landscape, his gaze fixed on the blurry horizon. "The Ancients buried theirs. We First Men hoard ours. The inhuman races like to be secrets themselves."

Aria wondered what her father would say if he knew *her* secret.

"Everyone you meet will have a secret, Aria. Nobody will be who they seem. Nobody can be fully trusted. No-one is on your side."

That would be why you intend to program an over-ride into me, the princess thought bitterly. *You don't believe in anyone.*

"Secrets are what give us power," the Black Sorcerer continued. "It was the secrets we First Men discovered that elevated us to rulership of this world. It is secrets that prevent us from destroying each other. Every secret that is found out takes power from someone and gives power to someone else."

Aria felt some reply was expected from her. "It seems to me that all secrets have their time," she said. "They remain hidden for years, for centuries, maybe for millennia, and then, somehow, it's as if their time is up. They are exposed and everything changes."

The Black Sorcerer nodded. He understood.

"Like the Hallows," Aria expanded. "One passage in the *Ojer Tzij* describing four ancient treasures that may have been tools of the Creator. Maybe they were the keys that programmed the Harmony Spires? Perhaps they were weapons of mass destruction, failsafes in case creation went astray? Or were they allegories, new iterations of ancient legends from old Earth itself? Nobody knew. And then suddenly the Sword of Light might be discovered, and here we are hunting another Hallow, and ancient secrets that have been kept for countless generations tumble into the open like an irresistible avalanche."

"It is good that you can see that, my daughter" the Black Sorcerer approved. "Arcane prowess will serve you well. Understanding the way the world works will serve you better."

And he stared over the wide range of the windswept mountains at the far lands beyond.

The blood-thirsters attacked by night, half-man half-bat, winging onto the Black Airship despite its defenses. Their strength was terrible, tearing through combat drones as easily as lizard-men, shredding the very hull of the dirigible itself.

"What's going on?" shrieked Coda as the vessel rocked crazily from side to side.

Aria was already out of bed and preparing for combat. "I'd say that the Sorcerer of Night's minions have located us. I think Lord Erebus might have got to Styxis before us."

"Oh!" gasped Coda. "But what about...?" She clamped her mouth shut. There was no secure space aboard the besieged Black Airship to wonder about Dane and Halifax.

The gondola pitched again. The screech of the bat-men came from right outside the princess' cabin door.

"Here's where we see if my recent combat training pays off," Aria noted. "When I say *go* pull the door open quickly, Coda."

The maid nodded and took position. Sharp claws raked through the panels.

"Go!" cried Aria and loosed an arcane bolt.

The dark indigo energies roiled across the space from sorceress to bat-things and slammed into them like a thunderbolt. The whole corridor was cleared for a short while.

"Follow me," Aria told Coda. "Stay close."

"No argument," agreed the maidservant.

They hurried along the charred corridor and made the main cabin. The fighting had gone hand-to-hand there, with the Black Sorcerer's elite guard just getting the upper hand after some brutal encounters.

"Where's my father?" Aria shouted to Nash'Tak the Many-Warred, the commanding general of the lizard-men troops on board. The grizzled warrior spat out a mouthful of man-bat and gestured to the pilot's deck.

Another blood-thirster closed on Aria. Rather than waste her meager remaining arcane power – her earlier discharge had almost exhausted her magic reserves – she sliced it open with the dagger from her hip and pushed the creature back into the general melee.

The Black Sorcerer was alone on the bridge; or rather he was the only living creature there. A dozen of the airship's crew and a score of the bat-men lay strewn about the deck. "Ah, there you are," he said to Aria without even turning round to look at her. "The airship is lost. The damage will bring us down."

"The Sorcerer of Night set an ambush for us," the princess recognized.

"Just so," agreed the Black Sorcerer. "I had hoped he might."

"That makes no sense!" blurted Coda before she could stop herself. She clamped her hands over her mouth too late to prevent her exclamation.

The Black Sorcerer turned and released a bubbling black energy cluster toward her. Coda squeaked, but it seared past her shoulder and fried the bat-men flapping up the ladder to take them by surprise.

The vessel rocked again. Gondola cables snapped.

"You *wanted* to provoke an attack, father," Aria realized. "You wanted Night's forces out in the open."

"Better here than in the dark tunnels of Styxis," the Black Sorcerer proclaimed. "Would you say that their main reserve is now committed to the assault?"

"It looks like it," the princess agreed.

"Then shield your eyes with your hands, Aria."

The princess obeyed. Coda mimicked her a second after. The Black Sorcerer thumbed a silver button on the steering console.

The light was so intense that it almost blinded the girls despite their covered vision. Each had a clear impression of the bones of their hands lit by the actinic flash.

The Black Sorcerer's troops dropped, overloaded into blind epileptic spasm by the appalling light. The creatures of the Sorcerer of Night burned away to ashes and less than ashes.

The flash washed across a ten mile area, destroying the legions of Lord Erebus camped below, devastating a whole battle force. What few minions could withstand the light retreated at the devastation of their allies.

The Black Sorcerer raised his staff and shielded Aria as the airship crashed down into the forest. Coda was protected too, but that may have been quite accidental. The dying dirigible cut a wide swathe through the virgin woods and slid for the better part of a mile before coming to a halt.

"I believe we have arrived," declaimed the Black Sorcerer.

The ruins of Styxis were mostly sunken in a black mire, a lifeless lake that was silted with wash from the mountains that ringed it. Too liquid to be called mud and too solid to drink, the foul waters ringed the fallen city and kept whatever secrets it might hold concealed beneath their midnight surface.

"Set the remaining robots and the lizard-men to guard the perimeter," the Black Sorcerer ordered his Robot-Caller and General Nash'Tak. "I want the tripods on a defensive guard pattern. Some of Night's creatures will doubtless have endured my infra-bomb. I would prefer if they did not disturb me." He turned to Elicogna and the other two Sensorines that flanked her. "Survey this place. I require a three-dimensional map of what lies under the water, and of course notice of any anomaly."

Aria sat quietly with Coda while her father made his preparations; but she noted the way he planned and the way he commanded, how he offered reasons to some subordinates so they could intelligently carry out their parts but withheld information which an agent who might be captured did not need to know. She listened to the inflection and timbre of his orders and how he projected his authority without ever needing to use his magics. She made mental notes.

"Did you know this place was flooded?" Coda whispered to the princess. "How could... anybody... get down there and find anything useful without the resources of the Black Sorcerer?"

Aria shot Coda a quelling look. "At Ulyxis there were clues to follow, like some ancient treasure hunt. The Sorcerer of Night's agents had to solve the puzzles to find the hidden complex. Of course, they cheated in the end by sending bodiless spirits to spy out what lay below, but clearly whoever hid that artifact intended it to be found only by one who could pass every test. It may be the same here."

Aria hoped that Corrigan was smarter than Halifax or Dane, then felt disloyal for the criticism.

Presently the Sensorines returned with their report. They had mapped the submerged architecture and located a series of hidden tunnels that lay beneath the obvious chambers. "There is also an unexplained tachyon residue in the lowest parts of the complex," Elicogna revealed.

"Chronal particles?" recognized Aria. "The Chalice of Time?"

"Perhaps," cautioned the Black Sorcerer. This wasn't his first artifact hunt. "Or a lure."

Herald Ambrius returned from the downed ruin of the airship with other news. "What sensors we still have left warn of movement to the west," he reported. "Energy signatures of powered machines. Probably troops coming over the mountains. They will be here by morning."

It was already the middle of the night. Constant Deimos in its equatorial orbit seemed to mock them.

"That would be the Lord of Fatal Laugher, come to see what the bright light was all about," judged the Black Sorcerer. "He will be too late."

"I don't think there's time for the robots to dredge out those tunnels, father," Aria warned. "By the time they have burrowed down and shored a way into the depths of Styxis..."

"I don't intend to wait for robot drainage projects," snapped the Black Sorcerer. "Not when I can do *this*."

He pointed his staff at the rim of the cauldron that contained the murky waters. No blast emerged at once. Instead there was a constant whine that rose in pitch. The eyes of the serpent that topped the stave glowed. A few stray flickers of dark energy escaped the ebony sheath. For most of a minute the Black Sorcerer controlled the build up; only then did he release it.

The side of the mountain exploded. Fragments of boulder tumbled to earth five miles away. A new channel sixty yards wide and a mile long was torn through the Martian bedrock, spilling the oozy black liquid down the hillside in a turgid sludge.

As an added bonus it created a new barrier between Styxis and the reported army.

"Locate me an entrance," the Black Sorcerer told Elicogna.

Coda stared at the molten channel that had previously been immovable mountain. "Did you *see* that?" she gasped at Aria. "Did you see what he did?"

"Yes," replied the princess distractedly. "He used a lot of personal reserves, even for him. It will be some time before his strength builds up again."

The Robot-Caller interfaced with his heaviest machines and set them to wade in the diminishing slurry and dig through into the hidden tunnels below. Twice more the Black Sorcerer sped things along with livid energy blasts, further depleting his energies. Aria began to think that she might even stand a chance in direct combat with him.

It still took two tense hours before the robots cleared a path into the passages of deep Styxis. As soon as the outer wall crumbled Elicogna twitched and looked down. "There is more in there," she reported. "It was shielded."

"Interesting," declared the Black Sorcerer. "What do you seen now?"

The Sensorines all crooked their heads to the side simultaneously as they brought their inbuilt detection apparatus to bear. "There is another lake," Elicogna revealed. "And a barge."

The Black Sorcerer considered this. "Aria, Elicogna, with me. The rest of you, stand guard." He gestured to the tunnel the robots had cleared.

Coda made to follow too but Aria shook her head. "Stay up top and keep watch," she ordered. "You know who for."

The maid's eyes widened then ranged around the dark forest edge. "You think they might be here?" she breathed.

"If they're smart they won't be carrying energy weapons we could detect. Knives and percussion guns can be almost as deadly, and we've been weakened in war against the Sorcerer of Night. It all depends on how smart that Corrigan is. Anyway, stay here, stay safe, and if anyone I know happens to turn up, well…"

"Give him your love?"

"Say hello." Aria flickered a smile at her friend and hurried after her father.

The tunnels were smooth-cut but decorated with strange geometric patterns. Aria recognized the style from the data package on Ulyxis that she'd passed on to the Runners. The Black Sorcerer generated a dim glow from his stave, less bright than Aria had seen him project before, and had Elicogna lead him to the underground lake.

There was movement ahead. Silhouettes flickered for a moment then vanished like ghosts.

"Time shadows," the Black Sorcerer recognized. "There is chronal power here. Those echoes are mere side effects."

Aria realized that she could never allow her father to gain command of the Chalice of Time. If ever he harnessed its power he would be unstoppable. If he found the artifact here she would have to challenge him while he was weakened.

On the shore of the underground lake a simple barge awaited travelers as it had for uncounted years. An impossibly-tall dark-mantled stranger waited holding a long pole.

"There is an old-Earth legend…" began Aria.

"The ferryman, yes," the Black Sorcerer confirmed. "He carries passengers across the river of forgetfulness to the timeless lands beyond. And he requires payment."

Aria and Elicogna followed the First Man aboard the barge. It rocked alarmingly at their weight. The waiting boatman appeared not to notice. The Black Sorcerer produced a data coin and pressed it into the ferryman's colorless hand.

The creature shifted and began to pole the boat across the water.

"What did you give him?" Aria asked her father.

"A secret."

The dark lake was also absolutely silent. Even the ferryman's pole made no splash. Occasionally the waters seemed to form faces, but they too faded.

Aria lost all track of time. The journey over the water might have taken seconds or days. Only when the barge nudged the jetty on the other shore was the spell broken.

She cupped her own hands and generated a better light. The darkness receded to reveal a small island, hardly larger than the cupola that occupied it. The wrought iron construction was so old it looked like it would crumble at a touch.

The Black Sorcerer stalked forward and examined the array in the center of the podium. Finely-etched metal cylinders with glass side-panels were wired together then linked to a reflective black screen. Other cables extended to an obsidian slab that occupied the middle of the assembly.

"What is it?" Aria wondered.

"It is redolent with tachyon energies," Elicogna sensed. "It is charged. Primed."

The Black Sorcerer traced the circuitry and concluded which the principal apparatus was. "Look at this," he called, indicating a circular groove that might have been designed to accept the bottom rim of a goblet. The indentation was riddled with microcircuitry. "This is where the Chalice of Time fitted; but it is gone."

A vast sense of relief washed over Aria. She need not fight her father to the death today after all.

"This apparatus though..." The Black Sorcerer examined the equipment carefully. "Yes, this must be preserved." He opened his robe and removed a black sheet which unfolded into an eye-watering hole in space.

"A pocket universe!" Aria recognized. Just how much arcane energy did her father possess to maintain such a thing after all he had done?

At the Black Sorcerer's instruction the equipment in the cupola was disassembled and packed into the sheet he had empowered. When he was satisfied that he had taken all he could he folded up the fabric again and stored it back in his gown.

When they climbed aboard the barge the boatman made no move to return them to the other side

"Perhaps he will not allow it to move with the property of the isle on board?" Aria ventured.

"Perhaps he simply seeks another secret?" the Black Sorcerer mused.

"Do you have another data coin?"

"Not like the one I gave him. I must pay him a different truth this time."

Aria wasn't sure she liked the First Man's tone, sly and subtle. She held her tongue.

"Here is a secret for you, ferryman," the Black Sorcerer spoke. "My beautiful daughter, Princess Aria, plots against me. She has cast in her lot with Runner rebels that seek to supplant me, and thrown away her heart at a brave young freedom fighter who calls himself Halifax."

Aria's stomach lurched. She turned round to find the Black Sorcerer staring straight at her.

"She betrayed my secrets to her new champion, her hero. She sent him and his Runners ahead of me to steal the Chalice of Time, although I do not believe they succeeded. None entered here before us and that cup has long been gone from this place."

"Father…" began Aria.

"Instead these bold rebels have gathered their forces and come en masse to slaughter me while I am weak and far from home. Whilst I have sought secrets of the Ancients in these sunken caves, they have sought to slaughter my forces up above. By now they may have routed my troops and captured my base camp. I expect they will have executed Herald Ambrius and the other Sensorines but they will have spared Aria's maid girl because she too is a traitor. All those deaths are upon her head, and my daughter's."

Aria fell silent again as the words impacted upon her. Had all those she had brought to this place with the Black Sorcerer truly deserved death? What if Nan had come? Was Elicogna similarly doomed?

The Sorcerer turned back to the ferryman. "Is that sufficient payment this time for a ride?"

Without speaking, the boatman hefted his pole and returned them to the outer shore.

The rebels had taken the camp, as the Black Sorcerer predicted. The Robot-Caller was dead, his cyborg frame sprawled lifeless beside Herald Ambrius' scorched hacked corpse. But not all of the Black Sorcerer's troops were accounted for. General Nash'Tak was missing with many of his lizard-men packs.

The Runners were waiting for the Lord of the West as he emerged from the tunnels. Three dozen weapons, mundane and exotic, were trained upon him now they need not fear detection.

"It is almost sunrise," the Black Sorcerer told them. "I trust you have a plan to likewise deal with the Lord of Fatal Laughter?"

None of the rebels responded. Only Coda skipped forward, shouldering aside a rifleman to come and claim her mistress. "It's alright," she assured the Runners. "She's with us. Ask Halifax."

Aria spotted the swashbuckling young man emerge from searching the wreckage of the downed airship. Dane trailed behind him, dragging some databanks, but he dropped them to embrace Coda as she scampered back to him.

Halifax strode over and took Aria in his arms. "Well?" he asked her.

"Not bad," she admitted, and allowed him to kiss her.

An older man, broad and bearded, strode past the couples and looked at the Black Sorcerer and his remaining Sensorine. "You'd be the First Man, then," Corrigan judged. "Thought you'd be taller."

"I am," replied the Black Sorcerer.

"You have one chance to drop that staff and surrender peacefully before we blow you away. And you better believe we've assembled an arsenal here that could blow away even a First Man."

"Perhaps. *You* have one chance to drop your weapons and pledge allegiance to me before I lose *my* patience. I have been seeking you for a long time, Corrigan of the Runners."

Aria was suddenly, absolutely certain that it was all a trap. She knew her father. It had all been too easy! She remembered herself on the battle-wrecked bridge of the Black Airship, saying "You wanted to provoke an attack, father." Why settle for merely crippling the Lord of Night's forces when he could destroy the Runners too?

"Wait...!" she tried to call out. Halifax stifled her cries.

The Black Sorcerer smiled at Corrigan.

"Take him down!" shouted the Runner's leader.

And the two men nearest him died.

The shots came from above, from the great dark rigid-frame dirigible that loomed over them. Aria looked up just as the blinding searchlights flicked on. *Of course*, she thought, *of course he prepared a* second *airship. How else was he getting home?*

A moment of panic washed over the exposed rebels on the ground. Then nothing. Each of them dropped as if he had been poleaxed. They slumped nerveless, brought down alive by a simple hypersonic barrage.

Elicogna toppled too, unprotected against the debilitating sound. Corrigan, Dane, Halifax, Coda, all fell. Only the Black Sorcerer and Aria could resist its crippling assault.

"So, daughter," the Black Sorcerer demanded as the two of them stood alone on the battlefield, "what are you going to do now?"

Aria had no choice. She stood over the fallen Halifax and prepared to defend him to the death.

The Black Sorcerer chuckled. "You still don't see it? Well, you are still young. You didn't listen to what I told you. And yet you saw the payment I gave the ferryman."

"A data coin," Aria replied. "Wait! Was it the *same* data coin I recorded from your system, the one I passed to the Runners?"

"Indeed."

"But how did you come to have it then? Unless… you took it from them?"

"Or was sold it," the Black Sorcerer suggested. "How do you think I came to know of your poor choices, of Corrigan's puerile ambush, of how to capture the leader of those Runners who have inconvenienced me for so long?"

"Somebody told you. But who?" Her mind worked frantically. It couldn't be Coda. She couldn't have returned the data coin. Perhaps it was some unknown member of Corrigan's Runners? Because otherwise it was either Dane or Halifax!

The Black Sorcerer followed her chain of thought with ease. "It wasn't Dane," he prompted her.

"I don't believe it. Halifax wouldn't do that. He's a hero. My hero. He'd never betray me!"

The Black Sorcerer didn't bother to argue. "Will you still stand over him now in a last-ditch attempt to defeat me, Princess Aria?" he wondered. "Why would you?"

"I won't stand against you for him," Aria replied, "but I *will* stand against you. For all these others. For Coda. For the wretches in your Inquisition Pits. For the dead of Daedal. *For Mars!*"

"Ah," said the Black Sorcerer. He sounded mildly disappointed. "Then defend yourself."

Aria conjured up a hasty barrier before the first of her father's arcane bolts tagged her. She was taken by surprise when it veered around her and slammed into a fallen rebel, slicing him to mince.

"You didn't protect that one," the Black Sorcerer noted. "Shall we try again?" He blocked Aria's counterattack with ease and launched twin blasts that snaked in unpredictable arcs until one hammered against Aria's defenses and the second shredded another Runner.

"Two down," the Black Sorcerer counted. "Shall we try for three?"

Aria actually managed to destroy one of the triple bolts that came at her next. The second sizzled off her shields, staggering but not dropping her. The third sheared past her and detonated another stunned rebel.

This time it was Dane who was reduced to diced meat.

"No!" Aria shrieked, rage coursing through her. She felt her powers quicken as never before. Chambers of her soul sprang open and poured their strength into her will. "*No!*"

The arcane bolt she formed was the most potent she had ever achieved. If ever her magics were to overcome her exhausted father it was now! She prepared to project her wrath in a single overwhelming strike.

But the Black Sorcerer said. "That is enough, Aria. Stop it." And just like that, the princess allowed the energies to dissipate and stood quietly awaiting other instruction.

Then Aria realized that the obedience commands to be implanted in her during her next immersion in the Cavern of Rainbow Waters were not the first to suborn her will. They were the *last*. Most of the failsafes were already in place.

"Some lessons can only be learned hard, Aria," the Black Sorcerer told her. He had her wait in silence while he summoned his second airship down to load on the prisoners that he had captured alive.

"Are you sorry for what you did?" the Black Sorcerer asked Aria back in his Bastion.

"I'm sorry I didn't do it better," the princess replied.

"Defiant. So very much like Rhapsody," her father mused.

"We both saw you for what you are at the end," Aria spat.

"You betrayed me. In that moment you justified my decision to place override commands upon you. You lost any moral high ground. You lost everything."

Aria knew it was true. "What will you do with me?" she asked. She knew that the obedience imperative could be transferred to anyone.

"Nothing," the Black Sorcerer told her. "That will be your punishment. But each day, all day, you will stand in the Holding Quarters and stare down into the Inquisition Pits and watch what happens to the rebels you led to Styxis. You will watch what becomes of them, what is done to them and what they are made to do. You will observe their slow, painful, degrading destruction. And when the last of them finally, mercifully dies only you will escape untouched, unharmed, to carry the memory of what was inflicted because they chose to ally themselves with you."

Aria opened her mouth to protest, to plead, but the words choked in her mouth.

"Yes?" prompted the Black Sorcerer.

"They are my people. I led them to this. I will watch their fates. And I will remember."

The Black Sorcerer's nod carried a grudging respect. "You begin to act like a Princess of Mars."

Aria watched as Coda died, bold beautiful Coda who was disfigured and broken by the end. She watched each of the Runners be taken apart, every one differently, every one betraying all they knew about others who would in turn be taken by the Black Sorcerer's guard. She watched a whole organization, a vital part of Mars' resistance to tyranny, crumble because of her. Corrigan was the last to die, and he cursed her name with his final breath.

Halifax did not go to the Inquisition Pits. Halifax took his reward and went free.

After Corrigan screamed his last and the Black Sorcerer was certain that Aria knew that she was beaten, the First Man allowed her to return to the blissful oblivion of the Rainbow Waters, to be cleaned and renewed and to awake generations later with a fresh new start.

Aria was already vomiting before the memory dump had even finished. She fell to her knees and retched then dry-retched as the things she'd seen replayed in her mind.

"Highness!" Nepenthe squeaked, more alarmed than she'd yet been. "Shall I summon a physician?"

"A doctor? No," the princess hissed. "Fetch me a chain gun. And grenades. I want to speak to my father!"

Nepenthe looked on in helpless panic as the fury washed through Aria.

"It's no good," the princess grimaced, tightening her fists so hard that her knuckles whitened. "Even if I had a nuclear explosive right next to him and the trigger under my thumb I wouldn't be able to push it! I'm collared by his obedience programming, subject to his will like the merest slave!"

The handmaiden backed away, making more apologies although she didn't know what for. In the end she fled to summon Nan.

"He's beaten me!" Aria moaned, naked on the floor, rocking herself. "He's broken me!

She recalled the rumors Nepenthe had repeated, of the Black Sorcerer's intention to wed her to one of his lieutenants or allies. Would he simply transfer his absolute control over her to whichever man was awarded her? Suddenly the new erotic theory awaiting closer examination in her learning centers seemed less like intriguing new data and more like a pack of tricks her owner could call upon for his personal amusement.

"I was supposed to *save* Mars. To aid the resistance. I got them all killed!"

Halifax had betrayed her. She could still taste his tongue in her mouth, more bitter than the vomit. She'd come so close to trusting him, to yielding herself to him. Now she knew that heroes didn't exist. Nobody was on her side. Everyone was less than they seemed.

Aria sobbed and sobbed, curled in a ball on her bathroom floor, until she felt her heart would burst. Surely it was already shattered?

"Now now," said Nan Vidi's familiar gruff voice. A fluffy robe covered the princess and large wrinkled hands lifted her easily from the ground.

"You betrayed me!" Aria spat, trying to resist the old nurse's guiding grip.

"Maybe I did, lovie. And now I'm cleaning you up and putting you to bed."

"Get off me! Only a monster would serve a monster!"

"We're all what we're made, sweetling, and that's the truth of it. Now hold still while I sponge you down. Such a mess you've made of yourself!"

Aria couldn't even catch her breath to speak. She surrendered to Nan's familiar ministrations and allowed herself to be washed, groomed, and tucked into her four-poster.

The princess looked over at the snag-toothed old Neanderthal woman. "I thought I could trust you, Nan," she said sadly. "I thought you at least were on my side."

"Creator! There's more sides than anyone can count in this world, Aria my pet, and we all switch sides all the time. That's life. But I told you straight I'm the Black Sorcerer's, and if I didn't obey him from respect I'd be obeying him for the same reasons you will."

How many bodies has Nan Vidi worn now? Aria wondered. How many opportunities had the Black Sorcerer had to put obedience contingencies into the old nurse?

"Halifax turned on me. I thought he… liked me." Aria realized that she sounded like a little girl confessing some indiscretion with the cookie jar.

"Well there's men for you, lovie. There's not one man on the planet fit for you, and that's the truth of it. Certainly not that Halifax."

"I thought he was my hero."

"He wasn't. You know that now."

Aria's tears were softer now, of regret rather than anger or loss. "I got Coda killed, and Dane. I watched everyone die as they were... I *watched!*"

Nan patted her hand. "You need your sleep now, Aria. Sleep's a great healer of body and mind. You've remembered your punishment, but that's behind you now. Tomorrow's another day, lovie. If you made mistakes, learn for 'em and don't make them again. If you let folks down yesterday, don't let 'em down tomorrow."

The old nurse smoothed the covers over her charge. "Coda's dead and Dane's dead and that Corrigan and all his Runners. You're alive. Hold to that, lovie. Wake up in the morning and live some more."

Aria slept, then Aria woke.

She lay in her satin-swathed bed thinking. Remembering.

"Aria, every beautiful princess should have a hero to quest for her. Someone who'll do the impossible to win her."

"I do want a hero. I need someone to save my world for me, to free my people. I need one man, just one, who I can trust with everything. Entrust not just with me, but with all I must do, the things I have to accomplish. Impossible things."

"There's not one man on the planet fit for you, and that's the truth of it."

"One of them let me glimpse a lost world and a forgotten hero."

"The whole of Mars may change because of General John Blackthorn."

Two:
Belief

Aria awoke from a troubled night knowing what she had to do. When she opened her eyes Halifax was looking down at her.

Her reaction was quite instinctive. She unfolded the arcane energies within her and hurled a blast at the intruder that would have slammed a hole in a brick wall.

Halifax moved very quickly. His right arm pistoned up to catch the magic on his vambrace. The black metal arm-sheath absorbed the magic. Red LEDs spiked all the way up its length to signify the power of the blast it had deflected.

"Good morning," said Aria's betrayer. "I let myself in."

Aria's second attack was indirect. She caught up the bread knife on her breakfast tray in a kinetic field and sent it directly at Halifax's throat.

The intruder shifted quickly again and caught the blade by its tip between his fingers.

"My, you're grouchy first thing in the morning, princess," Halifax smirked. "Pretty though."

Aria grabbed her bedsheet around her and glared at him. "Why aren't you dead a century years ago?" she demanded. "Tell me quickly so I can put that right."

Halifax handed her knife back to her. "You're the clever sorceress. You tell me."

Now that Aria's waking shock was receding she was able to take in other details. Halifax was dressed in rakish black leathers, his hands swathed in fingerless gloves. In addition to the magic-deflecting vambraces he was equipped with a force shield belt, a pain wand, and an electro-whip. Aria recognized the uniform. "You are a Herald of the Black Sorcerer!"

Halifax made a little mocking bow. "Your father keeps his deals. All those years ago I gave him Corrigan and the Runners and he gave me a place at his side. I'm stronger, fitter, more powerful than I ever imagined. I'm virtually immortal. This is my fourth body."

"You're not immortal," Aria promised.

Halifax leaned back on the wall of the princess' bedroom. "Come on, Aria. No point holding old grudges. All of that was a long time ago. I've served your father loyally ever since, risen high in his inner circle. I'm his Prime Herald now, his voice and ears across the whole of the West. You're back as his faithful daughter. We're on the same side again."

"You betrayed my friend and your comrades to weeks of torture and slow death!"

"Better them than me. Your father was on to your treason all along, you know. Right from the first time you hacked his data systems. Even if I hadn't saved myself he'd have found another way to wipe out the Runners."

Aria glared at the former rebel. "Is that how you sleep at night?"

Halifax grinned. "Still keen to know my sleeping arrangements. That's a good sign."

Aria snarled. Then she realized that the Herald had somehow walked right into her private apartments, past security, past her staff, to watch her sleep in her own bedroom. "Where's Nepenthe?" she demanded.

"Cowering outside. She knows better than to say no to me."

An unpleasant question came to the princess. "What's your official Herald name, Halifax? What do they call you now?"

"I'm Maximal. Prime Herald Maximal. But you can still call me Halifax."

"I'll call you the bastard who abused my handmaiden."

"I didn't know she was going to end up serving you, Aria. I just saw her in Tempe, fancied her, dropped some hints to the Governor that it might be a good idea to include her in the next tithe, and had her when she got here. She's quite a pretty little thing, your Nepenthe."

"You destroyed her life because you lusted after her?"

"I saw what I wanted and I took it. Eighty cycles as the Black Sorcerer's Herald gets you used to having your own way."

The princess' experience of being close to her father was different. "I should kill you for what you've done, to Coda, to Nepenthe, to Dane, to Corrigan… to me."

Halifax snorted. "I didn't do much to you, princess, though it wasn't for want of trying. Why couldn't you have been more like your slutty friend? We could have had some good times before your house of cards collapsed."

"You taught me that I can't trust my heart. Or trust anyone."

"Then I've done you a favor, Aria. Anyway, I've not come to talk about what I've done or failed to do to you in ancient history. Ask me why I am here."

Aria gritted her teeth. "Go to hell, Halifax. And don't count on that Herald kit you're wearing to protect you if I decide I really want you dead."

"You won't kill me. The Black Sorcerer would have to punish you for the murder of one of his Heralds. As you know, that tends to get painful for people you care about. Maybe you haven't really had time to bond with frightened snively Nepenthe yet but I bet it would matter to you if Nan Vidi was skinned."

Aria looked at the intruder with loathing. "Why are you here?" she asked, hating herself for it.

"Well, I just got back from scaring the crap out of some delinquent sub-governors in Acidalia and I heard you'd been washed out of the Rainbow Waters again, so I decided to say hi. And I wanted to tell you what I'm going to do with you."

Purple sparks rippled across Aria's hands. "Make your threats," she said.

Halifax shook his head. "It doesn't have to be like that, princess. I don't want to be your enemy. I know how much better it is to be your friend. You're a pretty good kisser. We'd make a pretty good team."

"Not interested. I'm wise to you now, Halifax. I loathe you!"

"That can be changed. Have you heard the rumor that your father wants you bred so he can have more magic-capable family? Turns out you and I are pretty well genetically matched. Right now I'm top of the list to get given my own personal bed princess."

Aria suppressed a shudder of horror. She daren't let her enemy see her fear.

"I know about the obedience upgrade, the one you tried to overwrite," Halifax confided. "Sounds pretty kinky. I'm really looking forward to it."

"Is that it then? That's the threat?"

"Not so much a threat as foreplay," the Herald snickered.

"Fine. Then here's *my* threat to you: I will destroy you. I will make you wish you had never betrayed the Runners. You will wish you had never met me. You will die, as awfully as I can devise it. Believe that threats to those I care for will curb me if it comforts you. Believe that obedience conditioning will tame me if you wish. But I *will* see you dead, Halifax, Prime Herald Maximal." Her intense eyes bored into her enemy's. "My word on it."

For one moment doubt flickered on Halifax's face. Then his standard swagger returned. "And how will you accomplish that, princess? *I'm* your hero, remember?"

"I am the Black Sorcerer's daughter. I am ingenious." She pointed to the door. "Now get out. I want my breakfast."

Halifax bowed again, his grin insolent and confident. "I'm looking forward to sharing breakfast with you sometime soon, Aria," he laughed as he left.

Three luminescent gestation tubes hung in webs of nutrient pipes and control cables. Inside them the flesh for the Black Sorcerer's new warriors was gradually coalescing. But today Aria's concern wasn't with the almost-shapeless lumps of protoplasm floating in the amniotic nanocyclinders. It was with the information that was programmed in to the machines.

"Watch this," Aria instructed Nepenthe. It was hard not to show off when the new maid was still so impressed with anything magical. The princess rippled her arcane aura into the control panel and three holograms blinked to life above the research platform. Wire-frame men changed resolution and gained skeletons, muscle, bones and flesh, until at last images of three warriors hung before them.

Nepenthe glanced at the glowing canisters behind. "Is that... them? Or rather will it be?"

"That's the idea. These are the designs for the bodies that whoever the Black Sorcerer scoops from the past will be put into. What do you think of them?"

Nepenthe blushed. "They're naked."

Aria rolled her eyes. "According to the notes so far, these bodies will have the top range enhancement package its possible to deliver and still keep them human. Muscle tone, stamina, excellent co-ordination, manual dexterity, resistance to disease, the works."

"They look very grim and frightening," Nepenthe decided.

Aria inspected the holograms. The maid was right. "They do look fierce," she agreed. "I think that's the idea. This flesh will house the Black Sorcerer's finest warlords. They'll be programmed in pretty much every fighting skill there is. Father wants his generals able to defend themselves."

"They look brutal."

Aria looked more closely at the images. "Yes. Well, we can always improve them."

Nepenthe's brow wrinkled. "How?"

Aria ran a finger over the program panel to make it more compliant. "The Black Sorcerer tasked me with sorting out what additional modules we need to plug in here. Obviously there'll have to be language packs. No point having a general who has to give orders to lizard men or ratkin via a translator. And they'll need some background on weapons they're not familiar with in their own time. But we can make other tweaks too, I guess."

Nepenthe looked uncertain. "Like what?"

Aria pointed to the middle figure. "Him, for example. What color hair should he have?"

"He doesn't have any hair."

Aria slid her fingers over the control interface. "Now he does. What color shall we make it?"

Nepenthe touched her own blonde braid. "This shade?"

"Fair, then. Skin color?"

"Caucasian. But tanned," Nepenthe suggested. "Like an Amazonis Sea pirate!"

"Romantic," Aria teased. "What else? Body type? Let's say lean and muscular for this one, shall we? Classic old-Earth pantheon deity." Her lips quirked up mischievously. "Which reminds me..." She made another quick adjustment.

Nepenthe's eyes went wide and she blushed bright red. "Oh my!" she said, failing to avert her eyes.

"Too much?" the princess asked.

"Just... quite enough," the handmaiden judged.

"More than Halifax – Herald Maximal?" Aria checked.

"Yes."

"Locked." The princess stepped back to admire her work. The hologram-man wasn't a hero. He just looked like one.

"He's very fine," Nepenthe approved. "Much better than before. Still fierce and dangerous-looking, but daring and exciting too. Can we do another one?"

Aria turned the controls over to the blonde girl for the second hologram. Unsurprisingly, Nepenthe's Adonis turned out to be remarkably handsome, with swept-back dark hair and brooding gaze. Aria quite admired his looks, but her eye kept being drawn back to the blonde one, who was less smooth but seemed to her to have more character.

They joined together in crafting the third, who ended up stockier and more muscular, with thick red hair everywhere. Before they'd finished, Aria and Nepenthe were overcome with giggles.

At then end, Aria turned sober again. "It doesn't matter what they look like, really. They're only tools, to use and throw away." She programmed the changes into the gestation equipment and stalked off.

The Loremaster barely classed as human any more. The greater part of his skull had been carved off, replaced with a translucent dome into which he could jack dozens of data-spikes to connect him with the various and diverse retrieval systems of the Black Sorcerer's library. The information poured straight through his cerebral cortex, leaving little time or room for personality, or dreams, or character.

He was programmed for politeness, however, and for obedience. He bowed formally as Aria entered his dusty domain and he said her name reverently.

"I have some enquiries," the princess told him. "Let's start with the oldest text of the *Ojer Tzij* you have. Quote me the passage about the Four Hallows, please."

The Loremaster's silver-flecked eyes went distant for a moment, and without further preamble he began to speak:

"The First Men walked amongst the ruins of the nations and amidst the dole of the peoples. In fire and blood the last works of the Ancients perished or were lost. The Hallows too vanished. Some say the First Men claimed them, others that they were taken from the world to deny the First Men; but they were gone.

"Four Hallows there were, greatest of the legacy of the Ancients that the Creator touched. The Sword of Light was sovereign over power; who wielded it could not be stopped. The Stone of Transmutation was sovereign over matter; with it all things could be molded that were. The Staff of Death was sovereign over life; when it was raised the doors of mortality opened. The Chalice of Time was sovereign over space and years; who drank from it controlled eternity.

"Each Hallow spoke unto the other, opposite and allied, the base of all that is. As there were four Hallows so were there four First Men, and of them we shall now speak…"

The Loremaster fell silent for a moment then added, "That is all the scriptures say on the Hallows."

Aria questioned the living database further in case variant versions of the *Ojer Tzij* or more recent codices offered any additional information. The only volume that offered any pertinent notes was a commentary by a scholar named Father De'bias, and that was incomplete to the point of uselessness.

"What happened to the rest of this?" Aria asked frustratedly.

"It was burned when the scholar's workshop was torched by Lord Ruin's men," the Loremaster reported. "Lord Ruin is not a big supporter of scholarship."

"Are there any other copies?"

"Not available to this facility, highness. If there were other editions of this work then they vanished with Father De'bias himself, forty-four cycles past."

"And he didn't leave a forwarding address?"

"I have some data suggesting he took refuge in or across the Amazonis Sea, but it has not been a matter of priority to investigate. Until now."

It was clear that Aria had hit a dead end. She pressed on. "What descriptions are there of the Hallows? Where did they come from? What do they look like?"

The Loremaster tilted his head to one side for a moment. A small circular lens-screen lit up and showed Aria the various woodcuts and engravings of the Hallows over the years. Imagination had clearly played a large part. There were few common elements, save one.

"Where are they all decorated with fives?" the princess wondered. "Five studs, five sigils, five indentations. I thought the *Ojer Tzij* was obsessed with fours? First Men, Hallows, Ages, that sort of thing."

"The Isidian theologian Atticcus suggested that the clue was in the phrase 'base of all that is'," reported the Loremaster. "Four connected points on a plane form a square or parallelogram. When all are connected through a third dimension there is a fifth node to form a pyramid."

Aria thought of the shiny cylinder with the crystal lens that lay in her father's sanctum. There were five colored buttons on it. "Assume for the moment that the Hallows are not mere allegory. Why then might they not operate now?"

The Loremaster had nothing to offer on that.

Aria pushed on. "What other wonders of the Ancients are still rumored to exist?" she enquired. "Ignore the ones under the control of the First Men or in the Crystal Dome, and exclude geographical artifacts like ruins and statues. What items are believed to exist or have existed? Collate me an indexed list, ordered by likelihood of credibility."

The Loremaster slumped for a moment then seized up a quill and began to write. His script was fast and uniform.

When he'd completed the top page, the most likely undiscovered surviving treasures of the Ancients, Aria interrupted him. She pointed to the top item on the list. "Pause that task for a moment. Brief me on the Light of Malador."

The Loremaster explained what was rumored and what little was known about the arcane-amplifying materials beneath the ruins of Malador in the Warfields most desolate contested tract. It did not sound like an appetizing place to visit.

"This then," Aria said. "What's the Voice of God?" Dane had mentioned that once, she recalled.

The Loremaster summarized the written material describing the Ancients' ultimate communications technology. Aria leaned forward. "This Voice of God, it could send commands anywhere on Mars? Irresistible orders, yes? At least according to the fragmentary records. Is there anything about it also being able to override implanted compulsions?" *Obedience packages, for example*, she did not say out loud.

"There is no data on that possibility," replied the Lorewarden neutrally.

"Anything on this Sleeping Army that's supposed to protect it, wherever it is?"

"There is no data there, either."

"But I bet Ancient technology trumps the cobbled-together orders we stamp onto obedience discs," the princess mused. She had the Loremaster describe the Voice of God in detail, including places where ancient sources hinted it might have been installed; but she made no notes and took no record.

It took a long time to review the whole list. At the end Aria rubbed her temples to alleviate her headache and she sighed heavily. "Problem is, the First Men have been hunting this stuff for centuries and haven't turned it up. If it's out there it's damned well hidden.

Most of the juicy stuff is lost in the marginal lands between the First Men's domains where it is most dangerous to go."

"Yes," agreed the Loremaster. It was as much opinion as he was interested in expressing.

"One couldn't go after the Light without dodging Lord Ruin's patrols, for example. Nor seek the most likely places for the Voice of God without encountering the Lord of Fatal Laughter's traps." The princess had to accept the truth: "It's just too dangerous to go treasure hunting without better information than this library holds."

That at least pricked some vestige of the Loremaster's professional pride. "There is no library with better information in the world!"

Aria consoled him then; but she wasn't sure that was true. There was no better library available to the Black Sorcerer. Aria was the Princess of Mars.

Phobos set in the east, a dull red fist descending into murky waters. The distant moon gave the algae-choked wetlands a melancholy feel that matched Princess Aria's mood.

"Homesick?" asked Halifax. He took his place at Aria's side uninvited and leaned on the rail to survey the view with her.

"Sick," she retorted, scarcely glancing at the leather-clad Herald. She had not been pleased when he had claimed the duty of escorting her on this voyage.

Halifax surveyed the seemingly-endless terrain of ragged red grass clumps and weed-choked water. At far intervals some scraggly tree managed a precarious growth, but mostly there was only endless Daedalian water meadows.

"I hear you're princess of this place," the Herald noted. "Isn't this where royal Daedal was once the capitol of Mars?"

Nothing remained of the shimmering City of Joy now except for some distant blackened stumps. Wars and centuries had taken the rest. The landcrawler's six steam-powered legs pistoned through sucking mud and sometimes stirred up old bones, but nothing else was left.

"I'm princess of everywhere," Aria told him. "My mother's line was the ruling house of Mars before the First Men and the Great Burn."

Halifax gestured to the desolate waste. "It's a fixer-upper."

Aria turned on him. "Your duty is to guard me on this journey and make sure I don't run off and meet unsuitable rebels. I made that mistake once before. Your duties *do not* include talking to me or commenting about my life!"

"I know that, princess. That's just pure pleasure."

Aria stalked away to the far side of the vessel. There were other places to stand. The view was the same in every direction.

The landcrawler was little more than a huge flat platform supported by hydraulic limbs. An engine shed occupied the center of the vehicle. Half a dozen cabins and staterooms ranged around it. An open balcony ringed the machine. The deck tilted with each step the multi-legged transport took.

Nepenthe was huddled on the lee side out of the wind, trying to make herself inconspicuous. She tended to slip away whenever Halifax was near. Aria didn't think he bothered her now but she was never quite sure. Would Nepenthe dare to tell if he accosted her again?

The maidservant came hurrying to attend Aria. "Shall I get you a cloak? It's getting cold as night falls."

Aria shook her head. "It's not the temperature that chills me. Not even having Halifax cling round me like a fly on a sore." She gestured to the broken wasteland. "I remember this very differently."

To Nepenthe, Lost Daedal was just as much a legend as the Creator or the Ancients of old Earth-that-was. Stories of the Knights of Daedalia were told to children as bedtime tales. "It's hard to remember that you were there," the blonde girl confessed. "What was the City of Joy like?"

"Beautiful. More lovely than anything I've seen on Mars today. Now everything is patched and mended and worn, as if we've lost the ability to make things new. We scrabble through the rubble piles to pick out the leftovers and discards of better years. We don't make high towers of fluted colored glass, or graceful bridges of amber and gold. Our soldiers don't wear hand-carved amour where every decoration has a meaning. So much has been lost."

Nepenthe spoke of her own distant home, of the crumbling manor her family so assiduously maintained. "The newer plaster is inferior to the older construction. The modern friezes are crude and gaudy next to the elaborate painted ceilings of the older rooms."

"Mars is dying, Nepenthe," Aria said. "Even before the Great Burn there were the declining centuries and the chaos times. The endless wars of the First Men give our world no time to recover, no chance to repair. We are so desperate fighting for the remnants of what was that there is no freedom to discover something entirely new."

The landcrawler lurched as one of its piston-legs mis-stepped into a sinkhole. Aria and Nepenthe had to grab the guard-rail to avoid being pitched over the side.

"Why did you come here if it makes you sad, highness?" the maid wondered.

"I told my father it was for a break from court. He knows I need time to process my distress at what he did to me and my friends before my last sleep."

"Then why did he send Herald Maximal with us? Isn't he a constant reminder?"

"My father is the Black Sorcerer, subtle and cruel. Who can tell what cunning games he plays?" Aria shook her head. "I need time to think. I hoped that some echo of my mother might remain in this place, but so far... there is only desolation."

"Do you remember your mother much?"

"Very well. And I remember what she taught me." It had cost all Daedalia to teach those lessons.

Phobos had almost set. Constant Deimos still shone a lurid purple over the equator. Fear comes and goes, Aria thought as she pondered the original meanings of the satellites' names, but Loathing is always with us.

It was time.

"Nepenthe, you must make a choice now," Aria warned her servant. "Neither option is pleasant or safe."

Nepenthe's brows lowered. "I don't know what you mean, highness."

"I'm about to embark upon an... adventure. You may accompany me if you choose, although the risks are significant. Or you may stay here, with Halifax."

Nepenthe blanched. "I will come with you, please, Princess Aria. But I don't see..."

The landcrawler rocked once more. This time it was no mis-step. Something massive had slammed into one of its legs beneath the waterline.

"What is it?" Nepenthe screamed as the vessel yawed.

Another impact on the other side caused it to tilt again.

"Stand with me," commanded Aria. Her eyes were flecked with violet as she drew upon the arcane field of Mars. "Whatever you do, keep close."

Halifax raced round the corner of the deckhouse, calling Aria's name. He had his energy whip coiled in one hand and a disruption tube in the other. The next collision bowled him off his feet but he rolled with it and sprang back into a combat crouch.

"Get inside, princess!" the Herald called. "We're under attack!"

"Good thing we have your training and experience to tell us that," Aria answered dryly. "Has the Prime Herald determined what it is that might be assaulting one of the Black Sorcerer's own imperial landcrawlers?"

The Captain emerged from the pilot-house, shouting obscenities at the Mock-Men deckhands who clustered on the aft-deck doing nothing. The great shaggy beastlings had worked out what was going on long before anyone else.

The first giant waterworm leaped out of the fetid lake and dived right across the deck. It snapped at one of the crew but missed.

"Waterworms?" Halifax gasped. He cast around for a bigger weapon. The amour-plated serpents grew up to a hundred feet long and would require rather more damage to stop them than an electrified whip could deal out. "Princess, seriously, get to your cabin!"

"This way, Nepenthe," Aria called, guiding the terrified maidservant away from the central rooms to the very prow of the crawler.

"What's going on?" Nepenthe shrieked. She clung to the princess for dear life, as if Aria were some magic talisman that could keep her safe from the huge monsters; perhaps she was right.

"As our dashing Herald escort so brilliantly perceived, those are waterworms. They do not usually disturb the Black Sorcerer's crafts." That was because usually a permanently installed vibration box sent out the ultrasonic frequencies that soothed and deflected the creatures. If someone had used sorcery to alter the signal to something which attracted and enraged the giants then the waterworms' intentions might be entirely different.

Halifax raised his disintegrator tube and launched a disassembler pellet at the next worm to raise itself to the deck. Fifteen cubic feet of monster was reduced to plasma but the creature hardly seemed to notice. It lashed out and knocked half a dozen crew off the landcrawler. The Herald himself barely avoided the strike.

Another waterworm veered up right in front of Aria and Nepenthe.

"Yes, that one will do," decided the princess. She raised her hand and snared its will with an arcane link.

The creature swayed reluctantly as its instincts were over-ridden by Aria's searing mind. It struggled for a moment then surrendered.

Its broad head, larger than a table, sunk down until it was level with the deck.

"Climb aboard," Aria told her maid. "Our ride is here."

Nepenthe couldn't speak. Aria shepherded her onto the flat spade-nose of the enslaved waterworm and commanded it to bear them away from the besieged ship.

"Aria!" shouted Halifax, racing over to intercept. He was so preoccupied with the princess' departure that he never saw the waterworm that swallowed him.

"Shame it won't kill him," the princess muttered. "His force field will protect him from too much harm. I hope he enjoys being an uncomfortable bowel movement."

The Mock-Men were organized now. Their formidable strength and undoubted physical courage allowed them to stand against the besieging sea-monsters. Before her personal waterworm swam her out of range, Aria hurled a hex to reverse what she'd done to the vibration transmitter. The Mock-Men's mournful battle cries echoed after her from the crippled landcrawler as she was carried away.

The Black Sorcerer had done a through job on Queen Rhapsody's Jeweled Palace. When he'd finished, even the blue glass support struts that held the elegant building above the sparkling waters were mere melted blobs of disfigured silicone. Aria hadn't expected to find much left and she'd been right.

She arrived just before dawn, soaked to the skin like Nepenthe, clutching the slimy brow-ridge of the waterworm that conveyed her. The huge creature slithered between the algae-stained stubs and part-submerged fragments that were all that remained of the place where the Black Sorcerer had first claimed his daughter.

Nepenthe asked no questions. She stared straight ahead without comprehension or knowledge. Aria had suspended the girl's mind. Coda had been a willing participant in the princess' plots and had died for it. What Nepenthe did not know she could neither confess nor be condemned for.

"I must be mad to try this," Aria told the blonde girl, although she knew that nobody was listening. "But I have to do *something*!"

She willed the waterworm to drop low to the waterline and slide slowly through the ruins. Aria opened her arcane senses to the full trying to find any signature.

She had a few words and a half-understood lesson from her mother to go on and nothing else. The Knight Commander of Daedal had once wanted to spirit the young princess away through the Shadow Door to hide her in the Hall of Reflections. Rhapsody had told her daughter of an ancient secret of their ancient house.

Aria had been through all the combat reports of the destruction of Daedalia. The Black Sorcerer had been most thorough, picking through the devastation to harvest what magics and machines he could before reducing the rest to mere rubble. Everything that was found had been catalogued and classified. There was no mention of a Shadow Door, nor the Hall of Reflections to which it led.

If I am to stand against the First Men, Aria thought, *I must have resources of my own. It is not enough to try and take the Sorcerers down with their own tools, nor set them to greater war between themselves. There must be another force on Mars, equal to theirs, with a power base not derived from the First Men's cast-offs.*

Aria had the beginnings of an idea how she might manage that – although she knew it was an absurd long shot. But to make even the opportunity possible the princess needed other things. Information and allies.

She rubbed the waterworm's eye ridge. "I could be Queen of the Slimy Monsters," she told it. "Except that the Black Sorcerer could wipe you all out in a fraction of a second." She'd chosen to travel by landcrawler because it would be particularly susceptible to waterworm attack. Whatever the Black Sorcerer sent to retrieve her undoubtedly would not be.

She glanced over to check on the entranced Nepenthe. She'd begun to like the quiet romantic from Scamander, but she couldn't trust her. Her father was no fool, and neither was Nan. They would hardly provide her with another confidante with whom she could plot rebellion. Aria would protect Nepenthe if she could but she would not confide in her.

The waterworm side-slithered through the shallow floods of murky ooze around ruined Daedal. Aria divided her attention between directing the beast, holding Nepenthe, and searching for any glimmer of arcane technology that the Black Sorcerer might have missed nearly a thousand years before.

Two hours later, just as she was beginning to despair, she found it.

It was so weak she might have just imagined it, a mere echo to her magical soundings. It took her a quarter of an hour after the first trace to locate the feedback again, then another half hour to triangulate enough to plot its source.

The faint arcane signature radiated from a spot of empty air some fifty feet above the water's surface. Aria calculated that it might once have been inside the central keep portion of the Jeweled Palace.

The Black Sorcerer should surely have found it. The Loremaster's records illustrated just how thorough then destructive the Black Sorcerer's forces had been in their search for Daedalia's secrets.

And yet there it was.

Directly beneath the spot, Aria balanced on the snout of the hundred-foot long armored waterworm and focused her perceptions. She was rewarded with a faint but definite tingle of recognition.

Then she knew why she had found this and the Black Sorcerer had not. If this was indeed the fabled Shadow Door of her mother's bedtime stories then it wasn't the Black Sorcerer's to find. It was hers. She perceived it not because of her arcane senses but because she was Queen Rhapsody's heir.

"Up," she commanded the waterworm. The great creature strained to raise its segmented bulk level to the place that Aria knew she had to be.

She held her hand out to the spot. Little ripples of arcane force hummed between her fingers and tickled her palm. But if this was the Shadow Door to the Hall of Reflections, how to open it?

The child in her knew. The best way to open a door was to push.

Aria sheathed her hand in magic and gently pressed it into empty air. She imagined a hinge turning, a portal creaking open.

The world around her turned monochrome, then dark grey. Shadow.

The door swung wide and she tumbled through.

It took the princess some time for her senses to accustom themselves to the Hall of Reflections. Part of her perceived a tall grey chamber, carved stone joined seamlessly up to an arched coffered ceiling a quarter-mile aloft. Another aspect saw shaped spirals of arcane force twisted like a sculpture into a glowing wire-frame structure. At the same time she balanced on an absurd entity that was merely a giant twist of DNA in a miasma of life forces that ebbed across the Martian crust; and she was also falling, falling into some kind of abyss from which there was no escape.

"I am Aria," she heard herself saying out loud. "Aria of Mars."

Ares was Mars, she suddenly realized. *Aria was of Ares, lord of war.*

The thought was new, alien to her. It appeared in her mind full formed, as if it had dropped in from outside.

Aria is the feminine of the Latinate suffix '-arius', she considered. It was used for so many important words: honorary, rosary, visionary, elementary, necessary, revolutionary…

That wasn't her thinking those thoughts, the princess realized. *Someone is with me in my mind.*

Another idea pressed upon her. Aria was a Princess of Crete, which some thought to be Atlantis. She was the lover of Apollo, the Light-Bearer…

It's not someone thinking those thoughts, Aria realized. *It's a reflection.*

"I must control this," she told herself out loud. Mirrors reflected everything before them all the time, but what mattered was what you focused on, the part you wanted to see.

"The Hallows, then," Aria said. "Show me them."

She staggered as hundreds of images of cups and spears and stones and swords riffled through her mind. She glimpsed the secret treasures of the Tuatha de Danaan; the four houses of the Tarot's minor arcana; the coronation stone of Tara which cried out when a High King came. She saw the Spear of Destiny and the Holy Grail. She saw Excalibur rising from the waters, except its blade looked more like a crackling tine of energy than enchanted steel. She saw the four fundamental particles of the universe dancing and the unified fields of creation bending time and space.

Aria forced herself to look away before she was lost.

"Not too helpful," she commented. "The Sword of Light, then. How can I use it?"

A sword is a tool, she considered. *You need a good workman.*

It is a warrior's tool, she told herself. *You need a champion.*

It's a royal tool, she thought again. *You need a king.*

There are no kings. And only one princess.

Princesses make kings. Kings make worlds.

"There are no heroes on all of Mars," Aria said bitterly. "Show me who still resists the First Men."

Again her mind was inundated with ideas and images. Ragged refugees sheltered under gaudy carnival stalls. Others hid in subterranean lairs. Free Corsairs dared the island waters of the Amazonis Sea's Dead Coast and merchant adventurers ranged far from Phoenix Landing peddling exotic wares and sedition.

She saw distant ice-caverns where the Hall of Tatters lay, the legendary repository of Ancient lore where blind keepers preserved the last glimmerings of wisdom that had perished in nuclear fire a thousand years before the rise of the First Men.

Aria gasped. The rush of information hurt. It threatened to shred her mind, to tear it open. Yet she dare not stop now.

More and more data hammered through her, so fast she couldn't process it. She had to hope that some of it might lodge in her subconscious for later, like the sleep-teaching Nan plugged into her in the Chamber of Rainbow Waters.

Only Aria's disappointment allowed her to break free of the reflections' allure. "There is no one out there," she mourned. "No one at all who can pull them all together. No one they'll all follow. No one who can win against the Sorcerers."

She looked and looked but though there was rebellion and sedition and a planetwide resentment to the First Men's rule there was no leader. Her mind flickered over phantom faces: a bald black man in tattered khakis, a fierce woman in Amazon silks, an old priest with a white beard, even the hairy twisted visage of a savage Mock-Man, but there was nobody in all her sight who could save Mars. Only her own pale reflection stared back at her from the dusty mirrors, bleak and lonely.

The visions dimmed. Too late Aria realized that whatever magics sustained this Hall of Reflection were very old and had not been renewed for close to a millennium. She was spending the very last of them right now.

"What should I do, then?" she pleaded. "I want to save Mars! I do! But I don't know how. If there's no one in the whole world who can help me then what else is there?"

There's no one in the whole world ... yet, Aria thought to herself, or was that thought *at* herself? The mirrors were almost black now but she maybe glimpsed an antique barbarian armored column progressing along a desert road under an alien sky. A rugged hand held the Sword of Light and it sprang to flame. A Harmony Spire shattered to the ground. Angry red mushroom clouds rose over the surface of Mars.

If you don't turn away now you'll be caught forever, Aria warned herself. This time the mental voice sounded *just* like her.

She forced herself to turn from the dying reflections and their infinite recursive counterparts. She flung herself back through the Shadow Door; or perhaps she'd never truly left.

She staggered and almost fell from the flat ridge of the waterworm's nose. Nepenthe caught her. "Highness! What's happening? Where are we?"

Aria gasped and blinked. It was night again, and the stars wheeled in the black Martian sky. She had been in shadow and reflection much longer than she thought.

Nepenthe handled awakening on a giant serpent better than Aria could have hoped. She wrapped Aria in her own cloak and helped the shivering princess to squat on its nasal ridge until she recovered.

"How did we come to be here?" the maid asked at last.

"We were seized by a serpent, but I used my magics to guide it away from the attack that was destroying the landcrawler," Aria lied. "I was able to direct it just enough to keep us alive but not to control where it took us."

She reached out with her tired arcane senses to feel for the Shadow Door above her, but there was no echo now. She had used the last of that miracle. If she wanted more she must look elsewhere.

"Can you keep the monster under control?" checked Nepenthe, trying to keep her voice from quavering.

"I think so. And surely it won't be long before the Black Sorcerer's searchers come for us."

Nepenthe nodded and shivered as well. Aria returned the maid's cloak. She could shift her own clothing to something warmer just by willing it.

They sat on the head of the giant serpent and waited to be found.

Nan must have been seriously worried at the reports of Aria's loss to the waterworms. She came in person on a Black Airship to check on her charge, and Nan hated traveling. The old nurse hurried forward as soon as the princess was hauled aboard the heavily-armed dirigible and wrapped her in an unnecessary blanket.

"And what have you done this time, child?" Nan scolded her.

"I was not eaten by a sea monster," the princess replied. "I thought that was good thing."

The Neanderthal nurse gave Aria a look that suggested she believed there was a whole lot more to the story than she was being told, then chided Nepenthe for not getting her mistress inside and into a warm bed after her ordeal.

Malathea the Sensorine had been dispatched on the rescue mission as well. The milky-eyed woman flexed her ebony fingers around the Black Sorcerer's daughter, checking Aria had come to no harm. "Your synaptic serotonin levels are significantly elevated," Malathea warned. "You have recently produced atypically high levels of adrenalin. Your arcane reserves are almost depleted."

"It's been a busy day," Aria replied.

"Your neural net is performing effectively," the Sensorine continued. "It is gratifying that your upgraded wetware sustained you under adverse conditions."

"Is that your way of saying that you're pleased I'm okay?"

The airship commander hovered near Nan awaiting orders. "Shall we divert to retrieve the crew from the damaged landcrawler?" he enquired.

"That won't be necessary," Aria told him sharply. "However, I will require a minor detour to Cocytus Market on the way back. All my luggage is on that damaged crawler and I intend to shop for more."

"I brought everything you might need, lovie," Nan Vidi assured the princess.

"But not everything I want. Look, I just survived twenty hours on the snout of a waterworm. I am going shopping!"

Nan could see she was wasting her time arguing. New shoes were a small price to pay for having Aria back safe and sound. "Shopping it is then, lovie. But get some rest for now. Even if the winds are right we won't be over Arcadia until mid-afternoon tomorrow."

Aria saw the sense in that. She allowed herself to be bundled inside and cosseted.

She lay back in her bed, reveled in her enhanced serotonin levels, and plotted.

Second harvest was home in Cocytus, and the people were gathered for the festival. In the last balmy days before the coming of autumn and the season of winds after it, farmers from the canyons streamed into the market town to trade, gossip, and celebrate.

Aria insisted that the Black Airship moor a league outside the settlement. A vessel of war hovering over Cocytus would not enhance the festivities. The princess rode into town on one of the horses stabled aboard the dirigible.

She wasn't allowed to ride alone, of course. Nepenthe was an excellent horsewoman and delighted at a canter across the dusty trail down to the verdant canyons. Four of the Black Sorcerer's royal guard and a pair of wicked-looking lizard-men accompanied them, the soldiers on hover-frames, the reptile warriors merely loping alongside and keeping pace with the horses. Finally, Malathea was also briefed to stay with the princess; of all of them she would be the hardest to give the slip.

Nan stayed on the dirigible. She drew the line at horses.

They arrived late in the afternoon, when the long shadows were already creeping across the crowded marketplace. Aria didn't allow that to deter her. She began a systematic and diligent programme of visiting each and every stall in the busy plaza.

Nepenthe seemed much recovered from her aquatic ordeal. In fact the handmaiden looked happier than Aria had ever seen her. Away from Nix Olympus and from Halifax, the blonde girl resumed more of her true character. She scurried beside Aria, pointing out interesting trinkets, chipping in to help with the bartering.

Malathea's presence was actually useful with negotiations too. The Sensorine's devastating and precise assessment of items for sale tended to disconcert vendors and give Area an advantage.

"Are you actually enjoying this?" Aria asked Malathea as they emerged triumphant from a merchant tent with a basket of ribbon for one of the royal guard to carry.

"I am experiencing enhanced endorphin levels and my heartbeat is nine percent faster than average, so it may be that I am," the Sensorine admitted.

"These country fairs can be great fun," Nepenthe promised. "In Tempe they'd light lanterns when night fell and there'd be a square laid out for dancing."

"It looks like they do that here," Aria observed. "That looks like a dancing square, wouldn't you say, Malathea?"

"It is not precisely a square, being off by some seven degrees from right angle, but the purpose seems the same."

"Do Sensorines dance?"

Malathea hesitated. "I have no instruction on the subject."

"You mean you don't know how to dance, or you don't know if you're allowed to?"

"Both."

Nepenthe smiled sunnily at the confused Sensorine. "I can teach you! It's easy. I bet with your diagnostic abilities you could pick up the Tenchman's Reel and the Waltz Ebullient in no time!"

Aria noticed that in addition to a dancing square and musician's platform there was a trestle stage raised up for a mummer's play. "Oh, they're going to perform one of the harvest morrises!" she cried. "Malathea, send word back to Nan on the Black Airship. Tell her we'll be staying a while longer for the theatre - and to teach you to dance."

"Yes, highness," replied the Sensorine as neutrally as she could manage.

Nepenthe found them a prime spot to watch the performance, with a good view but some protection from the jostling crowd. Lizardmen guards ensured them personal space but were very conspicuous. Aria suggested the creatures instead found high vantage points to offer missile cover in case of trouble.

The harvest pageant was traditional. A local girl was elected Autumn Bride and gave out prizes to the winners of the day's contests. Awards were presented for wrestling, weightlifting, climbing a greasy pole, hurling, seed-cake baking, marrow growing, and a children's egg-and-spoon race. The yarning contest would come much later in the evening when everyone had eaten and drunk their fill. A young man who'd won an award for best-trained herd dog also received a kiss from the Autumn Bride, to tremendous cheers from the crowd.

"I bet she'll be a Winter Mother," Nepenthe giggled into Aria's ear.

Then the mummers came, dressed in rags and tags, to weave amongst the crowd and act out some traditional play that involved a good deal of ribald pantomime. A fair maiden was courted by Death in his grim robe with his black spear. A handsome hero wielding a brightly-painted sword was guided by an old woman bearing a cup of prophecy to go to the heroine's rescue. He fought the villain and won the damsel. She brought him to a flower-strewn throne and gave him a vine-leaf crown like hers. The throne turned out to be a hamper filled with rich spicy fruits for the audience so that everyone could share in the happy couple's bounty.

Nepenthe laughed so hard and clapped so loud that she was red in the face by the end of it. "I *love* that story!" she told Aria. "It's so passionate when the Knight rescues the Princess with his Sword of Light!"

Aria's heart skipped a beat. She looked again at the mummer cast taking their bows and receiving flagons of foaming ale for their efforts. The heroine wore a flower tiara like that awarded to the Autumn Bride. The hero carried a wooden sword painted as if it were ablaze. The old woman who saw the future carried a chalice, and Death – or was that a Sorcerer in grim black robes? – carried a staff. The new king sat on a throne of earth that transformed into a larder of bounty for all his people.

Aria gulped back a startled laugh. The First Men had spent centuries stamping out all resistance to their rule, and yet in every village across Mars simple folk were gathering to play out *this* story. Did the commoners even know about the Hallows of the *Ojer Tzij*?

And yet every man, woman, and child here in Cocytus knew about this!

Aria pointed. "Who's that meant to be, Nepenthe?" she asked.

"Why she's the Princess," the blonde girl answered without even thinking. "The Princess of Mars... oh!"

"Oh indeed. And who's he?"

Nepenthe looked at the hero in his new-won flower crown. "That's the Bold Champion," she answered, a little less certainly. "Highness, it's just a play. A bit of fun."

"So it is. If only real princesses had glorious heroes with Swords of Light, eh? But we only have Halifaxes." Aria realized she was sounding bitter. "I'm going to find a latrine trench. Wait here and teach Malathea some basic dance steps, will you?" As the Sensorine rose to object the princess added, "I do not need my next activity scanning. Honestly."

She told the perfect truth. As Aria slipped away into the milling throng she sorted through the things she'd seen at the ruins of Daedal.

The image she wanted was still fresh enough for her to dredge up easily: a shaven-headed dark-skinned man with a casual air that concealed a formidable intelligence. She'd seen him in the Hall of Reflection, but she knew that he was here, now, amongst this throng, meeting his contacts and passing instruction.

She spotted him on the other side of the dancing square. He whispered something unobtrusively to a baker passing with a tray of spiced rolls, then resumed his casual lean against one of the barter wagons.

Aria glanced back to where Nepenthe was walking the stricken Malathea through some basic moves. There was no better way to distract an all-seeing Sensorine from surveillance than by placing her out of her comfort zone and making her direct her attention to her unprecedented situation.

Aria wove her way across the market and came straight up to the black man. "Reith," she called him by name.

The loafer's attention fixed on her, but one hand went straight to his pocket and the other made a subtle signal. Aria guessed that he'd already marked her as an outsider right back when she was shopping, and her guards and attendants had not gone unnoticed.

"It's alright," she told him. "I won't hurt you."

The blade came from Reith's pocket straight at her throat. She easily caught it with her magics and left it hanging there six inches from her neck.

"A sorceress!" the black man hissed.

Aria nodded. "Worse. A sorceress who knows who you are, Edar Reith. I'm pleased that the Runners have re-formed and are carrying on their business."

The Runners' current leader made another seemingly-random gesture. Aria rightly interpreted it as 'I'm blown. Get the hell out of here.' A dozen revelers began to make inconspicuous exits.

Aria pressed on. "I don't have much time so I'll be brief, Mr. Reith. You can check what I say later with whatever resources you have. I am Aria, Princess of Mars, from the court of the Black Sorcerer. I am that same Aria who tried to help your predecessor Corrigan with such tragic consequences. I am sorry for my failure in that matter."

Reith's lip pulled back into a sneer. "You're Princess Aria? I'm the Crystal Lady!"

"You're not. I've met her. I've sat on her knee. Now listen carefully and I'll give you vital assets to help you in your fight. Do I have your attention?"

"You're number one on my to-do list, duchess!"

"Princess. Listen then. On this data coin are some of the access codes to my father's Bastion. There is a schematic with a route that will take you to weapons vault five. The vault door over-ride sequence instructions are in a separate appendix at the end. I will undertake to mute what alarms I can so you can get in, grab something useful, and escape."

Reith spat. "Sure. And this isn't in any way a trap like the last time you helped us, 'princess'?"

"That's for you to decide. I'm telling you it isn't. But read my instructions carefully. There's a specific time window for infiltration. We need to be co-ordinated so I can shut off the automated defenses. When I hang this red scarf from my balcony, that's the go signal."

The Runner commander flicked his gaze around the crowd and the town's rooftops. "You think I don't know you've got two snakeheads up there with laser rifles?"

"They're lizard-men. The Sorcerer of Night uses snakeheads and they're *completely* different." Even as she spoke Aria realized how bizarre her existence was. She was a mummer's play! "Anyway, I've said my piece. The rest is your choice. I can't help people who don't want to be helped. You may go now."

Reith shook his head in disbelief. "You want me to run off now and lead your men to my whole organization?"

"I really don't care where you run off to, Mr. Reith. Stay and dance the Tenchman with the Autumn Queen if you want. *I* need to get back to teaching a Sensorine how to waltz. Good evening."

Aria could feel his gaze burning into her back all the way over to Nepenthe and Malathea.

"Fascinating," said the Black Sorcerer when Aria gave her account of her Daedalian adventure. "A truly extraordinary account."

Aria wasn't certain whether her father merely meant that she had endured a singular adventure or whether he was passing comment on the selective version she had offered him. With the Black Sorcerer it was impossible to tell.

"They found me quickly enough once Herald Maximal crawled out of his waterworm and thought to send for aid," Aria sniffed. She considered whether to ask the Black Sorcerer about his intentions for her marriage or breeding, but her pride restrained her. She had no intention of allowing her father either to gift her like property nor to make her some brood mare. There was no advantage in letting him know that.

"Shall I execute the captain and crew for not maintaining an adequate vibrational deflector beacon?" the Black Sorcerer enquired.

Aria spotted the trap. "It seems wasteful. You know I don't like it when you casually slaughter your people for things that might be beyond their control. It seems like bad policy."

"Tyrants rule by fear, not affection, my daughter."

"So you admit yourself tyrant then?" she challenged.

The Black Sorcerer was uplit by the green glow from the time-screen apparatus on which he'd been working. As he put down his multi-tool and turned to Aria he looked like some devil from a woodcut version of the *Ojer Tzij*. Maybe he was.

"The term 'tyrant' is an interesting one," he said. "On old Earth, in their own legendary times, the Greek nations would sometimes willingly surrender their freedoms to a tyrant in order to survive some menace that would otherwise destroy them. The first tyrant of Athens was Cypselus, seven centuries before the start of Earth's dominant calendar count. After civil war had cast down that city's rulers and invasion threatened it with annihilation, one man rose to hold back the tide of anarchy. In Archaic and Classical times there was no pejorative connotation to his title of Tyrant. It was necessary for one man to hold all power to address the larger issues of the time, so one man did."

"You are suggesting that your tyranny is a necessary evil, better than the alternatives?" Aria understood. "Better than Lord Ruin's doctrines of evolution by conflict, maybe, or the Sorcerer of Night's obsession with the boundaries of death. Certainly better than anything that the Lord of Fatal Laugher might do if he ruled all Mars. But better than *every* alternative, now or ever?"

The Black Sorcerer considered for a moment. "Better for me," he answered at last. "Now, since you are in a philosophical mood after your visit to Daedalia, let me pose you a moral question with a practical application. Step over to the time-screen, daughter."

Aria moved to stand beside her father, looking at the flickering black and white images that flashed over the main monitor. Smaller pictures on other restored displays scrolled sensory data or showed supplementary views of much the same scenes.

"The chronal energies in this device we found at Styxis are almost exhausted," observed the Black Sorcerer. "Without the Chalice of Time or whatever artifact it was that charged up this equipment it will soon be useless. If we are to draw consciousnesses through the veil of years to occupy those lumps of meat in the nanogel vats behind us then it must be soon."

Aria glanced at the gestation tubes. The forms inside had developed now into grown males, complete except for a guiding sentience to spark their brains. That elusive intelligence, be it mind or soul, was impossible to synthesize. It had to be harvested from elsewhere.

"Do you really think you can do it?" Aria wondered. "Drag a dying man's mind all the way here from the barbarian past and use it for your new war-general?"

"I am confident in the process," replied the Black Sorcerer. "My question for you regards the choice of candidate."

Aria realized that the biometric data referred to three men, not one.

The Black Sorcerer keyed up the information to show her as he spoke. "Three warriors command an army in an obscure and primitive theatre of conflict. Their names are Blackthorn, Yuei, and Morningstar. It is these three men upon whom I have now locked this apparatus."

"Blackthorn is the senior," Aria noted. "He is ranked their General."

"All of them have the necessary skills and capacity. It is their secondary traits that will decide which I place into my new General's body. If sufficient charge remains thereafter I will draw the others here too to be his subordinates."

"And you want me to pick which should lead?"

The Black Sorcerer tapped a fingernail on the monitor's glass. "Blackthorn is an inspiring general. He is admired and trusted by his troops, respected by his enemies. He has excellent strategic and tactical skills and an exemplary record of mission successes in difficult environments. On the other hand he is reluctant to take casualties and resistant to techniques of war that he holds to be dishonorable."

His finger shifted to the next man. "Major Anton Yuei. He is considered an exemplary combat soldier, cool under fire, fierce in achieving his operational objectives. He has resisted enemy interrogation and recovered from significant injury to continue his warrior career. However, he is somewhat narrow in his vision with a tendency to focus on the smaller rather than the bigger canvas."

Finally he indicated the last candidate. "Colonel David Morningstar, Blackthorn's second. He has risen fast and is ambitious to rise higher. He considers every order an opportunity to excel. He has shown formidable lateral thinking and a capacity for enlightened self-interest. In fact he has just sold details of his General's troop deployments to the enemy and intends to discredit Blackthorn so he can step into his command. I admire that kind of initiative in a man."

Aria thought of Halifax's rise to power. "It means you always have to watch your back," she warned.

"I have obedience discs already programmed, ready to implant. Nothing as refined as your contingency programming, Aria. Heavy duty wetware that will bond with their central nervous systems and be impossible to erase without killing them."

So mine is not? Aria wondered.

The Black Sorcerer returned to the fuzzing images on screen. "That is the day they all die. Morningstar underestimated the usefulness of the intelligence he sold on. He expected an ambush of forward columns, not a direct attack on the command module where he would be. Blackthorn, Yuei, and Morningstar all perish in the first ten minutes of combat. One of them at least will be reborn here tonight. But which?"

Aria ignored the frozen portraits of three long-dead soldiers. What they had looked like, whom they had been did not matter. What they could become here and now on Mars was all that counted. Which would be the best choice for her purposes?

Yuei might be the toughest, the one that could be thrown into savage combats with creatures and machines he had never even heard of before. He was used to adversity and had withstood pain and loss. But there were many here on Mars of which that was also true. Just as well promote the lizard-man Nash'Tek the Many-Warred to lead the Black Sorcerer's armies; the result would be little different.

Blackthorn then? He was the obvious choice, the most experienced commander, the military historian, the battlefield strategist. He had a long lifetime of army discipline and combat experience to draw upon. He would probably be best for the Black Sorcerer's purposes once he was compelled to obedience, but would he suit Aria's nascent plans? The princess was not confident that Blackthorn would be easy for her to suborn.

Morningstar? He was versed in treachery and had a Byzantine mind. If any would naturally wish to cast down the First Men who ruled the red planet it would be him. He might wish to supplant them and rule in their stead, but perhaps he would be a tyrant in the Athenian fashion? Aria could make him a king if it would save her world.

The princess' eyes strayed over to the gestation tube where the subject the Black Sorcerer had selected as host for his General floated waiting for a soul. Her father had chosen the blonde body with the lean tight muscles, Aria noted with approval. Somehow that one had come out best from the modifications she and Nepenthe had programmed in a silly hour months before.

Did he look like a Morningstar, though? Aria's gaze was drawn to the dark haired rogue in the left-hand cylinder.

The Black Sorcerer watched his daughter's deliberations but said nothing.

This is important, Aria mentally chided herself. *If Mars doesn't have a champion then you must make one. You only get a single shot at this. Which barbarian will you have to spearhead your war on the First Men?*

She thought harder. Really, how could it be anyone but brilliant, devious Morningstar?

"I have selected," she told the Black Sorcerer.

"And who will have the honor of being my General, my prime warrior, my puissant right hand?"

"Blackthorn," Aria answered before she could stop herself. "Call John Blackthorn."

Massive geothermal turbines throbbed so hard they could be felt through the Bastion's very walls and floors. Energy transfer spines dug deep into the solar system's biggest volcano, sucking heat from lava pits twenty miles under the planet's crust. And still the lights flickered in the palace above.

Everything non-essential was powered down. The machine shops ground to a halt mid-assembly. Elevators and gravity tubes shut off. Viewscreens turned to static fuzz then went dark. All energy in the huge volcano-side base was diverted up to the iron and copper dome where the Black Sorcerer himself stalked between his ancient machines about his mighty works.

Aria knew she didn't have much time. The minimal-energy protocols meant that the defense grid would be in its most passive mode, but even that wouldn't be enough to assure Reith's intrusion was effective without some additional precautions.

"Go to the Loremaster," Aria told Nepenthe. "Here are a list of items I want researched. Show him my requirements and wait there for his responses. Wait with him all night if you have to." The enquiries were meaningless, a mere diversion to keep the maidservant well away from what came next. Aria wanted no blame to fall on the blonde girl.

With Nepenthe absent, Aria was able to pass unchallenged into the Security Suite where she asked sharp questions of the Internal Logistics Duty Officer about what else could be diverted to supply yet more power for her father's vital experiment. It wasn't an idle enquiry; the last tachyon particles in the Ancient's time-viewer would only be as effective as the energy that projected them.

The harried officer was already distracted by red-lining system gauges and the task of manually levering various vital circuits on and off to balance a strained network. While he scurried off to a gallery to check what could be safely diverted from the cryogenics floor Aria had easy access to his open security panel.

A few minor changes laid open a path that the Runners could use to infiltrate to the weapons depot – if only they chose to come as Aria had instructed them.

Aria swept out of the Security Suite and back up the Iron Staircase to her own chambers. She snatched up the red scarf that she'd acquired at Cocytus Market and knotted it round the wrought-bronze stanchions of her balcony balustrade.

Aria had most things in place for her escape now. She'd even programmed her personal flyer for an unmanned journey far out over the Amazonis Sea and a crash in deep water. She intended to actually depart on horseback. Horses were much harder to spot on energy scanners.

She came back inside to check her saddlebags. She found Halifax checking them first.

"Planning a trip, princess?" the Herald enquired. "Your father's got a storm brewing."

Aria hadn't expected Halifax. "Why are you intruding in my quarters again?" she demanded.

"I asked first," Halifax smirked. "Another accidental adventure, princess? Where are you off to this time? And why?"

"What I do and where I go are not your business."

"Oh, Aria! Everything and everyone are the business of the Prime Herald of the Black Sorcerer. I'd want to know what you were up to even if you weren't going to be my beautiful bride."

"I'm not going to be your anything, Halifax, except your death if you don't get out of my rooms *now!*"

"Oh, must we rehearse this scene again, Aria? Do you *really* think the Black Sorcerer doesn't know that you plot against him still? Do you believe he wouldn't back me up in whatever I have to do to thwart you?"

The princess wasn't sure, but this was no time for gambling. "What do you want?" she asked the Herald.

An unpleasant smile bloomed on Halifax's face. "Why princess, what are you offering?"

"I don't want you poisoning my father's mind with your paranoid fantasies about me," Aria said. "Must we be enemies, Halifax?"

"I never was your enemy, princess. I've been pretty clear that I want to be your very good friend."

Aria unconsciously wet her lips with her tongue. "Once you could have been."

"I still can be, Aria. I will be." The Herald moved closer. "I know you liked it when I kissed you."

"Maybe."

"You did. Another meeting and I'd have had you. It's a shame things moved so fast back then." He smoothed a finger over Aria's cheek. "But there's no time like the present."

Aria bit her bottom lip. "I can't trust you, Halifax."

"This isn't about trust, Aria. It's about need and want. You need me. You need me to keep silent about your visit to the Security Suite today. You need me to overlook your intended abscondment to wherever you planned to ride tonight. And you need me to look after you because there are predators out there much worse than me. And I *want* you."

Aria said nothing, but she did not shy away as he took her in his arms.

"No more defiance, princess?" Halifax asked as he bent to kiss her.

As their lips touched, Aria knew she had the direct contact that would bypass Halifax's magic-deflecting vambraces and his personal screen belt. She discharged as much arcane energy as she could through their interlocking mouths, slamming Halifax into and partway through her bedroom wall. It was one hell of a kiss!

"One all, Halifax," she told the scorched, unconscious Herald as she stepped over him to repack her saddlebags. There were data coins and survival aids there that were essential to her plans.

The lights dimmed again. The Bastion's energy weave was almost at capacity. The Black Sorcerer would be decanting the minds of those barbarians into their new bodies within the hour and he would expect Aria to be there.

Aria scampered out of her chambers and hurried to join him.

"Engage the wild lightning snares!" shouted the Black Sorcerer. Minions scuttled to turn the giant wheels that opened up his laboratory dome to the skies. Others activated the heavy gears to push the catcher rods upwards into the raging storm.

Hail pelted into the open rotunda but melted from the heat of two million diodes and cathode tubes. On the main operating deck the Sensorines scuttled from panel to panel regulating the massive forces with which the Black Sorcerer played.

"Open the genesis valves!" the First Man commanded. "Gear in the soul engine on my mark!"

Aria stood beside her father as the trestles containing the three soulless bodies were winched into position. She helped Nan to connect the transfer helmets to the host flesh, ignoring the noise of the thrumming energy vats that steamed directly beneath the racking they stood on.

"Test the reception nodes, Nan," she called over the thunder.

The old nurse peered at a series of liquid-filled tubes to check that the measuring bubbles were in the right places. She flicked one with her finger until its display matched the others. "These are clear, dearie," Nan reported. "There won't be an accident like last time."

"What last time?" Aria frowned. Had the Black Sorcerer used this time-shifting mind-transfer apparatus before?

There was no time for answer. Lightning slammed into the catcher rods and fizzed down into the conceptual buffer reservoirs below. The liquid computers in the plasma tanks began to froth.

"*Now!*" howled the Black Sorcerer. He slammed home a six foot metal lever. The closed circuits came live, spraying showers of sparks across the various tiers of his sanctum workshop. Rubber-suited minions shied out of the way as terrible, immense forces shifted and rippled around them.

The images on the time monitor went mad, becoming mere retina-searing micro-flashes. Red warning lights blossomed across the equipment retrieved from Styxis' buried lake. The containment ovens made a high shriek of tortured metal as the last of the chronal energies mixed with the fundamental forces raised by the Black Sorcerer's engines. The projection array throbbed with an unholy negative glow.

Aria checked the encephalograms on the blonde body she'd wired in to the circuit. "Nothing's happening!"

"Patience," warned Nan. "Time does not leap to our rhythms."

"More power!" demanded the Black Sorcerer, raising his arms to the heavens. "Come on! Pour it on! More! *More!*"

Maybe it was coincidence or perhaps the First Man had ways of provoking the tempest, but new lightning sizzled into his gathering equipment, pushing the gauges past their red lines, bending their needles.

The blonde body shuddered and gasped. Brainwave monitors burst into activity.

"It's worked!" Aria gasped. "Nan! He's here!"

The old nurse signaled over to the Black Sorcerer on the main experiment platform that the transfer had succeeded.

The Black Sorcerer examined the readouts on the vibrating equipment around him. "Hold all steady!" he boomed at his servants. "We shall go again!"

More power breakers burst but the back-ups cut in. The dome shook as the storm raged round it. Aria quickly changed over the transmission coils to connect to the red-haired body.

"Let time itself serve me!" screamed the Black Sorcerer as he slammed home the second activation lever.

One of the energy transfer coils exploded, spraying lethal shards through the minions below. One servitor caught fire, his rubber suit burning around him.

The second body pulsed and came truly alive.

"More!" demanded the Black Sorcerer. "The chronal charge is almost done, but while the way lies open we can harvest one more mind. Engage the reserve cylinders. Knock off the last regulators! We shall reach through time that my eternal dominion be assured!"

"He's really enjoying himself," noted Aria.

Her fingers danced over the last connections until the dark-haired body was fitted for transfer. Even as she completed the work, wild electrical discharges earthed themselves from the skies above, ignoring the collectors and slamming into the copper dome itself. Skittering ball lightning rattled along the support girders like hunting ghosts.

"Now!" cried the Black Sorcerer, closing his final lever.

The first of the thinking tanks ruptured, spraying its sickly green nano-ooze out over the main workshop floor. A second column followed suit. The third cracked but held, boiling furiously.

Power monitor needles that had so recently strained at maximum plummeted as the system's final energies were exhausted.

The last of the three bodies shivered and began to breathe without need for external machine support. A moment later the time monitor winked out and went dead.

The noise levels in the sanctum fell until only the angry howling of the storm remained. Straining servants cranked shut the segmented dome and cleared away the bodies of their fellows. Steam rose up from overheated equipment and twisted into the returned darkness of the high ceiling.

"All three subjects are nominal," Nan reported to the Black Sorcerer as he climbed over to inspect his new creations. "They're progressing through first stage neuro-trauma at the moment, finding their way through different cerebral architecture than what they're used to. That usually takes a couple of hours, and another hour or so to adopt non-autonomic functions. Then we can see how well the consciousnesses translated. They should be awake before dawn."

The Black Sorcerer gestured for Malathea and her kin to make their inspections. "This is the day that history will record as the end of the rule of the Four First Men," he declared. "Soon there will be but one!"

Aria remembered that boast for a long time afterwards.

Aria made a quick return to her chambers to make sure that Halifax was still down. She slammed more energies into him to make sure. She told herself it was merely prudent.

When Nepenthe returned Aria kept the maid away from the wrecked master bedroom. She sent the girl on another urgent errand right away, heedless and seemingly uncaring that Nepenthe had been up all night too.

Aria allowed herself one luxury, that of a final hot dip in the thermally-heated spring-bath that formed part of her suite. If things went as she planned this might be her last ablution for a long time. Even that indulgence had to be a quick splash rather than a long soak. The princess was on a schedule.

If only the lure had worked!

As if on cue a distant shudder rumbled through the fortress. An alarm bell tolled its sonorous warning.

"Intruders!" someone shouted on the Iron Staircase. "Intruders at Weapons Vault Five! Rebels!"

A slow smile invaded Aria's face. So Reith had overcome his skepticism and made his move. The last distraction was in place.

She drew on a cloak and hood to mask her identity and slipped like a specter up to her father's secure sanctum. She had worried about bypassing the defense system but she was still logged in from her earlier efforts that night.

The three subjects were still in their gestation coffers, she saw, but they'd been winched or wheeled down onto the main floor. And they were awake.

"If you can think of another way to get free, by all means share it!" one of them growled. Aria shied into the shadows so they would not see her. They were communicating with each other, discussing their situation, striving to break loose.

The Black Sorcerer had been interrupted before he could install their obedience wetware. One by one the variables of Aria's mad scheme were falling into place!

The princess climbed a gantry ladder so she could look down on the three men from the concealed security of the darkened upper tier. From this bird's eye position she could see that it was Blackthorn — the new-bodied, young, strong Blackthorn — who was struggling to escape. The three barbarians had been dressed in top-of-the-range multicombat suits that could resist laser fire, sonics, and projectile attack. Blackthorn's was mostly black trimmed with silver, a General's livery. The other two wore gold-trimmed red.

The subjects were restrained with kinetic web. No amount of force would set them free, not even the impressive level of muscle that Blackthorn was testing on it. Aria focused her will and hurled an arcane bolt to scramble the fabric and denature it.

Blackthorn said something that the translation-ware in his new brain could not handle. Interesting that the barbarian knew profanities too horrid for modern ears! He blinked to clear his eyes from the blue flash that had enveloped him then began his struggles again. This time one of his wrist-straps snapped. A moment later he was free.

Aria waited to see what the man might do now. Would his first instinct be to run, to hide, to search, to grab a weapon, or what? Earlier, the princess had left a selection of suitable equipment on an illuminated shelf near enough for him to notice it.

Blackthorn looked to his comrade first. He tried to find some way to free him too.

Aria couldn't launch another arcane bolt without being seen. Besides, after participating in the night's scientific endeavors and searing Halifax twice her personal reserves were very low by now. She watched to see what this John Blackthorn might do for himself.

He stared around his unfamiliar environment, obviously seeking some tool to help him release Morningstar. His traitorous former second officer had wisely not identified his new flesh to his General.

Blackthorn's eyes were drawn to the illuminated display shelf. Aria watched his hand pass over a force decoupler and an agony wand, ignore an energy brace and a pack of disruption needles. Any of them might have released the captives. Evidently the additional programming on modern weapons hadn't yet clicked in for the General. He didn't recognize the tools.

Blackthorn's hand closed on the last object on the shelf, the one that Aria had only put there at the very last minute on a mad whim. It had no place amongst the others and was the one item that would be useless to the awakened General.

Blackthorn seized up the silver-white cylinder that might have been the Sword of Light. "Too heavy for a flashlight, I think," he muttered to himself.

Aria almost cried out. She only caught herself at the last minute and reminded herself of the plan. Blackthorn and the others were just tools, like the ones she'd laid out on display. If they were to be of any use they had to escape on their own from here. Besides, the Sword of Light was utterly useless now that...

Blackthorn thumbed the green square on the cylinder's edge. A bright dagger of yellow light flared from the crystal disc.

"That's not possible!" Aria gasped to herself. Fortunately the barbarian was too occupied with his new discovery to hear her squeaked denial. Why should one of the holy Hallows work for John Blackthorn when it had not operated for a First Man or for the Princess of Mars?

Because it's for him, a small seditious part of her argued. *A hero needs a magic sword.*

He's not a hero. He is a tool, nothing more.

Down below, Blackthorn sliced Morningstar out of his coffer. Then they both heard movement in the third container.

Aria listened with interest. Morningstar recommended ignoring the noise and making a hasty retreat. That might have been sensible, but some tiny part of Aria thrilled when Blackthorn instead chose to investigate. They found Yueh's container and released him too.

Now there were three potentials free in the Black Sorcerer's sanctum. That meant three possible figureheads who might lead a revolution to cast down the First Men. Aria crouched in shadow and waited to see what they would do next.

They *introduced* themselves to each other. Aria was surprised. It was such a human thing to do!

"*General* Blackthorn," Morningstar said skeptically when he heard his rescuer's name.

"You know me then?"

"I know General Blackthorn, yes," Yuei interjected. "But *you* are certainly not him."

Aria waited impatiently as they sorted out the idea that they may be in unfamiliar new bodies in an unexpected and strange new place. Morningstar declined to give his name, knowing his comrades would suspect him of the treachery that had led to their destruction.

Then they moved to planning their next actions. Like the barbarian warriors they were, the three men determined on escape. It became clear to Aria that each of them would offer her a very different approach to the situations they faced. Yuei was a pragmatist, addressing each problem with practical utility as it presented. Morningstar was an opportunist with a healthy sense of self-preservation. Blackthorn... well, Blackthorn seemed to appreciate the big picture, Aria had to admit.

The escape attempt had got as far as speculating how to open the sealed doors to the service laboratories when the portal pistoned open and one of the lizard-man orderlies entered the chamber.

Blackthorn killed him without a moment's hesitation. A clean neck-snap dropped the unfamiliar monster to the floor.

Unfortunately the lizard-man was not alone. The reptilian clean-up crew with him switched from domestics to warriors with the ferocity bred into their race and came at the escaping barbarians.

Aria had intended that the men should escape unaided from here, but her whole plan teetered as the lizard men overwhelmingly outnumbered them. The humans weren't even armed except for the dubious advantage of a supposed Sword of Light that acted like a laser-knife. The princess span off another bright energy bolt, the best she could manage, to dazzle rather than damage the incoming assailants. She directed a supplementary tiny energy packet to glow like a luminous eye and draw the fugitives' attention to the secondary service staircase.

That was all the advantage Blackthorn and the others needed. They took the hint and clattered onto the metal spiral ahead of the dazzled lizard-man host.

Aria tried to review what the roofs of the Bastion were like if the barbarians could force their way out through one of the dome's maintenance hatches. Was there any chance that the fugitives could reach the flyer bays or the main courtyard from there?

The main entrance to the sanctum irised open. Aria's heart fell. The Black Sorcerer re-entered his laboratory and took in at a glance the lizard-man hunt and the escaping test subjects. He raised his serpent-headed staff and floated himself up to end the conflict.

Aria knew that she must flee. It was over. Her plans had come to naught.

She scrambled down the ladder on her father's blind side. She could no longer see what he was doing to recapture Blackthorn, Yuei, and Morningstar. She had to get away!

She would be punished, the princess knew, punished worse than she had been for her plotting at Styxis. Even as she admitted it, she guessed what her penance might be: *Father will give me to Halifax. I shall be his obedient slave!*

Aria had to leave, to escape the Black Sorcerer's Bastion as the barbarians would not. Her grand design had failed. Now mere survival was all she could hope for.

Blackthorn and his men might not need the three horses she had sent Nepenthe to arrange outside main gate, but the pair for Aria and her maid at the lava gate might allow the princess a chance for freedom.

Aria slipped from the sanctum while the conflict raged above. She caught a last glimpse of Blackthorn defying her father. He had somehow converted the Sword of Light's energy knife to a full-blown blade like the one in the mummer's play. Aria didn't want to think how or why he could do it.

She raced down the Iron Staircase heedless of who saw her. At one point she thought she heard Nan Vidi calling after her but she fled on.

The fortress was still on high security but diminished power. The princess gathered from the swarming minions and courtiers that a rebel foray had made it as far as one of the weapons depots. Most of the intruders had escaped with plunder before the Black Sorcerer could arrive. Aria was glad.

She made it to the inner seal of the lava gate, where Nepenthe nervously and obediently waited with a pair of saddled mounts. "I don't think this is a good time to go riding!" the girl blurted when she saw the princess arrive. "There are rebels on the mountainside and all the outer doors are sealed. There's not even anyone on the lava gate to open it for us."

That was what Aria had been counting on. It was one of the least of the fortress' entrances. A standard security shutdown would simply deadlock it, allowing vital defenders to be redeployed at other, more sensitive posts; except that Aria had omitted this exit from the deadlock commands when she'd visited Security earlier.

If only she wasn't excised from the security passlist! Aria wasn't clear whether her father had perceived her back in his sanctum. Perhaps Halifax was awake now too, wrathful and vengeful? Or else her tampering with the systems to allow the rebels to penetrate so far might have been found; it was only a matter of time. The princess touched her hand to the control glass with trepidation.

The inner doors hissed open. "Come on, Nepenthe," Aria called her handmaiden. "It's time to escape."

Nepenthe paused. "Escape? What do you mean?"

"We are leaving. I have turned my back on the Black Sorcerer. His wrath will be terrible. We must go, right now!"

Nepenthe hesitated. "But... if I run then my whole family will be executed! Do you not know the penalty for tithed thralls who betray their gifting? I cannot leave, Princess Aria, n-nor allow you to depart either!"

The princess felt like she'd been punched in the gut. How could she have been so stupid as to forget that Nepenthe had concerns and feelings of her own? "I'm sorry," she told the blonde girl. "You're right, of course."

She slammed a palm into Nepenthe's cheek then downed her with a nerve pinch. The bruise should be enough to demonstrate that Aria had used force to escape from a loyal servant of the Black Sorcerer who had tried to prevent her departure.

Aria tethered the horses together, led them into the corridor between the inner and outer doors, and activated the evacuation sequence.

The sulky night seemed endless. After the storm came heavy rain, enough to soak Aria to the skin despite her magical garb and a heavy cloak. She lost her path twice and had to redirect her mount back along tenuous muddy trails to reach the treeline that abutted the upper reaches of Nix Olympus.

She almost cried when she saw that the twisting tracks had brought her right round to the shallow shelf beneath the main bulk of the many-domed Bastion. An hour's hard traveling had put her back on the path she might have taken if she'd departed from the main courtyard.

That at least sparked an idea. The other horses, the ones she'd arranged for the barbarians to find had they escaped this far, would be just down the road from here. If she could not make use of Blackthorn and his comrades then Aria could at least make use of the rations that she'd ordered Nepenthe to pack into their saddlebags.

She approached cautiously. The removal of some prime riding stock might already have been detected now that her plots were exposed. Lizard-men guards or Herald Maximal's personal troopers might be lying in wait.

She heard voices and froze.

"This is handy," someone said.

"Too handy."

Aria recognized that tone. The speaker was David Morningstar!

"I agree," chimed in Blackthorn, " but seeing as these literally are 'gift horses', I don't think we're in a position to refuse them. Especially considering that loon and his lizard-men are going to be on us any second now."

The princess tried to think, despite her cold and exhaustion. *How* had the barbarians escaped the Black Sorcerer? *How* had they managed to leave the Bastion when it was on high alert? Nobody defied the Black Sorcerer and lived.

Except you, Aria reminded herself. *And now them.*[6]

Her reverie was interrupted by the echoing howl of a hunting lizard-man pack. They had caught Blackthorn's scent – or hers – and were closing fast.

Blackthorn leaped onto a white stallion and seized the reins. "Alright gentlemen, let's ride!"

The barbarians took the horses and thundered away down the steep trail. Aria had no choice but to climb back on her bay mare and follow after them.

Aria had never been alone before. The princess had always been surrounded by people. As a tiny child in the Crystal Lady's court and later with her mother in Daedalia there had been attendants and courtiers, playmates and guardians. With the Black Sorcerer there were her tutors and the ever-present Nan. As she'd blossomed to womanhood she'd had confidante-maids like Coda, noblewomen who'd served as her attendants and perhaps as her friends.

Aria had never spent a day without anyone to talk to if she'd wanted. She'd never had to prepare her own food. She'd rarely had to look to her own safety.

From Princess of Mars to cavewoman in three days, Aria reflected as she coaxed flame from damp brushwood for her evening's meal. She still had supplies with her from the palace kitchens, but she'd deliberately omitted any power-operated devices from her equipment, including any food heater. The Black Airships could detect standard artificial energy sources from a mile away, even through the pervasive static that blocked long-range sensors.

Aria struggled to roast a chicken leg without burning her fingers. She could have used magic but she was afraid the Black Sorcerer might have dispatched Sensorines to hunt for her too. They might track an active arcane signature.

Everything is harder out here, the princess admitted. Comforts she had always taken for granted like warmth, nutrition, and a place to sleep all required much more effort and planning. Aria decided that the tent-dome she'd packed in her saddlebag had definitely been

---

[6] An account of these events from Blackthorn's perspective is offered in Van Allen Plexico's "Bastion of the Black Sorcerer" in *Blackthorn: Thunder on Mars*. Dialogue and action from that story are reproduced here with thanks and credit.

designed by the Black Sorcerer's inquisitors as a means of driving prisoners mad.

Something shifted in the undergrowth. It was too big for ground game, but there was nothing visible through the thick forest foliage. The horses stamped nervously, but that might be because the princess had omitted to pack grain for them amongst her escape provisions. They could survive on turf but they weren't used to it.

Aria very cautiously extended her arcane senses to test the area. Her mind connected with an adolescent brown jumpbear snuffling mere yards from her tent. She crafted the right encouragement for it to forage off in another direction and launched the idea into the creature's fuzzy brain.

"This won't do," she told herself out loud. It helped to hear a human voice, even if it was her own. "You have a plan. You're certainly committed to it now. Why won't you go and see it through?"

Because I am afraid.

The barbarians had made good their escape, at least for the moment. Aria presumed that her father must be more concerned for now with the weapons stolen from his vault than with three timelost refugees. If the Runners managed to get away with whatever they'd liberated from the Bastion's arsenal they might equip resistance across the West. Every patrol would have to be doubled if a sniper might have access to a disruption snarl or a detonation pellet.

Blackthorn, Yuei, and Morningstar had made it as far as Domrik, one of the dozens of supply villages that were permitted to exist in the shadow of the great volcano to service the Bastion's needs. Aria had seen the barbarians there through her binoculars just that morning, interacting with the villagers as welcomed guests. She'd had to stifle a pang of jealousy.

The next logical step was to meet with the warriors and recruit them to the liberation of Mars. She'd have to convince them to trust her then lead them to the places where they'd need to go. Eventually she'd need to hook them up with Reith and the Runners, and through them to whatever crude tentative alliances existed between the ragged rebels. After that she'd have to support her chosen candidate in his war with the First Men until her planet was free.

Whatever it cost. Aria was very aware that these were barbarians and she was an attractive woman. If *that* was what was required to win their trust... well, her mother had made that sacrifice, and the Black Sorcerer was surely worse than John Blackthorn or David Morningstar?

There was always the chance that the villagers of Domrik might just try to burn her, of course. Sorceresses were not popular. An unprotected sorceress with no guards was likely to end up buried at a crossroads with a spike through her heart. Aria couldn't begin to guess how the peasants might react if they knew she was the Black Sorcerer's daughter. If they didn't kill her they would certainly betray her to her father.

An unpleasant burning smell roused the princess from her brown study. The chicken leg was smoldering, blackened on one side, still pink and raw on the other. Aria quickly rotated the stick she'd skewered it on. The meat fell from the charred branch and dropped into the fire.

She cursed and tried to salvage her meal before it was burned beyond redemption. She was so busy with the campfire that she didn't notice the approach of hunters until they were in the clearing and pointing crossbows at her.

"Who are you?" one of them demanded.

Aria dropped the scorched chicken and sucked her fingers. "Who are you to ask?"

The leader pointed to the men ranged round the princess. "We are eight armed hunters that are asking your name and what business you have in our forest."

"Your forest? This is the Black Sorcerer's domain. And I am... from his court." Aria gestured to her clothes, a finer weave of much better quality than anything these peasants could hope to possess.

"And what are you doing in the forest... milady?"

Aria watched her chicken leg blacken and burn. "Failing to cook supper, it seems. You are men from Domrik?"

The leader pursed his lips to silence but one of his comrades answered "Aye."

"Well then, men of Domrik, I am Princess Aria, formerly of the Black Sorcerer's court, and you will take me to your village to speak with the barbarian they call General Blackthorn."

Aria wasn't sure if the men who brought her into the village that evening were escort or warders. They flanked her vigilantly as she entered the central square, then made her wait there while the common populace gawked at her and their leader vanished into the refectory.

Domrik was typical of the little farming centers ringed on the fertile larval plain round Nix Olympus. Thick lush forest had been cleared for fields and a circle of houses clustered behind a high thorn hedge. The buildings were a ramshackle mixture of brick, wood, and whatever metal had been salvaged from older, sturdier constructions. Probably three hundred people lived here, with as many more out in the woods using this place as a market and home base.

Aria thought that Blackthorn had been lucky in his choice of refuges. A half day more would have brought him to Bandusae, the military and administrational headquarters of the Pyriphlegethon region. He and his companions would certainly have been noticed there. If they hadn't been detained they would undoubtedly have been reported. Smaller settlements might have sent messengers for advice about what to do with three unauthorized strangers. Only a semi-independent village like this would have waited a few days before deciding what to do with such unorthodox visitors.

The senior hunter spoke with another, older man. Aria rightly concluded that this must be the local headman; she later learned his name was Ardin. The village elder indicated the eating hall and sent the hunter inside.

The delay was longer than Aria cared for. She was becoming more and more nervous, and the wait made it harder for her to disguise it. When men emerged from the longhut again she was ridiculously relieved to see the tall blonde shape of Blackthorn amongst them.

Morningstar and Yuei appeared too, each approaching from a different way.

Surrounded by three barbarians and the men of the village, Aria felt absurdly outnumbered.

"She was camped in the forest nearby. We think she'd been there for at least a day," the hunter reported.

"Three days," she corrected him, then wished she hadn't. "There was no need to arrest me, or whatever you're doing. I was on my way here anyway. I need to talk to General Blackthorn."

The barbarian met the questioning stares of his hosts with a shrug. "No, I don't know her. Never met her before."

"No. But I know you."

"How?"

Aria took a deep breath. "I was there when you... arrived!" As the barbarian reached for the Sword of Light that hung at his waist she quickly went on. "Settle down. I'm not with *him*. I escaped too. In fact if it wasn't for me, you three probably wouldn't still be alive." She transfixed Blackthorn with what she hoped was an imperious stare.

Blackthorn met her gaze as so few did. Then he looked at Morningstar and Yuei. "I see..." he said thoughtfully, then turned to Ardin. "Take her to the jail. She and I need to talk."

Aria masked her fear. This wasn't going the way she'd hoped! She fixed on what she hoped was an alluring smile and turned it on the General. "The pub would be better," she coaxed. "Assuming that these... *people* have a place here where we can get a drink and a private table." There it was, she thought, the moment she bartered herself.

Blackthorn nodded. Everybody relaxed a little. Aria found herself shepherded towards a rickety lean-to with a live green branch nailed over the door; the traditional sign of a place that served alcohol.

Morningstar and Yuei followed after her and Blackthorn. All of them sat around a greasy table in the chimney alcove.

So seduction wasn't first on Blackthorn's mind, Aria noted with a wild relief; unless these barbarians had *really* primitive mating customs. "Not what I had in mind," she began as the three men looked at her, "but I suppose it will do."

"You seem to know who I am," said Blackthorn. "Who are you?"

"I am the Princess Aria."

"Princess of what?"

A thrill of good fortune shivered through Aria. He didn't know! How could he? He was new to Mars. Even the peasants here hadn't connected her with the daughter of the Black Sorcerer, not for sure. The names of legendary queens and of the last princess were popular choices amongst the children of the nobility.

Aria stammered out the cover she'd decided on during those cold rainy nights in the forest. She talked about the tithe, the tribute of noble slaves that was levied by the First Men. She managed to imply that she was one such victim, recently brought to the Black Sorcerer's court and now run away. She described how she'd seen the barbarians' revival in their new bodies, confessed to loosening Blackthorn's bonds and speeding their departure. She told how she'd taken the opportunity to escape after them.

At last she fell silent and waited for a response.

"Okay, assuming I believe any of this," said Blackthorn, "you have my thanks."

The General had more questions, of course. He wanted to know how he'd come to Mars, so Aria had to describe the Black Sorcerer's mechanisms to him as best she could. She also had to warn the barbarians that the memories of their past would gradually fade, leaving their expertise and character but losing the context that had formed it.

"Describe any of your former life for me," she challenged them. "Your home. Your family. Your friends." It disturbed them to learn that they could not.

At last Blackthorn asked the vital questions: "What do you want? What did you want from me?"

Aria composed herself and answered. "I want to go with you. You and your friends. I want to join you."

"Go with us where? Join us in what? We're not *doing* anything!"

"You will," Aria promised.

"We will *what?*" Blackthorn demanded. He was growing irritated.

"You'll go. You'll do." Aria surrendered her pretence of poise and spoke from her heart for once. "And I want to be a part of it!"

Aria lay in the smelly hut they'd assigned her and delicately probed the bruises on her neck. She didn't think there was any permanent damage but they hurt a lot. Mock-Men were strong!

Everyone knew about the Mock-Men – except barbarians torn from some primitive past on old Earth-that-was, Aria supposed. The huge fur-swathed bipeds had opposable thumbs and near-human faces but their size and strength were those of a shaggy bear. Like the lizard-men, they'd been genetically created as shock troops in a First Man's army. The Lord of Fatal Laugher had held high hopes for them.

But for once the joke had been on him. Some miscalculation made the Mock-Men pacifists by nature, unless stirred to rage by direct attack or threats to those they loved. Designed with the bodies of savage killers, the Mock-Men turned out to be excellent gardeners and farmers, naturally forming rural communities where they lived in peace and harmony.

No wonder the Lord of Fatal Laugher had culled them by the thousands, and that now every First Man used them for brute slave labor.

The Mock-Man who'd left the bruises on Aria's throat had been no slave, though. He'd moved with all the lethal ferocity bred into his race to slam her to the ground as soon as she'd begun to gather up her arcane power. Blackthorn had convinced the Mock-Man, Oglok, to release the sorceress at last, but it had been a near thing.

I didn't even want to demonstrate my magic, Aria complained to nobody in the darkness of her straw pallet. *It was Blackthorn who wanted proof that I have arcane power.*

One minute she'd been levitating a table in that malodorous pub, the next she'd been under four hundred pounds of snarling Oglok.

Still, the bruises and the Mock-Man's reaction that had caused them seemed to have convinced General Blackthorn to take her seriously. She'd explained what she could bring to his cause, the knowledge of the red planet that she'd gleaned from the Hall of Reflections, the rare sorcery of those who tapped into the energy fields of the Harmony Spires, the contacts and prestige of a Princess of Mars.

"You need me as much as I need you," she'd told Blackthorn, then blushed like an idiot as she'd realized how her words might be construed.

In the end Blackthorn had agreed that the First Men needed removing, but she wasn't sure that was more than mere expedience. The General was still coping, surviving. He didn't have any other reason to care about Mars.

Aria huddled into a miserable ball and tried to sleep. Every time she used her magic to remove fleas from the straw matting reinforcements seemed to arrive.

It was the middle of the night but Aria was still awake when she heard the scraping at her door. "Aria? Princess Aria?"

She recognized the voice. She'd helped create it. "Colonel Morningstar?"

The rush door was lifted aside and someone slipped into the hut. Aria sat up and generated a small witchlight in her palm.

"That's better," David Morningstar approved. "Sweet power, princess."

"It's a great comfort to me," Aria admitted. "Why are you here?"

Morningstar smiled. "I was thinking about all that stuff you and Blackthorn were talking about before. About the First Men and technology that seems like magic and how there needs to be new leadership on this funky new world. I was thinking a lot."

"There has to be change or we will diminish and die," Aria insisted. She shifted her knees to make room for Morningstar in the cramped little hutch. "The First Men rose out of the chaos of generations of civil war. Their first unregulated conflicts scorched the planet. Their long rule has not lifted us from the dark ages but rather entrenched us in them."

"And you think there needs to be new management."

"I do. The First Men must fall. Mars must be reunited so it can rebuild and survive."

Morningstar nodded. "And you think General Blackthorn will do that for you?"

Aria hesitated. "I think he could do it. I do not think he will do it for me."

Morningstar seemed satisfied with that answer. "I was hearing the guys talk. They seem to think you know all about the lives we had back on Earth that we can't remember."

"I know much of your bio-data," the princess conceded.

"So you know who I really am. Not the guy I'm claiming to be to Blackthorn and Yuei. You know I'm David Morningstar."

"Of course."

"But you didn't tell them. Do you know what I've done?"

"Providing secrets to your nation's enemies. Yes. That was why my… the Black Sorcerer considered you as his commander in chief."

"Really?" The soldier's eyes went up. "Well damn! So what do you think about that, princess?"

Aria searched her feelings. "You could be king of this world," she decided at last. "I think it is in you to plot and achieve the overthrow of the First Men."

"I think it is too. And I heard all the things you promised Blackthorn, how you could help him with intel and connections and that mage-tech you've got going there. If him then why not me?"

It was just what Aria had planned. One of the barbarians would take up her standard and displace the Sorcerers. If she cleaved to him, he would make her co-ruler of Mars.

And it was *wrong*. If she helped Morningstar to supplant the First Men she would simply replace four tyrants with one; and Mars needed more than that. Aria didn't know what, but Mars needed more.

"Blackthorn's an idiot," Morningstar told her. "A beautiful sorceress princess offers him the world on a plate and he stops to *think* about it? Well I guess he was an old man when you dragged him to that new body of his. He's had his day. I, on the other hand, know exactly what to do with beautiful sorceress princesses when they come my way."

He reached out for Aria to draw her to him.

"What are you doing?" she asked. The light in her palm fluttered.

"Well from what I recall about Earth, we'd say this was sealing the deal, honey. Afterwards it'll be you and me kicking the First Men off their thrones and ruling the world!"

"No," said Aria. She pushed the soldier away.

"Don't deny it, princess. I could see it in your eyes before you let the light go out. You want Mars so bad I can taste it. Well so do I. A man doesn't get another chance like this and just let it slip away. And you want me, too. I know that as well."

"I said no. Mars needs saving, but not for me, not for you. It's not my destiny to *rule*. It's my duty to *serve*." Aria shook her head. "You're not the one, Colonel Morningstar."

"You sure?" the soldier asked.

"Yes."

"I can't convince you different?"

"No."

Morningstar waited half a beat then slapped her hard across the face. "Shame, that," he told her as he folded his hand around her already-battered throat. "We could have been great together!"

She heard the metallic hiss of Morningstar's knife leaving its sheath. Aria was half-stunned, too fazed to draw upon her magics to protect herself. She battered at Morningstar but he was an experienced combat soldier in the body of a superman. The princess' eyesight darkened. She felt herself slipping away. The point of the blade came down towards her jugular.

Mars *cried* to her. For a brief moment as she approached death she felt it all, the whole planet, throbbing to the song of the Harmony Spires, wounded and battered like she was, on the edge of extinction.

Her magic flared up and twisted the blade from Morningstar's grip. She sliced the dirk blindly, hoping to gash her attacker.

Morningstar's fist hammered all the air from her chest. She'd never been punched before. The knife clattered uselessly on the straw.

An alien howl came from outside. Guiltily, half-conscious Aria realized that the fierce Mock-Man who didn't like magic had sensed her arcane projections and was objecting again. *Too bad, hairy*, she thought to herself in her pain. *You can't strangle me 'cause I'm already being strangled...*

There was movement beyond the hut. Morningstar broke away, bursting through the back of the flimsy dwelling to make his escape.

Aria slumped to the ground and waited for the Mock-Man to finish her off.

Aria woke late and wished she'd not moved. Her whole body felt like a giant bruise.

The events of last night flooded back to her. Her meeting with Blackthorn. Morningstar's night visit and his assault. The Mock-Man's warning cry. Her assailant fleeing into the night.

She examined her blurry memories of the conversations after that, when Blackthorn, Yuei, Ardin and the others had come to see what was going on. She suspected she had been rather obnoxious, revealing Morningstar's true identity to the General then berating his stupidity. She'd defaulted to ice-princess to mask her fear and shock and hurt.

It was evident from village gossip that Morningstar had gone. Hunters had been sent to track him at first light. Aria believed they were wasting their time. Even before he'd received a perfect new body, David Morningstar had been an excellent ranger. Creator help the hunting party that actually found him!

She forced herself to rise from her stale pallet and groom herself for the day. A purpling ring of bruises and some abrasions were hardly an excuse not to turn herself out properly. She willed the stains and creases out of her dress and decided it would be emerald today. She opened her travel case of costly make-up and applied it to her face and nails.

Only when she felt sufficiently armored did she push aside the covering of her little hut and step out into the new day.

Blackthorn was in the tavern, at the same table where he'd interviewed her yesterday. Yuei and the Mock-Man Oglok accompanied him. They were chatting amiably, even though the hairy beast communicated only in growls and howls. Aria surmised that the translation packets she'd programmed into the barbarians' new bodies allowed them to understand his speech. She wished she could interpret more than the occasional general gist.

"Good morning, Princess Aria," Yuei bade her. He rose with literally old-world courtesy as the lady approached. "Some late breakfast? The harvest's just in here so there's plenty for everyone."

Aria shook her head. She went and stood directly in front of Blackthorn. "When do we leave?" she demanded.

"Leave?" the General questioned. He glanced at the others.

"To begin preparing for the rebellion," Aria clarified.

"Rebellion? What rebellion is this?" Blackthorn took another pull at the dark sour ale he was drinking.

"The one you're going to lead, of course." Aria took the mug from him. "The rebellion against the Black Sorcerer and the other First Men."

"Hold on now…"

"No. Shush. I have something to say and it's hard for me, so just listen please. I don't know if you still remember why you're a soldier, General Blackthorn, but I do. You volunteered because you believed in some ideals that your country held as self-evident. You believed that people everywhere should be free. You believed that evil should be fought. You believed that there should be justice, and compassion, and opportunity for all. Didn't you?"

"That's enshrined – was enshrined – right there in the Constitution of the Unites States of America."

"So then." Aria spoke directly to Blackthorn, but Yuei was listening as well. Even Oglok leaned forward to hear what the princess had to say. "My world, this world, is not free. Evil rules it, and has done for a very long time. There is no justice, no compassion, no opportunity. There are only people clinging to life, suffering, then dying. There is no hope, John Blackthorn, and no end to the misery – unless *you* give it to us."

The man from old Earth opened his lips to speak but Aria covered them with her fingers. "This world needs a hero. A champion. If one man can stand against the Sorcerers then all men can." She gestured to Oglok. "In the Mines of Deuteronilus and Cryse's Foundries his people labor and die every day in abject slavery, but nobody cares. The dead walk in the Forests of Utopia and prey upon the living by night, but nobody resists. Conscripted armies clash in endless wars for the amusement of their overlords but no-one cries 'enough!' Someone needs to stand, Blackthorn! *Someone* needs to show us the way."

Aria snatched the Sword of Light from its place at Blackthorn's belt and held it before him. "This is a weapon of heroes. It's a light for a man who is a beacon. If it has come to you then you have to be that man. Here on Mars you were literally made for it!"

"Hold on now…" Yuei objected, but Aria still wasn't finished.

"John Blackthorn, your army is gone and your country is gone. Even your world is dust. But if you still believe in the things your army and your country and your world stood for then you have to stand for them here. Mars cries out for aid and as Princess of Mars I am *calling* you, and *begging* you, and *anointing* you to save it from destruction!"

Aria slapped the Sword of Light into Blackthorn's hand. The blade flared out, bright and golden.

Oglok roared. He roared that he would follow Blackthorn and save the world.

"You too?" the General asked the excited Mock-Man.

"Oh wait," Aria said, falling from that lofty place she'd climbed in her fiery speech. "*He* wants to come?"

They left the following morning; but not all of them. Major Yuei chose to take a different road. He was tired of war.

Aria was surprised when Blackthorn let him go. Her father would have compelled his obedience or punished his desertion. He would not have shaken hands and walked off in the other direction.

They took the horses on which Blackthorn and Morningstar had escaped and the pair that Aria had brought and set off on the northern track that put Nix Olympus at their backs.

"Is there a plan, General Blackthorn?" the princess enquired as they cantered.

Blackthorn had declined to answer any questions about his strategic intentions back in Domrik. That was basic operational precaution. Nobody could be forced to reveal intelligence they did not know. Now he was able to give the princess a response.

"Every operation needs four things, your highness. First it needs information. Then communication and logistics. Then materiel and personnel. And last of all opportunity. So practically we are working on developing those things."

Oglok groaned something in his fierce-sounding language. Aria thought it was probably a wry comment about needing food and beer as well.

Blackthorn went on. "Now if we intend to foment revolution there's a few things we need to set in place. First off we've got to let folks know there's resistance in the offing. They've got to know what we're out to do, and why. We need popular support."

"That's why you sent those messengers from Domrik to the other villages," Aria supposed.

"Yep. And then we have to make people believe that what we're about is possible. They have to know that the Black Sorcerer and those others aren't unbeatable or indestructible."

"And we have to hope they aren't," Aria added.

"One guy with a Sword of Light, a magic princess, and a furball can't save a whole planet," Blackthorn warned. "But maybe together we can mobilize a whole planet to save itself."

Oglok growled that he was not a ball, but rather a handsome prime specimen of steely muscle and lightning reflexes; at least that's what Aria thought he said from the context and from Blackthorn's snort of acknowledgement.

She spent the morning dredging her memory for every detail of the various scattered resistance groups she'd glimpsed in the Hall of Reflection. She didn't mention the source of her information and Blackthorn didn't ask. It was another of his compartmentalized security precautions, the princess realized.

Oglok suggested that it was a priority to find the Runners, who seemed to be the link between the various freedom fighters and refugees.

"Not right now, buddy," Blackthorn told him. "Not with that weirdo Black Sorcerer probably still on our tail. We don't want to lead his guys right to the resistance they're hunting. Besides, we need to build a rep first. When we're famous enough this Reith guy will come to us."

Aria rode her bay alongside a would-be hero on a white charger and wondered how she had ever got herself into this.

They left the main path before sunset to find a secluded campsite. They discovered Oglok had a natural talent for picking such places. The big Mock-Man led them to a sheltered hollow where a fresh stream trickled down to a basin pool. Thick brush protected their flanks and the overcrop would obscure them from aerial observation.

Blackthorn scouted the area, set some warning snares, then returned to supervise setting up the camp. He was much more adept at raising Aria's dome-tent than she was, the princess noted. She wondered if he would expect to share it with her tonight.

The General climbed the rock behind them for an overview of the terrain. Aria busied herself with unpacking some more of the food-stores she still hoarded. She glanced nervously at Oglok.

"I need to use magic to heat these," she told him. "It won't be detected here round all this granite. The signature will be masked."

The Mock-Man growled warning. His teeth were bigger than Aria's fingers.

"Look, if we're going to travel together we need to come to some sort of understanding," the princess insisted. "I'm a sorceress born – and created, I suppose. But magic is part of who I am, just like big claws and massive muscles and that horrible stench are part of you!"

Oglok growled that his big claws and massive muscles could tear the sorceress apart if she tried her magics on him.

"Not on you! On this dried ham. There is a difference, you know." She tried and failed to reign in her temper. "The dried ham is smarter!"

For a moment she thought the Mock-Man might tear her head off. Then he made a snorting sound she'd not heard before. Oglok was *laughing!*

The princess had never considered that the huge shaggy beastlings might have a sense of humor. It absurdly encouraged her. "Look, I don't know your reasons for suddenly deciding to follow the General, but I assume you really want to help him. Well so do I. Can't we agree on that at least?"

Oglok growled his explanations, but Aria couldn't follow all of it. "You and your... uncle? You uncle disagreed that it was time for the Mock-Men to resist the First Men. Your people are pacifists. When the... hunters? The hunters come and take your kin as slaves and you do nothing. But you think your people should fight."

Oglok folded a fist the size of Aria's head and howled defiantly.

"Nobody would listen to you, so you decided to leave and do something about it yourself?" The princess snorted. "We might have more in common than we thought, Oglok."

The Mock-Man snarled that he would never have anything in common with a magic-working sorceress.

"Well you do," Aria argued. "And whether you like it or not, a magic-working sorceress is traveling with you and your new boss. If I'm to be as useful as I can to General Blackthorn I have to be able to use that power – without you ripping my throat out."

Oglok's growls were too fast and passionate for Aria to follow, but she made out a few words.

"I don't worship any devil. I won't and can't steal your soul. I certainly don't get my power from human sacrifice. I know that some magic-workers do all that - or claim to. Those are second-rate amateurs. I'm not." She held out her hands. "Under my skin is a microscopic arcane fiber-net. It runs through every nerve of my body. It's part of me. Those filaments pick up magic from the very air of Mars, all around us. They store it up for me like a battery until I want to use it. Then I use my natural gift to channel those energies to do work, just like your muscles store up energy for when you want to lift something or strangle a princess."

Oglok said nothing; but he listened.

"Great warriors with great strength can use it in all kinds of ways. They can be good or bad. It's not the strength that's good or evil, it's the purpose to which it's set and the man who harnesses it for those ends. Magic's the same. Some methods are pretty horrible, I grant you, implicitly nasty because they steal life-force or whatever. I know your people have had some bad experiences about that. But not all magic is like that, and not all people who use it."

Oglok made a skeptical sound, but not a fierce one.

"Really, I have to use my magic. It's a part of me, and we're going to need it. Watch carefully, Mock-Man, and you'll see I do no harm."

Aria held out the silver food-packet and very slowly drew the arcane energies to her hands. The Mock-Man growled deep in his throat and the hackles on his back rose, but he made no move. The princess willed the ham to rise from her fingers and float an inch above her palms. Then she slowly heated it, regulating the energy flow so it was properly cooked inside and out.

"Well?" she asked the Mock-Man. "Is that evil?"

Oglok made a strangled, severe noise.

Aria glared at him. "Well I didn't *pack* any ketchup!" she snapped.

Blackthorn returned in time for supper and shared in the ham and roots. They ate in a companionable silence until Oglok has finished his share and headed off to scout – or possibly to find a bathroom. Aria didn't want to imagine the Mock-Man's ablutions.

Blackthorn turned to Aria. He'd clearly been waiting for a moment when they were alone. Aria braced herself.

"Are you doing okay?" the General asked her.

"What? Yes. Yes, I'm… fine."

"It's pretty obvious that you're not used to living rough, your highness."

Aria glanced back at the dome-tent and at the damped-down campfire. "I won't slow you down. I can learn."

"It's not a criticism. You're trying hard, I can see that. You've ridden all day without complaining and I know it must have been tough. You're way out of your experience but you're handling it like a real trouper."

Aria wasn't quite certain what a trouper was but it seemed like a term of approbation. "I knew it would be difficult when I elected to walk this path."

Blackthorn paused a moment. *Here it comes*, thought Aria. *The move.*

"You know who I was," Blackthorn ventured. He actually sounded uncertain, nervous. "Who I was back on Earth, before my whole life went crazy."

"Yes. The Black Sorcerer had full biometric and historical data on you. I… saw it."

"I can't remember it now, except in snatches. Little pictures in my head, and they're fading. I remember baseball but I can't remember who won the world series in '69. I remember going to high school but not its name, or who I sat next to in twelfth grade Geography."

"That's a consequence of the transfer, I'm afraid." The Black Sorcerer had told Aria that. She wondered now how he knew that if this crop of barbarians had been his first subjects.

"I get that. Since I was going to be dead without this body-swap I guess I can't complain too much. And I can hardly bitch about turning up in Captain America's skin. But I still… there's stuff I need to know about who I was. Important stuff I shouldn't forget."

Aria hadn't thought that the barbarians might have such sensibilities. She hadn't really thought of them as people at all, she realized. They were more than pawns or symbols or tools. "What do you need to know, General Blackthorn?" she offered.

"First off, call me John, or Blackthorn. General's fine when we're impressing the masses, but it wears a bit thin in everyday use."

"Then call me Aria. I know I'm a princess. I don't need to be reminded of it every sentence."

"Okay, Aria. Then tell me this. Was I married?"

"You were married once. Your wife was dead at the time we took you."

Aria could see in Blackthorn's face that the truth resonated with him. A look of hurt and grief crossed his countenance, so poignant that for the first time the princess wanted to hold him.

"Kids?" Blackthorn asked.

"Grown up. You were quite an old man, on your last command, when Morningstar betrayed you. You'd lived a long, good life. You were a good soldier, a good husband, a good father. You left behind a good legacy. There's nothing to be ashamed about, no work left unfinished, no dependents who couldn't survive without you. Your tasks back there were done." Aria was surprised how important it was for her to give Blackthorn closure. She didn't want him hurt.

Blackthorn didn't ask for any more details. "What about you?" he asked her. "You got any family?"

Aria looked down. "Not any more," she answered.

Blackthorn showed more perception and understanding than she'd have expected in a barbarian. He didn't press any further.

"So here we are," he said to Aria as they sat side-by-side in the dusk watching the low flames crackle over the campfire.

"Here we are," agreed the princess. Her heart was pounding. *Perhaps it will be no bad thing to belong to this warrior,* she told herself. *He is more honest than Halifax, and there is a kindness to him that I had not expected. If I must go to a man's bed to save my planet then let it be his. I shall be content, almost.*

And you know he's well equipped for the job, a subversive part of her added. *You made sure of that.*

Blackthorn looked over at her. She blushed guiltily.

"Well, good night, Aria," the warrior bade her. "Get some sleep. We've got another tough journey tomorrow." He unfolded his bedroll near the flap to her tent. "I'd like you to take last watch if that's okay. I'll wake you a couple hours before dawn."

"Right. Good... good night, John Blackthorn."

Princess Aria crawled into her sleeping furs with a strange feeling of relief – and disappointment.

Her dreams were vivid.

Apocta was a village much like Domrik, except there was a wider river that allowed for a water-driven sawmill. The settlement clung to the edge of the water, surrounded by another thorn hedge between the decaying remnants of an old stone wall.

Blackthorn asked a few pertinent questions of his traveling companions before they rode into town, but then he made straight for the central green.

"He's very brave or very dumb," Aria whispered to Oglok the Mock-Man. "Maybe both."

The huge hairy fighter growled back something about being happier battling a whole clan of lizard-men then trying what Blackthorn was here to do.

Aria peeled away as the barbarian strode to a broad tree-stump at the edge of the village market. She was swathed in a full-length cloak with her hood drawn forward to conceal her face. She didn't think anyone could recognize her - at the worst they might spot she was from the Black Sorcerer's court - but she really didn't want to complicate things with Blackthorn any more by telling him that she was the daughter of 'that crazed loon' who'd shanghaied him to this strange new world.

Blackthorn hopped up onto the stump and clapped his hands for attention. "Afternoon, ladies and gentlemen, boys and girls!" he called in a voice loud enough to carry over the marketplace. "I've got a few things to say that I reckon need saying."

A few heads turned, but it was the busiest part of the trading day.

"First off," Blackthorn announced, "I want to tell you that the Black Sorcerer stinks. Except I don't need to tell you that, because you already know it. You just daren't say it out loud, because his bullies will come after you and yours."

That got him some attention. The noise level in the market dropped considerably as people stopped to listen to his blasphemy.

"The First Men want us to think they rule by right, because they've got magic and armies and all that. I'm here to tell you they rule by force, which is why they *need* the magic and the armies. If they didn't have the power to crush you would any of you pick to be under their boots? Of course not. The Black Sorcerer and his cronies reign by fear and force, nothing else."

A few people hurried away, perhaps afraid to be associated with such sedition – or to summon guards. Oglok watched and growled low in his throat.

"Now my name's General John Blackthorn, and I say it's time we got rid of these First Men for good. I'm putting together a resistance that will do the job. Right now you don't need to do anything but listen, and maybe talk about what you've heard with folks who aren't here today. It's enough that you know I'm in business, and what I intend to do. Later on, when you know I'm for real and can do what I say, then there'll be other stuff you can help with."

It was a good stump speech, Aria had to admit. More people were nodding and listening carefully than she'd expected.

"As you hear this, there's probably a few objections spring to your minds," Blackthorn noted. "I'm going to tell you what I figure a few of them are and answer them. If there's more you want to ask after that, then go ahead and…"

He was interrupted by a zap of laser-fire discharged into the air. An officious-looking man in the saffron robes of a local administrator had emerged from a tax house to break up the meeting. He was flanked by a pair of lizard-men bearing wicked two-bladed weapons. A vast clanking war robot stomped behind them all, solid and intimidating.

"Hold right there, rebel!" the administrator called. "The rest of you disperse. This sedition will be dealt with harshly!"

"You got a play, make it," Blackthorn challenged. He gestured with his fingertips: bring it on.

The administrator aimed his firearm at Blackthorn and discharged a stun packet. Let the loudmouthed fool wake to explain his wild proclamations to an Inquisitor Unit.

Aria wondered if she should intervene, but Blackthorn had asked her to hold herself as a tactical reserve. She remained amongst the crowd as a passive observer, although her every instinct was to go to the General's aid.

Blackthorn's arm blurred. By the time the energy packet reached him the Sword of Light was in his hand, the button that formed it into a full combat blade depressed. The stun packet fizzed uselessly as it was sliced out of the air.

Blackthorn leaped in a high somersault and came down right in front of the lizard-men. A pair of lightning slices cleft them in two.

The administrator squeaked and retreated back behind his heavy warbot.

Oglok charged over the distance. He actually *grappled* the industrial-grade combat machine. Though it overtopped even the mighty Mock-Man he hefted it off the ground and lifted it above his head, then tossed it away over the village green. The crowd scattered as he raced after it to continue his attack.

Blackthorn sliced his energy blade right through the administrator's laser-gun, leaving the man staring stricken-faced at the mere stump of it sparking in his grip. The official looked up just in time to meet the General's incoming fist.

Aria considered stepping in to assist Oglok as he wrestled the warbot. It soon became evident that no aid was required. The growling Mock-Man tore the machine's limbs off one by one. By the time he finished and ripped out its central processor care the crowd was cheering every blow.

Blackthorn dragged the broken-nosed administrator back to the stump and tossed him down on it. "Confess now," he demanded of the sniveling overseer. "You know what you've done."

"I've done nothing!" the man blubbered, cringing from the General. "I only did what the Black Sorcerer told me! Please!"

Blackthorn turned to the crowd. "Is that right? Nobody's got as complaint against this guy?"

There was angry muttering. At last someone broke out with an actual accusation. "He takes bribes so he doesn't falsify our output records to make us pay more tax!"

There were shouts of affirmation.

"He expects the company of our daughters or he cries sedition," a woman shouted. There were more angry cries.

"He had Nevis blinded for staring him down!" someone cried bitterly.

The dam broke. It was as if everybody in the village had some personal grudge against the visiting administrator.

Aria watched the petty official grow paler and paler as the charges were laid. Then her attention was drawn to Blackthorn. She saw the narrowing of his eyes, the tightening of his grimace. He'd planned to turn the village against whatever authority was here. He hadn't expected to be so outraged by the stories they told, the princess realized.

Before, Blackthorn had been conducting an exercise, by the book. His rebellion had been a mission necessity to secure his survival. Suddenly it was becoming more.

He is taking up their cause, Aria told herself. *Before, rebellion was only personal. Now it had become...* personal. The two senses of the term were clear in her observation.

When everyone had taken their chance to speak against the administrator, Blackthorn turned back to the cowed prisoner. "You got anything to say in your defense?" he demanded.

"I only... my orders... everyone does it..." the man stammered.

Blackthorn shook his head. "What's your name?"

"Divisional Sub-Administrator Adwin, of the..."

"Adwin, I find you guilty of crimes against humanity. The sentence is death. You've got two minutes to make your peace."

The crowd cheered at first, but then they went deadly quiet as the magnitude of what was happening came home to them. A few more villagers slipped off. Most stayed.

"I'm going to execute this man," Blackthorn told the crowd. "That way you can't be held to blame for what happened. And every time I find another guy like him I'll do the same thing. I'll bring 'em to justice whether they're a petty crook hiding behind some thugs and a warbot or a First Man with a mutant army of killing machines. That's my job. That's what I'm here to do."

Aria did not turn away as he killed Sub-Administrator Adwin.

Blackthorn didn't linger in Apocta. He retreated quickly back into the depths of the Arcadian Forest where Oglok could obscure their trail and pursuit would be hampered by terrain. The General made good use of Mars' limitations on distance communication and sensory technology.

They camped that night in a rotted tree-bole, the hollowed trunk of a giant redwood whose base was larger than most of the huts in

Apocta. Camp was set up in much the same way as the night before. Soon it would become routine. Oglok vanished at sunset.

"It's a religious thing," Blackthorn explained to Aria. "The Mock-Men gather in their villages as the sun goes down and they sing something called The Song of Mourning that remembers all the kin they've lost. They believe it unites them with the spirits of all the Mock-Men who came before, and maybe all who'll come after."

"It seems strange that such fierce-looking creatures have beliefs and customs," Aria confessed. "I suppose everyone is more than they first appear."

"The Mock-Men are limited by the jokes their creator played on them. Their language seems like nothing but roars and growls to humans, but for them it conveys wisdom and emotion and a rich mischievous humor. Their puns are outrageous. They love art and green growing things and they bond in complicated family units that they would gladly die for."

"You've spent a lot of time talking with Oglok," Aria concluded. *More time than you've spent with me.*

"I'm trying to figure why he should join the crusade. I know he argued with his uncle and the rest of his kin about resistance to the First Men's exploitation, but there's got to be more to it than that. I guess he'll tell me in his own time, when he's ready."

And what conclusions have you been drawing about me and my motives? Aria wondered. What she actually said was, "Oglok was certainly useful in that fight today. I never thought anyone could toss a warbot like a rag doll."

"Today was only a start. It was easy, bush-league. It sent out a first message. Next one's going to be tougher."

"The next one?"

Blackthorn scratched a crude map on the soil in front of them. "Tell me if I got this right. Down here's the big volcano, Nix Olympus. That's where the Black Sorcerer's Bastion is, right? We're northeast of that, somewhere here. This is Domrik and this is Apocta on the river. Now you said that somewhere this way there's a regional admin center?"

"Bandusae," Aria supplied. "It's a grim little town, mostly a shipping depot for timber and ores that come from the further settlements. There'll be substantially more than one administrator with a pair of lizard men and an old 'droid to deal with if you take us there." *We'll all die*, she managed not to add.

"Bandusae," Blackthorn repeated. "Yeah, well that's where we want to be in about six weeks time. We keep working the villages, especially the ones where there might be a minor imperial presence we can deal with, and we work up a head of steam. We want there to be buzz. That's the right time to hit the Black Sorcerer where it hurts, in his regional headquarters."

"Will there be an army backing us up by then?" Aria enquired.

"No. An army would just slow us down. It'll be you, me, and Oglok."

"You have a very high opinion of our capabilities."

Blackthorn grinned at her. "Princess, are you telling me you don't think you can handle a big mess of guards and robots and lizard-men and whatever?"

"General, are you making it a personal challenge?"

"What if I am?"

"Then, as you like to put it, bring them on."

Blackthorn chuckled. "That's my girl!"

Aria retired to her furs with that last phrase resounding in her mind.

Martian fall had come, and in Arcadia that meant sudden squalls, unpredictable winds, and a long slow change in the deciduous forests. Aria dreaded the coming season of windtide and the bitter winter snows that would follow it: five and a half long Martian months of bleak chill[7]. It would be a hard time to live rough. But she discovered she loved picking the autumn berries off the wild brambles that fruited beneath the giant trees. It was an unexpected pleasure.

She'd traveled with Blackthorn and Oglok for six weeks, long enough for novelty to become familiar routine. She'd never imagined that danger might become ordinary.

The pattern was regular. Blackthorn would walk into a new settlement and announce himself. More and more often his name had arrived before him. He would speak out against the First Men and outline his intention to cast them down. If there were agents of the Black Sorcerer present to challenge him then he'd take them on and defeat them. If there was local justice to be done then he did it.

---

[7] The additional season of Windtide is counted from 22nd October to 40th December, with Winter officially ending on 57th March before Fool's Feast.

Then he'd move on, leaving rumor and gossip in his wake. In a world with no mass communication except word of mouth it was an effective way to build a legend.

But it could only go so far, and that was why, exactly on the General's schedule, Aria passed through the city gate of Bandusae and scouted out the regional center.

She'd transmuted her clothes to her dress-chain's limits to match the shabby peasant garb of the local women and swathed her head and hair in a hideous check scarf. She walked in at the tail end of a train of wagons bringing ore for smelting. The gate-guards barely gave her a look.

Bandusae was bigger than anywhere Blackthorn has visited so far. The population was in the thousands and it boasted all the secondary services of a major urban site. As well as the common open marketplace there were dedicated shops, smithies, potteries, and butchers. Aria steered clear of the seedy street of tavern-brothels but she happily visited a sweetmeat store and purchased a treat for later.

The main government buildings were obvious, the only structures constructed from gunmetal steel and connected to a power distribution grid. Three tripods were parked outside the main control center and a dozen war robots were alert and active. Aria counted five full packs of lizard-men, well over a hundred of the fierce killers. The fenced-off barracks behind the admin square suggested yet more might be available.

Aria couldn't get an accurate tally of human troops; she didn't want to get too close to the secured areas. Most of them wore the standard black metal combat gear of the Black Sorcerer's rank and file, but a couple of them sported the stylish leathers of the Herald Corps. She saw at least two cyborg robot-callers, which made sense given the large combat machines that stood sentry. The administrators that ran this settlement were well protected.

Conscious that she needed to do a through job, Aria found a little restaurant that didn't look too dirty and took an outdoor seat under the twining trellis. She ordered hot tea and a half-loaf bun and sat back to eavesdrop on the conversations around her.

Most of the talk was unremarkable, but she perked her ears up at news of another incursion in the far south by Lord Ruin's mutate hordes. It was rumored that the Black Sorcerer's legions had taken more heavy casualties. Southern Diacria might be lost.

Father won't like that, Aria considered. No wonder he'd been slow to track down his escaped barbarians or his absent daughter.

Another useful piece of news was that the regional governor had returned to Bandusae. Count Leptis had been 'investigating trouble in the valleys'; Aria hoped that referred to Blackthorn's efforts to foment discontent. However, the return of the Count meant the return of his personal guard retinue as well. The odds were stacking up.

Aria had finished the grainy bread and was draining the last of her cup when someone actually mentioned General Blackthorn. The princess' heart leaped as the conversation ran to half-formed rumors of the rebel warlord. She was surprised to learn how large his army of followers apparently was.

Emboldened by her General's fame she dared to enter the tax building and examined the public notices pinned on the information boards. Many of the posters were mere pictograms, reflecting the low literacy rate amongst the peasantry of Arcadia, but the pictures told a story. Every third item produced was to be tithed. Travel without permission was not allowed. Thievery and loose talk were punished by death.

There was other information there too, though, for those who were educated enough to comprehend it. The current exchange barter values for the main products were posted. Right now pelts and green vegetables were down while carved wood and worked metal were high. The tax collection dates for each sub-district were displayed. Aria made sure to memories them.

And there, pinned in pride of place, was the hierarchy diagram of the Pyriphlegethon District. Aria examined that closely.

The Black Sorcerer was at the top, of course, as he always would be unless Blackthorn did the impossible. Off to one side was his Prime Herald and the Herald Corps. Below was Count Leptis, who ruled this region in his master's name, and under him the divisional chiefs responsible for security, order, industry, and planning. Again to one side was the Senior Accountant and his staff; they operated semi-autonomously from the Count so that there was always a watch upon what he was doing. Aria fixed the name of Senior Accountant Pardelin in her mind.

The building was filled with a steady stream of functionaries coming to render their accounts and a queue of people bringing their tithe fees. In an economy that largely operated on goods-and-services barter rather than minted coinage this made the main tax office a noisy, crowded, and sometimes messy place. When a peasant arrived with three wheelbarrows of chickens, the princess decided she'd researched enough.

She left the way she'd come and reported back to Blackthorn and Oglok in the forest.

The guard barracks was commanded by a smartly dressed Captain on his first duty posting. His day went quickly downhill.

"Ten-hutt!" shouted Blackthorn, striding into the watchroom like the wrath of God. "Stand to attention, trooper, when a superior officer enters the room!"

The Captain and every other soldier present sprang from their seats as if they'd been kicked.

Aria and Oglok stood at the doorway and watched the show.

"What in the name of the Black Sorcerer do you think you are doing here?" Blackthorn yelled into the Captain's face. "What kind of soldiers are you? Do you *want* to spend the rest of your service in the Sirenum swamps? Well do you?"

"Sir, no sir!"

"I can't *hear* you, soldier!"

"Sir! No, sir!"

"Then get off your fat lazy behind and call a full inspection parade, Captain! I want a full garrison out there for me to review ten minutes ago! And Creator help any man who's kit is not in perfect condition when I come to look at it! *Move!*"

Blackthorn still wore the uniform of a General of the Black Sorcerer's elite guard. The memory implants told him exactly how to behave with the Black Sorcerer's armies. Thirty years of military service had taught him exactly how to ruin the day of junior officers caught with their pants down.

Oglok growled something to Aria to the effect that he hadn't realized humans ate each other.

Blackthorn pushed things forward on sheer force of personality. The Captain's panic transmitted to his troops. Within two minutes from the parade horn sounding, over a hundred men were standing to attention on the cobbled yard outside the watch-house.

The General turned to a grizzled master-sergeant and jabbed him in the chest. "Your name, soldier!"

"Top Sergeant Jarrik, sir!"

"You know the Accountant called Pardelin?"

"Sir, yes sir!"

"You take some good men, you bring me Pardelin here right now. Do it quietly, do it quickly, and don't take no for an answer. You got that?"

"Yes sir!" Jarrik had made master-sergeant by not asking for reasons. He saluted and yelled for half a dozen men to peel off parade and jog away with him.

Blackthorn swung round on the nervous Captain and the other officers who'd been turned out of barracks. "Which of you maggots has taken bribes from Count Leptis?" he demanded.

There was a chorus of denials. A couple of the officers looked worried enough that the accusation might even have been accurate.

"You better have told the truth," Blackthorn growled, "'cause when the Inquisitors get here the liars will scream their apologies for the rest of their short miserable lives."

Aria wondered how many dress parade pants would need changing before the General had finished.

Blackthorn began his inspection of the rows of troops. He knew how to keep up the scare. The duty Captain and a pair of nervous NCOs paced him as he marched along the column.

"Name?" he snapped at a random soldier.

"Trooper Neshim, number 37792773-D, sir!"

"What's that you're holding, Neshim?"

"Sir, it's a Mark III Phase Pellet Rifle, sir!"

"No, Trooper Neshim, what you are holding is a *dirty* Mark III Phase Pellet Rifle, with a badly maintained focus filter and grubby greasy stains on the butt. There's enough dirt on there, Trooper Neshim, to start a municipal dump!" Blackthorn slapped the rifle to the floor. "Pick that up!"

As the unfortunate Neshim bent to retrieve his weapon Blackthorn brought his knee to the soldier's chin and sent the man sprawling on the cobbles. Then he stamped down, shattering Neshim's wrist. He moved on, leaving the stunned trooper groaning.

By the end of the row Aria was actually feeling sorry for the soldiers for the first time in her life. Master-Sergeant Jarrik's return with the very worried Senior Accountant came as a relief.

Blackthorn turned and stalked towards Pardelin.

"I don't understand what all of this is about!" jabbered the Accountant. Blackthorn's approach chased the self-important complaints held been about to make right out of his brain. He saw death bearing down on him. "I haven't done anything!"

"Accountant Pardelin," challenged the General. "Are you loyal to your master?"

"Yes! Yes, of course I am – sir."

"Are you? Then why have you not informed the Black Sorcerer of the crimes of Count Leptis?"

Pardelin's jaw dropped. "Crimes? I... I don't know of any..."

"Peculation, receiving bribes, trading information to agents of the Lord of Fatal Laughter?"

"No! I can't believe the Count would... that is, I never suspected..."

Blackthorn loomed over the Accountant. "Are you testifying that Count Leptis is innocent of the charges brought against him? Are you offering me your personal assurance of his honesty?"

Pardelin went pale. "I can't... that is to say, I couldn't swear to it, no. I, um, had suspicions, of course, nothing I could prove, nothing worth reporting to the Inquisition..."

Aria couldn't believe what she was seeing. One man, one terrifying man, was convincing a whole garrison to turn against their commanding officer.

Blackthorn eyed Accountant Pardelin until the man was a sweating lump of terror. "I believe you," he said at last. "Now is the time to make up for your incompetence. I'm making you acting commander of this division pending a full investigation. You will take charge once Count Leptis is arrested."

The duty captain blanched. "Arrested? Sir, Count Leptis is..."

"Leptis is rotten!" Blackthorn snarled to the soldiers. "He's got those damned lizard-men right under his thumb, and probably the heavy robotics as well. So when we take him down we've got to be fast and smart and damned tough! You want to be a hero and rise up in this man's army? Well today you got your chance, all of you. You want to see some lizard-man ichor? You better have cleaned your gear better than Trooper Neshim!"

He had the absolute attention of the whole compound. Aria was as enthralled as the rest.

"Now pay attention, 'cause if we go in dumb against Leptis and his goons we're gonna get hammered. Pardelin, this starts with you and your people. You go into the headquarters building like it was any normal day, but then you trigger screamer units by surprise. At that point I want squad one with anti-robot weapons gunning for the war-droids and squads two and three going in against the lizards. Amour-busting artillery brings down the walkers – that'll be you leading the charge, Captain. Leave Leptis and his personal guard to me. Now let's get to the detail..."

War burst over Bandusae. The front of the imperial headquarters exploded as the first barrage of heavy ordinance went in. The lizard-men at the gates were mowed down. Two of the three tripod walkers were detonated before they could even react.

But the duty officers at HQ were alert, Aria had to admit. Even Blackthorn was impressed and irritated by how quickly they reacted to sudden attack from their own forces. Soon battle was joined, a confused melee that quickly degenerated into a free-for-all.

Blackthorn seemed well pleased with it. As the civilians raced for cover the soldiers lost all discipline and descended into every-man-for-himself grudge matches.

"This way," the General told Oglok and Aria as he took advantage of the new entrance that had just been blown in the steel and concrete command bunker.

Oglok stopped to down an approaching trooper; a single arm-swipe did it. Then the Mock-Man hefted a heavy disruptor cannon in each arm and followed the General. Aria brought up the rear, extending her arcane senses and neutralizing the remaining automatic defense systems before they could orientate.

The building had been designed to be defended. Count Leptis and his personal cohort were in the control suite, still protected by reinforced steel and a single easily-held entrance. They were fighting off the incoming soldiery and racking up an impressive body count, but were too preoccupied to hear Blackthorn slicing through their amour to the rear with his Sword of Light.

The General thumbed the red button on his weapon and hurled a single explosive blast into the defenders' midst. The fireball not only burned away the main cluster of Leptis' personal guard but detonated the fragmentation magazine they'd been loading into their field gun.

Oglok hurled himself bodily into the remaining mass of soldiers. At close quarters their rifles were useless. The massive Mock-Man had an absolute advantage. Blackthorn pushed on into the inner chamber where the Count himself was on the short-wave radio trying to raise assistance from any forces not yet engaged in the chaos.

"Who are you?" he demanded as Blackthorn faced him. "What is the meaning of this?"

Blackthorn never got to answer. Crackling orange magics slammed into him from the side, pounding him from his feet and tumbling him like a doll into the far wall.

Aria looked up sharply. A sorceress!

She silently cursed herself for not realizing that a magic-user wouldn't appear on any hierarchy chart or roster. Such a skilled and unique individual would be outside and beyond any system, answerable to the Black Sorcerer alone.

And there she was, a tall, skeleton-thin woman with a silver plate stapled to the front of her skull and long metal talons grafted to her finger-ends. Even as Blackthorn struggled to rise – his suit offered him a limited protection from arcane blasts – she pointed again and loosed another spray of malevolent energies.

Aria hurled out a defensive screen. Her violet web crackled and buckled as the orange fury seared into it. The other sorceress whirled round, realizing there was another arcane-worker present; her next blast came straight at the princess.

Count Leptis sprang forward, his vibra-foil cranked up to maximum, to carve Blackthorn while he was down. The General rolled aside and came up fighting, matching Leptis blow for blow, Sword of Light against sonic blade.

Aria loosed an arcane pulse at the gaunt sorceress. The emaciated witch clutched a jeweled necklace with one hand and easily sidelined the princess' attack with the other. Her own counterblast shattered Aria's defenses and laid the princess on her back.

Amplification crystals! Aria had seen them, of course, but never encountered anyone who used them. The gems stored arcane energy like external batteries, available for a sorcerer to draw upon in addition to personal bio-resources. They made the gaunt woman significantly more powerful than Aria.

"But I bet you've not been trained by the Black Sorcerer!" Aria snarled, spitting blood and rising again.

The next attack on the princess was crude and powerful. The gaunt woman had no need of subtlety. She had energies to burn. Aria deflected the bolt with a precision shield that made best use of her position and required as little effort as possible, then replied with a designer arcane bolt.

The other sorceress was confident she could block it. Her eyes opened wide as the single shimmering ball split into two then four attacks, each twisting round on its own intelligent trajectory. She wasted vast quantities of energy creating a full-body shield, the only way she could keep out each of the hex-balls at once.

Aria kept up the pressure with a long snaking strand of force that required more blunt force defense to deflect, then sneaked through the tiniest kinetic event while the sorceress was distracted.

The emaciated witch neutralized Aria's force strand and sneered. She focused a single overwhelming blast that could punch through anything her opponent might muster and launched it at the princess.

Except she didn't. The effort sucked all the strength from her and dropped her to her knees. She didn't have the power to put together an assault that vast! Her hand reached for the crystals at her throat – and found them gone!

One tiny kinetic spell was sufficient to undo a delicate chain-clasp and let the necklace fall to the floor.

Aria slammed home a final arcane bolt that seared the witch back into the communications array on the far wall. It was probably the high energy equipment rather than the magic that killed the mage.

The princess stood for a moment in shock. She'd never had to fight an arcane battle in earnest before. Apart from man-bat monsters, she'd never had to kill.

Then she remembered Blackthorn and the Count. She looked round just in time to see the General slice through Leptis' armored tunic and punch the Sword of Light out of the regional commander's back.

And then it was all over but the shouting - and the setting of emergency self-destruct codes to be used in the event of the base being over-run by another First Man's forces, a warning to the people of Bandusae to take cover, and a message to the Black Sorcerer that General Blackthorn said hello.

And a very large explosion.

Oglok drank deep from a captured skin of some disgusting alcoholic brew and growled happily.

"Yeah, I think he'll get the message," agreed Blackthorn. "Bandusae's the one he won't be able to ignore. After this he's coming after us."

The trio were hidden out in a tiny fishing village called Anx, two days hard ride from the regional center, and they were keeping their heads down. The lake-folk all knew who they were, but so far they'd welcomed the man who'd done such terrible things to the tax officers that made their lives a misery.

"You *want* the Black Sorcerer to come after us?" Aria worried. "You were lucky to survive him once. Do not underestimate him, Blackthorn."

"I don't intend to, Aria. But remember what this is all about. It's showing people that the First Men can be fought. It's showing they can be beaten. We've demonstrated that resistance can work on a micro-scale. Now we've shown that it can work at a regional level too. Word on that's going to spread far and fast, you can bet. Next up we've got to prove that the First Men can even be defied face-to-face."

Oglok mournfully enquired what would happen if it turned out they could not.

"Then we look damned stupid and die pretty miserably," Blackthorn shrugged. "But think of it like this. If I were this Reith guy, the Runner leader, I'd be very interested in what we were doing. Interested but cautious. On the one hand we're a serious asset to anyone interested in defying the First Men. On the other we're a sure-fire trouble magnet due to get stepped on real hard, real soon."

"So you reason that he will be holding back to see what the Black Sorcerer does and how we cope with it," Aria surmised. It made sense.

"That's right. If I was Reith I'd put a couple of agents close to us. Some of the fishermen out on the lake, or that fur trader who's hanging around the tavern maybe. Just to keep tabs and report back. I'd be waiting for one more confrontation, Blackthorn versus the Black Sorcerer, before I made my decision."

Oglok groaned that it might be nice to have a little support for once before the entire army of the Black Sorcerer arrived to kill them.

"Yeah, well, that's the downside of the plan. We can only hope that the First Man underestimates us as well."

Aria hesitated but decided that for once she had better tell Blackthorn an unvarnished truth. Keeping things from him was becoming more and more uncomfortable. "There is one problem, John. I should have mentioned it before."

"Go ahead, princess."

Aria swallowed. "I think the Black Sorcerer... that is I, I know that when I was his... his captive, he had them put some dormant obedience programming in my mind. It's just sitting there, waiting to be activated. I don't think he can do that remotely, but face to face, well, I might end up working for him, John."

Oglok made an I-told-you-she-couldn't-be-trusted snarl.

"I can!" snapped Aria. "You people have no idea what I've done for you, what I've suffered, what I've given up! These last few weeks I've trudged with you and slept rough with you and spied for you and fought for you. I've bled for you. I've killed for you, and I didn't like it one bit! I have done everything you asked and tried my very hardest to be a good companion."

"Aria..." Blackthorn interrupted.

"Shut up! Maybe I haven't told you everything about myself. Maybe I can't! Maybe I have secrets, but who doesn't? You do, Oglok. Why don't you tell us why you suddenly decided to follow Blackthorn and turn your back on your family and your people's pacifistic beliefs? And so do you, John Blackthorn, with your grand plans to get us all killed in spectacular memorable ways! But I am trying – *trying* so very hard to do the right things. I *am!*"

Blackthorn caught her hand and held it in his. "Hey, Aria, listen to me. It's okay. I'm a dumb idiot not to realize that you hadn't seen combat before. I should have seen how hard all of this was on you. I'm sorry."

Oglok made a complicated noise that Aria couldn't follow. She chose to take it as an apology.

Blackthorn tried to comfort the princess. "It's good that you warned us about what the Black Sorcerer did to you. You were right to tell us now. All it means is when we get into the big fight we just make sure to keep you away from him. There'll be plenty of other stuff for you to do. Leave the big guy to me and Oglok."

Aria wiped away a tear. "I'm as dumb as you are," she snorted.

"You're not. C'mon princess, it's your war we're fighting here. You set us on. You gave me a job and I'm doing it. Frankly, if it wasn't for you always being a step ahead of the rest of us, being smarter and sneakier and knowing stuff that keeps us out front, we wouldn't know what to do."

They are just your tools, Aria told herself. *Don't get carried away because they say nice things about you. Remember the lesson the Black Sorcerer taught you. Remember Halifax. Nobody is really on your side.*

It was lovely to pretend, though.

"Fine. Let's go do whatever stupid folly you're setting up next then, John Blackth…"

The door of the fishing hut clattered open. A breathless lad of twelve or thirteen rattled in. "Soldiers!" he squeaked in a breaking voice. "*Lots* of soldiers over in Keplis, only two miles round the shore! And they've got tracker cats and ratkind and hover-cars and whole packs of lizard-men, hundreds of them! And warbots! And Sensorines!"

Blackthorn was already on his feet. "That'd be the Black Sorcerer taking us seriously then," he declared. "Let's run!"

The next fortnight was nightmare for the Princess of Mars. It seemed to be an unending series of desperate escapes, hurried flights, cramped hideouts, and unremitting tension. There was little food and less sleep. Blackthorn swore the constant rains helped them to avoid capture but they did nothing to help Aria's mood.

When they had to, the three rebels approached the small settlements in the thick Arcadian woods. Sometimes they were rebuffed by frightened village guards who closed the wicker gates and stood behind thorn hedges with bows and staves. Other times they found entire hamlets abandoned, the people fled into the forest for fear of getting caught between the Black Sorcerer and his prey. But thrice they found houses where brave men and women had remained behind, and there they received shelter and supplies before going on their way.

Twice the pursuers got too close. The first time a big hunting cat sprung out on Oglok, only to be torn apart by the Mock-Man's surprising strength. The ratkind with it attacked, confident of their numbers. None were allowed to escape and report back.

The next time the rebels were spotted from the air by one of the Black Sorcerer's flying cars, a military version of the personal flier that Aria had sent off over the Amazonis Sea a seeming lifetime ago. It flew in low enough to bring its lightning cannon to play on Blackthorn, Aria, and Oglok, not realizing that the Sword of Light could project laser blasts at a significant range.

A third close encounter was averted when Oglok scented robot oil downwind and Blackthorn shattered a dam to inundate the pursuers.

Blackthorn seemed to be moving with a purpose, but he didn't reveal it to Aria and Oglok. Each day sapped more and more of their reserves and brought their tired horses to the edge of exhaustion. On the fourteenth night of the chase, when the treeline opened up to reveal the shores of the great lake and Aria recognized the village of Anx again, the princess almost wept.

"We've come full circle!" she cried. "All that running and we're back where we started! They'll find us here for sure!"

"Yeah," agreed Blackthorn. "Come on."

The villagers of Anx didn't seem surprised to see them return. Aria, on the other hand, was shocked to spot Elder Ardin, the headman of Domrik, waiting for Blackthorn beside a heavily-laden ox cart.

"You got the message, then," the General grinned, striding over to clasp Ardin's hand.

"Yes. We were a little surprised, but we decided to come."

Elder Renk, headman of Anx, stood beside him, bearing a burning torch. "We too were taken aback, General, but we have voted," he reported. "We will have evacuated our homes by nightfall. We shall take our boats across the lake to safety. The village is yours."

Oglok beat Aria to it with a roar of incomprehension.

"Back when we were decamping from Bandusae I made a few arrangements," Blackthorn explained. "Remember how we raided the barracks weapons depot and Oglok got his new shock-sticks and pellet-caster? And remember how much more stuff there was there than we could never carry?"

"You found some likely lads from the town and had them port it off," Aria recalled. "So now Bandusae has an armed resistance."

"Yes. But I also paid a carter to ship this wagon-load of the good stuff back to Domrik, with a request for them to hang on to it until I sent for it."

Ardin took up the story. "Which the General did, two weeks ago, when he quit this place. He asked that we transport it here, to have it arrive today, and that we reveal to the people of Anx what it was that he proposed to do."

"We are proud that General Blackthorn intends to make a stand against the Black Sorcerer," Renk proclaimed. "If our simple village must be the battlefield then that is not too great a price to pay."

Oglok tore away the blankets covering the wagon's load. The cart contained a treasure-trove of military equipment: smart-mines, surface-to-air detonators, anti-robot grenades, fragmentation skimmers, shrieker drones, even black matter bombs.

"The Black Sorcerer expects to be going up against a handful of ragged rebels armed with sticks and stones," Blackthorn pointed out. "He'll be walking into a full-scale killing zone equipped with the best tech his own arsenal can provide."

Aria recalled that she herself had installed the special weapons training module into Blackthorn's brain. Of course the General knew how to set up and prime every item in that wagon; and exactly where best to place it for maximum effect!

Oglok stamped around like an excited child at a birthday party, picking up first one then another lethal killing device. Two weeks of retreat hadn't sat well with the Mock-Man. Now the running was over.

"Careful, Blackthorn," Aria warned, teasingly. "It's starting to look like there's a small chance of surviving this!"

Blackthorn shot her a grin that made her heart flip. She turned away quickly. *Business,* Aria told herself. *He is not on your side. You are not on his.*

You are not.

Blackthorn clapped the Domrik elder on the back. "Okay, Ardin, you've done your part. Thanks for everything. Now make yourselves scarce while we get things set up to give the First Man a proper welcome."

The two headmen exchanged looks. "Actually, we wondered if you might need a few extra hands," Elder Renk admitted. "My people know this area. We could be useful. Especially if you could spare us some weapons from your marvelous horde."

"And my volunteers knew what they'd be getting into when they stepped forward," Ardin added. "If this is where the line gets drawn, where history turns, they all want to be able to say that they were here."

"Be clear. This is deadly dangerous," Blackthorn warned them. "There will be heavy casualties."

"We have heard your words, General Blackthorn. *All* of them. We would like to stay, please."

Oglok hammered Ardin on the back and nearly knocked him over.

Aria felt the distant probings of a Sensorine and carefully masked her aura. "You'd better hurry, Blackthorn," she warned. "They know you're here. They'll be on us by sunup."

Blackthorn clapped his hands. "Right then. To work!"

The Black Sorcerer's vanguard walked straight into the smart mines, but the explosives waited to detonate until the robo-walkers were right in the middle of the field. Blackthorn followed through at once with all the surface-to-air materiel he had, clearing the skies in one fell swoop.

It was clear that the Black Sorcerer still didn't realize he was up against such heavy defenses. He sent in two robot divisions flanked by lizard-man packs and lost them all to black matter explosions and sonics. Thereafter he took things more seriously and as the hours passed the battle became hard.

"He's through the frag skimmers!" Aria shouted across to Blackthorn. "He's used his warcrawlers to take out the shriekers and they're flanking us to the west."

Blackthorn nodded acknowledgement. "Ardin! Renk! Time to bug out. Fall your guys back to position three! Watch out for any remaining hunting cats that might be running loose. Oglok and I will give you covering fire. Move!"

Aria saw that the General wanted the villagers gone now. The guards had done well but the tide was turning. If they stayed they would be overwhelmed and cut down en-masse. She was absurdly pleased that Blackthorn didn't try and send her away in the evacuation.

The village guards managed an orderly retreat down to the shore, where a common sailboat had been hastily modified with the addition of a grav-engine. It would make an effective if short-range escape vehicle. Aria watched Renk herd the others on board while Ardin gathered stragglers.

Not everyone was assembled when the lake behind the boat bubbled. A high wave rocked the vessel at its mooring as a great mass of water was displaced.

"Blackthorn!" Aria shouted warning, pointing.

A warcrawler broke above the surface of the lake. The force-field around it fizzed and shimmered as it burned the energies it had used to survive beneath the water.

Blackthorn blinked. "That's not part of a warcrawler's capabilities," he objected as if it were a rules violation. "How could it...?"

The crawler fired, reducing the escape boat to fragments. Dead rebels littered the shore. Suddenly the orderly evacuation became a rout.

"The Black Sorcerer!" Aria recognized. "Only he has the power to place a protective magic screen around something that size!"

"You told me not to underestimate him!" Blackthorn spat. "Damn him!"

Oglok emptied the last of the detonator rounds from the field gun he was carrying like a rifle and growled another warning. Lizard-men were charging past the shredded outer defenses now with nothing to stop them.

"We're bracketed," Blackthorn realized. "Onto the horses! Fast!"

They abandoned the command post from which they'd operated the remote equipment and galloped diagonal to the shore, trying to avoid being ringed by robots, lizard-men, tripods, spider-drones and the warcrawler. The noose closed around them.

Blackthorn stood up in his stirrups and fired a laser pulser in one hand and the Sword of Light in the other. "No!" he shouted. "No, not yet! It won't end here! Aria! Oglok! *Fight!*"

Aria didn't know how the barbarian warrior was able to ride and shoot and give orders at the same time. It was all she could do to control her panicking mare, and that was with the enforcement enchantments she was pumping into the terrified beast's brain. Attackers seemed to be all around her and she was getting separated from Blackthorn and Oglok.

The crawler detonated a line of fishermen's huts along the water's edge. Aria's bay shied and a lizard-man sliced a vibra-spear through its neck. The princess fell heavily, rolled, and took the lizard-man right in the chest with a searing arcane bolt. She staggered to her feet, firing blindly; her enemies were pressed close enough around her that every random shot hit.

She felt a warm spray across her shoulders, then realized it was blood. A herald trooper had got close enough for an assassination lunge but had instead been eviscerated by Oglok the Mock-Man.

"Thanks," she said tersely and stood back-to-back with the hairy berserker as their enemies surrounded them.

In the corner of her eye she saw Blackthorn riding straight at the warcrawler as if he could joust it like knight against dragon. "He's mad!" Aria cried, somewhere between despair and admiration.

Then the crawler's forward cockpit opened and a familiar black-robed figure sprang out. Aria cried aloud as she realized that Blackthorn directly faced the Black Sorcerer!

Her own adversaries pressed in, evidently trying to take her alive. Oglok exhausted the last of his firearms and resorted to his own natural claws and teeth. The Mock-Man was so matted with blood and ichor it was hard to tell how injured he really was. Aria touched her hand to the necklace she'd taken off the sorceress at Bandusae and burned away the stored energies in it to cast back her attackers.

It became impossible to see what was happening across the battlefield. Ardin and the surviving villagers were scattered, surrounded; soon they would be cut down.

A huge explosion ripped across the war zone. The light and sound momentarily stunned both sides. When Aria's vision cleared she saw the crippled crawler staggering to stay aloft. Blackthorn's Sword of Light had clashed with the Black Sorcerer's serpent stave and the combatants had been blown apart into the melee below.

"He didn't realize what Blackthorn was carrying," Aria said aloud. "Nothing could resist that staff – except a Hallow!"

It was little comfort. Blackthorn had fallen. Already the Black Sorcerer was levitating back to the crawler's command pod. His black cloak fluttered raggedly in the crosswind.

"John needs me!" Aria suddenly knew. She called to Oglok, "This way! Blackthorn's in trouble!"

The Mock-Man howled acknowledgement and began to clear a path through the robots and lizard-men. Aria threw out a wild spray of magic, profligate of the stored energies of her captured necklace, and pounded towards the shore.

By the time she got there the Black Sorcerer had regained control of the crawler. Aria's senses allowed her to see that he had taken complete arcane control of the wounded vehicle. Now he possessed it entirely. It was part of him.

Blackthorn was somehow still fighting. Bloody and torn, the warrior had burst free of the troops that surrounded him and leaped again to engage her father's war machine.

He couldn't know it was now much more deadly than before! Aria yelped involuntarily as she saw the under-turret swivel towards the attacking barbarian then fire right into his chest.

Blackthorn fell hard, but he was confined, not killed. A thick gooey containment webbing solidified around him. Of course the Black Sorcerer would want his General alive. Blackthorn had more than demonstrated his effectiveness as a war leader. Once he'd been fitted with obedience technologies he could still be the supreme commander that the Black Sorcerer had designed him to be.

Unless Aria prevented it.

Unless Aria faced her father.

If I fight him and he uses his obedience over-ride upon me I am lost, the princess warned herself. *I will be his forever, or bound to whomever he gives me. I will be Halifax's slave and he will breed me like a sow and my children will be monsters. John Blackthorn is only a tool. I can find others, another day. I cannot fight the Black Sorcerer!*

I must.

Aria turned to Oglok. "Get down!" she warned the Mock-Man. "You won't like this!"

Oglok hadn't even hit the ground before she'd touched the arcane storage necklace and sucked all its remaining power out in one single burst. She hammered it with all her will into the underbelly of the crawler her father was possessing. The backwash splashed out over the army below, shredding tanks and robots and lizard-men alike. Everything in a ninety degree cone ahead of the princess was reduced to fragments of shrapnel.

The crawler staggered and sank down into the lake. Aria fell to her knees, exhausted, spent. She might have blacked out, except that rough hands clamped onto her and dragged her to her feet. She was bundled in containment netting set to disrupt any further magic use; they might as well not have bothered for all the arcane power the sorceress had left.

Oglok still resisted, but the lizard-men surrounded him with shock wands and discharged them until even he could not stay conscious any more. He was dragged after Aria down to the waterline.

To the princess' horror her father waited for her there, not far from the captured Blackthorn.

"Well well, Aria," said the Black Sorcerer, stroking his chin. "So. Here you are."

Did I impress you yet, father? she wanted to ask. "Here I am," she said.

"Your insolence has never gained you any special favors in my court. And if you ever needed my favor it is now – for I am most unhappy with you."

Aria's stomach churned. She had felt the Black Sorcerer's displeasure before, and then he had shown forbearance. Every time she had defied him he had found a way to hurt her worse.

I hurled enough magic at him to blow a hole in Nix Olympus. Surely he must be as exhausted as I? Just how powerful are the First Men? How did we ever hope to beat them?

Her eyes flicked over to Blackthorn, her failed tool. She had almost believed in him.

Blackthorn was utterly tangled in the thick strands of containment webbing – except his hand still groped over the scrubby turf to reach his fallen Sword of Light!

The Black Sorcerer glared at Aria with an expression of distaste and disapproval. Behind him John Blackthorn refused to give up. And the Princess of Mars was suddenly filled with a wild, giddy elation. "You're an idiot!" she told her father defiantly, to his face.

The First Man's sour expression became darker still. He approached her. "Such foolishness, Aria. Such foolishness to speak to me so."

Aria had heard him use those tones once before, the last time she'd ever seen her mother.

The Black Sorcerer's lips curled into a snarl. "Can you imagine the punishments I shall inflict upon you, once we have returned to my sanctum?"

"Not so foolish at all, actually," Aria snarled back, not realizing how much like her father she sounded at that moment. "I needed you to keep looking over here a little longer. But now you can turn around." She nodded over the Black Sorcerer's shoulder to where Blackthorn had retrieved the Sword of Light and had cut himself free.

The First Man whirled as Blackthorn leaped. Hallows blade and serpent staff clashed again – and the Black Sorcerer's stave was torn from his hand!

The Black Sorcerer leaped back just in time as Blackthorn's follow-up slash cut across his chest. Layers of the best-enchanted fabrics on Mars were sliced open by the searing blade. Hidden circuitry sparked and shorted.

The First Man feinted and reached for his dropped staff. Blackthorn got there first, jamming the Sword of Light's point into the serpent-head. The bright blade glowed even more. Aria felt the surge despite her debilitated magics. All of Mars wheeled beneath her, and the Harmony Spires sang.

The serpent staff glowed orange, then white, then shattered! The explosion was not as large as the last detonation, but it was concentrated. It demolished the Black Sorcerer's stave completely.

And the Black Sorcerer ran. He turned and retreated to the waiting crawler, leaving his troops to cover his exit.

Blackthorn turned on the lizard-men that held Aria and Oglok. The reptiles backed away and fled. Suddenly the Black Sorcerer's forces were in rout.

Blackthorn helped Aria to her feet. Her legs trembled. "Nice work, Aria," he told her.

She managed a brave smile so he didn't know how scared she'd been. "Wasn't hard. I could see what you were up to."

The sound of the crawler rising from the sand warned them that the danger wasn't past. Blackthorn turned in irritation as the Black Sorcerer coaxed the groaning machine back to its feet and turned the turrets at them once more.

"Again?" asked Blackthorn incredulously. "What does it take to put this guy down?"

Aria saw the cowling slide back on a sleek midnight sphere that lowered out of its casing. She wanted to warn Blackthorn what it was, but there was no time. No time at all.

The black matter bombs that Blackthorn had used were the size of marbles. This was the size of a cart. Nothing would survive for a hundred miles in any direction. The Black Sorcerer looked directly at Aria as he lowered his finger to the trigger. Was that regret on his face, or merely vengeance?

The explosion wasn't the one Aria expected. The black matter detonation would have ended Blackthorn's rebellion right there, but this blast blossomed across the warcrawler's flank, shivering it to the side. Subsequent attacks destroyed its servos and main engine.

The war machine crashed to ground again for the last time. The Black Sorcerer thumbed his detonation trigger in vain.

A bright red personal flyer hovered over the fallen crawler. Its guns strafed the vessel, trying to end the Black Sorcerer's life. The First Man had to make an undignified scramble for the emergency evacuation pod and blast away while his remaining magics could protect him. His escape device shot off and vanished into the sky.

Oglok asked if they had really just made the Black Sorcerer run away like a little girl.

"With some assistance from our unexpected air support," Blackthorn answered. "I wonder who our mysterious benefactor was?"

The flyer adopted a hover position twenty feet above them. The canopy slid back and David Morningstar leaned over the side and flipped them a casual salute.

Blackthorn glared back without amusement. "Colonel Morningstar. Your timing was excellent. We appreciate the assist."

Aria found that she had some arcane power in reserve after all. Her hands crackled with blue energies. "Why don't you come down here and let us thank you personally?" she offered the man who'd tried to seduce and kill her.

Morningstar had other ideas. He clearly had things he wanted to say, things he'd rehearsed in the long weeks since his flight into the dark. "It's every one of us for ourselves now. Our old world is dead and gone, Blackthorn. This new one is all that matters! And I intend to carve a place in it. A particularly large place, as it happens."

A revelation struck the princess. Morningstar was wrong. It *had* been every man for himself, before. But not with Blackthorn. Blackthorn was for her, and for Mars.

Nobody was on her side – except him!

Then maybe I am on his side too?

Morningstar was still mouthing his self-justifications. It seemed that he felt his last-minute appearance to stop the Black Sorcerer made things right between him and Blackthorn. "We're even now. Square," he told the General.

"You think so?" his former commander answered.

"All bets are off, Blackthorn. Next time we meet, may the best man win."

"Understood."

"That'd be you, John," Aria insisted as the red flyer skimmed away with the traitorous colonel in it. "Why didn't you blast him?"

"He helped us. He drove away the Sorcerer."

"So?"

"So it was my decision."

"But… if he pops up again, we are taking him down."

"Hard."

Aria had to be satisfied with that.

Oglok limped over, using a robot's leg as a crutch. The Mock-Man howled that there were wounded to attend to and escaping lizard-men to hunt down. The battle was over but the clean-up was just beginning.

Blackthorn nodded. "Time to check the butcher's bill," he sighed.

There were two campfires. The one outside town, downwind, was the gory pyre where the dead soldiers and lizard-men burned. The villagers had dragged the dead there, separated from the local heroes who had given their lives in the Battle of Anx. Renk and his neighbors would receive funerals of the highest honor; their names would never be forgotten.

The other fire was the celebration blaze. It burned all the higher because so much of the material came from broken machinery from the Black Sorcerer's assault force.

"We shall take word back to Domrik and everywhere!" Elder Ardin promised, elated despite his burns. "Already word is spreading of what you did here."

Relin Renkson pointed to the bonfire where the returned village children toasted lumps of cheese and danced with excitement. "This is not a flame that will be easily put out."

"That's the idea," Blackthorn told him. "We did it once. We can do it again. And again. And again, until the First Men have run out of ways to run away. Send out the word."

"Build your armies of revolution," the new headman replied, "and our people will rush to your banners when you call."

Aria touched Blackthorn's arm. "There's someone here to see you," she said in his ear. "Down by the fallen crawler."

"The day is coming," Blackthorn told the elder. "Be ready!"

He paced beside Aria down to the shore without speaking. The princess didn't mind the silence. Blackthorn needed some peace after his campaign, and Aria herself had a very great deal to consider. She had once thought that only a long sleep in the Rainbow Waters could fill her mind with so many new thoughts to examine. She had come a long way since then.

Aria led Blackthorn into the shadow of the wrecked war machine, where a shady figure lurked and waited. "John Blackthorn," she introduced, "this is Edar Reith. I think you need to talk."

The leader of the Runners held out a tentative hand. "Heard a lot about you, General. You've impressed some people. Including the princess, it seems."

"Yes," Aria admitted. "Yes he has. You should believe in him, Mister Reith." She took a deep breath and took the leap. "I do."

Three:
Passion

Two months later:

The stench from the slave pits was overpowering. A stale odor of unwashed, frightened bodies packed tightly in the spiked cages and the rank musk of the broad bulky ogrin mutates that guarded them rose up even to the superior walkways where the buyers stood. Aria wrinkled her nose in disgust.

"There is fine stock down there today, milady," the cringing city guide promised the princess. If he crouched any lower to look up at her he would be bent double, Aria thought. "There are many strong males from the capture of Southern Diacria, suitable for laborers or organ donors or... leisure activities."

Aria ignored the insinuation and stalked on towards the Circus Terminus. The Challenge Horns were sounding so all the crowd was moving that way.

"Or girls, if your highness prefers, beautiful nubile captives new to the whip and the brand, who..."

"I'm not here to buy," Aria snapped. "I'm here to compete."

The guide glanced back at the huge Mock-Man who followed behind them, and the naked muscled warrior he led on a long silver chain. For a moment he wasn't sure which was intended to be the lady's entry to the great melee.

"The man, of course," the princess said scornfully. "The Mock-Men look fierce but they are pacifists at heart. Besides, this one is fitted with a control collar. And he's neutered."

Oglok barely suppressed a growl but managed a stare that promised a conversation about that comment later.

Blackthorn merely looked down at the captives below with a grim, deadly demeanor.

"You have entered livestock into the Games before?" the guide enquired.

"No. I am not familiar with the process. That is why I hired you to assist me in registering this entrant and placing my wagers."

The guide nodded. "I will be pleased to assist you in any way possible, milady." He pointed to a different arch than the grand entrance that most of the crowd swarmed through. "We shall need to register your livestock at the challenge gate. There is a fee of one thousand bloodmarks."

Aria gestured to the Mock-Man who carried a purse at his belt. It would be a bold pickpocket that attempted to steal from that satchel.

The guide continued his instruction. "Your candidate will enter the arena with all the others. There will be hundreds, possibly thousands. The Challenge Horns will sound one final time, and then the battle will begin. Warrior will fall upon warrior, scrambling for weapons dropped randomly into the ring. The battle will rage until a mere hundred and twenty-eight contestants remain. Those will be the combatants who face each other in single conflict in the games proper."

Aria glanced back to check that Blackthorn was taking this in. He gave her a slight curt nod. She could tell from the set of his chin that he was not happy about anything he saw or heard in the city of Hades.

"I understand that Lord Ruin himself sometimes attends these games," the princess mentioned casually.

"The master is present whenever he can be, milady. He loves the slaughter and highly rewards the victors. When he cannot be here in flesh he will sometimes project his image as conditions allow so that he can still view the carnage."

"What about today?"

But the guide didn't know.

Aria entered the challenge gate and went through the procedure for registering her slave as a combatant. It was a remarkably simple task. Lord Ruin did not require the complicated paperwork so common in the Black Sorcerer's domain. In Ruin's lands force and power determined all.

Oglok made a mournful farewell as Blackthorn was hustled away to the warrior cellars by more of the tusk-mouthed ogrin.

The guide steered Aria to her private box, a shell-like projection above the common stands that afforded an excellent view of the bloodshed below. She could also see the imperial platform. The grand iron throne remained empty.

Oglok sniffed the air and growled down at the teeming throng on the benches beneath them. For the citizens of Hades this was just another day's entertainment. For the captives and criminals in the warrior cells it was death or glory.

"He'll be fine," Aria assured the Mock-Man when she'd sent the guide away to place bets with the touts. "He agreed to this, remember? If his message is to reach the whole of Mars then we have to strike against all the First Men. Where better than here, where the decimation of Diacria must be avenged?"

If Blackthorn could do what the Black Sorcerer had not then the mission would serve the additional purpose of shaming her father too.

The guide had barely returned when the Challenge Horns sounded their final brassy discord. Six gates opened around the oval circus. Chained warriors shuffled into the arena. Aria tried to spot Blackthorn but there were too many captives.

Hovering grav-bots released a hundred or more weapons randomly into the throng. The shackles restraining the arena combatants were electronically deactivated. As the chains tumbled away the killing began.

Aria forced herself to watch. It was all she could do for the people who were dying down below.

Oglok groaned and pointed. Aria followed his extended claw and spotted Blackthorn. The General was still unarmed, relying on his combat-hardened body and martial techniques to deflect whatever assaults came at him. He was restricting his attacks to those who deliberately came at him, but those opponents received no mercy.

"Your livestock is fighting smart," the guide commented. "He is reserving his strength for later."

He is avoiding harming the innocent, Aria thought. *Colonel Morningstar would not show that weakness. How curious that with John it seems more like a strength.*

The battle was fast and furious. The no-hopers fell quickly. The arena sawdust was stained red.

The Challenge Horns blasted out again. A stasis field clamped over the combat ring, pinning all the survivors in place. A barely-bruised Blackthorn was amongst them.

"He is into the contest proper," the guide approved. The obsequious little man had ventured a small personal wager to that extent.

"What happens now?" Aria demanded.

"There will be some small entertainments while the main games are prepared. Prisoners torn by ur-bears. Some public executions. A novelty act or two. It will be around an hour before the lots are drawn to see who each of the warriors will fight."

"I shall take some refreshment and come back then," said Aria. There were limits to how much of this she could stand.

Blackthorn's opponent stood half a head taller than him and had an extra set of arms. The random draw said this combat was to be on foot with only blunt weapons. The mutate selected four wicked-looking shillelaghs, each capable of splitting a man's skull with a single blow. Blackthorn chose a quarterstaff and tested its balance.

He and his adversary were not alone in the arena. For the first two elimination rounds the circus was quartered with a match in each quadrant to speed up the action.

"First round match, Nestorr of Alcyon against Ah-nie of the Duchess Coda!" cried the heralds. Aria wasn't sure why Blackthorn had chosen that particular barbarian name to fight under, but she hoped her old maidservant would have approved of her elevation to duchesshood for the princess' disguise.

Oglok grumphed that Nestorr's four arms would cause him upper-body balance problems that Blackthorn should exploit.

Blackthorn avoided the first brutal swings of the giant's clubs, moved inside Nestorr's arc of attack, and made painful use of his stave on the mutate's pressure points. The creature dropped, poleaxed, and lay unmoving as the crowds cheered Ah-nie. The General had finished his match before the other combats in the arena had barely begun.

The second round was delayed by the arrival of a large warlord in spiked crimson amour into the imperial box. Aria feared for a moment that Lord Ruin himself had come. That would be a complication the rebels were not yet ready for. But her guide identified the newcomer as Bloodmaster Bale, Lord Ruin's current favorite war-leader, the glorious conqueror of Southern Diacria.

"Oh, that's *much* better then," Aria said softly. She flicked a glance at Oglok and the Mock-Man purred agreement.

Blackthorn's second bout was against a lightning-fast bladesman from Tyrhenna. Fortune favored the bravo when the random battle conditions were drawn for short knives on foot. Aria thought she saw Blackthorn attempting dialogue with the captured killer but when the battle began the man went straight for the General's throat.

That combat allowed no quarter. Blackthorn had no opportunity to be merciful. In the end he caught one of the Tyrhennan's arms, shattered it, and bent it round to plunge the bladesman's own knife into his chest. The crowd knew his pseudonym by now and shouted it in celebration. "Ah-nie! Ah-nie! Ah-nie!"

"You didn't say you had a potential finalist," the guide chided Aria. "You should collect some of your winnings now and place them again for your Ah-nie to achieve a rank in the final four."

"Collect them and bet on him to win it all," Aria replied fiercely.

The third round was unarmed on high-wires, and Blackthorn faced a razor-toothed woman who moved like a cat and fought like a tiger. The ground of the arena was electrified so that any fall would be fatal. Aria watched with mounting concern as the cat-woman literally ran rings around the General, hopping from line to line with apparent ease. When Blackthorn stumbled and almost fell, Aria leaped out of her seat as if she could jump from her box and catch him.

Sensing victory, the cat-girl got too close. Blackthorn's ruse worked perfectly, and he rendered her unconscious and left her dangling on the wires as he took his bow.

Bloodmaster Bale noticed him and leaned forward.

For round four Blackthorn drew Domak Regan with power amour. The crowd jeered and booed Regan as he stomped into the circus. This was the notorious criminal's third time in the arena for crimes of rape and murder. On each of his previous visits he had walked free as champion.

Blackthorn had evidently heard about Regan as well. He showed none of the delicacy he'd reserved for the cat-woman. He slammed into the murderer hard and kept going, heedless of his own safety as he smashed through the combat plating that protected his enemy.

As always with power amour clashes it was a long bloody fight. The crowd roared as Blackthorn tore away Regan's helmet – and his head with it.

After that, Blackthorn's victory in round five seemed almost anticlimactic. Nanzak, captured chieftain of some itinerant gypsy clan, might have proved a formidable opponent with his own weapons on foot. Instead he faced Blackthorn with sword in zero-g. Nanzak could not fight tumbling in free-fall. He seemed more shocked when his opponent spared his life than he had been at Blackthorn's mastery of weightless combat.

Aria was disturbed by ogrin guards entering her box. Oglok growled warning. "What's this?" the princess demanded.

"Bloodmaster Bale congratulates the Duchess Coda on her livestock's performance," a guard-sergeant proclaimed. "He invites the Duchess to join him in the imperial box to witness the remainder of the contest."

Aria's guide went pale. If he'd cringed much more he would have melted to liquid. "I'll just… wait here for you then," he told her.

Aria gestured for Oglok to follow and allowed the guards to convey her to the butcher of Diacria.

She arrived in time for Blackthorn to take on a cyborg mercenary in the semi-final. The draw was for swords on horseback so the two warriors each had to control a spirited warhorse as well as strike at the other with vibra-blades.

"Ah, duchess," Bale greeted Aria as she was ushered to him. "You arrive just in time. Your Ah-nie is performing well."

"I hope so," the princess replied coolly. "I have a lot of bloodmarks wagered on him."

Bale nodded in appreciation. "Where did you find him? He fights like a warrior born but I do not recognize his nationality."

"I came across him in the Black Sorcerer's lands," Aria spoke with strict truthfulness. "As soon as I saw him I knew I'd have to bring him here."

"He will defeat this cyborg," the Bloodmaster predicted. "The man-robot fights with programmed precision. Your warrior has passion and courage. That always tells."

"I hope so."

Blackthorn finally made good the prediction and put the cyborg down. The crowd voiced their approval loudly and long. The unknown stranger had won their support by his valor.

"This is where it gets interesting," Bale told Aria. "Now your slave will face Baron Kemak's Drush-na-Vor. Have you seen a wight in action before?"

Aria's mind flashed back to that terrible night when the Black Airship had gone down as the undead fluttered through it. "Once," she confessed.

"Not like this one. He is a prince amongst undead, surely one of the Sorcerer of Night's finest creations before his capture and indenture. You will have received fine odds if you betted against him in the final contest."

"I'm sure the evening is going to be instructive," the princess promised.

Aria was somewhat perturbed by technicians entering the box and attaching heavy machinery to the vacant throne.

"You are very privileged, duchess," Bloodmaster Bale revealed. "In addition to gaining my attention you will share the imperial box with our glorious master himself. Lord Ruin will project here to witness the final battle!"

Aria checked the exit. Oglok was by the door and might take down the ogrin guards there, but beyond that there were a thousand more like them.

The iron throne sparked with static. Massive engines drew upon the interconnected systems of the iron city. The huge chair filled with a hologram of Lord Ruin's broad bulk.

Everybody kneeled. Aria kept her head down and hoped he would not remember her from that long-ago conference at the Crystal City.

The First Man was grotesquely muscled. Steel spikes grew through the skin of his arms and legs. His face was a bolted horror of rivets and steel. "What do we have, Bale?" Lord Ruin demanded in an impossibly deep voice.

"A greater wight against a baseline human, master. The odds favor the wight, of course, but the human is a superb all-round warrior. It should be a good contest."

"Excellent. Tell them to begin."

Aria watched in trepidation as Blackthorn re-entered the arena with a vibrasword and buckler. Drush-na-Vor ghosted in from the opposite side, clad in silver amour, bearing a bone-white blade. The crowd fell silent. It was as if the wight had sucked all the noise out of them.

Oglok's hackles were high.

The heralds proclaimed the combatants and called out their victories today. Lord Ruin gestured that the fight should begin. The adversaries closed upon each other.

Aria was torn between watching Blackthorn fight for his life against an undead opponent that could drain the very strength from his limbs and glancing at the First Man to check he had not marked her as the Black Sorcerer's daughter.

"The human does fight well, Bale," Lord Ruin commented as the combatants closed. "More, he fights intelligently. He knows what the ghost-blade can do in the hands of a wight and uses his shield to block while testing the weaknesses in Drush-na-Vor's armor."

Aria tried to follow the combat but both warriors were mere blurs now. She wondered how anyone human could possibly match the speed and fury of the wight, but somehow Blackthorn did.

"The mortal must tire," Bale predicted as the battle wore on. "Drush-na-Vor is pushing him back."

"He husbands his strength," Lord Ruin argued. "He has analyzed the wight's fighting style and is trying to compensate. He has abandoned slashes and thrusts. Now he seeks for a chance to strike clean and sever the undead's head."

"The wight is too wily to allow that."

"Yes. I wonder if the human realizes it and is relying upon Drush-na-Vor believing that is his whole strategy? You chose your champion well, Princess Aria."

Aria froze as she heard her name on the First Man's lips. Bale turned to stare at her in amazement.

"I would hardly come to Hades unprepared for what I must face, Lord Ruin," the princess managed to reply.

The Emperor of the South chuckled. "I had heard you were gone from your father's court. It is rumored that he is most displeased with you, Aria. He has dispatched his Prime Herald to seek you out."

"I doubt that Maximal will come looking for me here."

"That is true. He would never believe you so foolhardy."

Aria pointed at the arena. "Like a human standing against a greater wight?"

Down below the crowd had overcome their spooked silence. Now they cheered and cried, encouraging the underdog human against the terrible pale undead. Blackthorn fought a defensive battle, giving ground until he could see a chink in Drush-na-Vor's technique.

"You have courage, daughter of Queen Rhapsody," Lord Ruin approved. "I do not understand your tactics, however."

"Well then, Lord Ruin, why not watch and learn?" suggested the princess.

Oglok rubbed a dismayed paw over his forehead. From the back of the imperial box he couldn't hear what Aria and Ruin were saying but he could read her body language.

Blackthorn feinted left and attempted the decapitating blow. The wight anticipated it, knocked the human's shield away, and clamped an icy left hand onto the General's head.

Blackthorn staggered as the strength and vitality were sucked out of him.

"He is finished!" proclaimed Bloodmaster Bale.

Lord Ruin jerked forward to watch more intently. "No. I see what he is doing! He has *allowed* himself to get too near so he can close with his enemy! Watch! Watch him!"

Blackthorn twisted his sword with his remaining energy and jammed it through Drush-na-Vor's throat up into his skull cavity. As the wight staggered, Blackthorn twisted the blade round and sliced it through the undead's spine.

Drush-na-Vor tumbled backwards, trailing white wisps. Blackthorn finally had the angle to arc round and behead him.

The crowd in the Circus Terminus went wild. Blackthorn dropped to one knee, exhausted, then rose and lifted his frost-cracked vibrasword to accept their salutes.

Aria stared at the Bloodmaster defiantly. "Aren't you going to proclaim the winner?" she challenged. "Your audience is waiting."

Lord Ruin nodded. "It was a fair combat," he rumbled.

Bale raised his arms for quiet. When the auditorium was hushed, he turned to the princess. His voice was amplified around the entire arena. "Duchess Coda... Princess Aria, name your champion."

There was a murmur round the crowd. Many of them had heard of the Princess of Mars.

Aria answered in a clear loud voice that carried to the furthest corners of the arena. "My champion is General John Blackthorn - Blackthorn, the liberator of Mars, who will cast down the First Men and forge a new age of freedom, peace, and justice! But you are wrong, Bloodmaster, to name him today's victor yet. He still has one more challenge to fight before he is triumphant over all."

"What? Who?"

Lord Ruin was ahead of his Bloodmaster. "*You*, Bale. He's come for you. He allowed himself to get this near so he can be close to his enemy! Very well played, princess. I am most impressed."

"Not as impressed as you will be when my champion spanks your champion's butt," Aria threatened. "The Black Sorcerer may have abandoned Diacria but *I* have not! Nor has General Blackthorn. He'll prove it on your Bloodmaster today!"

Lord Ruin's red eyes burned. "Then let there be war!" he proclaimed.

Bloodmaster Bale rose from his seat and stepped onto the rail around the imperial box. He jumped down into the arena, his crimson battle amour growing and sealing around him. Thick epaulettes and shoulder-pads expanded to activate the weapons platforms within them. A black hilt became a six-foot-long kinetic blade that would hit with the force of a war-tank.

"Nice," said Blackthorn. "You want to run home and get some more toys before we start?"

"Any one of my weapons can shatter your vibra-blade," taunted the butcher of Diacria.

Blackthorn held up his hand. Aria slipped the Sword of Light from beneath her skirts and tossed it to him. He switched it to laser-blade and swirled it in the air. "I think I'll just stick with what I know," he told Bale.

Oglok shook free the ogrins holding him and voiced a full-throated bellow to the effect that the General should kick the Bloodmaster's ass; except it was much ruder in Mock-Man.

"You made one error, champion," Bale told Blackthorn as the two of them circled. "You assumed you could stand against me."

"Oh, I've made lots of errors," the Earthman admitted. "The worst ones haunt me day and night. But I've seen Diacria. Facing off with you? That's no mistake!"

"Are you going to cry over slaughtered cattle?" mocked Bale.

"I'm going to avenge murdered people."

Lord Ruin turned to Aria. "You have chosen well, princess. Your weapon is a fine one. How did the Black Sorcerer cope with his insolence?"

"The Black Sorcerer went scuttling back to his Bastion at the end," Aria reported. "I imagine he described his retreat as prudent."

Ruin snorted. "I imagine he did. You have grown up, Princess. You are strong now. There would be a place for you at my side."

"I wouldn't want to be at your side when the storm I'm brewing against you hits," Aria warned. "The First Men are going to fall."

Down below, Bale peeled off a pair of combat drones to bracket Blackthorn. The General blasted them out of the air and came in for a direct attack.

"And he is your Last Man, is he?" Ruin asked Aria. "Is *he* to be the new ruler of Mars then?"

"Perhaps."

Bale slammed Blackthorn aside. The General rolled and got his Sword of Light up fast enough to deflect the missile pellets that came after him.

"He is a strong warrior," Ruin judged. "And a fair tactician from what I have seen. He fights with courage and passion. But I do believe that passion is for rulership. *That* is why he will fail."

Aria would have liked to rebut the First Man but she couldn't think of a reply.

Bloodmaster Bale loosed a series of smart missiles to ring round and take Blackthorn from the rear. Blackthorn dived in close and slid beneath the warlord's legs so the bombs burst across Bale's combat amour. He switched the Sword of Light to its short-blade setting and carved it through the battle-suit's primary power pack.

Bale's razor-edged arm came out and caught Blackthorn across the ribs. The crowd howled. Aria gasped.

The Earthman rolled aside to avoid a ground-shattering strike from Bale's kinetic blade. He flipped up and landed on the Bloodmaster's shoulders, tearing at the bolts that pinned Bale's helmet in place.

Bale shook him off, but Blackthorn took the helm with him. Without the command unit the combat suit's higher defense functions were neutralized.

The Bloodmaster was unfazed. His power-enhanced boot smashed into Blackthorn's chest like a mule-kick. The General flew backwards, tumbling in the bloody sawdust. His vision blurred.

Aria gripped the rail of the imperial box and bit her lip to stop from crying out. Any distraction could be fatal now.

"So he is more than your weapon," Lord Ruin observed. "Interesting."

"He is my chosen champion, the liberator of Mars. Nothing more!" Aria flared.

Ruin chuckled.

Blackthorn discharged the Sword of Light in blast mode. The red fireball hammered Bale backwards, spilling him over onto his back for the first time. As the Bloodmaster sat up Blackthorn *hurled* the Sword of Light at the butcher of Diacria.

The Hallow blade cut right through reinforced polytitanium power amour and flared as it lodged into Bale's chest. The warlord looked in surprise and horror at the energy tine that transfixed him. "That's not... not..."

He slumped down dead.

Blackthorn limped over, retrieved his weapon, and turned to the cheering crowd.

"I believe the custom is that the champion walks free," Aria reminded Lord Ruin. "Or do you intend to be a bad loser?"

Ruin's stitched and riveted countenance screwed into an angry mask but he knew the princess had outmaneuvered him. If he did not honor his custom then he would lose face; better to save his rage for another day.

"Blackthorn is the winner!" he publicly proclaimed. "He is the strongest here." *If I were present as more than a mere hologram there would be a different outcome*, his undertone promised.

Blackthorn raised his own arms for silence, and got it. "I didn't come here today to prove I was the best fighter," he told them. "I came here today to do justice on the butcher of Diacria. And to send a message to Lord Ruin there and all like him who think that force entitles them to whatever they want. It doesn't. And from now on, whenever you try it, whatever you do, *it will be answered*. And that answer will be *No!*"

Ruin stood from his throne and raised a fist at Blackthorn. "You insolent nothing! You dare to threaten me, here, in my city? What forbearance can there be for one who incurs my wrath?"

Aria saw her moment. Ruin's image was no longer occupying the iron chair connected to the First Man's machinery. She reached down to the interface nodes and grabbed them with both hands, then jammed every iota of arcane energy she could muster into the system.

Ruin's hologram vanished with a squawk of feedback. But more, systems all across Hades crashed into critical shutdown. War machines exploded. Guard towers went dead. And every imprisonment shackle in the city dropped from the wrists of every captive.

Oglok grabbed the ogrin beside him and hurled them off the balcony.

"Beware!" Blackthorn shouted. "Justice has come to Hades!"

And the riot began.

Two months after that:

"What *did* you do to Lord Ruin's city?" David Morningstar asked Princess Aria as they sipped tinoro leaf tea together. Aria was a captive in the Lord of Fatal Laughter's city-sized mobile headquarters, *Fatality*, and the Colonel was… his guest?

"We gave it a taste of freedom," Aria replied. "They will not soon forget it."

"I've seen Fatal Laughter's intelligence reports. In one day you and the good General managed to kill Ruin's favorite war-toy, release ninety thousand slave captives into the wild, and set half the structures of Hades on fire. Our host was most amused."

"It made Ruin think twice before pursuing his campaign in Diacria. He had to draw units back to deal with his problems at home." *And gained Blackthorn new support and new allies, like that gypsy chief Nanzak.*

"That would be the ninety thousand fugitives you left to starve or be hunted to death at the South Pole, would it? You're good at making messes but you don't seem to think through the clean-up."

"Those people had more chance that way than they would have as slaves in Hades," Aria argued. "We did what we could. It's still early days in this campaign."

Morningstar sipped his tea. "And how's ol' Blackthorn working out for you, Aria? Are you keeping him well satisfied in exchange for him fighting your battles?"

The princess tried not to blush. "Blackthorn and I are not lovers."

"Really? That guy's even dumber than I thought. I'd have had you barking like a seal by now, begging for more."

"You could not have done what John Blackthorn has, uniting the people of Mars."

"What, hooking up with the Runners?" Morningstar grinned as Aria's face betrayed her. "C'mon. Fatal Laughter's got the best torturers on Mars, and the most inventive. Or course he's got a collection of half-dissected Runner couriers somewhere on this hulk. It's going to take more than enthusiastic peasants and a bunch of long-distance mail carriers to take over the planet." He paused then added. "Which is why you want the Voice of God, right?"

Aria pursed her lips and said nothing. How did Morningstar always manage to put her on the back foot? Why was she always helpless with him?

Well, she reminded herself, *you are a captive in the Lord of Fatal Laughter's mobile stronghold, and as soon as he finds you're here he'll be devising all kinds of merry torments for his rival's daughter. And there is a suppression field active here that prevents anyone but him and his agents from being able to access the arcane field to do magic. And when you just tried to plant your foot in Morningstar's face he slapped you down like a trainee.*

"I'm not here to answer your questions, Colonel Morningstar," Aria said.

"Actually you are. As I believe you heard, I haven't yet drawn our host's attention to your... availability aboard *Fatality*. As long as you keep interesting me it'll stay that way. Bore me and... well, I'd also be interested to see what the First Man does to you."

Aria shuddered. She'd seen the Lord of Fatal Laughter at a summit two hundred cycles ago when the Crystal Lady had called together the First Men to review the terms of their conflict. Ruin had intimidated the teenage girl and Night had chilled her to the bone but Fatal Laughter had *terrified* her.

"More tea?" offered Morningstar as if he hadn't just threatened to give her over to a monster who would destroy her in every painful and humiliating way that could be devised. "You never did say how it was going with Blackthorn. Apart from the abstinence, of course. I never understood why you decided to run off with him instead of me."

"I can trust him," answered Aria.

"Trust is overrated. Mutual need, that's much more effective."

"So another too-handsome traitor once told me."

"It's not too late to jump horses, you know. You're welcome to jump on me." Morningstar stretched back with his arms behind his head and grinned at his captive.

"You're not my type."

"But I am," the Colonel recognized. "I'm *exactly* your type. Don't pretend you haven't thought about it, on those wet lonely no-sex nights fighting the good fight with General Blackthorn. Tell me, is it just you he doesn't fancy or is it women generally?"

Aria pursed her lips. Morningstar caught the tell.

"There *are* other women!" he crowed. "What, kinky little Sihla of the Nots, from the grubby little refugees scraping a life in the ruins of that Martian theme park out there? I hear she really knows how to warm up a dark windtide night. Is that who your champion's 'liberating' right now?"

Aria had *not* cared that Sihla had been all over Blackthorn at the victory celebration after they'd helped the Nots overcome the robot presidents[8]. Aria had *not* been bothered how Sihla's hands had kneaded Blackthorn's shoulders as the rebel-girl whispered in his ear. Aria had *not* minded when the freedom fighters had closed the great blast-door on her so they could escape with Blackthorn and the wounded Oglok, leaving her alone against an army of monsters to be captured and dragged to *Fatality*. She *hadn't!*

"They abandoned you, didn't they? Blackthorn made is choice, and he went with the grubby little Not hottie."

"I *told* Blackthorn to retreat with Oglok while I held the rear," Aria protested.

---

[8] These and subsequent events are described in more detail in Mark Bousquet's "Cradle of Atlantis" in *Blackthorn: Thunder on Mars*. Some dialogue is also quoted with thanks and credit.

"And here you are, while he's snuggling with his raggy little rebelette." Morningstar shook his head. "Everyone finds their level, princess."

Time for a different line of attack, Aria decided.. "Why isn't Fatal Laughter dissecting you right now, Colonel Morningstar?" she enquired.

The barbarian smirked. "Because I amuse him. I come from old Earth-that-was, and I still remember all kinds of terrible things that people did to other people back in the day. Enough of them are novelties to our First Man host that he's simply dying to try them – or at least other people are dying. Can you believe he'd not come across the Chinese wire torture, where they continually wind a mesh tight round you and slice off the bits that bulge out?"

"How fortunate that you were able to instruct him," the princess replied coldly.

"Well, like you, I'm disciplined enough to work to a long term objective. If I want to take Fatal Laughter and his cronies down I need an edge. Same edge I bet you've come to Atlantis for, right, princess? Did you actually *tell* the General why you'd led him to the Lord of Fatal Laughter's chuckle-a-minute killer robot amusement park? I bet you didn't."

"What makes you say that?"

"Because the Voice of God is a weapon in the right hands. A tool – the only tool – that allows Mars-wide communications? A means of reaching the whole population and telling them what to do? Those Ancients really knew their powerful artifacts, didn't they? But what would noble John Blackthorn do if he got his hands on it? Institute democracy? The United States of Mars?"

"You think I'd do different," Aria recognized.

"I know you would, *princess*. Your mother was Queen of Mars, right? You can trace your family line back through kings and queens to, well, I dunno, probably Earth, can't you? I don't think democratic republics are what you've got in mind as a happy ending, Aria. That's why you want the Voice and you won't be sharing with Blackthorn."

Aria neither confirmed nor denied Morningstar's accusation. "How do you even know about the Voice of God?" she wondered.

"Because I ask the right questions and I listen to the answers. For example, I asked myself: princess? Princess of what? And if her mom is the legendary Queen Rhapsody then who's her pa? And then I listen to the screams of this little dismantled Sensorine that Fatal

Laughter keeps as a personal hobby and, hey, it turns out you're royal twice over, Aria."

"Sensorine? Elicogna?"

"There's nothing left to rescue, princess, so don't bother. I nearly put her out of her misery myself, except I'd have ended up replacing her. Your close friends sure do end up in some bad places, don't they? Coda tortured to death by the Black Sorcerer. Elicogna is Fatal Laughter's chew toy. Nepenthe given to the Sorcerer of Night…"

"What? What's that about Nepenthe?"

"You didn't know? As a consequence of Blackthorn's derring-do your daddy and Erebus had a brief treaty. Nepenthe was part of the exchange. I think it was arranged by that Herald who's so keen to find you."

Aria thought of innocent Nepenthe as she'd been at the harvest dance, her blonde plaits whirling, her face beaming. The Sorcerer of Night would devour that joy and drag her to grey cold eternal nightmare.

Aria's hands doubled to fists.

Morningstar snickered. "Sucks to be you, huh? Sucked to be Nepenthe more, I'd guess. Kind of makes you wish you had access to some kind of ultimate weapon, doesn't it? A Voice of God or something?"

"I admit that it does."

"And you know it's likely somewhere in the catacombs below us, right? You've decided the Voice of God lies in Atlantis."

Atlantis was part of the long-ruined theme park where the Lord of Fatal Laughter had modified the entertainment robots to be hunter-killers; or it was memory of an ancient Earth colony; or a secret treasure-store of the Ancients that might hold a sleeping army and a weapon that could forever free Aria from the fear of mental slavery to the Black Sorcerer.

"Maybe." The princess sipped her honey-soaked tea and eyed the Colonel. "What now? If you're attempting to keep secrets from the Sorcerer of this craft, you are not long for this world."

Morningstar smiled at her. "We're going to be allies."

"Why on Mars would we do that?"

"Because neither of us can find the Voice of God alone."

It was very different with David Morningstar.

Aria rode with him in the confined claustrophobic metal shell of the deep digger, rattling and juddering through the Martian soil into the catacombs beneath the Atlantis park. She felt like she was betraying Blackthorn and Oglok just by traveling with the traitor, but the portable magic jammer he carried was just as effective as the one on *Fatality*. Besides, only a combination of the equipment Morningstar could commandeer from Fatal Laughter's ship and the visions Aria had gleaned from the Hall of Reflections could find the Voice.

Being with Morningstar also felt *dangerous*. She'd somehow become accustomed to Blackthorn's barbarian bluntness, even to Oglok's bestial growls. Colonel Morningstar offered no comfort and no compromise.

I thought I'd decided he was not for me? Aria chided herself.

Better a short alliance with David Morningstar than a lifetime's servitude to Halifax, she answered. If only the Voice of God could do what she hoped…

The rock crusher rattled out into the undercaverns. The Colonel flicked on the bright arc lights and drew back the canopy so they could see around the massive Ancients-carved chambers. A quarter hour's travel took them to the largest cave, where natural light from sinkholes from the surface shone down across a tangled forest on the cavern floor. Shattered spires rose from the undergrowth, the last remnants of whatever Atlantis had been.

Aria felt a surge of excitement. This could be the turning point in the history of Mars! If the Voice of God, whatever it was, lay amongst those ruins, or if the Sleeping Army waited to be woken to her cause, then…

Morningstar blindsided her with a two-handed push that toppled her out of the grinder. She fell hard to the dust-thick floor twenty feet below. The breath went out of her. It was a moment before she could kneel up and see what the Earther was up to.

The Colonel waved the scanner unit down at her, his handsome face twisted with fury.

"What is the meaning of this?" she demanded. "Come with me! Help me find the Voice of God!"

Morningstar's rage became mere contempt. "Go away, Aria. The Voice of God is yours. If you can find it, it will be useless. But you won't find it." He showed her the scanner feed. "This place was stripped centuries ago." He tossed the console down at her. "What a waste of time. A joke!"

He returned to the drive column of the rock grinder. Aria had to scramble aside to avoid being crushed by its tracks. "You're just giving up?" she demanded.

"You don't get it, do you?" Morningstar spat. "You will." He shifted the gears to drive the digger back into the crust of Mars, but not back to the Lord of Fatal Laughter. "I wonder how much of this you'll tell Blackthorn when you slink back to him?" he pondered. "Since you haven't even told him who you really are, I'm guessing not much. Then again, since he couldn't even be bothered to try and save you from Fatal Laugher, I guess that's what he deserves!"

Aria ignored him. She scurried aside to avoid the spray of rocks as the machine bored away, and counted herself fortunate to have got out of her encounter so lightly. She felt the tingle of magic return to her as the jammer moved out of range.

She picked up the discarded scanner with a growing sense on anticipation. Even if the Voice of God was gone, there was still the Sleeping Army. Morningstar hadn't even known about them.

It was only when she examined the scanner again that she knew what he had seen.

The joke.

Blackthorn had discovered a space rocket, and a weapons cache, and possibly the site of the first colonist landing on Mars; except the vessel was a rotted shell, the weapons were rusted beyond repair, and the astronauts' descendents had degenerated into the desperate rebel Nots. Whatever secrets the Ancients had left here had long since been found and stripped out by the Lord of Fatal Laughter. Even the killer robots in the park above only hunted the Nots for amusement, while the Nots spent their lives and blood protecting a Great Rocket that meant nothing.

"The Sorcerer of Fatal Laughter really knows how to pull a prank," Aria admitted sullenly after she was reunited with Blackthorn and Oglok - and Sihla. "He had Morningstar, and me, and you, and the Nots all running around dancing on his strings." *And he showed me parts of myself that I don't really like. Only really good jokes make you think.*

"You don't know that it was the First Man," Sihla objected.

Aria handed over the scanner Morningstar had launched at her. The cracked screen was filled with little bouncing smiley faces careening madly over the data.

Once again, Aria felt beaten. The obedience programming could make her turn against everything she cared about – but worse, she knew now that she could do that to herself as well. Her passion for her quest gave her power - but it could be a killer.

Blackthorn crushed the scanner in his hand and laughed. It was a good-humored guffaw, so different from Morningstar's smug snicker. Then he became more somber and gestured for Aria, Oglok, Sihla and the Nots to gather round him.

"All is not lost," he told them.

"The weapons..." began Sihla.

"This vessel must have been stocked with the flora and fauna you see around you. There is food to gather and game to hunt. You can feed your people with what you see here and grow strong."

"The Sleeping Army... they were to be our best hope!"

"The scriptures prophesied it," added Aria, "The Sleeping Army guarding the Voice of God. All gone."

"Really?" asked Blackthorn. He looked into Sihla's eyes. "Sihla, you *are* the Sleeping Army."

"What?"

"Somehow the message has been lost down the ages." Blackthorn explained how the children of the astronauts, the ragged Nots, could forge themselves into an organized resistance to fight for the freedom of Mars. In a few sentences, there in the shadow of the rusty useless hulk that symbolized their failure, Blackthorn gathered together an people and gave them a destiny. "*You* are the army that shall overthrow the First Men and deliver Mars back into the hands of its people."

"Only us?" Sihla was close to tears, close to giving up. "If we are the chosen ones... what chance do we have against the power of the First Men?"

"Strength in numbers. Courage even to death. A future for all Mars if only you can win it."

Oglok roared his defiance of First Men and prophesy and everything that stopped Mars being free.

"Wake up, my Sleeping Army," Blackthorn told the Nots with a quiet, compelling intensity. "It's time."

Nobody could deny that call, Aria thought, *nobody*.

Not me.

Aria saw Sihla's face change, and the faces of all the Nots behind her. Desperation transformed to determination. Not today or tomorrow, but one day General Blackthorn would have his army.

The princess blinked back a tear. John had somehow taken a moment of defeat and made it a moment of victory. He'd turned a cruel joke into a moment of grace.

He was not David Morningstar. He was more than that.

And then Aria got the other joke, the one that even Fatal Laugher hadn't seen, and she began to giggle, then chuckle, then guffaw.

"What's so funny?" Blackthorn puzzled.

"The Voice of God?" Aria choked. "The communication that can cross all of Mars, and can't be denied, and can't be silenced? The words that cast down enemies and echo across history? The Voice that was rumored to be here but could never be discovered, that no scanner could detect, that Morningstar couldn't find, that *I* couldn't find?"

"Yes?"

"I've found it now," the princess testified. "The message is sent: Wake up. It's time!"

Those were the words that would burn across the red planet, from rebel to rebel, from oppressed people to oppressed people, whispered, treasured, passed on, until all Mars rose, and united, and fought.

Maybe they could even set a princess free?

Three weeks later:

"There's Albus up ahead." Captain Korzan gestured at the tiny nub of blackened rock that rose out of the mists of the Amazonis Sea. It was still early in the morning and the red tides cast a strange uplight on the lonely island. "Why anyone should want to visit this godsforsaken place I don't know. Why anyone should want to live here I know even less!"

Oglok groaned agreement. The desolate rock was hardly hospitable.

"Wait here for us, Captain," Blackthorn instructed the corsair. "Oglok will wait with you." That way there'd be a boat still there when they wanted to leave.

Korzan glanced up at the huge beastling. "No problem. We'll launch an, um, launch. Sorry about that little misunderstanding earlier."

"As you say, no problem. Sorry about your fingers."

Aria and Blackthorn climbed into a flimsy dinghy and rowed across the red water to the rocky shore. The princess reached out with her arcane senses and located the only human on the island. "He's waiting for us," she sensed.

Blackthorn made a pretence of straightening his hair and shining his boots on the backs of his pants and followed Aria between the smooth black rocks.

Albus was an eerie sort of place. No plant grew there. All was beaded black rock, jutting up in fantastic melted stalagmites ten yards high. Blackthorn and Aria encountered no bird, no animal. Even the tide-tossed Amazonis seemed muted when it broke upon this alien shore.

The lack of other life signatures made it easy for the princess to locate the man they'd come to see. She scrambled up a set of ridges that layered like steps towards an elevated center of the island. There the fantastic pillar-spikes formed a natural circle with a shallow basin inside. Aria was put in mind of an old wax candle. If so then the scholar who awaited them was the wick.

A bespectacled white-bearded man watched them scramble into ring of stones. Aria had seem him before – in the Hall of Reflections!

Blackthorn saw his companion's expression but couldn't known the reason for her shock. "This is the guy?"

"Oh yes. I'm certain of it now."

The scholar sat at a wooden table stacked with manuscripts. A pair of books laid open, ready. Two more stools were set out for visitors.

"How did he know we were coming?" Blackthorn asked uneasily.

Aria shrugged. "Father De'bias?" she ventured.

"Yes," the old priest replied.

"We've come a long way to see you," the General told him. "We had a tough time tracking you down."

"Yes."

"We weren't sure you would still be… alive," Aria ventured. After all, it was forty cycles since this scholar had fled Lord Ruin's purge.

The old man looked from princess to warrior and made a note in red ink in the volume before him. Aria thought it might have been the *Ojer Tjiz*. If so he was *correcting* it. "Are you ready for the tests?" he asked.

"Tests?" Blackthorn tensed and looked around. His experience of tests on Mars tended to involve brutal axe-wielding ogrin or trap-floored dungeon labyrinths.

"We just want to talk with you about your work," Aria told De'bias. "It wasn't easy to find you, but we've done it at last." The Runners had taken nearly five months to locate the scholar, and Reith's Runners could find anything.

"And so the tests," the old man said.

"No-one mentioned tests," Blackthorn objected.

De'bias pulled off his spectacles and examined his visitors. "Nothing's for nothing, General Blackthorn. You want what I know.

I want to know that you're the kind of people I'd want to know it. So, tests."

Aria rubbed her forehead. Something here didn't seem right. She was missing something. "What do we have to do?" she sighed.

"Oh, terrible things!" De'bias warned them. He leaned in confidentially "You have to tell the truth! And you have to make sacrifices! And then there's the ordeals!"

"I don't like the sound of that," Blackthorn answered. "How about you just tell us what we came all this way to find out?"

"And what's that?" the old man asked. "Or shall I tell you? You look like the sort of skeptic who'd prefer some proof that I know what I'm talking about."

He knew Blackthorn's name before we told him, Aria noted. But if he was using magic she couldn't sense it.

"Talk, then," Blackthorn prompted.

"Why you think you're here, then," De'bias said. "Princess Aria's trying to make sense of prophecies from the ancient holy books of Mars. She's pored over the *Popol Vuh*, which frankly says very little about the First Men and an awful lot about misbehaving twins and girls getting pregnant by skulls - which can be confusing for a young woman[9]. And she's read the *Ojer Tzij*, which has appalling grammar and jumps between history, allegory, and legend so fast that specially trained stunt-readers can strain a thinking muscle. Now she wants to find out how First Men really happened, how to grab the Hallows to stop them, and how to mend Harmony Spires."

"Well... yes," admitted the princess, taken aback.

De'bias pointed his quill pen feather at Blackthorn. "You, General, are hoping there's more practical information can somehow be gleaned from the scrapings of the Ancients' bookshelves. You want to know about that Sword of Light, why it works only for you, and what its true capabilities are. You want to know how to beat unbeatable magic-workers and break their grip on this world. And you'd quite like a hint about why Princess Aria is really traveling with you and what she's truly up to. Am I right?"

Aria glared at Blackthorn. "You want to check up on *me?*"

"You're not exactly forthcoming, princess. I was just... curious." The warrior turned to the old man. "Okay, you're probably the real deal and you know how to cause trouble. Want to tell me *how* you know all this?"

---

[9] References to actual content of the ancient text.

"No. I want you to do the tests."

"The tests then!" surrendered Aria. "What do we have to do?"

"I've already covered this. You each have to tell the truth. You each have to make a sacrifice. You each have to face an ordeal. Then you'll know what you need to know."

"What truth?" Blackthorn asked.

"Oh, nothing hard," De'bias promised. "Just tell me whether you love Princess Aria?"

Aria's heart lurched. She looked at the Earthman with mounting panic. What if he said yes? What if he said no?

"I'm… very fond of her," Blackthorn answered. "She's one of my closest friends."

"I see," De'bias answered as if what he'd heard was very significant. He made a marginal note in his book. "Aria, do you love Blackthorn?"

"*No!* Not like *that*, anyhow. I don't think I *can* love anyone like that any more. It's like John said, a friend, but…"

"Sacrifice, then," the old man pushed on. "General, will you surrender the Sword of Light to me?"

Blackthorn shook his head. "Not likely."

"Why not?"

"It's mine. Well, mine now. The Black Sorcerer couldn't make it work. Nobody can but me. Aria thinks it's one of these legendary Hallow items, which is what we want to talk to you about."

De'bias scribed another comment. "The Sword does indeed serve you alone. Its Light is yours to command. *Remember* that. It'll be important." He turned to Aria, "Sorceress, will you yield me your arcane gifts?"

"That's not possible," the princess argued. "I've been implanted with an arcane neural net, grown right in…"

"There are Ancient devices that could rob you of all the magic you have," the old man assured her. "Will you sacrifice your birthright to achieve what you seek?"

Aria reluctantly shook her head. "Magic is a part of me, Father De'bias. If I give it up it won't be me who's seeking."

De'bias raised his eyebrows as if to say *this isn't going very well, is it?*

"So to the ordeal. Are you ready?"

Aria didn't feel ready. The other questions had shaken her, and her arcane perception was almost finding something that she really should know about…

"Get on with it," instructed Blackthorn.

"Very well then. General, will you die for Aria?"

Blackthorn frowned. "Die trying to save her, I guess yes, if I had to. Die fighting this revolution of hers, yeah probably. If you mean lie down here on a sacrificial slab or something so she can get answers about some crummy books written thousands of years ago, then no way."

You didn't die to save me in Atlantis, Aria silently accused him. *You didn't save me at all.* Morningstar's jibe still stung.

"Aria, will you surrender everything for Blackthorn?" De'bias asked.

"I don't understand the question," the princess prevaricated.

"Will you give up everything you are? All your hopes, your dreams, your future? Will you surrender to your greatest fears and allow yourself to be destroyed for him? Will you accept that ordeal?"

"She doesn't have to," Blackthorn interrupted. "I wouldn't want her to."

Good, Aria thought. *I do not think I would.*

Father De'bias clapped his hands together. "Fine!" he said. "Now I know you."

"Did we pass?" Blackthorn asked uncertainly. "Did we pass *any* of them?"

"Some, perhaps," the old man conceded. "The rest... well, there are always re-sits."

"Can you answer our questions then?" Aria begged. "Some of them at least?"

"Some I've already answered," De'bias told them with a twinkle in his eye. "Others will come when you know yourselves better. Some things you can only know at the moment you face death. Don't be in a hurry for those."

"We've come a long way to get fobbed off with cryptic, Father," Blackthorn objected.

"Yes," agreed De'bias. "I wonder, Aria, do you think you came in the right direction?"

The question hit the princess like a punch, right on the guilty spot that had been there since that confrontation with damned David Morningstar. *No*, she confessed in her head. *I know where I should be.*

Blackthorn hadn't been privy to that dialogue "Why shouldn't we be here?" he demanded.

"Because the Princess of Mars has other obligations, and for her this is a repeat journey," De'bias answered. "And if *that* wasn't cryptic enough, try this..."

Then he, his books, and his table, all melted away like the fog on the red waters.

"What?" gasped Blackthorn, activating his Sword of Light just in case. "Where did he go?"

The radiance from the sword glinted off the black glass rocks, reflecting rainbow arcs along their cracked ruin. And then Aria knew when she had been here before.

She rushed to the smooth time-rounded material from which the island was made and touched a palm to it. No purple spark responded to her call.

"No…" she whispered.

"Aria?" Blackthorn checked. He'd been spooked by De'bias' vanishing act but Aria was really distressed.

"No wonder he knew so much!" the princess told Blackthorn. "No wonder he saw into our hearts. How could he not?"

"Aria, you have to explain what's suddenly bothered you. We've come across worse sorcery than an old guy going the ghost bit."

The princess gestured round to the bleak black stones. "This is a special place, John, special and terrible. A man who dwelled here for many years, he would be changed. How could he not be? He'd see things and know things. He'd face truths, and sacrifices, and ordeals. In the end he'd be consumed by it!"

"Still not following," Blackthorn admitted. "Was he a ghost? Does Mars have ghosts?"

"He was an echo, say. I *have* voyaged here before, John. A very long time ago, with my mother, when I was a little girl. When this black jagged tooth was the best thing I'd ever seen, a glistening, singing Harmony Spire!" Aria shuddered as the chill got to her.

Blackthorn looked around at the desolate stump. "What happened to it?"

"What happens to all the Harmony Spires eventually. What's happening to all of Mars. It died. It fell. Its wonder was lost."

The Earthman tried to make sense of things. "So the old priest came here, took refuge here, spent decades here, in this strange atmosphere, amongst this… skeleton of a Harmony Spire. So what is he now? Alive? Dead? Mars' spooky spokesperson? The ghost of Christmas Past?"

Aria forced her fingers off the melted silicon shards and faced her fears. "It's time I stopped questing for arcane knowledge and short cuts," she told Blackthorn. "De'bias was right about me having to be somewhere else. Somewhere important. Will you take me there?"

"Yes," said Blackthorn before he ever asked, "Where?"

Six weeks after that:

Winter was hard in Utopia. Snows piled ten feet up the sides of houses and wolves and worse-than-wolves came out of the forest hungry for prey.

Oglok drove the dog-sled hard through the Vargo Pass, racing the blizzard that threatened to block the last route through the Sabaen Mountains. The temperature was twenty below zero without the wind-chill factor and dropping fast.

The grey snow-laden skies grew even darker as night threatened. The sled half-slid half-skidded down the steep slopes. Only Oglok's huge strength kept control of the pack-dogs enough to prevent the team dragging the vehicle over the breathtaking precipice drops.

It was Aria who sensed refuge, her arcane perceptions strained to the limit. "That way!" she gasped, pointing a frost-rimed mitten to the left. "Human life. I'm sure of it!"

Oglok reigned the dogs round and cut over the white snowfield as the storm caught up with them. By the time the travelers could see a flickering light the snow had become hail pellets the size of marbles.

It was another twenty nightmarish minutes before Oglok wrestled the sled through the gates of a tiny mountainside village. A crooked signpost suggested that two roads crossed here, but the deep drifts of snow obscured any sign of the joining tracks. The settlement itself was no more than six houses, all of them covered on two sides by the banking white blanket.

The light came from the building closest to the gate, a larger two-storey structure under a steep frost-white shingled roof. Wings on both sides and a rear wall formed a stable courtyard. A swinging sign announced it was The Vine of Life, a tavern and inn.

"Get the dogs round to the kennels," Blackthorn shouted to Oglok over the winds. "Aria and I will see about getting us rooms."

The Mock-Man honked a wry comment about some people getting the warm jobs and turned to coax the exhausted pack a few more yards.

Blackthorn grabbed the carpet bags from the rear of the sled and hefted them up the stairs to the inn porch. Aria knocked on the door, then pushed it open when there was no immediate answer. She discovered a small lobby leading into a large low-roofed timber common room where a dozen or more patrons turned to examine the newcomers.

A bewhiskered innkeeper put down the pewter mug he was polishing and hurried over to meet them. "Where on Mars did you come from?" he marveled. "I thought nothing could move in this storm."

"We traveled the Vargo Pass," Blackthorn explained, "and we damn near didn't make it."

There was a general murmur of agreement from the company in the common room. Apart from a young barmaid and an older woman who bustled with a landlady's authority everyone else had the air or travelers. The storm had stranded them all.

"I can let you have a room," the innkeeper offered. "It's nothing fancy but it's the last space we've got. Food's included from the common pot but you buy your drinks and any extras. Half a grain a day for the pair of you and I won't take a scruple less."

"There are three of us," Aria explained. "Our companion is kenneling the dogs."

At that moment Oglok came in, stamping his feet and shaking the snow off his fur. A couple of travelers rose in panic and reached for their weapons.

"Oh no!" insisted the innkeeper fiercely. "You don't bring that thing in here. Strictly humans in the Vine of Life! No demiwolves, skinshifters, werekin, cursemorts or anything else."

"Oglok's a Mock-Man," Blackthorn argued, angry at the reaction to his comrade of many adventures. "He's no danger to anyone who's not a threat to him."

"Not in my inn!" insisted the landlord. "I won't have it! My patrons won't have it No devilspawn under this roof!"

Blackthorn folded his arms. "Fine. *You* throw him out then. I'll stand here and watch."

Oglok growled a disconcerting challenge.

"Get him out, mister," one of the visitors warned. "That creature's not coming under the same roof as my children."

"Because they might grow up to be less ignorant than you?" sniped Aria. She was surprised how upset she was at the prejudice against the Mock-Man. A few months ago it wouldn't have mattered; she might even have taken the travelers' part.

The landlord reddened but tried to keep things calm. "Look, sir, there's no way that... thing can stay in this house. But if you want he can lodge in the stable or the kennels. It's warm with the dogs. I'll not make any charge." He eyed Oglok worriedly. "'Less he eats some of them, of course."

Oglok cut off the argument by growling that he'd prefer to sleep with the pack dogs. The company would smell better. He scratched his armpits to show his contempt of the guests and stamped out again.

"So do you want this room or what, mister...?"

"Smith," said Blackthorn grimly. He reached into his purse and dropped granules of silver onto the counter scales until he'd paid the demanded fee.

"Right, Mr. and Mrs. Smith," the innkeeper said, "Come with me and I'll show you to your room."

Aria settled down on the thin mattress under the low eaves and glared at Blackthorn as he returned from checking on the Mock-Man.

"Oglok's plenty mad, but not at us," the Earthman reported. "The half-ham I took him pacified him a bit."

"Mr. and Mrs. Smith," quoted Aria. She sat cross-legged on the double bed that occupied most of the tiny attic room. "Mrs. and Mr."

Blackthorn winced. "This was the only space. Even the common room's booked for the night. It was this or the kennel with Oglok."

"I'm thinking," retorted the Princess.

"C'mon Aria. You know you're safe with me. I'd sleep on the floor only there isn't any."

"I know I'm *safe*, John Blackthorn," snapped the raven-haired beauty. "I suppose my question is *why?*"

Blackthorn blinked. "I'm sorry?"

"Less than two minutes with Morningstar and he was trying to get into my bed. Two minutes."

"Morningstar? Aria, if that bastard did anything to..."

"Colonel Morningstar did nothing I didn't want," scowled the princess. "Except that time he tried to stab me and that other time when he pushed me off a rock crawler. Anyway, why should it matter to you what happened between me and David?"

"*David?* Aria, that guy's a treacherous snake. He'll use you and dump you and laugh in your face as you cry!"

"And you care because...?"

"Because... you're a key ally in this war of liberation we're running. Without you that sorceress back in Bandusae would probably have fried me. We'd never have worked out that the Light in Malador amplifies magic, but only in that one spot[10]. You got us

---

190

safe out of the Canyon of Night – from what I remember.[11] And at Anx you went toe to toe with the Black Sorcerer for us. Hell, we'd never have got started on all this without you!"

"So I'm a valuable strategic asset."

"And a friend. I don't get what…"

"Not an *invaluable* asset though, General Blackthorn. I mean, when I was taken into *Fatality* to face the Lord of Fatal Laughter you didn't rush to rescue me, did you? Who was it that actually got me out of there? Oh yes, it was David Morningstar!"

Blackthorn winced. "Aria, I had a tough call to make. If I went after you I'd have been abandoning the Nots to die, maybe Oglok too. I knew you'd want me to see them safe first before I sorted out a rescue for you."

Aria's angry response choked in her throat. "That's what you knew, was it?"

"Of course. I know you always put other people before yourself. *Noblisse oblige* or whatever it's called. You reckon because you're a princess you have to take care of the whole damn world. It's gutsy and stunning and I admire you for it more than I can say."

Aria felt worse than when Morningstar had slapped her down. "Well, I'm not that good," she admitted. "I kind of wanted a *little* rescue."

Blackthorn nodded. "I'm sorry. You know I'd die to save you, right? Without question."

"Well, maybe *some* questions, according to what you said to Father De'bias."

"Hey, wasn't that just before you ducked the challenge about whether you'd give up everything for me?"

"Give up everything, face my worst nightmare, and be destroyed was what he asked. All for someone who sees me as 'one of his closest friends' but wants to know what I'm really traveling with him for."

"I'd sure like to know why you don't think you could love anyone ever again – except maybe David Morningstar!"

---

[10] This refers to Bobby Nash's "The Minefields of Malador" in *Blackthorn: Thunder on Mars*, which takes place between Aria's search for the Voice of God and the present voyage.

[11] The memory-sapping chasm was described in Danny Wall's bonus story "Into the Canyon of the Night" in *Blackthorn: Thunder on Mars (e-book edition)*.

They glared at each other over the quilt eiderdown. Blackthorn relented. He gestured at the cramped confines of the Vine of Life. "Hey, we came all the way here on your say-so, didn't we?"

"Yes." Aria felt guilty and stupid, and she didn't like it.

Blackthorn sat carefully on the edge of the bed. "As for why I never come on to you, there's a bunch of reasons. Want to hear them?"

"I'm sure I'd be fascinated."

The Earthman snorted. "First off, I don't want you to think you're obligated to me for anything just because I'm fighting in your corner. You don't owe me anything. I'm standing up for Mars because it needs standing up for. It's the right thing."

Aria nodded to concede the point. She remembered that first night, so long ago now, when she'd expected Blackthorn to join her in her tent. She'd been so relived when he'd said good night – hadn't she?

The General went on. "Second, we have to work together. Romantic relationships get in the way of that, cloud decisions, color responses. It's bad discipline. It's forbidden in the service. We're on serious business. No time to fool around."

The princess was pretty sure that the no-sex-while-adventuring rule would eliminate three-quarters of the legends ever written but she held her tongue.

"Third, I'm old enough to be your grandpa, even if I don't remember most of my life and feel like a young wild buck again."

Everybody who was born when I was has been dead for eight hundred years, Aria thought.

Blackthorn risked a hand on her arm. "And last of all, princess, you're a real class act, way out of my league. I reckon when you go with a guy that's it, you're in for the long haul. You'll fall big time, heart and soul."

"Perhaps," said Aria neutrally, admitting nothing.

The Earthman shook his head. "Now there's a good chance I won't be alive a month from now, maybe not tomorrow. Even if you had any interest in me it'd be real dumb of you to let yourself give in to it."

"Yes. Dumb."

He patted Aria's hand. "Anyway, you're not interested. You already said back on Albus Island that you don't think of me like that. Right?"

"Right. Those are all very sensible reasons," Aria agreed. "You take that side of the bed, Blackthorn. Goodnight."

The snow fell for three days and three nights, isolating the little village even more, with no way in and no way out. Even so, on the third night a coach arrived at the Vine of Life.

"Impossible!" objected the innkeeper as the sound of hooves echoed outside the front door. "Nothing could pass in this weather!" He scrambled to the leaded-glass windows and tried to peer through the obscuring ice.

A heavy knocking resounded through the inn. The guests in the common room all turned round, suddenly nervous. Blackthorn and Aria looked up from their chess game.

A second set of raps were louder still, threatening to damage the stout elm door. With a desperate glance at his wife, the innkeeper reluctantly went to answer.

A tall thin man in a long snow-spotted black coat and top hat addressed the landlord. "My mistresses seek shelter. May they come in?"

Through the partially-open door Aria glimpsed a black coach with silver highlights and rich red livery. Midnight horses stamped in the snow.

"We… we are full," the innkeeper stammered.

"Look at the crest on the carriage," the tall man warned. "Will you deny my mistresses entry?"

The innkeeper swallowed hard. "I am a simple man…"

"May they enter?"

The innkeeper trembled and nodded, defeated. "Yes - may they have mercy - yes."

The tall man pushed the door wide so that three cloaked ladies could pass into the common room. They seemed to glide rather than walk. Grey hoods covered their faces. Everybody present sat utterly silent as the women occupied the inn.

Aria and Blackthorn exchanged alert looks.

The ladies looked around the country inn, at the stranded travelers, the faded décor, the hearth-fire that was grown suddenly cold. One of the woman crooked a silk-gloved finger to the young barmaid. The girl walked across to her as though drawn on a leash. "Pretty," the stranger said.

The landlady took a step forward as if to intervene but jerked up short as the hooded women glanced at her.

"Do you know who we are, pretty?" the first lady asked the barmaid.

"Yes, mistress."

"Say it."

"You are Brides of the Sorcerer. The Brides of Night."

"And who are you?"

The barmaid's eyes were frightened but her voice was calm. "I am yours, mistress."

"Yes."

Aria snapped out of the lethargy that had come upon her and Blackthorn as it had everyone in the chamber. "Alright, that's enough! Leave her alone!"

The Brides turned in unison on the princess. One of them pulled back her hood to reveal her lovely flaxen hair. "Why hello, Aria," said Nepenthe of Scamander.

"Hello, Nepenthe. I'm *so* sorry."

The cold lovely lady with Nepenthe's face tilted her head a little. "Sorry? Not yet, Aria." She glided towards the princess. "I do not know how you come to be here at this lonely crossroads; but now you have come there is no turning back."

Nepenthe reached out to brush Aria's cheek. Blackthorn caught the Bride's wrist and held it firm. "Hold it there, lady. The princess is with me!"

The cold numbed his fingers to the bone.

The first of the Brides glided in too. "Is she?" the lady questioned. "With you? I can scent an innocence that says not. I smell confusion and guilt and shame and passion. Such delicious odors. I cannot wait to taste."

Aria summoned up magics. Her hands began to crackle.

"Don't," asked Nepenthe, staring into Aria's eyes. The arcane conjuring faded away again."

Blackthorn still gripped the bride's wrist, though his own hand was numb and dead now. "Back off, Vampirella!" he warned.

The inn door swung open again. Oglok's huge bulk filled the space. His growl rumbled round the common room.

"Last warning, ladies," Blackthorn told the Brides. "There's no easy prey here."

The third Bride swung round to the snarling Mock-Man. "But there is," she contradicted the General. "This poor creature is entirely defenseless. Can you not smell his pain? How exquisite it will be to drink it down."

Oglok managed two leaps towards her then fell trembling on the floor, huddling and whining.

"What pain?" demanded Blackthorn. "Oglok?"

"Why, the loss of his kin," the Bride replied. "His whole family unit taken. How could you travel with him so long and *not know?*"

"We talk all the time," Blackthorn objected. "He never said anything!"

"Perhaps you never asked. Perhaps he never trusted you."

"Some things are too terrible to speak of," Nepenthe confided to Aria. "Those taste the best of all."

The first Bride held out her palm to the quivering Oglok and sniffed the air. "Oh, I perceive it now. His whole family raided by slavers, sold in bondage to the Lord of Fatal Laughter for the furnaces of Cryse. And him away on some foolish errand he thought important, so he was not taken with them. How willingly he would have accepted the chains only to be with his kin! And his tribe, unwilling to hear his arguments for resistance and revenge, had no pleasure in him after."

"He bleeds from his heart," the third Bride whispered, "and you never saw. Thus now he is ours."

The Mock-Man whined again and shuffled up to her. He knelt, shoulders slumped, swaying, defeated.

"We should have known!" agreed Aria. "Now we do, so we'll do something about it. We're his friends. We look out for each other."

"As Blackthorn did when you were taken by Fatal Laughter?" asked Nepenthe. "Or as you did when you abandoned him to partner Morningstar to gain the Voice of God?"

They can see our thoughts, Aria realized. *They can read our hurts and our shames.*

"You will taste very good," Nepenthe told her former mistress. "Perhaps the Sorcerer of Night will permit you to join our sacred sisterhood?"

Blackthorn tried to release the bride's wrist but his hand was locked tight. "We do stand by each other!" he gasped through gritted teeth. "You can look into minds? Okay then. Do it! See why we're here!"

Nepenthe's milky eyes turned on Aria again. Her serene expression faltered. "You... you came to find me!" she perceived. "Aria came to try and save me, and the barbarian and the Mock-Man came to aid her!"

"We did," agreed Aria. "I'm so sorry we were too late."

"And I'm sorry we didn't figure what had happened to you, buddy," Blackthorn told Oglok. "We've got so used to you being there, tough and dependable, that we never looked any deeper. But listen, we're here for you."

"Too late," echoed the First Bride.

But Oglok made a tiny noise in his throat and forced his head up just a fraction.

"No," declared Aria. "Just in time." She opened her hands and the arcane power that was her birthright welled out in bright lightning crackles. It pulsed through the three ladies, pushing them away shaking and spasming. Their spell was broken.

The gaunt black-coated coachman snarled and leaped for the princess. Oglok caught him in mid-spring and brought him down. The man morphed into something worse, part-spider, part-wolf, and tore at the Mock-Man. Oglok leaned in and bit out the creature's throat.

Blackthorn pulled the Sword of Light. He thumbed its simplest button, the white one that emitted pure illumination. The shadowed inn was suddenly lit like brightest day. The Brides screamed.

Aria hurled an arcane bolt that punched right into the First Bride. When the princess jerked her fist back, the grey lady's heart was ripped from her chest. The Bride disintegrated into rags and cobwebs.

Oglok came at the third Bride, the one that had beguiled him, hurt him, shamed him. Massive claws tore at her, rending her undead flesh. In shadow he would have passed right through her. In the radiance of the Sword of Light her defenses were gone.

That left Nepenthe, cowering in the brilliance, last of the travelers from the black coach. "Aria," she pleaded, "I never meant to wrong you."

"Nor I you," the princess confessed. "Halifax will pay for his deeds, and the Black Sorcerer after him."

Nepenthe blinked in the brightness. Tears glistened on her cheeks. "Finish me, highness," she pleaded. "While I am myself again for an instant, let it end."

"Be at peace," said Aria, weeping too, and ended her.

Fifteen weeks after:

The heat from the furnaces was intense. The air shimmered.

The icefields of Utopia and the humid swamps of Secunda Prevura[12] were a distant memory. They seemed like terrestrial paradises compared to this red burning inferno.

Blackthorn stood on a high internal ledge and looked down on the Forges of Cryse. The first cavern was the smallest and it had room for a sixty-foot-wide crucible winched by giant gears over a natural lava vent. Beyond that the smelting and fractioning rooms were larger still. Smithies and workshops ranged off into the heat haze.

As well as the fumes the deafening noise made standing even this close to the Forges uncomfortable. Above the roar of the lava channels was the grinding of rusty machinery, the turning of antique cogs, the hiss of molten metal into pig moulds, the clattering of countless hammers on cherry-red steel – and the crack of whips on the backs of the slaves that toiled along the rickety walkways between the mighty industrial machines.

"This is hell!" gasped Aria, gazing down at the sweltering naked captives who toiled under the lash. Their warders had been human once, but now most of their main organs and limbs had been replaced with clunky machine parts. Unlike the elegant ticktockmen who served the Black Sorcerer these cyborg tyrants were chaotic tangles of wires and tubes, each different from the last.

"These are the Forges of Cryse," Edar Reith told them. "This goes on, every day, every night, without cease, without respite. Slaves work eight hours, rest four, then work again until the die. Average lifespan of a prisoner here is seven weeks. Their corpses are tossed in the vats."

A cloud of steam burst up from one of the cooling troughs, filling the whole cave with fumes.

"Try not to breathe," Reith went on. "There's copper, lead, arsenic, mercury. If people didn't die of exhaustion and dehydration then they'd be poisoned anyway."

Oglok's strangled cry of fury was drowned by the machines. This was where his kin had come, months before he ever met Blackthorn. The chances of even a Mock-Man surviving that long were slim to none.

Blackthorn studied the processes, trying to work out what each step of each production line did. Crude ores were chuted in from mines and supply dumps above. The raw materials were refined through five or six stages to create a purer product, then admixed as required for the project of the day. The wretches who worked the mine tunnels were little better than the foundry slaves, emaciated,

---

[12] Blackthorn's exploits in Secunda Prevura are chronicled by Sean Taylor in "City of Relics" in *Blackthorn: Thunder on Mars*.

half-blind and desperate. Quota shortfalls were punished with amputations.

"This is the Sorcerer of Fatal Laughter's arsenal," Reith supplied. "There are other centers, of course, but the Foundries of Cryse are larger than everything else on the planet put together, excluding maybe a couple of Lord Ruin's industrial gaols. In one day this place can turn out three hundred laugh-track medium combat vehicles, five thousand roboclowns, thirty thousand homing gigglers. And half the swords, guns, bombs, and warbots on the planet get exported from here."

"Wait a moment!" Aria objected. "Fatal Laughter sells weapons to the other First Men so they can fight him?"

"Oh sure. Sanity's not big on his to-do list. As far as he's concerned, war is fun." The bald black man spat. His spittle sizzled on the rock and evaporated.

Oglok described in explicit detail what the Lord of Fatal Laughter should do to himself. The growling language of the Mock-Men could be very graphic.

"This isn't only a production center, of course," Reith went on. "A major strategic asset like this is a prime target, so its extremely well defended. Drones, sonics, energy fields, smart mines, you name it. Its surface to air cannons could blow an armada out of the skies. There's even robot splatterpillars deep underground to prevent burrowing attacks. And the whole thing's linked via a web of half-sentient computers. Don't even *think* about trying to hack those." He gestured to the vast forge-caves and the mines beyond. "This place could defend itself without a single soldier – but Fatal Laughter's got about twenty thousand of them here anyway."

Aria winced. "This would be quite a power base, though, if it were captured. Enough to kick-start a revolution, do you think?"

"Not my department. Ask your wonder-general. But since it can't be captured it's really pointless to speculate."

Blackthorn took no part in the conversation, Aria noticed. He just stared down at the cavern and at the endless conveyor belts.

The princess spoke quietly, right in his ear. "What are you thinking?"

"I'm thinking that Reith was right. We're crazy to come here. But it's for Oglok, right?"

"Yes. He's been there for us. It's really his revolution as much as ours." Aria remembered those visions of potential rebel leaders that had ripped through her mind in the Hall of Reflections. One of them had been a Mock-Man, and now she thought she knew which. "I admit though, I'm at a loss as to how we can put a dent in this operation."

Blackthorn used his binoculars to examine the distant ledges where the smiths worked at their anvils and the technicians at their desks. All were shackled to their benches by thick iron leg-chains. It was clear that even the specialists too valuable to be allowed to starve, parch, or cook did not serve here voluntarily.

"We do have a problem," he told Aria. "It's this: Now that I've seen what's happening here I'm not going to stop until this place is shut down for good. I want everyone rescued and the bastards behind this destroyed."

"John, think. If we *held* this place, if we had access to the machines and weapons this forge can turn out…"

"This slave-labor powered hell-hole of a forge?"

"This significant fortress with the firepower to hold off a floating war city," the princess argued.

Blackthorn turned to her. "Aria, it's an abomination. I'm going to see it gone. Are you with me?"

Aria looked down into the blistering heat. Men toiled in agony down there, forced to feed the very war machine that enslaved their kind. "I'm with you," she said. "I am starting to learn that the smart thing is not always the right thing. It turns out that we are fighting this revolution based on right not smart." *Of course, that means we die horribly on the moral high ground.*

"You wanted to see this," Reith said, unaware of the private conversation. "You've seen it. Now let's get out of here. I told you it was dangerous creeping in this far. Only a matter of time before the Jokers or the Chucklehounds detect us. I don't know 'bout you folks, but I'd prefer not to end my days down there on that treadmill."

Oglok made a complicated sound something between a cry and a snarl. Aria's heart went out to him.

Blackthorn took a last look and turned away. "Okay, Reith, you came through and got us in. Now we need out again, but only to get some preparations laid. You're going to have to work the Runners like they've never worked before."

"Who made you the boss of me and the runners?" Reith demanded.

Blackthorn jerked his thumb at Aria. "Her. So listen up. You've seen what we can do. We chased off the Black Sorcerer. We freed Lord Ruin's slaves in Hades. We've even taken out three of the Brides of Night. We have seriously pissed three of the four First Men and we want to go for the set. Are you going to help us?"

Reith stared at the General. "You're one screwed up soldier, you know that?"

"Is that a yes?"

Reith snorted. "What did you have in mind... boss?"

Four weeks after that:

A hundred candles lighted the top floor of an abandoned watchtower on the shore of the Xanthe Sea. Soft petals had been sprinkled over a four-poster bed. A carafe of mellowed Isidian white was opened to breathe in a bucket of ice.

Morningstar lay back on satin pillows and stretched his naked frame. "Come on, honey," he called out. "Come to me and I'll make you forget all about John Blackthorn."

He smiled as he saw the feminine silhouette move behind the gauze curtain. Princess Aria pushed it aside with a rattling of beads. "Here I am, David," she said.

Morningstar's eyebrows rose a little. "You're not the date I was expecting," he admitted.

"Paula?" asked Aria dismissively. "She went to sleep." It was probably something to do with the arcane discharge the princess had released through the former Eternal Light of Secunda Prevura.[13]. It had felt very satisfying.

"Did she now?" The Colonel stretched further, not bothering to cover his body. "And you thought you might jump in?"

Aria tossed him a sphere the size of a golf ball. He caught it by reflex.

"You might want to hold on to that carefully," the princess advised the Colonel. "It's a souvenir all the way from the Forges of Cryse. They call it a tactile neural shredder. It's fine as long as you grip it, but if you let go it burns out your central nervous system."

"What?" snapped Morningstar.

Aria looked lower down the Colonel's body. "Not as keen for me to jump in now," she noted. "You have a little problem."

Morningstar held the globe carefully. "What are you here for, Aria? What are you doing, apart from ruining my sex life?"

---

[13] Twenty-third century Earthwoman Paula Winterbourne was reborn on Mars in a beautiful cyborg shell. Her career as a local deity terminated after her encounter with Blackthorn and Aria in "City of Relics".

"Because you were in no way romancing poor Paula to try and learn what secrets she'd gleaned over all those years ruling the serpent-folk of Secunda Prevura."

"And if I was? Besides, she's a spanking hot piece of very lifelike android who's not had a date for several centuries. But now you've gone and spoiled the mood."

Aria smiled sympathetically. "The shredder's just insurance, David. Call it leveling the field. You have your localized magic-inhibitor, I have my localized physical-inhibitor. If you do something I don't like I can trigger the neural shredding remotely, by the way."

"So now you've got me, princess, do you intend to have your way with me?"

"In a sense, yes. I've been thinking about our last conversation. The part before you quite literally dumped me."

"Sorry about that. I was a bit upset at the time. Somebody played a bad joke on me."

"Old news. But you pointed out that Blackthorn might have some different ideas and objectives to those I have. And that perhaps I wasn't able to... convince him enough to see things my way."

Morningstar sat up, still nursing the globe. "So you've woken up and smelled the power, have you Aria? What wised you up?"

The princess settled on the edge of the bed and absently ran her fingers over the satin covers. "The Forges of Cryse," she told the Colonel. "You know of them? Of course you do, you're the one who does his research. You were flying around in a hoverbug while Blackthorn was still working out why there were two moons up there."

"Big munitions fortress controlled by the Lord of Fatal Laughter," Morningstar summarized.

Aria nodded. "It's a very powerful stronghold in its own right. It would make a very useful start to an empire. Blackthorn intends to destroy it."

"How?" asked Morningstar.

Aria snorted. "Like I'm going to tell you, David. But he's got a way to neutralize the computers, set them randomly generating gibberish. Those things control everything in the Forges from the steam pressure pipes to the blast doors, from anti-airship batteries to lava chutes – plus about half the guards. If he takes those systems out then he'll grab the fortress before Fatal Laughter can hit the reset button. And then he'll destroy it."

"Madness!" frowned the Colonel. "All that power captured then thrown away?"

"I know, David. That's why I came to you."

"So that we can leap in before he blows the place up and rule in it harmony together?" Morningstar allowed his skepticism to show in his voice and face.

"No. It's a powerful place but I don't think it could last forever against *Fatality* backed by the Lord of Fatal Laughter, or opposing my father's Black Armada, or any First Man's really concentrated force. I have another ploy in mind."

"I'm listening."

Aria leaned forward. "David, I want to go home. I'm tired of trudging round dirty ruins fighting ridiculous monsters for ungrateful peasants. I want a long bath and tinoro leaf tea and a proper bed and feet that don't ache all the time. I want to be allowed back to the Black Sorcerer's Bastion. But for that to happen…"

"You have to get back into your father's good graces," recognized Morningstar.

"And what better way than to give him the Forges of Cryse?"

The cunning Earthman considered the concept. "It might work – assuming the Black Armada swoops in between the time the General brings the defenses down and when he sets the volcanic vents to overload, or however he intends to kill the place. Except… Blackthorn won't fall for that. He's dumb in some ways, but not when it comes to tactics."

"That's why you're going to get me an obedience pack from my father. The wetware implant that hardwires loyalty into its subject? The Black Sorcerer's always wanted Blackthorn as his faithful army commander. Who but me could get close enough at the vital moment to slap a controller on him?"

"You'd do that to him? Really?"

"The alternative would be killing him, and for all his… failings, I'd prefer not to see Blackthorn dead. And wouldn't you *enjoy* having the General obedient to your control, David?" She flicked her eyebrows mischievously. "I know I would."

"It has… possibilities," owned the Colonel. "If you're serious."

"Oh, I am the Princess of Mars, of a line that was old before the First Men were created. I'm deadly serious. My time is come."

"And you really think you can steal the Forges from Fatal Laugher and Blackthorn both and sell them to the Black Sorcerer?"

"I think it's possible," Aria admitted. "I need an intermediary, though, to get assurances from my father. I want amnesty for past actions and a guarantee, his personal word, that I won't be forced into any kind of marriage alliance or be subjected to any kind of obedience programming. I don't want Blackthorn harmed if that's possible, or the Mock-Man Oglok. They could both be useful afterwards. And when this is done I want the Herald Maximal's head on a spike."

Morningstar looked at her. "And that's all you want, is it?" He was suspicious.

Aria's cheeks dimpled as she grinned. "Well, that's all I'll ask for. You should ask for a place in the Black Sorcerer's retinue too. It'll be very useful later."

"Later?"

"It has occurred to me, during all this tedious time trudging around after John Blackthorn, that there's an alternative to raising a rebel army to overthrow the four First Men. That's to command an existing army against the three First Men as the one First Woman."

Morningstar whistled softly. "If anything happened to the Black Sorcerer you are his heiress!" He shook his head admiringly. "You should have run with me from the start, princess. We could've been *magnificent!*"

"We still might be," Aria twinkled. "But sadly for you, not tonight. Maybe you can revive dear Paula? Just get to my father, do the deal, get that obedience wetware installer to me, and tell the Black Sorcerer to have forces ready to enter Cryse two weeks from now. That's all I ask."

"And I don't get an advance payment on account?"

"I'll deactivate the neural shredder as I leave."

Two weeks later:

Aria returned to Blackthorn just as Oglok got back from his own mission. The huge Mock-man was riding an even huger ferocious quadruped with a chitinous hide and a shaggy golden mane. He declined to explain how he'd acquired it on his journey.

"Did you actually manage to get what you were sent to find?" the princess asked him, avoiding the horse-thing's teeth.

Oglok grunted assent and handed over a small linen-wrapped package from D'iurk Crefarn, the Chief Miner of Malador[14].

---

[14] Blackthorn met and befriended Crefarn and the miners guarding the mysterious magic-amplifying 'Light' mineral in "The Mines of Malador".

"Did it work?" Aria asked excitedly. Her fingers examined the packet and told her that her instructions had been carried out. "Oh my!"

Their reunion was by a high pounding waterfall on the eastern edge of Tempe. The nine hundred foot drop brought water from one of the wrecked canals down to the broad Red Canyon River. The caves behind the torrent offered a good place for rebels to assemble.

Aria handed the reins of her tired bay to Judan, one of the earnest young men fired by the burgeoning resistance. He picketed the mare with a dozen other horses, all well away from Oglok's mount. Aria concluded that Blackthorn had several guests.

She passed under the waterfall into the stalactite-filled lime caves beyond. Shielded by the geology, the rebels had installed lighting and power to their forward command base.

"Hello, Elder Ardin," Aria greeted the headman from the village where it had all started. The ageing leader still had scar tissue from the Battle of Anx but he carried his disfigurements with pride. The princess was surprised how pleased she was to see a man who'd treated her as a witch the first time they'd met.

"Greetings, highness. I have come to tell the General that all is in readiness. Provision has been made and villages across Mars stand ready."

"That's good news, Ardin. Thank you, and thank them." Aria's smile faded and became fixed as she saw the next visitor. "Hello, Sihla."

The Not warrioress nodded formally at the sorceress princess. There was little else to say.

"And Chief Nanzak. Recovered from your ordeal in Lord Ruin's combat arena, I trust?"

"Recovered and ready, dear lady. I owe you and Blackthorn more than a little bit of smuggling," the gypsy leader replied. "But since smuggling's what's required, I'm glad to contribute."

Reith was there too, briefing a whole knot of Runners who were huddled round a map-table. He seemed to be giving each of them specific and individual oral instructions. One by one the men and youths – and two women – broke away, retrieved a horse, and galloped off.

When the Runner-Chief looked up for a moment Aria asked him, "Where's John?"

"Out on the high ledge. Brooding."

"I'll go disturb him, then."

"Generally, yes."

Aria filed that oblique comment away for later consideration. She climbed the cut rock staircase to the highest of the lookout points. The view was spectacular over the scarlet river basin and the distant cliffs of Cryse. Blackthorn abandoned his staring contest with the horizon and turned to the princess.

"Aria! You're alright?"

"Yes. Why?"

Blackthorn shrugged awkwardly. "You were gone a while. I thought something might have happened."

"Nothing happened."

"Fine. I just… worried."

"Thank you."

Blackthorn paused. Aria saw the little throat movement that meant he was trying to find a way of saying something. But then he straightened his jacket, turned back to the view, and became more businesslike. "We need to get prepared for the mission. The whole plan depends on you being able to do what's required. We still don't know if everything will come together. A lot of things have to go right."

Aria showed him the packet that Oglok had ridden across half a planet to deliver. "Crefarn returned these," she said to encourage Blackthorn. The jeweled power-stone necklace that she'd taken at Bandusae sparkled in her hand. "I was right! The magical energies under Malador fade away outside that region, but when *that* magic is used to basically pack magic drawn from Mars' *regular* arcane field into these storage crystals then the charge crammed in here holds good anywhere!"

"So you'll get the power boost you'll need?"

Aria fingered the stones. They were warm to the touch. "About a thousand percent, while it lasts. Should be quite a buzz."

"And the spell?"

"I've been practicing. I won't know until I try it for real, but… well, it'll be a really interesting few seconds."

Blackthorn's black mood broke. "*Every* few seconds with you is really interesting, Aria!"

"Why General Blackthorn! Did you accidentally give me a compliment?"

"No, Princess Aria, I did not *accidentally* give you a compliment."

"Reith says you were brooding. And Reith is really good at gathering information."

Blackthorn's half-smile faded again. "I guess he was right. It's guilt. It's taken us six weeks to put this operation together, Aria.

That's pretty much a slave's life expectancy in Cryse. How many innocents have died while we were setting up?" He turned away.

"John, do you remember when I was prisoner aboard *Fatality*? When you chose not to come and rescue me straight off because you needed to get all the priorities sorted? I was so hurt by that at the time, but eventually I saw that it was the proper choice. So is this. We only get one chance at this mission."

"What comfort is that to the slaves stoking the blast furnaces and choking in the volcanic fumes?"

"None. But us dying and getting all our allies killed wouldn't comfort them either. At least this way we maximize the chance of saving the next victims due to be sent to that hell. Concentrate on that."

Blackthorn looked as if he had the entire world upon his shoulders. "You don't give me easy jobs, Princess of Mars."

Aria put her hands round his neck. "I save the very hardest jobs for my champion, John Blackthorn. For my hero."

Blackthorn stiffened. "I thought you didn't care for heroes any more?"

Aria ran her hand over his stubbly cheek. "I care about this one."

Her lips moved in without her permission and kissed him. It was sweet.

The other time I kissed a man I thought heroic he betrayed me and most everyone I cared about, Aria thought.

Blackthorn isn't Halifax, she told herself.

Isn't this a scene from that country morris play?

Nan Vidi was right. Practical experience is essential to understanding.

Shut up. Just enjoy it.

Blackthorn broke away at last. "That was… an innovative way to snap me out of a funk."

"Glad to be of help."

They both hurried away to make their preparations.

One week later:

The splatterpillars were the largest of the Forge's robotic defenders. Sixty feet long, segmented like the lepidoptera they resembled, and bristling with grinding robotic weapons arms, the gaudily-painted machines crawled through the deep service tunnels that honeycombed the caverns of Cryse. They hunted by vibration, sprayed nitric acid at their prey, and were operated by a human brain hanging in a latticework of biofibres.

They also had an internal space just large enough for three intruders to carve out non-essential equipment and conceal themselves inside to ride in secret into the foundry complex.

Blackthorn, Oglok, and Aria ambushed one of the splatterpillars in a fumarole at the Forge's very outer edge, where the ore-filled rock already hampered easy radio transmission and a jamming field could be mistaken for natural interference. Oglok directly charged the massive machine with a pulse lance, knocking aside its forward urticating bristles, jamming the weapon right through the outer skin of the foremost segment. Aria confused its sensors with spurious inputs of dozens of false attacks while Blackthorn carved his Sword of Light through its outer sheath and wormed his way inside towards the computer core.

The splatterpillar sensed internal intrusion and released a horde of clockwork chatterspiders to tear the interloper to shreds. Blackthorn melted them with projected fireballs from his weapon then cut a route straight for the central processor brain.

It's now or never, Aria told herself. She slipped the obedience pack from her bodice and willed it out of dormancy. As Oglok wrestled with the forelegs of the squirming robot she hurled herself into the rent Blackthorn had made and wriggled after him to the splatterpillar's core.

The General was crouched beneath the bloated organic brain that was wired to the splatterpillar's control matrix. His Sword was in laser-knife mode, welding shut the toxic vapor vents that could otherwise flood the compartment with lethal gas. He had his back to her. "Ready?" he asked the princess.

Aria fingered the palm-sized circle imprinted with microcircuits and magic. On direct contact and it would bury its control fibers deep into human flesh, adding tiers of new imperatives that would soon over-ride any personal desires or ethical choices. It was rare technology, reserved only for the most vital of the Black Sorcerer's minions.

"Ready," said Aria, and slammed the coin home – directly onto the gelid brain hanging in the bioweb controlling the splatterpillar.

The robo-beast went mad, rolling over and randomly firing all around it. Oglok dived for cover just in time before it demolished the tunnel roof above and managed to half-bury itself.

And then it fell silent.

"Ouch," said Blackthorn, who'd been tossed around the cramped service cabin while the machine spasmed. "It worked?"

"Ouch back at you," complained Aria. She reached out with her arcane senses. "It worked. Faster than it would on you, because it's gone directly into the cerebellum. If that brain wasn't mad already it soon will be, but it'll do what we tell it for a couple of hours first."

Blackthorn looked at the twice-enslaved brain and shuddered. "And this is what you planned for me?"

"On you it would have been much subtler," Aria promised. "So that's all right, yeah?"

Oglok scrambled in after them. The crowded space got considerably fuller. The Mock-Man showed them the acid-scorched patches of his fur and complained loudly.

"But we did it, big guy," Blackthorn consoled him. "We've got control of this splatterpillar and nobody can tell. We can ride this thing all the way into the Forge's control crucible before anyone knows we're here." He turned to Aria. "Take her forward, princess. Time to liberate Cryse!"

"My my!" shrieked the Lord of Fatal Laughter. His face lit up all the monitor screens inside the captured Splatterpillar and all the external monitors overlooking foundry platform seventy-six. "What's this? Guests? If I'd known I'd have had cream buns ready, and agony jackets!"

Oglok wheezed a terse sound that meant *Busted*.

"I'd have had jelly and balloons!" Fatal Laughter added. "After all, its not every day that the famous General Blackthorn comes to infiltrate my facilities! And beautiful Aria, my, how you've grown! And… whatever that rug thing you've brought with you is. We'd have found some red carpets – or stained some red!"

"Get this thing moving," Blackthorn told the princess. "Forget subtle. Turn on all the armaments it's got and make straight for the control crucible!"

"You're controlling my splatterpillar? Ooh, clever! I just love what you've done with the place!" The First Man's stitched-together face was a bizarre mixture of machinery, mutated flesh, and corpse-pale rot. Every time Aria had seen it he had looked a little different; Fatal Laughter enjoyed redesigning it. His yellowed teeth were crooked in his smiling mouth.

Jokers and Chucklehouds poured out from the side galleries and zip-wired or leaped down from the gantries above. The

Splatterpillar's weapons decimated the first wave but there were plenty more to follow.

"Still going for the goal? That's the spirit, General! Remember the Alamo! Death or glory! Morituri te salutant! Never give in! Never surrender!"

"Does he ever shut up?" Blackthorn asked Aria.

"Not so far, no," replied the princess.

"Oh come on, General! A little banter's expected between arch-enemies. We are arch-enemies, aren't we? Do say it's me, not that tedious Black Sorcerer. What's he got that I haven't? The Lord of Fatal Laughter can speak in the third person too!"

"You're really in the love with the sound of your voice, aren't you, you pathetic murderer," Blackthorn scorned. "I'm going to put you down like the mad dog you are."

"No, nooo," denied the snickering First Man. "Mad Dogs are Lord Ruin's. I think he patented them. And they're sooo last century. And the mess! They piddle everywhere. Give me an incendiary baby any day."

The Splatterpillar dropped from the collapsing deck it was on, down to the gallery below. Oglok groaned as he saw another pair of the huge multi-segmented combat machines moving to flank them.

"How much further?" Blackthorn demanded.

Fatal Laughter answered. "Just over that next bridge, through five inches of sheet steel and a huge army of my elite Joker cyborgs. Or weren't you asking me?"

"What he said," admitted Aria. "We're not going to make it."

"Oh, the drama! The pathos!" gasped the First Man. "Will our handsome hero escape the lethal death-trap that he's walked himself and his brave comrades into? Or will he get eviscerated in a fiery inferno as his compromised war machine is torn to a million pieces around him and all the hopes of a desperate world die with him? Tune in next time for..."

Blackthorn shattered the nearest monitor screen. "I'm getting cramped in here, guys. Shall we step out?" He blew open the side of the machine, hurling a dozen Jokers off the platform to perish in the molten crucibles below. "Oglok, don't forget the gizmo!"

The Mock-Man groaned affirmation and hefted a heavy backpack onto his shoulders before dropping out of the dying war toy after Aria and the General.

"Five feet of solid steel," Aria pointed out to Blackthorn. "Did you factor that in to the plan?"

"I really thought Fatal Laughter would let us get nearer before dropping the boom," the warrior admitted.

"Fatal Laughter?" shrieked the First Man who watched the entertainment from every viewscreen. "Don't be so formal, Johnny. Call me Fatal. We don't stand on ceremony round here, not unless we want our legs chopped off! Or call me Big FL!" He wiggled his nose and the impenetrable sheet-gate that blocked the way to the control center opened up again. "There you go, J-dog! Never let it be said that good 'ol F.L. didn't give his bestest enemy a fair shot at the brass ring!"

Blackthorn cleared a path with another ranged detonation from the Sword of Light. He was burning its energies at a frightening rate but it was his only advantage in this mismatched struggle. Aria risked an arcane discharge onto the metal grill walkway, sending a quartet of chucklehounds into spastic spasms.

Oglok lowered his head and charged like a quarterback straight for the control crucible. Anything in his way went down.

"The big guy's at the fifty yard mark!" Fatal Laughter narrated. "Forty! He takes a laser shot to the leg but keeps on coming! Thirty yards, and he rips the guts out of a gigglepuss and just storms on. Twenty! Ten! Oh, at the last minute the neural interference nets have taken the Mock-Man *down!*"

Blackthorn switched his weapon to laser mode and carved Oglok out of the silver webs that were playing havoc with the beastling's central nervous system. The pain-wracked Mock-Man shambled to his feet and unslung the box from his back. He fumbled a communications jack into a socket and struggled to connect it with the Forge's main control system.

"Oh help!" cried the Lord of Fatal Laughter, his hands at his cheeks in feigned dismay. "Blackthorn's carpet has got to the command interface with his box of whatever-that-is! I'm doomed! Doomed!"

Aria was starting to reconsider her opinion that the Black Sorcerer was the First Man she hated most. "Ignore the pathetic attention-seeking mass murderer," she called to Oglok. "We can hold these monsters off for a minute, tops! Get the device working now!"

Oglok hammered home the connector then slammed his hand down on an activation pad atop the silver box.

Fatal Laughter bounced with glee. "Uh oh! Unforeseen problem ahead! It's almost like someone warned the First Man master of this place that the good guys were coming! It's almost like Colonel Morningstar sold out his allies yet again and left them walking into a big stinking trap! It's almost as if the Lord of Fatal Laughter had time to install a bypass so he could reboot his systems if somebody did this! Wait…! He *has!*"

As the silver box lit up, the entire command center went dark. Even the mocking screens blinked out for a moment as the Lord of Fatal Laughter reset the operating systems of the entire Forges of Cryse.

"At last he shuts up!" spat Blackthorn angrily. "Oglok, haul that useless decoy box out of there! Princess, you're up. Make it count!"

Aria and the General took advantage of the brief downtime many of their enemies endured during system reset and raced into the command crucible. Aria clutched her crystal necklace in one hand and laid her other palm on the dormant machine.

"John," she called. "Kiss me!" She'd not got a hand spare to make contact with him and this seemed as good a way as any.

Blackthorn folded his arms round her and locked his lips to hers. *Contact!*

Aria pressed her arcane-amplified mind into the dormant command systems that laced the vast Forge complex. She'd seen her father do this once with a warcrawler at Anx, watched him possess the machine and become one with it. What she attempted now was levels of magnitude more ambitious.

It wouldn't have worked unless the Lord of Fatal Laughter had shut down his systems for a moment. That was why Blackthorn had risked everything to bluff the First Man into resetting his thinking machines. He'd played the mad tyrant to get Aria to this place at this time to cast this spell.

The whole network of command systems opened up to her, a bewildering array of control choices from industrial processes to weapons hives. She gasped as she *became* the Foundry, then floundered as the vastness of her new domain overwhelmed her.

A tongue flicked over hers. A wild elation burst through her, both flesh princess and twisted labyrinth of circuits and mechanisms. John Blackthorn, General Blackthorn, the champion of Mars, the oh-so-serious military commander of the resistance to the First Men, was *slipping her some tongue!*

He's probably doing it in he cause of Mars, she told herself as she dragged him with her into the possessed systems. *It's probably so we make proper contact for the transfer.*

She twined round him and drew him with her into the machine. She felt Blackthorn spread his thoughts out to inventory the sprawling array of devices connected to the system he now occupied.

Aria's job was to project their minds into Cryse's self-contained command and control systems. Blackthorn's job was to command and control them!

"Got it?" she asked him in the labyrinth of the system.

"Got it," he assured her. "Round two."

Somewhere in real time the Sorcerer of Fatal Laughter was realizing his mistake, understanding that this joke had turned sour. Everything, even Morningstar's inevitable betrayal, had set this moment up!

"Yeah. Shut up," Blackthorn told him and locked him out of the system. Every viewscreen switched to fuzz.

Oglok turned on the remaining guards in the control crucible. His part was to protect the physical forms of the General and the princess while they were in the machines. That had become a lot more feasible now that every computer-assisted defense and remote-operated sub-routine had suddenly stopped supporting Fatal Laughter's minions.

"Get him!" a green and purple-clad cyborg Joker shrieked. "He is only one creature, all that stands between us and triumph!"

Oglok was one furious, vengeful, battle-crazed creature defending his friends against the murderers of his kin. The Mock-Man could finally vent his long-pent fury on Jokers and pain technicians, overseers and chucklehounds.

Blackthorn located the external point defense grids and fired them up again. A Joker deathsquad hurrying up entrance tunnel 622 was the first to know about it – briefly. He twitched on the anti-airship batteries to assure himself of a friendly sky.

"Very impressive, John," admitted Aria. "It's like you've always had this inner industrial center just waiting for expression."

"Honestly, it's not that different from running a brigade. Logistics, deployments, duty orders, tactical overview. Even having had extra knowledge files plugged into this body's brain before helps, because what I'm experiencing now is like the same on an epic scale. I can handle this."

"You're basically a country and you're taking it in your stride. Meanwhile I'm burning off magic like there's no tomorrow to keep this link gong. I won't be able to summon a thaum on my own for weeks after this, assuming I don't burn out and die from holding this link together[15]."

"Just keep doing what you're doing, Aria. I'm powering down the shackles on the prisoners now, and neutralizing as much of the slavers' weaponry as I can do remotely. It'll take a few minutes to reprogram the robots to kill the overseers but I'll get there."

What Blackthorn *was* doing was holding Aria in his arms in the most destructive kiss in history. *I might have thought this one through a bit better, since we intend this possession to go on for around a day*, the princess considered. Still, as ways of defeating planet-oppressing tyrants went, it was not unpleasant.

The perimeter alarms reported in – twice. Aria peered with Blackthorn through the strange extended senses that the Cryse network gave them. "Can you see that?" the General asked her.

"Fatal Laughter bring up an armored column from the south," the princess recognized. "A very large armored column. And the Black Armada from the west, backed by, it looks like about six divisions of the Black Sorcerer's elite legions."

"When Morningstar sells you out he does it properly," Blackthorn scorned. "I hope you were suitably convincing when you went to him." For a moment his consciousness flickered to the intimate flesh embrace they were engaged in. "Not this convincingly," he added.

"I've never smooched Morningstar while controlling a war complex," Aria promised him. "You're definitely my first."

As if to live up to that, Blackthorn started to make things go with a bang. He triggered the emergency destructs at most of the main entrances, burying the guards in tons of debris as he permanently closed those gates. At the same time he opened up six of the smaller emergency tunnels that led out high into the hillside.

"Hello there," he called through one of the monitor screens at hatch 917. "What's the weather like topside?"

Reith's crumpled face stared back into the camera. "You actually *did* it? Sonofabitch! I knew one of us was a crazy fool but I was hoping it wasn't me!"

---

[15] Aria references this debilitation in James Palmer's "Indistinguishable From Magic" in *Blackthorn: Thunder on Mars*, wherein she is still unable to utilise arcane force at that point without the aid of her crystal necklace. She has clearly recovered her prowess by the time she encounters "The Ghosts of Acheron" in I.A. Watson's concluding tale of that volume.

"We're in and we're running things for now. We've got control of the command crucible, most of the internal defenses, and the outer guns. There's still a lot of Fatal Laughter's people running loose in here, but the prisoners are free too. It's your turn."

Sihla's face appeared in the camera lens. "The Nots stand ready, John Blackthorn. Our warriors will enter the complex now and hunt out those minions of the First Man that do not depend upon machines. This is the moment where our Sleeping Army awakes to fight!"

Elder Ardin was there too. "My folks are prepared for the evacuation, General. We've got medical supplies for the slaves, even stretchers for those too wounded to walk. You won't believe how far some of our rescue volunteers have traveled! Everybody who ever lost a loved one to these mines, they've all come to bring these people out. To take them home."

"The Runners are primed," agreed Reith. "Skilled smiths and technicians who can make weapons and machines are like gold in the far villages. We can spirit them away to a thousand hidden forges and workshops where they can live free and make supplies for the revolution. You couldn't possibly hold them all in Cryse, even if you could hang onto the fortress, but distributed in a secret network all across Mars…?"

"Smuggling away experts at making stuff to blow up First Men?" added Nanzak. "We're there."

Aria laughed at the sheer joy of the rescue. "Then get to work, Mister Reith. Get my people out of here!"

"And fast," warned Blackthorn, flexing sensors west and south. "Hell's riding in and by night it'll be here."

Oglok interrupted Blackthorn and Aria's machine communion only once. Not, as Reith suggested, to throw a bucket of water over them, but to plaintively ask for access to the data records for Mock-Men captives admitted to the mines.

Aria unlocked the console and the big fighter painstakingly tapped his way through the information with clawed fingers far too big for the job. She knew he'd found the data he was seeking when he sank to the ground with a mournful wail then howled a full-throated roar up to the heavens.

Maybe if we'd been quicker coming here, the princess blamed herself, *we might have saved them. And thousands like them. But you led Blackthorn off seeking the Voice of God and the Light of*

Malador and Father De'bias and every other shiny thing you thought could save your pathetic hide. What does that make you, Aria?

Changed, she hoped.

Blackthorn had clearly been monitoring the Mock-Man's search too. "I'm sorry, my friend," he said from one of the viewscreens; his actual mouth was still occupied. "I wish I could think of something to say that would help with the hurt."

Aria flashed her mind through more of the data-screed. She pushed her image into the monitor with Blackthorn. "Your kin may not have survived this place but there are other Mock-Men that still live," she reported. "Down in Galleries 17 and 41, in some of the worst, most dangerous sections of the tunnels. They're weak and wounded, and they won't let any humans near enough to their downed kin to be able to help. They're going to die."

Oglok looked up. His hairy face crumpled into a determined glower. He growled the Mock-Man equivalent of 'I'll be back' and loped away, dropping from gallery to gallery with amazing dexterity.

"That was well done, Aria," Blackthorn approved.

"A day like today we need all the grace we can find," the princess replied.

And grace there was, amongst the hurt and horror and suffering. Even as Sihla's freedom fighters cleared out the remaining slavers in bloody running battles along the lower tunnels and automated defense systems turned Fatal Laughter's sacrificial vanguard to shredded meat, common people of Mars carried tortured captives away into the light and helped long-chained slaves stagger out to freedom.

This is not my revolution. It is theirs! Aria exalted. *And it is not fought only with the harsh weapons of the Forges of Cryse but with the overflowing hearts of the everyday folk of Mars. Whatever happens now I am proud of them.*

She was the Princess of Mars. Mars did not belong to her. She belonged to it.

"Colonel Morningstar to Princess Aria. Is that you that's running the whole damn Forges of Cryse by remote control?"

The message came over the radio, distorted and faded by the usual omnipresent Martian static. Sensors located the source as a fast-moving Black Airship running ahead of the fleet, straight for Aria's position.

"Here I am, David. I told you Blackthorn had a way of taking down the system. But someone leaked everything to the Lord of Fatal Laughter."

Morningstar was unrepentant. "Well sure. I needed insurance that you wouldn't cut me out at the last minute. With Laughing Boy and his mad clowns battering on your doors you can't afford to go solo. You need the Black Sorcerer's reinforcements to avoid an unpleasant visit to Fatal Laughter's Toyroom of Delights."

"So you betrayed Blackthorn to the Black Sorcerer, then me to Fatal Laughter, then Fatal Laughter to the Black Sorcerer? Can't you ever walk in a simple straight line?"

"Where's the fun in that, honey? Anyway, I'm coming in. Open an envelope in your aerial shield to let me through. I should mention that I've got Nan Vidi and the Sensorine Malathea aboard too, just in case you decide it would be a good idea to blow me out of the sky."

"Probably wise to mention it, yes," Aria admitted. "Very smart, David."

"Open up a landing bay. I'll be with you in an hour. Loosen your panties."

Aria cut the connection.

"*This* time I kill him," Blackthorn snarled.

Aria switched her consciousness to the cameras recording the Black Airship's descent to the caverns of Cryse. She was hoping for a glimpse of Nan and Malathea to divert her from the growing discomfort of maintaining the mass-possession spell. She knew the pain would get much worse as time went on.

The long dirigible made a vertical landing into the docking port. Steam pistons hissed overhead, vented clouds of vapor, then pushed the reinforced steel roof back into place to shield the airship from the escalating aerial conflict above. The Sorcerer of Fatal Laughter had sent his Ho-Ho-Harpies to test the automated anti-aircraft defenses.

Liveried sailors made fast the war-balloon to the mooring posts. Colonel Morningstar strode onto the deck. And beside him…

"Halifax!" Aria recognized. Her exclamation echoed from the speaker horns all around the hangar. She hadn't intended that.

"Hello, darling," the Prime Herald called out. An irritating smirk covered his face. How had the princess ever found that attractive? "I hear you want my head now. It's a start."

"Morningstar can't keep a confidence to save his life," Aria objected. "Why are you here, instead of on a pike somewhere?"

"We can't all have everything we want," Halifax pointed out. "Only me."

Armed lizard-men escorted Nan Vidi and Malathea onto the hurricane deck – unnecessarily since both of them would have come willingly. "We brought some folks to talk with you," the Herald pointed out. "And to make sure you keep your end of the bargain."

"The guns were his idea," Morningstar added. "I have more class."

Malathea looked up at the chamber, her milky eyes flickering with static. "The Princess Aria is currently tele-bonded with the entire complex system," she reported. "A class-one inorganic possession crafting very similar to the one the Black Sorcerer developed, but cast on a massive scale. She is necessarily augmenting her abilities with an external power source, but I am not able to determine how any storage crystals could be so massively overcharged as to support such an energy expenditure. I'm picking up discharge costs in excess of one terrathaum per second, that…"

"Yes, yes," interrupted Nan Vidi. "Aria's always been a clever little thing. Haven't you lovie? Now are you going to listen to your old Nan?"

"I'm monitoring the whole room, Nan," Aria confessed. "Say what you want."

"The Black Sorcerer is pleased that you want to give up that foolishness with the barbarian soldier and come back to the Bastion. He's impressed that you are able to achieve this and that you were willing to obedience-lock that Blackthorn warrior. He's willing to forgive you your trespasses and meet your demands."

"Except for my head," added Herald Maximal with a smirk. "Some other bits of me are available to you for the asking."

"I got you your deal, Aria," Morningstar pointed out, "and the rest of what we talked about… that still stands too, if you want it." He eyed Halifax with a rival's dislike.

"Open the blast door seals," the Herald commanded. "We need to take this complex quickly before the Lord of Fatal Laughter realizes we're coming in."

"Yeah, about that…" Aria began.

"Open the seals or I start to cut bits off your old nursie, Aria," Halifax threatened more pointedly. "I'm not allowed to kill her, of course, but I can make sure she suffers quite a lot before she gets a new body."

Malathea looked up sharply. "There is a second presence in the control system!" she sensed.

"Yes," agreed the second presence. "That would be me."

Morningstar's head jerked up. "Blackthorn!"

"He's not neutralized!" Halifax realized.

"Well spotted, knuckleheads. And it's not Princess Aria in actual charge of the systems right now. It's me!"

"Aria betrayed me!" Morningstar declared. "*Aria* betrayed *me!* Hah!"

"Step down and turn the Forges over to the Black Sorcerer, General Blackthorn," warned Halifax. "Otherwise very bad things happen to this dear old Neanderthal lady."

"So what?" asked Blackthorn. "She's nothing to me. And I have to balance you threatening the life of one of the Black Sorcerer's minions with the thousands who'll suffer if I hand this site over and the millions who'll regret it for centuries to come. Do the math."

The Prime Herald looked as if he'd just walked into a post.

"Now I'm pretty busy right now," Blackthorn told the people in the landing bay. "So here's the deal. You sit still and don't do anything – I mean anything – while I get on with fighting a war. The walls are blast resistant solid rock, so if you fire your ship's weapons it'll only reflect back on you. And if you try and escape there's some really nasty gas canisters I can trigger into your air supply. I think they're one of Fatal Laughter's flesh-eating toxins but who knows for sure? So sit tight, don't annoy me, and we'll talk again when I can be bothered with you, okay?"

Aria waited until the speakers were silenced to ask Blackthorn, "You wouldn't really harm Nan, would you? She serves the Black Sorcerer but I don't want her hurt."

"But they don't know that," the General replied. "Let's hope my threats keep Morningstar's ingenuity stymied and hold back Herald-boy's nastier urges for a while."

"Did you see David's face?" the princess ventured.

"Yeah. He seemed to think you might… team up. That maybe he'd have a chance with you. Would he?"

"Maybe once. Before I knew what I needed." Aria giggled despite the growing pain. The agony in her limbs was strangely at odds with the tingling contact her lips were making. "What do you think David and Halifax would do if they knew exactly how I'm teamed up with you right now?"

With no further communication from Prime Herald Maximal, the Black Armada advanced in combat formation. Aria and Blackthorn watched them move into range of the perimeter defenses.

"Looks like your deal is off, princess," Blackthorn pointed out. He cycled in the ground to air cannons and began to fire. Suddenly the western skies were a battlefield.

"I wasn't even tempted," Aria revealed. "My mother forged me into a weapon when I was a child. She showed me things that would set me against the Black Sorcerer forever. I would never return to him."

"Good to know."

"Good for me to know too."

She felt Blackthorn flinch. "The Black Airships are bringing their black matter arsenal to bear," he reported. "The outer perimeter won't hold much longer."

"The evacuation's nothing like finished!" Reith warned as he paced the command crucible and co-ordinated resistance units. "It'll be hours yet. Nightfall at least."

"You'll have to be ruthless," Blackthorn told him. "We just don't have that long. Triage. Those who can't get out, offer to ease their passing."

A near blast shook the roof of the great cavern beyond. A gantry toppled and smashed down into one of the vast smelting pots.

"Fatal Laughter's made it as far as the southern ridge," Blackthorn reported. "From there his heavy warbots can push a way into the outer sections."

"But you're going to do something clever, right?" Aria checked.

"I'm weakening our defenses to the south-west. Fatal Laughter can push in faster and further that way, and so can the Black Sorcerer."

"Until they bump into each other," recognized Reith. "Nice."

"The Black Sorcerer must be wondering by now why I've not debilitated the General and dropped the defenses for the Black Armada," Aria noted. "He committed his attack the second that Fatal Lightning powered down Cryse for a reboot - but then everything came back on."

"I hope he's blaming Morningstar," Blackthorn answered. He frowned and concentrated. "The Black Sorcerer's ground forces are penetrating faster and further than I anticipated. Whoever he's got doing my job there knows his business."

He peeled off a pair of monitor drones to survey the battlefield. In the seconds before they were destroyed he got one clear snapshot of the enemy commander.

"Yuei?!"

Aria studied the image. "He's wearing the uniform of an imperial general, like yours. And that *seal?* He's been made a Kan, a First Man's warrior-prince. It means that energy axe he's thrashing our defense-bots with draws directly upon the power of the Black Sorcerer himself."

"Anton didn't want anything to do with either side," Blackthorn objected.

"Looks like the Black Sorcerer's obedience implants have convinced him otherwise."

"He's what you were intended to be, General," Reith commented. "And every bit as deadly."

"That remains to be seen," Blackthorn snarled.

Another explosion rocked the control crucible.

Aria ignored the growing pain in her nerves and continued pushing Blackthorn into the systems around them. *For my mother and the Knights of Daedal*, she rehearsed in her head. *For Coda, for Dane, for Corrigan. For Nepenthe and Eelia. For Oglok's kin and Coda's brothers and the Not's fallen. For the victims of Cryse. I will not forget you and I will not fail.*

She repeated the mantra again and again as the effort got harder. The overcharged power crystals seared her hand. She could no longer feel Blackthorn's body pressed to hers; only the agony of magic.

For Mars, she told herself.

For John.

"Okay, that's it!" Blackthorn called at last. "We're done here. Time's up. Get your people away, Reith. Tell Sihla to bug out any way she can. Have Ardin and Nanzak get everybody out on the mountainside under cover."

It was midnight and the bombardment was constant. Cryse's air screen was gone and a battle for aerial dominance between the Black Sorcerer and the Lord of Fatal Laughter raged. General Yuei had breached all but the innermost perimeter around the forges. The lower workshops were already under his control. Splatterpillars and rock grinders had burrowed into the mines and would soon break the seals into the main caves.

"We could use a few more minutes, maybe half an hour," Reith suggested.

"We don't have 'em. I'm getting some sketchy new readings from what's left of our surveillance capability. A new column to the southeast closing fast with some huge power signatures that might be Lord Ruin's fast-attack fleet. And a power drain on the easternmost sensors that could be the Sorcerer of Night on the move. *Everybody's coming to the party.*"

Aria didn't say anything. She was locked in her personal agony, oblivious even to Blackthorn supporting her limp twitching frame.

Oglok roared warning that everyone else could evacuate but the last people in the command crucible would be cut off as soon as they tried to leave. He was willing to stay behind and hold off pursuit while Blackthorn and Aria tried to get away.

"Thanks, buddy," Blackthorn told him, "but let's try something else." The General shot off a last few orders through the remarkable network to which he'd been connected then pushed himself out of it back to that tiny mortal body. He jerked his head away from Aria and cradled the slumped girl in his arms. "The job's done, princess. You can let go."

Aria's snapped back to her flesh. Her eyes shot open. She gasped for breath and clung to Blackthorn as if she were drowning and he a rock.

The Earthman stroked her sweat-matted hair. "It's okay, Aria. You did it. It's over." He popped a field dressing out of one of his belt-pouches and wrapped it round the burned flesh where Aria had held the power crystals. The shimmering gems were dull and lifeless again now. Blackthorn didn't ask when they had tapped out or how long Aria had been using her own personal energies and sheer willpower to sustain him.

She managed to focus on the warrior holding her in his arms. "How did I do?" she croaked. "S'only my fifth time kissing a man. Nan says I'll get better with practice."

Blackthorn grinned. "Aria, if you get any better at that they're going to have to discover whole new planets to detonate!"

Reith was gone. Only Oglok remained in the control center with Blackthorn and Aria.

"Are you ready for the last toss of the dice?" Blackthorn asked.

"No," the princess replied. "Let's do it."

The gas that Blackthorn had released into the Black Airship's docking bay wasn't the Lord of Fatal Laughter's airborne necrosis. He'd instead selected a simple odorless pacification toxin; the prankster First Man often preferred his enemies captured alive so he could be creative. When Oglok hand-cranked the blast door open enough to squirm under it, the whole crew of the moored dirigible lay slumped on the ground.

Blackthorn gestured for Oglok to release the pressure valve that would spring open the roof doors so the ship could fly. The whole point of letting an airship land here was to have a viable getaway.

Colonel Morningstar lay near the pilot's station, slumped over the body of the crewman he'd killed for his gas mask. It hadn't helped; Blackthorn had made sure to use a toxin that worked on skin contact. Aria noticed Blackthorn twitch as the urge to pull the Sword of Light and end the helpless traitor almost overwhelmed him; but he would not murder an unarmed, unconscious man, even this one.

Aria climbed up behind the General. "I've nothing left, John," she warned him. "I can't possess this vehicle and get us out of here."

"Then we do it the old-fashioned way," Blackthorn replied. "There's thaumic energy in the envelope and power in the ailerons and vents. Plenty to get us out of this mountain before Fatal Laugher or General Yuei gets here." He moved to the main steering column and jammed home the lever to power the struts.

Nothing happened.

Oglok hauled himself aboard, honking dismay that the last part of the mission had hit a serious snag.

"What now?" Aria demanded. "It landed just fine."

Blackthorn ripped off the column cover and looked at the mechanism. "The main converter coupling's gone," he said, frowning. "How…?"

A disruptor-whip caught Oglok round the neck and pulsed enough energy into the Mock-Man to kill an elephant. The beastling went down hard. He crashed off the bridge and tumbled to the lower deck, then toppled off the ship entirely to slam down on the hangar floor.

Aria and Blackthorn whirled round to see the grinning Herald Maximal discarding his lash and drawing his pain wand.

"You didn't think a Prime Herald would be susceptible to simple aerial toxins, did you?" Halifax jeered. "I can survive in absolute vacuum if I have to. I'm very hard to kill."

"I'd like to test that," declared Blackthorn. He switched the Sword of Light to actual sword mode and rounded to face the Herald.

"I'm sure you would, barbarian. But this is a more sophisticated world, and your kind of conflict is rather passé." Halifax looked over to the princess. "Aria, draw your knife."

Against her will, Aria's hand went to the blade strapped at her shoulder and pulled it loose.

"If I don't say otherwise, carve your eyes out in thirty seconds time," the Herald ordered her.

Aria realized that she was going to do it. *He has my command programming over-ride!* she realized with horror. *My father has given me to the Prime Herald!*

"I'm sorry, John," she told Blackthorn. "He's got me. I have to do it."

"The obedience conditioning!" the General gasped.

"Turn that Sword of Light off, kick it over here, and kneel down," Halifax told him, "and I'll allow her to stop."

"John, don't!" Aria gasped. Her treacherous hand positioned the dagger point an inch from her cornea.

Blackthorn flicked off his weapon, skidded it over to the Herald, and knelt.

"Very good. Aria, don't move now. But do watch. I want you to see this."

"What, see that you're too scared to face me like a man?" sneered Blackthorn. "Stop hiding behind hostages, Maximal. Dare to face me!"

Halifax pretended to consider it. "No," he decided. "This is much more satisfying." He pointed to Aria. "She's utterly mine, now. She'll do anything I say. Can you imagine how much fun that will be? And if you don't do exactly what I say too, General, then I'll make her do things to herself that aren't very nice."

"I'm going to kill you," promised Blackthorn.

"You keep saying so. You're really not." He picked up the Sword of Light and pushed a button. Nothing happened.

"You're not worthy of it," Aria told him.

Halifax shrugged. "Oh well. By the way, Aria darling, if any harm should befall me, I command you to kill yourself instantly. That'll make your mighty hero think twice about jumping me. Whether I'm hurt, unconscious or dead, you die. Clear?"

"Yes."

He reached into the steering column and replaced the unit he'd removed before. Power returned to the airship. Halifax nudged it upwards. As the dirigible began to rise he produced a small gaudily-decorated cube and threw it to Blackthorn. "Open it."

Aria watched as her champion flipped the catch aside. The top popped back and something leaped out! It jerked and bounced and wobbled from side to side, giggling: a jack-in-the-box.

A jack-in-the-box with the head of the Lord of Fatal Laughter!

"Hellooo again, Earthman and the lovely Aria!" the tiny representation of the mad First Man greeted them. "Surprise!"

"You work for the Black Sorcerer!" Aria objected to Halifax. "You're his herald!"

"Turns out that obedience wetware can be repurposed after all," her first love shrugged. "The Black Sorcerer overlooked me and made a Kan General of his new Earth-toy Yuan. A mere barbarian got all that power, and I got left on the side. So I took a better offer. The Lord of Fatal Laughter will make me immortal."

"There's an entrance fee, of course," the jack-in-the-box crowed. "Noir's favorite Neanderthal and another delicious Sensorine. And the Sword of Light. And of course the beautiful Princess Aria. That should take care of the cover charge. Thwarting the Black Sorcerer's pitiful attempt to grab my Forge is just jam on the cake. Mmmm – cake!"

The airship rose through the exit hatch into open sky. Flares and detonations in the middle distance showed that the First Men's forces had finally met up close.

Blackthorn glared at Halifax with contempt. "Just another turncoat!" he sneered.

"Oh, not *just* another one," the Herald promised. "After all, I get a promotion, and revenge, and power… and I get the girl. Yay me!"

"No!" gasped Aria. Her worst nightmares were coming true, one by one.

"Yes," gloated Halifax. He spoke to the jack-in-the-box. "I'm bringing them to you now, master, and I'm leaving the hangar doors open. You can bring men in that way and easily retake the control crucible, then use the fortress systems to wipe out the Black Sorcerer's legions to the last man."

"Oh goodie!" applauded Fatal Laughter. "They can retrieve that Mock-Man for me as well. I want a throw rug!"

Halifax carefully closed up the jack-in-the-box again and put it away. "I'm sure the First Men would like you too, Blackthorn. But I can't afford to give you to them. You might just end up getting rebuilt into some useful minion who'd end up competing for my pre-eminence. So I'll do you a favor."

"I doubt it," Blackthorn snarled.

Halifax tossed the confiscated Hallow cylinder he'd back to its owner. "Put your magic sword through your chest in the next thirty seconds, Blackthorn. Keep me waiting and Aria will start carving her fingers off."

"No!" cried the princess again. "Halifax, you don't have to do that! I'll do anything at all…"

"You'll do that anyway," the Herald pointed out. "You've nothing left to bargain with, sweetie! And as I said, I want you to see this."

"John, don't do it! Mars needs you! You're its only hope! You must save it, John! I'll die for that, and for you! Please! *I I*…"

"Oh be quiet!" Halifax ordered her. "Women! Always chattering! Fifteen seconds until Aria cuts herself, Blackthorn. What are you going to do?"

Blackthorn looked into Aria's tear-streaked eyes. "Not the smart thing," he answered. "The right thing."

That was Blackthorn's passion, Aria saw at last. Not ruling, or killing, or power. Blackthorn's passion was for *right*.

And it was going to kill him!

He reversed the silver cylinder to the middle of his chest and stood up. "Goodbye, Aria," he said.

She couldn't answer. It was forbidden.

"Time's nearly up, General," smirked Halifax.

Blackthorn pressed the yellow square. The fiery laser blade sprang to life, blazing through him, bursting out between his shoulder blades.

Aria would have screamed but her throat closed up.

Blackthorn staggered backwards, stumbled over the guard rail, and fell as Oglok had. He tumbled down into the darkness of the landing bay far below.

"Tsk," Halifax disapproved. " I'll have to send someone to get that Sword back." He turned to Aria. "And now, princess, you are truly *mine*."

Nan Vidi woke when Aria's tears splashed down onto her face. The old nurse opened her eyes and looked up. "Now then, lovie. Don't take on so."

Aria forced herself to get a grip. Nan's Neanderthal physique and a millennia of the Black Sorcerer's enhancements meant she had shaken off the sleeping gas long before anyone else. Malathea was still insensate on the forward cabin's other bunk; her enhanced senses made her most vulnerable to such attacks. On the airship's decks, Halifax and the half-dozen agents whom he'd revived because they were personally loyal to him were stabbing the unconscious crew and hurling them overboard after Blackthorn.

"Nan!" Aria blurted; Halifax had removed the prohibition on her speaking so he could hear her beg. "He's won!"

Halifax had bundled her into the stateroom with direct orders: "Wait for me. Don't try to escape. Don't harm yourself. Don't try anything stupid." The obedience programming compelled her to comply.

The nurse struggled to rise but was hampered by heavy security shackles. The apostate Prime Herald was taking no chances with his valuable captives. "How rude!" Nan commented disapprovingly.

"Nan, Blackthorn's dead!" Aria blurted. "He said once that he'd die to save me, and I wanted him to be willing, I suppose, even though he said he didn't love me *like that*, only as a friend, but I didn't want him to kill himself for me. He should have to lived to save me rather than to die to save me. And I told him I didn't love him and I wouldn't give everything for him and now he's gone…!'"

"Calm, petal," Nan told the princess. She lifted a leathery hand to stroke her charge's cheek. "This isn't the time for distress."

"Nan, I'm enslaved to Halifax! And now he serves Fatal Laughter! My magic's burned away, probably for weeks, and even if I had it I couldn't use it to get free. I got John into this and then I got him killed. He was Mars' last hope and he was a hero and I…"

"Yes?" asked Nan.

"I never told him what I should have."

The old nurse chuckled. "Lovie, you ran away for the man. You traveled beside him through hardship and danger. You bled for him. You burned for him. You spent every last iota of your strength for him and sacrificed all you had. You walked into nightmare for John Blackthorn. If that's not saying 'I love you' then I do not know what is!"

Aria's jaw dropped. "But… that's what De'bias was asking for! Truth and sacrifice and ordeal! Too late now. All too late!"

Nan's hand tightened on Aria's face. "Come now, child. Get a grip. Your hero may have fallen but you're still here. Your magic may be spent but your brain isn't."

"I'm under that obedience compulsion the Black Sorcerer had you put into me," Aria objected. "Can it be cancelled, Nan? Herald Maximal's obedience protocols were hardwired in like General

Yuen's, much more blunt than mine, but somehow the Lord of Fatal Laughter overcame them!"

"There's no way past the Black Sorcerer's wetware obedience implants," Nan insisted, "for any sane person."

"Ah." Aria understood now. "The Lord of Fatal Laughter's little joke on Halifax. Father twisted Halifax into Maximal. Fatal Laughter has twisted him again into something even worse." *And I belong to him!*

"As for your programming, Aria, well like everything else the Rainbow Waters teach you while you're sleeping, it has to be put to practical use through experience."

"I'm ordered to die if Halifax is harmed. That would be better than living as his slave."

"True, lovie. What else?"

"He told me to wait for him… but not where. He said not to escape, but he never said I couldn't do other things. He said not to do anything stupid…"

"But?" Nan prompted.

"He never said not to do anything *smart!*"

"Well now, what might that be?" Nan speculated.

"Vengeance for John Blackthorn. Death for Halifax and me. A chance for you and Malathea to get away."

Nan shuffled to her feet, her hands and ankles hampered by heavy fetters. "Keep on thinking, lovie. *I* don't see any better plan, but you're *you*. Meantime, there's one of Maximal's loyal troopers guarding the door. Ask him to step in for a minute, would you?"

Aria obediently summoned the soldier. "What?" he asked insolently.

The bound and shackled Nan Vidi grabbed him and snapped his neck. "What an ill-mannered young man," she commented as she dropped the dead trooper on the cabin floor. "Well run on then, lovie! But don't spend your life carelessly. Your Blackthorn wouldn't have wanted it. Spend your life *well*."

Aria hugged Nan, flashed her a brief, brave smile, and slipped away onto deck.

Herald Maximal had disposed of the last of the Black Airship's crew. He kept Morningstar till last and revived him with stimulants from his belt pouch so the Earthman would know his end had come.

"I might give you one of these grav-harness parachutes if you beg for it," Halifax told the Colonel.

"No you won't," Morningstar answered. "You're just the tedious sort who likes to gloat too much. Now I don't mind the odd smirk and snarky remark myself, but I like to think I know when it's getting boring. You... not so much."

Aria heard the sound of Maximal striking the Colonel. "I could turn you over to my new master," the Herald told Morningstar. "How many times have you tried to double-cross him now?"

"You won't let him have me for the same reason you daredn't let him have General Blackthorn," the Colonel retorted. "We both outclass you."

"But Blackthorn is dead."

"So you say. Have you seen the body, Maximal? Have you checked it?"

"He fell."

"Ooh! Well then. Good thing he didn't have a utility pouch with a magnetic zip-wire attached to it like I have in my standard combat uniform. Oh, wait..."

"He impaled himself on his own Sword of Light."

"Okay, that would sting. But still, I wouldn't settle until I'd seen his splattered corpse, got the DNA results, and buried him under six feet of reinforced concrete. Maybe not then."

Halifax snorted. "His broken form lies in the landing bay of the Forge's control complex - which my master's forces have now retaken. The command crucible is back under the Lord of Fatal Laughter's personal control. His will drives the death machines of Cryse now."

"Yeah. What I said before about the gloating? Still good. Some people have the gift, and others... are you."

Another smack. "Take his 'standard utility pouches'. Let's see how ingenious the old-Earth barbarian is at learning how to fly on his way down to Mars."

"I could be Martian street pizza and still be smarter than you, Maximal. Oh, and Princess Aria's going to kill you."

Aria ducked back. Had Morningstar seen her?

It seemed not. Halifax slapped his captive again. "Princess Aria is enslaved by her own father's obedience programming. She has to do everything my twisted hot imagination can think of," he promised Morningstar.

"Yeah, she's got daddy issues alright. But there's a big difference between the stuff you got hardwired with and the software upgrade Aria had. Hardware's forever. Software gets overwritten."

Aria caught her breath. Everything she was taught by the Chamber was theoretical. Experience made it real. Experience modified it.

I have had many *experiences since I woke from the Rainbow Waters this time.*

Could she defy the programming if she really had to?

One way to test it: grab Halifax and jump off the edge with him. Or might a Herald survive even that fall?

"You've prevaricated enough, Morningstar," Maximal decided. "Toss him over."

"Yeah. Toss me. The conversation round here's really dull."

Aria decided she had to intervene to save David. He was crooked and devious but he might be her best remaining chance. She hurled herself round the corner, dagger in hand, straight at Halifax.

And came up short. Harming him would harm her, and that had been forbidden.

"Why Aria," mocked the Herald as the princess failed to stop him. "I didn't know you cared!"

Aria held the blade in her trembling hand. "I won't be your slave, Halifax. Never. *Never!* Like Mars... I will... be... free!" She tried to turn the knife on herself despite the compulsion.

"Drop it," the Herald ordered, and she did.

"Better," Halifax leered. "Now stand there and watch again. Do you think Morningstar would stab himself to save you as well?"

"No."

"Shame. Ah well. Tell you what, princess. Pick up that dagger again. Why don't *you* go stab him instead? Right through the chest, just like Blackthorn."

"No."

"That's an order."

Aria trembled. "No."

"I said, do it."

"And I said... *no.*"

"You cannot resist me!"

Morningstar was handcuffed between two guards but he still laughed. "Evidently she can."

"Aria, I own you. You are mine! Obey me!"

"I'm not yours. I never was. I never will be. I belong to Mars. I belong to myself. I belong to..."

Halifax struck her, spilling her to the floor. "*You belong to me, bitch!*"

"Oh," Morningstar winced, "you should not have done that!"

"Why not?" sneered Halifax, turning on the Colonel.

Morningstar raised his cuffed hands and pointed behind the Herald. "Zip wire. Big villain. Damsel in distress. It's like Blackthorn catnip."

Halifax whirled round. General Blackthorn was climbing over the side of the vessel, Sword of Light in hand. He showed no sign of a blazing laser blade seared through his chest.

Aria felt herself come alive again. Better than alive! Better than anything!

The Prime Herald took a step back. "H-how?"

Blackthorn dropped onto the deck. "I was told once that this Hallow served me. It was mine to command. I figured under the circumstances I might as well test that out. Turns out I can command it not to harm me."

"He can be irritating like that," admitted Morningstar.

"Had to fall down to the hangar floor to grab Oglok. My zip wire rewinder couldn't cope with the added weight of an unconscious Mock-Man so I had to climb back the hard way, hand over hand. Sorry for the delay, Aria."

"Your timing seems pretty good to me, John. I was just needing a hero, but all I had was Morningstar."

"We've played this out before," Halifax warned. "Surrender now or the princess harms herself."

"I really don't," Aria denied. "John, please kill this man now. For me."

"My pleasure."

"Guards!" called Halifax. "Grab the princess!"

Morningstar was still ahead of events. "And cue the Mock-Man," he announced.

Oglok sprang over the banister-rail right at Maximal's goons.

"Told you," the Colonel smirked. "Ooh! That had to hurt!"

"Fine!" snarled Halifax, raising his pain wand and disruptor whip. "Let's do it the hard way, Blackthorn!" He jumped in and cracked the lash at Aria's defender.

Blackthorn caught the cord on his Sword of Light and vaporized it. He headbutted the Herald back and came in fighting.

"Last chance, Blackthorn!" Halifax warned. "Fatal Laughter's recovered the mines. He's already undone the commands you left to cause the volcanic vents to rupture and destroy the forges. Soon he'll send out his hunters to recapture all your runaways on the mountainside and everyone who helped them. If he must he'll blow this ship from the skies, with you, your monster, and the precious princess with it. It's time to make a deal!"

"Fatal Laughter's in the crucible?" Blackthorn checked. "Aria?"

The princess unhooked a bead from her costume and held it up to show the tiny button embedded in it. "We didn't just set the vents to overload, Halifax. We left an explosive device too. This is the detonator."

"You have nothing that can harm the Forges or the Lord of Fatal Laughter!" scorned the Herald.

Morningstar frowned. "What about that vast black matter bomb the Black Sorcerer had at Anx just before I zapped his crawler into scrap?" he suggested. "Whatever did become of that device, General? Because when I slipped back for it, it had already gone."

"Guess."

Halifax swallowed hard.

Oglok twisted the last guard's head round and dropped him with the rest.

"You can't destroy the Forges," Halifax told Aria and Blackthorn. "Think of the power they represent – as a military asset or a bargaining chip. How can you walk away from that?"

"Those forges turn out half the armaments that fuel this insane feud between the First Men and oppress a planet," answered Blackthorn. "We're taking the Sorcerers' toys away,"

"Command me not to push the button, Halifax," Aria told the Herald. "Go on. Tell me *not* to avenge all the dead of the mines, not to destroy the living hell that feeds the bloody wars which ravage this world. Tell me not to strike a blow that will make all of Mars hear about General Blackthorn's rebellion. Go on, *tell* me. Let's see if the command codes the Black Sorcerer stamped into my head really take precedence over everything I've worked for, fought for, lived for. See if they can overcome everything I love. Let's test programming versus *passion!*"

"Do not push that, Aria!" ordered the Herald.

"Again."

"Do not push it. Drop it!"

"Say it one more time. With feeling."

"Don't!"

Aria turned to Blackthorn. "What do you say, John?"

The Earthman grinned. "Hey, you're the Princess of Mars. It's your call."

Aria thumbed the trigger.

The Black Sorcerer's device detonated deep in the lava-pits that fed the Forge's fire. Its antimatter core met the energy around it, releasing mass destruction. Searing plasma fire burst into the caverns above. Rock bubbled and vaporized. Anything and anyone in the caves or mines survived less than a second. The Forges of Cryse were utterly destroyed.

The reinforced walls of the fortress were good for one thing. The refugees on the mountain above were knocked from their feet by the earth tremor. A few boulders fell. But the blast was contained and concentrated below ground, turning a figurative hell literal for one actinic moment.

Then all that remained was the Lord of Fatal Laughter himself, seared, broken, buried beneath a quarter mile of rock and rubble. He was not laughing.

The shockwave rocked even the Black Airship ten miles distant. Morningstar took advantage of the latest disruption to grab a grav-harness and hurl himself overboard.

"So much for my command programming," noted Aria. "Congratulations, Halifax. You've finally done something useful for me. You've shown me the truth I've been denying for so long. Thanks."

"I can still kill him, though?" Blackthorn checked.

"Oh yes. That's fine."

The General dived in low under the Herald's pain wand. It was clear that despite his advanced weaponry Halifax wasn't expert in its use. He'd never needed to be.

Blackthorn brought the Sword of Light up through Halifax's chest. "See if it'll let you command it too," the champion of Mars suggested. "No? Too bad."

At Oglok's growled recommendation, the General cranked the Sword's output up until the fallen Herald was utterly incinerated, beyond any technology that might bring him back in any form.

Aria remembered Coda and Dane and watched.

Nan Vidi took control of the airship. "All four armies fielded by the First Men will have taken significant casualties today. With Fatal Laughter's troops shredded and the Forge fortress destroyed, the Black Armada will likely gain the upper hand in the next few hours," she considered. "Of course, it would probably be best for *some people* not to be aboard this vessel when the master reclaims it."

Oglok had already collected three grav-chutes. He growled something that Aria hopefully mistranslated as *I have urinated all over this vessel* and indicated it was time to go before the six pursuing airships caught up with them.

"We'll go," Blackthorn told the old nurse. "But warn the Black Sorcerer that this is only the start. We'll be coming for him one day and he'll pay for his crimes."

"I'll be certain to mention it, dearie." Nan turned to Aria. "And you, lovie, try and be a little bit more careful, will you? You did very well today and I think you grew up a little bit. Remember what you learned *and put it to good use!*"

"When the time seems right, maybe I will," blushed Aria. "I'm fighting a war, you know."

Nan whispered in her ear as they embraced. "It feels like that sometimes, with matters of the heart."

Oglok growlingly enquired if the new plan was so sit in the sky and help the Black Armada with target practice. Blackthorn and Aria hauled on their harnesses and plunged after him over the side.

"Make for that lake!" the General called. "It looks like a soft landing."

"There'll be flesh-eating monsters and robot sharks then," Aria predicted. She knew how these things worked by now.

"We'll fight them off and go check Reith's got the evacuation in hand."

"And send word by the Runners that the First Men are going to be short on weapons for a while so now's a good time to strike."

"Maybe hunt down De'bias again if there's any way to find him. A bit more spooky advice might be useful.

"And get that pirate Korzan on side. We need naval support."

"We'll need to factor Major Yuei into our plans. He could be almost as serious a threat as Morningstar."

"Did you see David's face when he realized I'd actually played him, John?"

"I saw Maximal's face when he realized you were more than he thought. As if you'd ever be a helpless victim or slave, or anything but our amazing *Princess Aria*."

Oglok screeched that the water was coming towards them very fast and maybe this wasn't the time for a plot summary. He also indicated just how unhappy he was about getting his fur wet.

"This whole mission was worth it just to get you to take a bath!" Aria told him, activating her chute, turning her fall into a dive.

The trio plunged down into the waters. Aria sank deep into the murky lake. She shrugged off the grav-harness and swam back to the surface.

Princess Aria rose from the cloudy waters, victorious and perfect.

Blackthorn was waiting for her, and Oglok, and adventure, and a whole world to save. She was free, and alive, and the Princess of Mars!

She laughed.

Epilogue:
Next Page

A dept Anselm wasn't used to people. He certainly wasn't used to the polyglot collection of extraordinary individuals who poured out of the ruined Isidic Bard-Hall to go their separate ways. In a few short hours he'd seen more strange men from foreign lands – and some who weren't even human – than he had in five cloistered years apprenticed at the Ghost Tower.

Naturally shy, untutored in social niceties, the young scribe found himself wishing again for the dusty solitude of his wonderful new home. The Hall of Tatters possessed the silence of ages. Here was cacophony.

Everyone was clustering around General Blackthorn, quite naturally since he had called this unprecedented gathering[16]. There were Amazonian pirates and brash Phoenix Landing traders, a richly dressed noble and a Not warrior-woman wearing little but leather straps and skins. Reith of the Runners slipped to each in turn, exchanging a few whispered words then passing on. The gypsy-prince Nanzak held court, spinning the most outrageous stories with an honest earnest face. The elders from various far-distant villages

---

[16] The meeting is covered more fully in Van Allen Plexico's epilogue, "Red Planet Blues", in *Blackthorn: Thunder on Mars*.

huddled off to one side conducting their own private business with Lucan, the brawny leader of the new-made Smith's Guild of skilled men rescued from the Forges of Cryse.

Anselm's own master, Father De'bias, was deep in earnest conference with Oglok the Mock-Man and another pair of that remarkable species. From their wide gestures and impassioned growls they clearly had something of importance to consult about with the old cleric-scholar.

Anselm felt overwhelmed. Officially present to record the first conference of Blackthorn's alliance against the First Men, he had sat through a tense two hours of bickering, cautious trading, and tales of horrors. Somehow Blackthorn had managed to keep anybody in the meeting from killing anyone else but Anselm did not know how.

The shy scribe slipped outside. He wasn't the only one to seek refuge from the noisy claustrophobic ruin that had once been the High Performance Hall of the legendary Bards of Isidis. The young partisan called Judan who'd been serving up the food and drink during the meeting hurried past him but thankfully did not pause to speak.

Anselm found a broken ionic column, perched on it, and allowed the silence of the night to soothe him. Irregular-shaped Deimos stared down on him from a starry sky. A broken stone face, long since splintered off whatever statue or cornice it had once graced, stared up from the weed-tangled ground.

"That's the muse Melete," someone whispered in Anselm's ear.

The scribe jumped, lost his balance, and toppled off his perch.

The whisperer was a young woman, or a girl about to become one. Her vivid red hair was filleted into a thick pony-tail and she wore the bright multi-patched waistcoat and leggings of a Meridian. She giggled as he fell into the undergrowth but extended a hand to drag him out again.

Anselm blushed deeply. He couldn't remember the last time he'd had to speak to a woman alone.

The girl tapped a contemplative finger on her cheek. "You're a scholar, right? So you know some Greek from old Earth-that-was? You know what the name Melete means?"

"To ponder or contemplate," the Adept answered. Here at least he was on sure ground. "Melete was one of the original three Muses in the Boeotian tradition[17]. Her sisters were Song and Memory."

---

[17] As described in Pausianus ix.29

"Not bad," the Meridian lass admitted. "I'm called Mel too." She leaned in close. "It means, 'think about it'."

"Right. Yes. Thank you, um, Mel. Nice to have, um, met you." Anselm glanced back towards the ruined hall. The crowd in there didn't seem so bad after all.

"And you're Anselm from Corozin, of the Dusty Legion of Stuffy Library-Crawling Scriveners, right?" Mel checked.

"I... I'm Anselm, yes. How do you know?"

The girl rolled her hands theatrically, gesturing to the length of her body. "It's a bard's job to know everybody, Anselm."

The Adept shook his head. "You're not a bard!"

Mel glared at him and stuck her fists on her hips. "I am so too! What, you think just because our Hall and city got blown up by the First Men there are no Isidic Bards today?"

"Yes. Because Isidis was bombed to ruin soon after Daedalia fell, eight hundred years ago. And between the Lord of Fatal Laughter and Lord Ruin and the Sorcerer of Night there was not a single one of them that got away! Everyone knows that. There are dozens of stories about it!"

"Epic tales, yes." Mel grinned. "Who do you think made them up? Who do you think told them?"

Anselm forgot his shyness in his determination for the truth. "Listen, I labored for five years in Lord Erebus's Ghost Library. Now I'm apprenticed in the Hall of Tatters itself! If there's nothing written there about the Bards of Isidis surviving..."

"The Bards have always had an oral tradition," the patchwork-clad girl interrupted. "Every bard was expected to know the thousand ballads note-precise and word-perfect. Nothing important was written down. If it's that significant you should remember it! You can blow up buildings, burn the scrolls, kill what people you find there, but if you destroy the Hall of Bards then you just scatter that living resource across the whole of Mars!"

Anselm shook his head. "You are not a bard! There are no bards any more! You might belong to some... cult that believes it preserves the old knowledge, but the true Isidian Bards died eight hundred years since! And their stories and songs died with them."

"Really? Says the boy who didn't even know the Hall of Tatters was real up to a few months ago!"

"You're a bard, you say?" the Adept challenged. "Go on then. Sing me one of the thousand songs, the lost songs that were silenced when Isidis fell. Let's hear one!"

Mel shrugged." Alright, here's one of my favorites:

A light shines down the ages as a guide for all to see
A champion arises who will stand for you and me
A hand lifts up a beacon so that all men may be free!
The truth is marching on!
Glory, glory..."

"That's not a song of the Ancients!" scorned Anselm. "That tune is the Tenchmen's Reel! It's a country wedding dance."

"Right. And this is a peasant doggerel for rocking babies to sleep," Mel countered:

"Needles of crystal reach to the stars,
Life's blood and hope for the future of Mars,
Promise and challenge for any who'll see
Heritage waiting the Princess who'll be."

The Adept stopped the retort that formed on his lips. Instead he said, "There are variations of that old lullaby all across the planet."

Mel grinned again. Her cheeks dimpled when she did that and her violet eyes twinkled. "If you're an exiled Bard and the First Men are trying to kill you and all your kind, if they're trying to wipe out all you know and all you saw, then what's the very best way to stop that happening? Isn't it to take the Ancient songs and *teach them to everybody?*"

Anselm considered this. "It's a lovely idea, romantic and appealing, but..."

The girl chuckled. "That's bards for you. Romantic and appealing."

"But nobody has seriously claimed to be an Isidic Bard for eight centuries. If your profession has been hiding out all that time then why reappear now?"

Mel jerked a thumb back at the conference. "Were you in there? All those people brought together in one place to speak out publicly against the Sorcerers and to discuss their overthrow? How could we not reappear? The times we've been singing about for so long are coming true."

"You were clearly in a different meeting to me. I heard the delegates insulting each other, arguing about everything, and refusing to do anything but offer General Blackthorn some logistics support and intelligence."

"This time," the bard-girl countered. "Don't you see how big that is? They agreed on something! All of them. In less than a year John Blackthorn has gone from overthrowing some local tax-man in a hole no-one's ever heard of to destroying the Forges of Cryse! Then for good measure he toppled a Harmony Spire that the First Men needed and destroyed the monstrous Acherim![18]"

"Father De'bias thinks highly of him," Anselm granted. "At least I think he does. It's hard to tell what my master's thinking sometimes. Most of the time. Always."

Mel snorted. "Well *I* think Blackthorn's the real deal. And I'll tell you another Bardic secret: the Bards know Aria too."

Anselm glanced back to the doorway where the Princess of Mars was in earnest debate with Lord Throg. The Adept had read so much about her that he felt he knew her; perhaps better than she knew herself yet. "What do you know?"

"The Bards remember when Rhapsody Arcantrix the Lost Queen brought her to them as a small child. As for the rest, that's a secret we have never yet told."

Adept Anselm shook his head. He'd never encountered anyone like the supposed bard-girl before. "How could you know anything about Princess Aria? How did you even know she was brought here before she visited the Hall of Tatters?"

Mel patted him on the cheek. "Listen, book-boy, you're going to be writing down everything that happens next. I'm going to be remembering it just as carefully. You'll record what you think about it. I'll preserve what I feel. We have similar jobs from different ends."

"I suppose so."

"Right. So we're going to be spending a lot of time comparing notes, Anselm of Corozin. That way I get made to think sometimes, which honestly I need." She winked at the scholar. "And maybe you get to feel."

Anselm blushed deeper than before.

And then it got worse. The Adept looked up and Princess Aria was there! The meeting had finally dispersed and she was making her final rounds of the guests.

"Hello, Adept Anselm," the Princess of Mars greeted him. "Nice to see you again. How are the books?"

"They... it... very good, highness," the young scribe managed.

---

[18] These events are described in I.A. Watson's novel, *Blackthorn: Spires of Mars* and in "The Ghosts of Acheron," respectively.

"He's great on Ancient languages, not so good on modern Martian," Mel grinned. "Hi, I'm Meleti Manysongs, out of Meridiani. It's a real pleasure to meet you in person, your highness. We're both big fans."

Aria raised an eyebrow.

"Very... yes... legendary, you know," Anselm managed.

"Anselm and I are both historians in our different ways," Mel covered. "It's our job to know things that aren't popularly remembered. So we have a question, if that's okay?"

"Please, ask it." Aria sounded amused.

The Bard made sure that no-one else could hear them and leaned in close. "Your highness, why haven't you told General Blackthorn who your mother and father are?"

Aria jerked back as if stung.

"It's okay! We'll keep your secret," Mel assured her hurriedly. "I'm sworn to it by ancestral oath and Anselm appears to have problems forming coherent sentences. We just wondered why the General and Oglok don't know that you're heiress of the throne of Mars or sole surviving offspring of Lord Noir the Black Sorcerer."

"We didn't wonder that!" Anselm managed to choke out. "She did!"

The bard-girl turned on him. "You were *so* wanting to ask as well, quill-boy! But first you'd have to develop vocal skills and stop hyperventilating."

Aria regarded the monk-cowled scribe. "You're with De'bias, aren't you? I don't suppose you can tell me what in Acheron he actually is, can you?"

Anselm shook his head. "The best scary thing that ever happened to me?" he ventured; except now he wasn't sure if there wasn't an even more terrifying contender.

"We're not just being nosy," the contender promised Aria. "This revolution is our last, best hope. It's got to go right. Do or die for the whole planet. And it all depends on you and Blackthorn. So why haven't you been honest with him?"

Aria sighed. "A good question deserving a good answer. So, then. At first I didn't tell the General because I didn't trust him – or anyone. Then I didn't tell him because I'd come to value his good opinion. I wanted him to want me beside him for my own qualities, not for my lineage. Now I don't tell him because it would shatter the delicate complicated détente between us and he cannot afford that distraction. And because when he knows the full truth about who I am and what I have been it will be over for us."

Mel nodded in sympathy. "Tough one."

Anselm disagreed. "No! You must tell him. Truth is the most important thing of all!" He quailed a little under Aria's glare but pushed on. "Princess, you are a creature of prophecy. Your coming was written of in the quiche maya books five thousand years ago or before. And possibly in some recent additional material. And arguably in some folk songs and popular dances if reports from certain quarters can be believed."

"So you noticed my certain quarters," Mel smirked.

"The point is, highness, that you and John Blackthorn between you – and possibly the large smelly Mock-Man – carry the future, the very survival of Mars! You have to tell him who you are!"

"And that's exactly why she can't," the bard objected. "It's too late for that now. The story's run too far. She's got to live with her concealment and pray to the gods that it doesn't doom her. I'm sorry, highness, but I'm right, aren't I?"

Aria regarded bard-girl and young scribe. Her face was inscrutable. "I won't tell you what I'm going to do," she told them. "That would be giving the plot away. I think there's been quite enough prophecy already. Let's have something unexpected for a change, shall we?"

Anselm flushed again. "As you say, highness. I... I apologize for the familiarity. It was not my place... not... overwhelmed by..."

"Yes, sorry," agreed Mel. "Sometimes I get carried away too. Bardic temperament and all that. Whatever you do, I've got your back, okay? Lots of us have. You've got friends you don't even know about yet. A world of them."

"Unexpected," Aria pondered. "Yes." She turned round to the ruined hall. Almost everyone had dispersed now, back to horses or personal fliers or whatever strange means had brought them to that unprecedented meeting. Blackthorn was alone at last, leaning on the conference table. For a moment he looked completely exhausted, the loneliest man in the world.

"John Blackthorn," Aria called to the Earthman.

"Aria," The warrior pulled out of his slump and turned to her.

She walked into his arms and kissed him. It was unexpected.

Prophecy was as blindsided as the General, but didn't recover and kiss her back like he did.

"Oh wow!" breathed Mel softly as she crouched beside Anselm. "Just... wow!"

Father De'bias limped over to retrieve his apprentice. "Time to go, Adept. Say goodbye to your friend and let's be off before the shadow door fades out."

Anselm fumbled a goodbye to Meleti of the Manysongs. She laughed and blew him a kiss. He retreated after Father De'bias through the shadow door to the Hall of Tatters.

There he went to his desk and arrayed his meeting notes to scribe out again in a fair hand. He arranged his quills and ink-pots. He unpinned fresh hide parchment from the stretching racks. He trimmed the candle-wicks to give a clear yellow light under the great cave dome of the silent hall.

He laid the broken statuary face on a shelf where he could look at it sometimes and think about the muse.

Adept Anselm turned to his work, glad that sometimes the Princess of Mars - that Mars itself - that life – could be unexpected.

Afterword

So there I was in the bath with Princess Aria. That would have been great, of course, except that John Blackthorn was also there, and Oglok the Mock-Man, and all four First Men and a bunch of other cast members from *Blackthorn: Thunder on Mars*, and it was getting a bit crowded. When Van Allen Plexico appeared as well I felt it was time to get out and do something else.

It was the day I finally got round to reading my shiny new-book-smelling fresh-from-the-US edition of the first Blackthorn anthology. I like paper books. I like how they weigh in my hands, how the paper feels, the reassuring habit of flicking the page to get more of a story I'm enjoying. And I can read paperbacks in the bath without electrocuting myself. So I'd taken *Thunder on Mars* to accompany a long soak. Bathing on the red planet.

I read all the stories we'd discussed, for the first time in order, all at once (it was a long bath). I remembered the things the authors had kicked about in correspondence, some of the things we'd decided to do, some of the flavours we'd wanted to bring to the mix. I reflected on what had worked and what hadn't, on what we'd managed to achieve and what we still had to do. I finally got to my story, the last in that volume, and went through "The Ghosts of Acheron" working out all the ways I could have written it better in hindsight. And then I got to Van's little epilogue, "Red Planet Blues."

It was clear from that story that Van had bathed before me. His ablutions had obviously turned up similar conclusions about the main things we hadn't covered in *Thunder* that we'd originally intended. We didn't firmly establish the four villainous First Men or set up Blackthorn as the leader of an ongoing and escalating resistance to their rule. By way of a promise to address that in future volumes, Van tossed in a meeting of the rebel alliance getting their act together and starting their campaign.

Excellent stuff. I wanted to read the next book straight away. I wanted to know who all these new people were, Captain Korzan and Chief Nanzak and Father De'bias and the rest. There was only one problem...

There was no next book. Lured by fame and success in his *Sentinels* superhero series and his various other projects like *Hawk* and *Lucian: Dark God's Homecoming* and stuff, Mr Plexico was too busy living a playboy lifestyle to get on with assembling and editing a second Blackthorn anthology. It was on his to-do list, along with initiating world peace and discovering who killed Kennedy, but it wasn't at the top.

I got out of the bath and e-mailed him immediately to point out this lapse.

We needed to know more about Princess Aria, for starters. I love archvillain's daughters. I'm fascinated by what that kind of childhood does to a girl. They unite into one desirable package the classic heroine, bad-girl, and villainous offspring romance interest tropes that go back at least as far as Theseus and Jason of the Argonauts. Aria needed more page-time.

We also needed to flesh out more of Mars, including its wicked rulers. We'd built a Kirbyesque playground where Conan, Randolph Carter, James T. Kirk or Luke Skywalker would be equally at home. Why would we go to all that trouble and not take it out for a spin?

And we'd got all those different visions of Mars from the contributors to our first anthology. Now it was time to combine all the ingredients that each had brought to the table to see what we could cook up next. Recombinant writing, a feast of stories.

For Van's ease of mind, I put on pants before entering into lengthy e-correspondence with him.

It became clear that Mr Plexico was committed to Mars, but that pushing him to more editorial work at this point would be tantamount to manslaughter. Who wants to rob the world of the next *Sentinels* book? And since I'd just spent quite a bit of time in the past, finishing *Robin Hood: Freedom's Outlaw*, *Blood-Prince of the Missionary's Gold*, *The New Adventures of Sinbad the Sailor*, and a forthcoming novel set in World War 2, I was ready for a leap to the far future for a while. So I agreed to write Blackthorn volume 2 to set out our stall for what was to come after. I accidentally wrote volume 3 as well; you can read *Spires of Mars* for free at the Blackthorn website at www.whiterockerbooks.org/blackthorn.

I like to have my backstories clear, and for a novel-length narrative it's important that the characters have the depth to allow each a story arc. That meant I needed to map out a little of Mars' past, some more history of the Mock-men, a fuller origin for Princess Aria, and some rationale for how the far future red planet had magic and monsters and haunted ruins and four megalomaniacs running the show. And that allowed me to revisit some of the events of our series so far and put them into the wider context of Blackthorn's campaign against the First Men.

It also gave me the opportunity to tell the story from Aria's side. In *Thunder on Mars*, our point-of-view character is John Blackthorn, a man from our own era and culture thrust into an extraordinary future under an alien sky. In *Dynasty of Mars* we reverse that; General Blackthorn is the strange visitor from a time of legend, as seen through Aria's eyes. He comes to a world where heroes have been all but stamped out, where our ideals have been forgotten, and he brings hope and possible salvation. For a long time the file with this tale in it was on my hard-drive under the title "Aria's Story", because it's about how that determined, troubled, glorious lady finally finds a champion.

Now I feel that *Thunder*, *Dynasty*, and *Spires* between them have brought us to where we need to be to move on. We've set out our stall. You know what we've laid out. We're all caught up with that meeting at the Bard-Hall where Blackthorn mobilises his allies. Next up: revolution.

More precisely: adventure, fun, mystery, romance, intrigue, disaster, passion, hope, horror, treachery, weird science, high drama, and revolution. Coming soon to a red planet near you. Watch for it.

Anyhow, it's no accident that Aria's first appearance in this book is in a bath.

--IW
Yorkshire, England
July 2012

About the Author

On **I.A Watson's** library mantelpiece there's a trophy for Best Pulp Short Story from the Pulp Factory Awards. It journeyed to Yorkshire, England from the "Ian can't be with us here tonight..." ceremony in Chicago, America and it arrived in pieces. There's one bit still missing, perhaps because that's the part that looks like a gold nib and a customs inspector might have thought was (a) valuable or (b) a terrorist weapon. But there the award stands, battered but unbowed, surrounded by thousands of beloved books and a few actually written by the library's award-winning owner; who is also battered but mostly unbowed, and who still thankfully has all his bits.

So, I.A.Watson is author of a *Robin Hood* trilogy: *King of Sherwood, Arrow of Justice*, and the soon-to-be-released *Freedom's Outlaw*. He's been a contributor to all three *Sherlock Holmes: Consulting Detective* anthologies. His stories have appeared in *Gideon Cain: Demon Hunter, The New Adventures of Richard Knight, Blood-Price of the Missionary's Gold, Sentinels: Alternate Visions, Sinbad: The New Adventures*, and of course *Blackthorn: Thunder on Mars*, which is what got him into this mess of having to write an "About the Author" piece here in the first place. All the rest and a scary photo are on his website at: *http://www.chillwater.org.uk/writing/iawatsonhome.htm*

About the Cover Artist

Adam Diller has held a wide variety of artistic positions within the video game industry ranging from Concept and Production Artist on through to Art Director, and working on everything from apps to RPGs to third-person shooters for the latest gaming consoles. When the realization hit that he hadn't had the opportunity to draw nearly as many Martian Princesses as he would have liked, he became an easy mark to recruit for this project.

BLACKTHORN
The Saga Continues!

BLACKTHORN: THUNDER ON MARS
The anthology that introduces Blackthorn, Princess Aria, and Oglok the Mock-Man with stories by Van Allen Plexico, I. A. Watson, James Palmer, Sean Taylor, Bobby Nash, Mark Bousquet, and Joe Crowe. Kindle edition includes bonus stories by Mark Beaulieu and Danny Wall. Cover art by James Burns; interior art by Chris Kohler. Nominated for seven Pulp Ark Awards! Winner of "Best New Pulp Character 2011!"
Paperback $15.95   ISBN-13: 978-0984139262
Kindle e-book $2.99   ASIN: B006FBRHG8

BLACKTHORN: SPIRES OF MARS
The serialized novel by award-winning author I. A. Watson, available for a limited time at
www.whiterocketbooks.com/blackthorn
And soon available in paperback and e-book editions.

BLACKTHORN: SORCERERS OF MARS
The second anthology, continuing the struggle against the dreaded First Men of Mars! Coming soon in paperback and e-book from White Rocket Books!

www.ingramcontent.com/pod-product-compliance
Lightning Source LLC
Chambersburg PA
CBHW050507260626
47157CB00004B/1229